Skipping Stones

ANANYA AND BRETT RIDENOUR

DEDICATION

*For my mom who inspired me to follow my dreams
and for the many lovely Sunday morning teas*

PASSING

I BEG YOUR PARDON, MISS," said the woman as she attempted to wake Claire. It was quite early in the morning, and Claire was fast asleep.

"What is it?" Claire responded without opening her eyes. She was very tired, having had little sleep the last few weeks.

"Mr. Stonewall is asking to see you, Miss."

With a quick turn, Claire moved herself off the bed. She stood up and rushed out the door. The thought that she was not there in his room when he awoke disturbed her. She had been so diligent in staying with him every night since he arrived home from London. It was a mystery to her how she ended up in her own room, the one time he had risen from his sleep.

Taking a deep breath at the door of her father's bedchamber, she knocked lightly and turned the handle. She looked inside and saw her father propped up against the headboard of his bed. Charles was standing on the other side of the bed, looking back at her. Dr. Michaels was at the foot of the bed with his head down in a prayer.

"Claire," her father exclaimed. His eyes widened and he did his best to hide his condition. He was far too weak to rise from the bed, and she went straight to him.

"I am here, Father. Not to worry. I am here." She returned to the edge of the bed, kneeling down on the floor and grasping her father's hand. "I am so happy you are awake. Do you need anything?"

"No, no, I wanted to see you," he said with a gilded smile. Claire saw the look in his face, and knew that he was not doing any better than he had been the last few weeks.

"Would you like me to read you a story, Papa? Perhaps 'The Evergreen', we have not read that one in a long time." Claire did not know if she was avoiding her purpose in being summoned to his room, or if she was deliberately trying to force the subject away from his health. In any case, she could not keep the tears from welling up in her eyes.

Her father, Edwin, could not hold back his own grief, and a tear fell down his cheek as he looked back at her. His opposite hand held a handkerchief and he covered his mouth with it as he began to cough. The dainty fabric was stained with blood as he hid it from her sight once again. Struggling to take a deep breath, his eyes closed for a moment, and Claire was frightened.

She glanced back at her brother Charles, then to Dr. Michaels, both of whom were silent with their heads hanging down. She wanted to denounce their behavior, but knew that there was little hope after so long. Instead, she attempted to regain her father's attention. "Papa?"

Edwin took a breath once more, and opened his eyes to look upon his daughter's face. "My little Claire…" he began. He would often call her that when he wanted to cuddle and read stories by the fire, or when he was proud of something that she had done. This was something different, and Claire could no longer hold back the tears in her eyes as she kneeled there listening to him.

"I want you to know, I love you. I am going to be with your mother now, and will be looking in on you time and again."

Claire's emotions poured out of her and down her cheeks. She had refused to accept that this illness would take him from her, and she was now faced with the reality that her only parent was soon to leave her. "But Papa," she begged, "I need you with me. Who will be there for me when I fall? Who will guide me when I am lost? You cannot leave me all alone!"

"You are not alone," he whispered, his breath failing him. He struggled to make it clear to her in that moment. "Charles is here, and Lily, and Mary. You have nothing to fear." He looked to Charles and then back to her once again. Claire had buried her face into his hand, not wanting to accept his admission.

"I love you, Papa."

"I know you do, my little Claire. I want you to know…" His handkerchief raised to his face once again as a fit of coughing overcame him. When it finally subsided, he looked to Claire and she returned his gaze. For a moment, it seemed to her that he was happy. But his hand dropped from hers, lifeless and still. His eyes were still open, looking back at her, but he did not move.

"Papa?" Claire called in her crackled voice. "Papa!" she called a bit louder, rising to her feet and leaning over him. "Papa, no!" she cried as she broke out in tears over him, her body lying over his as he lay lifeless in his bed. Charles kneeled to the bed and placed one hand on his father's shoulder, and the other on Claire's head. Dr. Michaels went to the bedside next to Claire, and gently closed Edwin's eyes.

GOOD MORNING

IT WAS A BRISK MORNING, a chill in the air that comes with the changing of the season. It had been so cold the previous months, some of the coldest that any could remember. The snow had already begun to melt, but the air was still sharp as it brushed along the frozen grounds. Looking upon the lands gave little hint that spring was coming. Animals were scarce, but once in a while the flitter of a bird or hint of a rabbit in the bush could be seen. The sun was bright, though clouds were quick to shield its warmth across the snow-covered grounds. The frost on the windows had gone, but the lack of direct sunlight made each morning long and bleak.

Even with the slow cold creeping along the grounds, within the house was warmth and comfort. Warmth was a luxury never forgotten, and always kept throughout the home. Fires burned fervently during the day in several of the many fireplaces that adorned the home. The floors were never too cold, even though made from marble and smoothed tiles. Movement of the household never faltered, for there was always more that needed to be done. The staff was busy, though never complained, they moved about their chores and tasks that needed to be done each day.

The home itself, although never filled to its capacity, always felt occupied. There was never anything amiss, as things always seemed to find their proper place. Based on its overall size, a tour of Brookfield Manor could take several hours. The staff were housed on the upper floors, in a comforting atmosphere. Although the staff rarely had visitors, their living quarters were kept clean and tidy, just the same.

The door to the bedchamber was opened slightly. Through the crack of the door, a softly spoken voice called out, "Good morning, Miss Stonewall." There was a rustle as the covers on the bed were pushed aside exposing a young woman lying there in her nightgown. As she turned to look to the direction of the voice that had called to her, a slow smile moved across her face, her eyes deep in thought yet bright and cheerful. The long strands of her hair draped across her back and shoulder even though they were tied in a ribbon behind her head. Her ears held back the last remnants of her long brown hair, except for a single tendril that fell forward across her brow. A glow about her face was evident, as she looked to the woman that called out to her. "Good morning," she said as she outstretched her arms and legs under the remaining covers. The woman at the door returned Claire's gaze with a pleasant attitude as always.

The woman entered the room briskly and headed to the curtains, still closed and blocking out the sunlight. She flung the curtains open wide, brightening up the room dramatically. Claire squinted as the light forced itself over her. The woman turned once again towards Claire and stood near the edge of the bed. "Is there something that I can do for you, Miss?" The woman was the lady's maid, and her attire reflected her position in the household. She wore a dark blue, finely pressed dress. The cuffs displayed white collars matching the neckline accents. Her sleeves were rolled up slightly, allowing her hands to be free to handle the tasks that she needed to accomplish throughout the day.

"Mary, is my brother about?"

"Yes, Mr. Stonewall is in the study."

"Thank you, Mary." Claire brushed away the last of the bed covers. Sitting at the edge of the bed, she looked to the window, glancing to the grounds in the distance. A few moments passed by before she rose to her feet and walked to the ornate door located near the back of the room. Opening the door, she exposed the insurmountable number of clothes that it contained. Though many of the articles were elegant and finely made, Claire quickly selected a more common dress from the available selection, and pulled it from the closet.

In the opposite corner of the room there was a dressing screen that seemed to be an import from a far-off land. It was bordered with colorful and delicately carved wooden edges, with thin but opaque paper walls that were painted with various colored designs matching the carvings along the borders. Claire took her selected dress behind the wall and took off her nightgown, tossing it lightly over the top of the wall, allowing it to hang on the wall itself. Mary joined her and helped Claire put on her chosen dress. "It's a beautiful day today, Miss Stonewall. Lily has prepared something for you this morning, and waits for you in the breakfast nook."

Claire's dress was a particular shade of blue that accentuated her slim form. She had an obvious beauty about her, but did not dwell upon it. Claire felt that she did not need to impress anyone. She walked over to the dressing mirror and pulled the ribbon from her hair, allowing it to fall and drape down over her shoulders and along her dress. Mary grabbed a brush with a pearl handle and gold inlays from the dressing table and began to brush Claire's hair. Standing before the mirror, Claire pressed herself to the chair and leaned towards the glass, glancing at her own reflection with her light brown eyes.

Mary continued to brush Claire's hair, straightening out the knots that were left from the night's sleep. Mary saw Claire examine herself in the mirror. "Beautiful as always, Miss Stonewall."

Claire looked to Mary in the mirror. "You are just saying that to please me, Mary." She mischievously stuck her tongue out of her pursed lips, and scrunched up her nose.

Mary giggled as she saw the reflection in the mirror and responded, "That may be, but it does not make it any less true." She placed the brush back down upon the dressing table.

Claire stood up straight in front of the mirror and jokingly responded, "Yes, I have my father's good looks!" Then she began to head out the door of her bedchamber.

Mary simply shook her head. There was much resemblance between Claire and her father, but her feminine beauty was more contributed by her mother. Claire was quite beautiful, a choice woman for any man, and definitely could stand on her own. Claire simply accepted who she was, and that was enough, as she felt it should be for everyone.

At the door of her bedchamber, Claire turned and slid her feet into a pair of slippers. The light from the windows brightened the hallway. The walls were lined with paintings of relatives that had passed on long ago. As she does each morning, Claire stopped for a moment before the centermost painting, kissing her fingers and touching the portrait of a man and woman, her father and mother.

She gazed upon her mother's image for just a moment, for the memory of it was always present in her mind. She never met her mother, as she had passed away during childbirth. Based only on the stories that her father had shared with her during her youth, Claire held hope that she lived her life to the expectations of her mother. According to Edwin, her mother Josephine was an exceptional woman. The bond that was between Josephine and Edwin was very strong, even many years after her passing. It had always seemed to sadden him when they spoke of her. It was evident that even though he missed her often, his love for her continued and would have until the end of time.

In the portrait, standing beside Claire's mother was her endearing father. He raised Claire as best he could, and as much as his position would afford him. It was only a year since his passing, having come home from a business trip feeling unwell. Claire spent the last remaining days with her father, tending to his illness. She would spend hours reading books to him in his slumber, tending to his fever and feeding him as it was necessary in his lingering sickness. Edwin read to her when she was ill, so Claire thought it was fitting to spend as much time reading to him during the last days of his life. They shared a very special bond between them that would forever remind her of him. Each and every day his voice was remembered by her, for it served as a conscience of her behavior and purpose in life. She loved him so very much, and to this day, her brother reminds her often of her father, both in mannerism and in appearance. Her brother had taken the loss as hard as she had, but seemed to find the strength to endure and take over the responsibilities of their holdings and business interests. Claire was very fond of her brother; she could not have hoped for a more loving family.

As Claire headed down the hall to the stairwell, she heard, "Good morning, Miss Stonewall." At the foot of the stairs, a rather tall looking man was standing and watching her as she started down the staircase. He was thin, wearing a white pleated shirt, a grey vest, and black coat with black pants, all neatly pressed and well kept. He wore a white wig, complete with curls just above his ears. There was a black bow in the back of a ponytail of the wig. The man smiled, his eyes bright and alert as he watched Claire walk down the stairs. His arms held firmly to his sides, his stance straight and narrow, with his feet together.

"Good morning, Samuel." She took each step one at a time, not in any rush or hurry, her hand gliding along the railing to ensure her stability. Her eyes glanced over the windows behind the man, which surrounded a large door. Through the glass windows she could see a glimpse of the grounds, the grass green and dewed. The cobblestone road that led to the door was empty. "Any visitors today, Samuel?"

"No, Miss Stonewall. Though I do believe Lily is awaiting you in the breakfast nook."

"That is unfortunate. I would have enjoyed company today. I will just have to find other ways to amuse myself. Perhaps I will follow you around all day and pester you when I can."

Samuel chuckled lightly under his breath. "Yes, Miss Stonewall." He held out his hand so she would reach the bottom of the stairs safely.

"You are too kind, Samuel," she replied softly, allowing him to see the fondness she had for him in her expression.

"You flatter me, Miss Stonewall." He led her towards the breakfast nook, allowing her to release her hand from his. Samuel watched her as she walked through the door.

Claire continued through the entry, and through the open doors of the drawing room. The room was filled with fine furnishings. The tables had vases filled with fresh flowers and the scent of the room was of a fine garden in the middle of spring. There were a few busts throughout the room, one specifically of her father, reminding her of his presence. There was another of her brother and she thought how he had changed since they had grown up together. Her thoughts moved to the times and life they shared when their father was alive.

As she entered the dining area she peered through the large windows. She could see the grounds extending before the home. The rectangular lake still had patches of ice. Centered in the lake was an elegant fountain, which still had a few icicles hanging from it. The fountain depicted a mermaid and a muscular man holding a trident, lifted from the lake by a rush of sculpted waves. The stone was well kept, and its color shifted with the passing of light and season.

Claire continued walking into the next room, passing by the long table that was the focal point of the dining room. The walls decorated with paintings and colorful arts, with a chandelier dangling from the ceiling, in its splendor and crystal ornaments. Typically, they used only a few of the chairs; however, one would be hard-pressed to identify which ones, for they were all in pristine condition.

The tableware garnished the table in neat order, ready whenever the need arose. The table stood upon a rug that Claire knew all too well, as she reminisced about crawling under it during the various games of hide and seek or when she felt like being under a tent, pretending to be on an adventure in India. Her childhood was filled with such fantasies as her father would read to her regularly, usually in the late of the day, just before she would nod off to sleep, dreaming of the events that would take place.

Claire passed the dining room and entered through the open door into the breakfast nook, situated with a round table and chairs. To her dismay, there was a single place at the table showing that she would be eating alone. She frowned for a brief moment before turning to the side door. Opening the door, she saw Lily, busy as usual with her many tasks. "Good morning, Lily," she said happily.

Lily turned to Claire. "Well it would be a good morning, if it were not so late already, Miss Stonewall."

"Very funny," Claire retorted comically. "Did you have something for me?" Claire was not sure what the two of them were up to. Mary and Lily always seemed to try to find ways of exciting Claire, at least surprising her once in a while with something she had not experienced before.

Lily looked to Claire. "Yes, Miss Stonewall. I will have it for you in a moment, if you please."

Claire reluctantly rolled her eyes, knowing that she would be hard-pressed to get what was going on with Lily. Instead, she would have to be patient and wait for the events to unfold. She returned to the breakfast nook and sat down at the table, where the place setting was already laid out for her. She glanced to the windows of the rounded room, looking over the southwestern corner of the garden. The sun was hidden by cloud cover, reminding her of the fact that it was still only March. The flowers would not be ready for full bloom for another few weeks yet. Claire always loved the look of the garden in the early morning, when most of the flowers faced the sun for their morning drink.

Claire took the napkin from the table and neatly placed it onto her lap. Soon Lily entered the room, carrying a covered platter. She placed it carefully in front of Claire and looked at her. "For you this morning, Miss Stonewall." Claire felt the anticipation build as she spoke, her hand on the handle of the platter keeping it closed. The aroma flowed from the platter and Claire was intrigued as to its contents. Lily lifted the lid, and the warm steam rose and reached Claire softly. "We have fresh toast, fried whiting, ham steaks, back bacon"—Lily pointed out the various items on the platter—"some spiced sausage, and for a special treat, baked halibut that Mr. Stonewall brought in last evening." Although the breakfast platter seemed more like a feast of flavor, each portion was particular to Claire's usual taking.

Claire responded with glee, "Lily, you have outdone yourself!"

"Anything for you. I do hope you enjoy your breakfast."

"I most certainly will, it smells absolutely splendid. Speaking of Charles, why am I so burdened to be eating alone this morning?"

"Mr. Stonewall had an early breakfast this morning. He expressed that he had somewhere he needed to be, and insisted that you not be disturbed."

"I do protest when he does that. I would much rather have some time with him. He has been so busy as of late. It seems like it has been forever since we shared any time together at all!"

"I did try to explain that to him, Miss Stonewall. But he was quite determined this morning, and would not speak of where he was going. Though he has since returned, and in his study, if you wish to personally express your disapproval. I am sure that you would have greater indulgence delivering the objection yourself."

Lily returned to the kitchen. Claire began to pick various pieces from the platter onto her plate, enjoying the splendor of the meal that was presented to her. Her brother's contribution made the breakfast all that more special, but also gave Claire reason to miss her brother's company on this fine morning.

IMPENDING BUSINESS TRIP

AFTER COMPLETING HER MEAL, Claire stood from the table and made her way towards the study where her brother was inside. She thumped her knuckles on the closed door of the study and waited for a response. She wanted to give her brother time to respond before bursting into the room unannounced.

"Come in," responded her brother.

Claire opened the door softly. "Charles?" she questioned through the crack of the door.

"Claire, come in, come in," he replied. "Are you just getting up this late in the day?" He stood from his seat, placing the papers he was reading back upon the desk. The study was fairly large, making the desk seem small and inadequate for such a space. Light from the window shone upon the various papers and books that surrounded the room. Cherry-stained bookshelves covered the walls of the study. There were a pair of lounge chairs in one corner of the room, separated by a small table and candlestick that would normally be lit in the late hours of the day. Claire visited this area often, to read in the quiet company of her father before he passed away, now with her brother in his stead. She did not have much to do with his daily business tasks, but enjoyed the company of family as often as she could.

As Claire entered the room, she was greeted with the open arms of her brother. He wrapped Claire in his embrace and kissed her gently on her forehead. "Did you have a good sleep, sister?" He was a bit taller than Samuel, but then again, most men were taller than Claire. He was wearing his pleated shirt, the one that she had picked out for him a year before, and a red velvet vest. In the vest pocket was his handkerchief as always, the one that was embroidered by her mother. Claire would always run her finger lightly over it, feeling its soft silky touch to her fingertips. Her brother was wearing his grey slacks, and his business shoes which were loosely tied.

Claire looked fondly up to her brother and kissed his bare cheek softly. "Good morning, brother."

Her brother reached his hand to Claire's shoulder, looking warmly into her eyes. He breathed deeply and spoke softly. "You look so much like our mother, Claire. She would be so very proud of you, as I am."

"Charles…" Claire blushed. "Please…" she requested. Her brother had a way of making her feel a bit embarrassed.

Charles stepped back half a step and chuckled lightly under his breath. He led Claire to one of the chairs in the corner of the study, and then sat beside her. "What?" he retorted. "Can't a brother bestow his admiration on his sister?"

"Well, not by giving rise to his sister's embarrassment," she responded in jest.

"To do so must we make special arrangements?"

Attempting to change the subject of her embarrassment, however slight, she asked, "Why did you not wake me, brother?"

"I had an errand to run this morning, so I headed into town early. Though I did not expect you to sleep so late into the day. Are you feeling all right?" he asked with concern.

"I am fine, Charles." Claire was quick to dismiss his worrisome tone. "I simply could not finish reading that book you lent me the other day. I have been reading it relentlessly and I do think that it is one of the best ones yet."

"So that is the reason for your apparent inability to sleep. I will have to strive to find you something else then while I am gone," he said nonchalantly.

"Gone? Charles, are you leaving again so soon?" Claire showed her concern. She missed her brother so, and he had been gone quite a lot recently. He had been going to the city lately on business, and in some ways Claire had found herself resenting their position, for it meant less time with her family.

"Unfortunately so. I have more affairs to attend to, which is why I needed to take care of business earlier this morning. I leave for London the day after tomorrow."

"But Charles, you just got home less than a week ago. Can you not stay home for longer than that?" Claire whined. Claire had always left business affairs to the men of the house, for she knew full well her place and her position. Though she was having difficulty adjusting to the increasing demand for her brother's time, she had newfound concerns for his wellbeing. "You deserve your rest too, brother."

"Soon, do not worry," he offered her in comfort. "Just need to take care of a few things, and will be gone for only a short time." He obviously knew that this was going to be hard on Claire. "I know that you and I have not had the time together that we used to. I need to deal with, and set order to, what would otherwise be chaos."

"May I go with you, brother?" Claire offered hopefully.

"I am afraid that would not be a good idea, Claire. You would be more of a distraction than a benefit, I fear." He loved the company of his sister to no other, but knew that it would be difficult for him to focus on his affairs. "It would serve me best to have you here at the house, maintaining the home while I am gone." Claire knew that this was a task that she would have to grow accustomed to. "And besides, knowing that you were here waiting for me would make me wish to return home sooner."

"But brother!" Claire tried once more to persuade him. Her demeanor was that of a child pleading for something from her parent.

"Now, Claire, not another word of this. I do not want to spend the next day in sorrow of my having to leave again. I have asked Aunt Sarah to come and check on you while I am gone. She will be coming to see you regularly, I suspect."

Claire stiffened and looked to her brother. "I do not need a governess. I am fully capable of watching over the house and taking care of things while you are gone. I may not like it, but it will keep me busy until your return." It's not that Claire did not like her aunt, in fact, quite the opposite. She had always been there for Claire when in need. Aunt Sarah had called on more than one occasion, and it was apparent she had the same love and care for Claire as her father had. Her father and Aunt Sarah had been very close and held the same regard for family ideals.

"If you think you can handle it without her." Claire could tell that Charles felt uneasy by the tone in his voice. His cautious regard to her independence reminded her of the way that their father had been as they grew older.

Claire nodded in return, her beautiful smile reduced to a blank gaze as the thought of her brother leaving came over her.

"Very well then, I will speak to her in this regard, and let her know to let you be."

Charles turned to the desk and pulled a rather large package from the top of it. He placed it upon Claire's lap, taking the seat next to her and sitting patiently. Claire gasped slightly, so blind she must have been to not notice the package when she first entered the room. "What is this?"

Charles held a straight face, watchful of Claire's curiosity, and then spoke to her in an urging manner. "Open it and find out for yourself, Claire".

Claire opened the package, lifting the top of the box gently to reveal delicate tissue paper wrapping an ornate fabric. Claire breathed in sharply, her mouth and eyes open, focused on the folded fabric within the box. She peeled away each tissue to reveal a beautiful gown, fully decorated with fine lace, warm enough for a winter's night ball. "Oh my!" The fabric was soft and silky to the touch, a masterpiece of beauty and elegance. She looked to her brother in complete surprise. "Charles?"

"What is the matter? Is it inappropriate for a brother to gift his sister with a fine dress now and again?" Charles sat back in his chair, looking back at her with a triumphant smile upon his face. Claire stood and pulled the dress to her chest, drawing the full length of the gown from the package. As she held it to her chest, she spun about the room. She lifted up the hem to watch in wonder as the beauty of the fabric flowed smoothly in the air.

"I came upon it yesterday, and had it wrapped for you. I am just back from collecting it for you. I thought that you would look absolutely stunning in such a gown. However, I am hoping that you would do me the honor of trying it on. It will do you great benefit at the Devereux Ball in the coming week. And I would like to see you in it before I depart for London." Claire knew that Charles was betting on the new dress to placate his departure. Though she could not be bought so easily, she allowed him this small victory and agreed to his request.

"Yes, yes, of course, brother. I will try it on straight away!" An obvious excitement had come over her. She headed out of the room, calling out in the distance, "Mary, Mary…come quickly, look what Charles has brought me!"

As Claire bustled into the next room, Charles followed her calmly and collectedly. The two of them came to a sudden stop as they saw Samuel standing in the doorway, stiff and honorable. "A Mr. Clayton to see Mr. Stonewall," he announced to the two of them. Claire turned around to her brother. Charles straightened his vest and then looked to Samuel. "Show him to the parlor, I will be just a moment." Samuel bowed lightly and turned around, closing the door behind him and returning to the visitor. Claire turned to her brother inquisitively.

"Yes, sister, a Mr. Nathaniel Clayton. I have been expecting him. You may know of the Clayton family. They reside in Belmont Terrace in Newstead. Unfortunately, you may need to wait until I have met with Mr. Clayton before trying on that gown."

Claire nodded and straightened her current attire. Charles walked to the door, raising his elbow to Claire as he waited for her to join him. Claire took her brother's arm and walked with him into the entry. Samuel stood in the center of the foyer, and Claire handed the boxed gown to him. "Samuel, take this to Mary and have her prepare it. I will be in need of it shortly." Samuel bowed to her, then took the box from her and travelled up the stairs in search of Mary.

Charles opened the door to the parlor, and they stepped together into the room. Nathaniel was standing near the center of the room. As Nathaniel noticed the two of them enter the room, he stepped to Charles and bowed lightly.

"Mr. Clayton," Charles declared. "It is my pleasure to introduce you to my sister, Miss Claire Stonewall," he said proudly, holding his open hand towards Claire. Nathaniel stood tall and turned to face Claire directly. His eyes glanced briefly over her before he responded, "A great pleasure to meet you, Miss Stonewall." Nathaniel bowed slightly but maintained his eye contact with her.

Claire looked upon Nathaniel intently, her eyes briefly catching a glimpse of his handsomeness as he stood there. He was roughly the size of Charles, with wavy brown hair and an obvious muscular frame hidden only by the fine coat that covered his shoulders. He was well kempt and clean, his sideburns trimmed and coming forward to a point just below his cheekbones. His jawline was prominent and squared, and he had a small dimple at his chin. His eyes were deep brown in color, clear, and full of charm. A handsome man to behold. Claire curtseyed slightly as she saw him bow. "The pleasure is mine, Mr. Clayton." Claire was mesmerized and intent on keeping her eyes focused upon the very attractive Nathaniel.

Charles watched as the two of them exchanged their introductions and smirked. It seemed particularly pleasing to him to see Claire be out of sorts with such a fine-looking gentleman. Charles turned his attention to Nathaniel in anticipation of his pending reason for calling. Nathaniel, standing before them, turned to face Charles. "I bring well wishes and tidings from my father Mr. Archibald Clayton."

"How is Mr. Clayton doing these days? I have hardly had a chance to share words with him." Charles waved his open hand to the couches in the room. "Mr. Clayton, please enjoy the comforts of our home, you are more than welcome."

Nathaniel bowed and walked to the nearest couch and took a seat. While Charles went to sit beside him, Claire took a seat at the couch opposite the both of them. Nathaniel acknowledged Charles' concern for his father. "He is unwell, unfortunately. He has been ill since the rough weather we had just a few days ago. Though the doctor does insist that he will be on the mend soon."

"That is unfortunate. Please send him our warm regards." After a brief pause, Charles continued the conversation. "Will you be attending the Devereux Annual Ball next week?"

"I will," responded Nathaniel cordially, looking briefly to Claire.

Charles continued, "It is a splendid event which we look forward to each year. Unfortunately, I will be unable to attend this year."

"I was informed as much," admitted Nathaniel, which took them by surprise. "My father has informed me of his duty to discuss with you specific interests that you may need take with you on your trip. He seemed quite adamant that I get the information to you personally."

"In that case," Charles declared as he stood from the couch, "would you accompany me into the study?"

Nathaniel stood at this request. "If you would but lead the way."

Claire arose and curtsied to them. "I will be in the music room. I have much need to practice."

"Very well," Charles said to Claire before turning to Nathaniel. "This way, if you please."

Claire watched for a moment, and then headed towards the music room. This was another large room of the house with several chairs and tables, similar to the drawing room. The windows shone brightly on a very dark-stained and ornate piano.

Sitting upon the piano bench seat, she thumbed through a few pages of songs before choosing one to play.

Claire continued to play eloquently on the ivory keys of the grand piano. Behind her the door opened and Samuel entered, making little noise. He approached Claire, and then called attention to his presence by pretending to cough slightly. "Ahem," he began. "Miss Hawkins to see you," he announced. Claire turned from the piano, looking to the woman he led into the room. "Vivian!"

Vivian happily moved towards her as they embraced tenderly. "Claire, so good to see you."

Vivian was dressed in the latest fashion trend. She wore a large bonnet adorned with flowers and pink ribbon. She looked her part, impressing her status and high position on all who saw her. She placed a kiss upon Claire's cheek. "Oh Claire! Where ever did you find that dress?" It was evident in her tone that she disapproved that Claire would be so underdressed, even in her own home.

"I was not expecting to see you or any other company this day!" Claire said in an attempt to excuse herself.

"It is a good thing I came by with time to spare then. Have you not heard the news?" Vivian continued in her typical excitement.

"No. What news? What has gotten you so excited, cousin?" Claire knew Vivian well enough that she could deduce that it would be some rather tedious task of mingling with other high-class members of society.

"Honestly, you must get out of those rags and put on something decent. We need to be on our way into town! It is absolutely the greatest news we have had in months!" Vivian urged Claire and took her hand, leading her out of the room and up the stairs.

"Cousin!" Claire felt the tug of Vivian, and found herself struggling to keep up with her as they travelled through the house. "What is it? Please tell me. You know I do not like it when you are so secretive!"

Vivian, with Claire in tow, opened the doors to the bedchamber and looked to the bed. She gasped in disbelief. "What is this?" Vivian stood at the edge of the bed looking to the dress that was laid out over the covers.

Claire had almost forgotten the gown that Charles obtained for her. "Something that Charles wanted me to try on for him."

Vivian pulled her gloves off, and touched the gown with her bare fingertips. Her mouth opened in awe. "Oh my!"

"What is it?" Claire wondered about Vivian's reaction.

"This dress… It is from Rowe's Garment Store, is it not?" Vivian showed her obvious obsession over the gown.

"I really don't know, Vivian, whatever is the matter? Tell me." Claire was eager to find out the news that Vivian was withholding from her.

"Well, in all honesty, this is the reason why I came to get you. Mr. Rowe announced that they had imported some of the most pristine dresses from Paris, France. These dresses were limited and only a few of them were available. I was going to have you accompany me to view the elegant and sublime articles for ourselves. It seems I am a bit too late." Vivian lifted the gown from the bed and held it up to her own chest, imagining herself as she would prance around wearing such a gown.

"I was going to try it on for Charles before the gentleman came to call."

Vivian perked up immediately at the mention of a visitor. "A gentleman? What is his name? What does he look like? Do you know his family? Do tell, do not leave your poor cousin in suspense!" Vivian pretended to pout with big eyes and sat upon the bed, pulling Claire down to the bed with her.

Claire felt the tides had turned and it was her turn to tease Vivian. Claire shrugged and looked to the dress, obviously holding back the information from her. Vivian grabbed at Claire, tugging her arm in hopes that her pleading would win her the information she sought. Claire looked to Vivian and grinned devilishly. "Well if you must know, dear cousin." Watching

Vivian nod overabundantly, she laughed lightly before giving in to Vivian's pleading. "A Mr. Nathaniel Clayton, if I do recall. And he is quite handsome. He came to talk to brother about some business, I do not know anything more about him."

"The Clayton family is so discreet. I think I do recall a gorgeous man once before traveling with a young Anne Marie Clayton. He is a thing of beauty, is he not?" Vivian was now more interested in Nathaniel than the dress.

"You would know more than I on that subject, Vivian. I only heard of the family this very morning, as Charles explained it to me."

Vivian sighed. "Oh Claire, he is one of the most eligible bachelors in all of England! He is to inherit Belmont Terrace when his father passes. Not to mention the rest of the estate." Claire could tell that Vivian knew more about the family than she alluded to, but chose not to go into further detail at the moment. Gathering herself up from the bed once again, Vivian digressed. "We still need to get to town to find you some gloves and ribbons to go with your new dress. Come, let us get you dressed more appropriately."

Vivian walked across the room and rang the bell for Mary to come and join them. Vivian opened the closet doors and proceeded to rummage through the fine dresses. She picked out a blue dress and placed it on the bed. Claire stood still and silent, imagining the various gossip that Vivian would inevitably regale to her regarding Nathaniel. At that moment, Mary walked into the room. Vivian turned around immediately and addressed Mary. "We need to change Miss Stonewall into more appropriate clothing."

Claire awoke from her daydream as she heard Vivian declare her orders to Mary. Mary came into the room, collected the dress, and waited for Claire. Claire reluctantly went behind the dressing screen and proceeded to change her attire. Vivian decided to assist in the endeavor and grabbed an undergarment for Claire before joining them.

Vivian began tightening the laces of the girdle. Claire scrunched her face as Vivian pulled on the string, looking over her shoulder. "Ouch!" Vivian ignored her protest and continued without delay. Pulling the blue gown over her head and arms, she tied the various ribbons with large bows, and took her to the dressing table. Vivian sat Claire down upon the chair and had her face the mirror. Mary stood back and watched as Vivian continued to hasten Claire's preparations. Vivian took the brush from the table and ran it through Claire's hair. "I do declare, you must learn to take care of yourself more than you do and be presentable at all times," Vivian exclaimed as she worked Claire's hair into a tight bun.

Claire looked to Vivian through the mirror as she dressed her up like a play doll. "What is the point of doing all of this myself? I have you to come dress me when it becomes important," Claire retorted to Vivian as she began putting various bows in her hair.

"One of these days, you will have to get dressed on your own. Without me, I am afraid you would end up looking like an old toadstool in a set of rags."

Vivian took a step back. "There, much better. If I do say so myself." Claire stood from the chair and looked at the dress that was upon her, then to her feet. Her slippers were not changed from before and she rolled lightly on her heels as a means of pointing them out. Vivian looked to Claire's feet and let loose a disapproving sigh, going back into the closet and retrieving a pair of nice shoes. She returned and pulled the old ones off Claire's feet and put on the new ones. "There, now my work here is done!"

Claire nodded in agreement. "Well you do have a way of making me look absolutely stunning."

"Let us be on our way then. I want to reach town and return before the rains come."

Claire looked out the window. The sky had darkened a bit since that morning, and she would have to agree with Vivian about the impending rain. Claire walked over to the closet and pulled a suitable coat from the rack. Vivian grabbed Claire's hand and the two of them walked from the room in tandem. They reached the foyer and Claire called out, "Samuel, have Forrester bring the carriage, we are headed to town."

Samuel bowed and headed out the door, walking towards the stables to inform the driver of the request.

SHOPPING IN TOWN

VIVIAN COLLECTED HER COAT and umbrella. They stepped onto the porch and watched as the carriage pulled by four large horses came to the front door. Forrester was dressed in a brown suit with a white, ruffled shirt and a brown hat. His hair was a dark brown, almost black, pulled behind his head and dressed in a ponytail with a bow. His shoes, black with a large copper buckle over the top, landed on the ground with grace. He stepped to the door of the carriage and opened it with his left hand, holding out his right to the two ladies who awaited him on the porch. "Good afternoon, Miss Stonewall, Miss Hawkins," he offered to them as they approached him.

"Good afternoon, Mr. Forrester," said Claire kindly. Vivian said nothing and took his hand in assistance into the carriage. Claire followed shortly behind Vivian. "Mr. Forrester, to Mr. Rowe's Garment Store if you please," she said as he helped her into the carriage.

"Yes, Miss Stonewall," responded Forrester. He then closed the door and climbed to the perch of the carriage, taking the reins in hand. With a flick of his wrist, the reins flapped the back of the horses, and they began to trot off down the parkway. Claire sat next to Vivian and looked towards the home as it began to fade in the distance. When they passed by the border of the land, she looked to Vivian and asked genuinely, "How is Aunt Sarah?"

Vivian looked down to her lap. Her fingers played with the seam of her gloves. "Mother is fine, and sends her best. You must come by Bedford Park, it has been far too long."

Claire watched Vivian fidget. "I should be by soon enough. I do miss your family. How is everyone since Simon?"

Vivian sighed heavily. "Mother and Father have been out of sorts since his passing. It has been a drain on the whole family, but we are making do. Michael has been busy helping Father with business. Mother tends to focus on the household, while little Anna Beth is growing up to be a fine young woman. You will be attending her coming out ball, will you not?"

"Yes, of course, I would not miss it. Charles should also be in attendance." Claire knew that it was difficult to talk about the situation with Vivian's youngest brother Simon. He was so young to have lived so little. He had been stricken with Scarlet fever and was never able to recover. It had been several months since, but it still weighed heavily on her aunt and uncle. "You know, if you need anything, you simply need to ask."

"We will manage just fine," Vivian said with certainty. "Honestly, Claire, I believe we have discussed enough about it. We must be on about our task and find you some gloves." Claire nodded at the comment. She knew that Vivian disliked talking about her family in general, so it was no surprise that Vivian would not entertain the subject for long.

The carriage continued down the dirt road. The path had been traveled quite often enough to prohibit the grass and foliage to cover it. Occasionally, the carriage swayed from side to side, as the road was a bit uneven. Claire looked out the windows of the carriage as she often did, staring at the grounds and wildflowers as they passed by. Vivian sat properly in her seat, straight and stiff, focusing herself on her own attire, fiddling with her gloves in quiet contemplation.

After a few moments of silence, Claire finally changed the subject to the impending ball. "Have you had words with Mrs. Devereux yet?"

Vivian sighed slightly, an obvious disdain about the lack of communication with Mrs. Devereux, but Claire pretended not to notice. "No, and I do hope that we have the opportunity to discuss the impending ball. It is quite strange, but each year I never know what to expect from her. I do hope we find more suitable subjects to dance with. Last year there was barely a soul among them who was worth a second glance."

Claire giggled slightly under her breath. She felt that there were plenty of eligible bachelors there for the both of them. In her opinion, Vivian was only disgruntled that Claire had been asked to dance more than she was. Claire knew that Vivian envied her of that particular night's attention. It seemed to be more often on Vivian's mind as the years advanced. "I am quite sure she has something planned. You know Mrs. Devereux. She never misses an opportunity to liven things up at these events."

"Do you remember the older gentleman who kept hounding me last year?" Vivian replied sarcastically.

"Yes, I do. How could I ever forget him? Does he still haunt you these days, cousin?"

"Yes! I can only hope that she has better taste in her so-called 'available bachelors'." Vivian huffed and looked out the window, attempting not to pay attention to Claire's amusement.

"What was that fine gentleman's name? You know, I can't quite remember exactly. Do you?" Claire teased Vivian about the situation, in hopes of lightening her spirit.

"No, I would rather forget it than attempt to remember the beast of a man."

"Ah, I remember now…" Claire playfully replied. "Mr. Gibbons, wasn't it?"

Vivian cringed at the name. She turned to Claire, and saw the playful expression upon her face. She took the paper fan from her side and slapped it lightly across Claire's knee. "How dare you bring up such a thing!"

"How could you ever turn down such a lovely and enduring gentleman?" Claire teased. "I mean to say, given a soap box, a shave, and well, a few pointers, he would have been a fine catch!" laughed Claire.

Vivian retorted, "And a bag over his face. Perhaps if he had money I might have done so, but would never be able to stay with the poor man."

Claire showed an overbearing, disgusted face. "You don't need to go that far!" They laughed together.

The trees became a bit denser and lined the road along their journey. The once-dirt road was now covered in smooth cobblestones, as they passed by the retaining wall entering the border of the town itself. As they travelled nearer to the center of the town, the buildings were closer together. The first few buildings were small and less cared for, then gradually they became larger and more ornate. As they travelled further into town, the carriage slowed, as people were walking along the sides of the road. Some well kempt and dressed for a fine day, others a bit more ragged and obviously not as well off as the others. There were a few who looked to the carriage as it passed on, in a state of wonder at its occupants.

Although it did not concern Claire of her status, it was apparent that they hailed from a higher position than the patrons of the small town. Eventually the buildings became a bit taller, some with signs hanging over their doors, painted with various words and pictures. These were the stores and homes of the merchants. At the very center of town was a large fountain surrounded by several streets. The road circled the fountain completely, and split off in five different directions. Each road was lined on either side with buildings, none of which were lower than the other, and all three stories. The upper floors of the buildings were used as the residence for the store owners. The stores themselves were located on the bottom floor of each building.

Forrester called out to the horses and pulled on the reins, slowing the carriage to an eventual halt. Jumping down from his perch, he walked to the door of the carriage and opened it. He held out his hand again to help them exit the carriage. "Welcome to Springhurst, Miss Stonewall and Miss Hawkins."

Vivian was first to exit with Forrester's assistance, climbing out of the carriage and straightening her dress. Claire followed suit and upon her exit of the carriage, looked to the sky, noting the time that they had before the rains began.

Forrester closed the door and bowed to the ladies before returning to his perch and heading off towards the stables. Claire watched the horses gallop for a moment, and then turned her attention to Vivian. Vivian was busily ensuring her perfection in the glass window of the shop nearest to them. Claire looked to her own reflection and verified that her dress was straightened as well. The two of them headed down the road in the direction of the garment store.

As Claire and Vivian got closer to Rowe's, the crowd of people seemed to get larger. There were several people looking through the window at the fine dresses and suits displayed in the window frame. Vivian took Claire's hand and guided Claire through the small crowd entering the shop. As the door opened, a small bell posted at its height rang loud and clear. Vivian turned to the side of the door and took off her bonnet, hanging it upon the available hook on the wall, and then placed her umbrella in the nearby brass container. Claire followed her actions, and removed her bonnet and umbrella as well. Vivian removed her gloves, and as she turned to the center of the store, she was greeted by an older gentleman.

"Miss Hawkins and Miss Stonewall!" he greeted them warmly. "Welcome to Rowe's!" The man was dressed in a brown suede vest, covering a white furled blouse. He had a pair of black pants that did not reach his ankles, white stockings, and a pair of black shoes that were a bit scuffed but otherwise clean. He bowed graciously to the two ladies in respect.

"Good afternoon, Mr. Rowe," said Claire.

Suddenly, a woman called out from the crowd, "Mr. Rowe!" He quickly responded, "Please excuse me ladies, help yourselves and have a look around. I will be with you in a few moments." He turned and shuffled off to the woman who called out to him.

Vivian turned to Claire, and they headed off in the direction of the gloves. Each section of the store had been separated in order for people to find what they were looking for. There was a separation between the men's and the women's clothing. The more common and everyday dresses and suits were separated from the gowns and fine accessories. Vivian knew the layout of the store better than most, as she went directly passed several of the overhead signs, and arrived shortly in front of the gloves. Claire followed her lead, as she was less accustomed to the store and would otherwise find herself having to ask for directions.

Just as they arrived at the section of gloves, "Miss Stonewall, Miss Hawkins" was called from a short distance away. Claire looked to see who it was, and noticed a stately dressed woman, full of spirit. Despite her advance in age she was much more boisterous, as if her childhood lasted much longer in her life. "Good afternoon, Mrs. Devereux!" Vivian greeted her quickly.

Mrs. Devereux was wearing a full gown with a flower pattern, which could have been easily mistaken for a summer dress. She was always under the impression that the seasons would change faster if she wore the appropriate clothing. She was a bit larger than most women but it was typical of those who were of her generation. Her cheeks were still quite rosy and she had obviously used a good portion of her reserved energy in attempts to reach the girls in a hurry. "I am so glad I have caught you both," she said finally. "Oh and good afternoon." She shook her head in amusement.

"How are things with you, Mrs. Devereux?" asked Claire.

"Fine, fine. I hope to see your attendance at our annual ball next week?" she asked inquisitively. "You did receive the invitation that I sent you both?"

"Yes, of course, Mrs. Devereux, we would not miss it. It is the grandest event of the year and I plan all of my activities around it," said Vivian, in attempts to gain favor with Mrs. Devereux.

"You should, but I have a special surprise for you girls," Mrs. Devereux said with a wicked smirk. She continued as if it were impossible for her to contain herself. "After last year's fiasco, in which there were hardly men worth attending in all of Europe, I made it my duty to ensure that there would be enough young strapping bachelors for all you pretty girls." She winked at Vivian, apparently remembering that Vivian had the unfortunate responsibility of entertaining a certain Mr. Gibbons the previous year. She placed a hand on Vivian's forearm. "I am so sorry, my dear," she whispered.

Vivian smiled softly at the comfort. Mrs. Devereux could not waste another moment with her description of her ultimate plan. "So, I have spent the majority of my waking time searching for the most eligible bachelors in the area, speaking with and interviewing most of them, and sending invitations and requests for their attendance." She prided herself on her accomplishment before continuing, "So I have confirmed with multiple men their promise of attendance, and in turn, I assured them that I would be having the most gorgeous of women to gain their favor."

Vivian's interest was piqued greatly at this news. "Who did you invite? Tell me, please, do not leave me in suspense. I shall not have a single wink of sleep without having at least some idea of who you believe will be in attendance. Surely you would not deny me of rest before the night's event," Vivian pleaded with Mrs. Devereux.

Mrs. Devereux did not give in. "Now, now, child, do not fret. I will not be confirming names of any who will be attending the ball. You will simply have to be surprised when you arrive. All I can say is that I promise you will be glad and thank me for all time."

Vivian pouted a little, in hopes of gaining Mrs. Devereux's confidence regarding those who had been invited. But Mrs.

Devereux saw past that effort and grinned devilishly at the attempt. Vivian cried out, "That simply is not fair!"

Mrs. Devereux laughed lightly. "Well ladies, I am off to see who else I can find in town. I must be on my way." She was obviously pleased with the torment that she bestowed on Vivian.

Claire payed little attention to Vivian's performance. "Good day then, Mrs. Devereux, and good luck." Claire knew that Mrs. Devereux had her plans in place, expecting nothing less than a grand evening.

Mrs. Devereux placed her hand on Claire's forearm. "Good day, Miss Stonewall." Giving her a wink, she headed to the other side of the room. Her voice was heard again calling out to some other person in the room, her white glove in the air waving about.

Vivian looked to Claire. "Very well, I will just have to get the information myself. I am not without my means of obtaining the information I want. I am quite sure I will know more about the people she has attending than she does, in due time." Claire knew full well that if Vivian ever wanted to get information, she always found a way. Regardless of the validity of her sources.

"Why can't we just simply be surprised at those who are attending?" Claire was not concerned with who would be present at the ball. The events themselves were always entertaining, but she often felt that the attendees were more interested in improving their own social importance. Claire began to fumble through the gloves lying on the table in an attempt to excuse the thoughts from her mind.

"Claire, you know as well as I do that the annual Devereux Ball is the one place where we are sure to find our future husbands. No other event gives us the opportunity to encounter such wealthy and important men."

Claire lifted up one of the gloves, and examined it in more detail. "I was only making an observation. It is quite apparent to me that Mrs. Devereux intends on matching all of us girls up with whom she deems worthy. She has already married off her own children, now it is we who get to be the brunt of her attention." She returned the gloves and continued looking for another pair.

"Honestly, Claire, I hope she does. The woman has exquisite taste and knows everything that there is to know about everyone. I just hope she takes the time to find a suitable man for me this time as well." She handed the gloves she had chosen to Claire, and urged her to try them on.

Claire took the gloves from Vivian and put them on her hands. The color of the gloves was very similar to the gown she had. "Oh yes, Mrs. Devereux has the most impeccable taste for us young ladies." She first looked to Vivian, then down past her nose as she lifted her chin, trying to keep a straight face. "Just look at Mr. Gibbons."

Vivian quickly responded with a painful gaze at Claire as if she had taken a stab at her and was completely caught by surprise. "Cousin! I will not take this torment from you!" Claire could no longer hold the laughter within and laughed lightly as they continued to look through the available gloves on the table.

Mr. Rowe walked to the table where Claire and Vivian had been spending their time and stopped. "Miss Hawkins, Miss Stonewall, is there anything that I can help you with?"

Vivian looked to him and responded mindfully, "Yes, I am looking for the newest fashion in gloves and ribbons. I believe you are familiar with the dress that Miss Stonewall received this morning."

"Ah yes. Mr. Stonewall came by this morning, and I had thought it odd that he would not also be looking for a matching set of gloves and ribbons. In fact,"—he raised his finger and looked to Claire— "I have already set aside a specific arrangement that I think you will find to your liking. If you would give me just a few moments to collect them, I will be back shortly."

Claire nodded to Mr. Rowe in approval. Mr. Rowe returned shortly with a box in hand, and placed it upon the table. He produced a pair of gloves that matched the color and accents of the gown, complete with frills and a fine lace. Vivian snatched the gloves and looked at them with glee. Claire watched as Vivian examined them closely. "We also have this set of ribbons…" offered Mr. Rowe as he pulled some ribbons from the box and handed them to Claire for her inspection.

Vivian placed the gloves down, and looked over to Claire as she too examined the ribbons. Mr. Rowe rumbled through the tissue paper that was neatly packing the objects in the box, searching for something. He eventually pulled out an oriental fan, decorated with similar patterns as the gown, and placed it on the table as well. Lastly, Mr. Rowe took out a hat from the box, well-formed and flexible, adorned with ribbons and flowers that matched the color of the dress and its overall design. Vivian took the hat and placed it upon Claire's head with delight.

Without a second thought, Vivian exclaimed to Mr. Rowe, "We will take all of it, place it on Mr. Stonewall's tab."

Mr. Rowe chuckled lightly. "Yes, Miss Hawkins and Miss Stonewall. Shall I box everything for you and have your driver stow it?"

Claire nodded graciously. "Yes Mr. Rowe, thank you, and include a pound for you and your family, for your generosity and assistance."

Vivian looked to Claire and shook her head, disapproving of Claire's offer to the storeowner. She turned toward the door and spoke plainly. "Good day, Mr. Rowe." Claire followed her and they gathered their belongings. Just as they reached for the door, Forrester entered the building. Claire looked to him. "Forrester, Miss Hawkins and I will be roaming the shops for a short time. Mr. Rowe has a package or two for us."

Hearing Claire, he bowed. "Yes, Miss Stonewall." As Claire fitted her gloves upon her hands and took her umbrella, Forrester whispered softly to them, "I would inform you that the rains are near."

Claire looked out the shop door and saw that the clouds had darkened substantially. "Very well, Forrester, bring the carriage to the streets in case we need a quick escape," Claire stated as she passed by him in the doorway, hoping not to have lost Vivian.

Vivian had already begun down the street when Claire caught up to her. They talked together nonchalantly about the coming and going of nearby patrons. It seemed as though Vivian was at her best when discussing the local gossip concerning everyone near the town, even from far-off places. It always amazed Claire how well she was informed, and although she never asked her specifically about her sources, she imagined that she kept a log with everything written down. There would be too much information for Claire to retain in her own mind.

Throughout the town, many people had begun to vacate the streets in fear of the coming rains. Claire looked back and could see Forrester sitting upon his perch of the carriage, watching them as they travelled the streets, ready at a moment's notice to come and collect them.

RAIN BEGINS

A BOOM WAS HEARD FROM THE clouds above, announcing the pending rain. This signaled Claire and Vivian it was time to go. Claire turned towards Forrester and caught his attention. Within seconds, he charged the horses, and the carriage came to the two of them. Again, Forrester jumped down from the carriage perch and opened the door, holding out his hand and urging them out of the weather. Vivian entered first, as per her usual, followed by Claire, who sat beside her. Before Forrester had the opportunity to close the door, Vivian called out to him, "Take me to Bedford Park."

Claire watched the landscape as the rain began to fall. The patches of snow that littered the fields faded away with the rain. The weather had warmed enough for the snow to lose its hold on the grounds. Spring was just around the corner, and Claire was quite ready for the start of the new season.

The rain increased as they came closer to Bedford Park. Tiny rivers of runoff from the hillsides were strewn about the surrounding area as they rolled past. A splash occasionally could be seen from the windows as the rains continued. Claire looked to Vivian who seemed to be in deep thought. "Please do give my regards to Aunt and Uncle."

Vivian awoke from her thoughts and looked to her. "Of course, and do the same for Charles." Claire and Vivian had been in confidence with each other for years and the thoughts of their time together were always joyous and happy. As the years continued, they seemed to be drifting apart in their own ways, but their childhood together was a fond memory for the both of them.

As they arrived at the gates of Bedford Park, several of the staff worked off the water as it pooled in various locations throughout the property. They wore specialized clothing to keep them warm and dry, but the rains still managed to get them wet. Claire saddened a bit at seeing them toil in the weather but said nothing to Vivian about it. The carriage arrived at the door and the doorman stood attentively, watching as they arrived. Forrester jumped down from his station once again, opened the door, and looked inside the carriage towards Vivian. Vivian grabbed his hand and allowed him to guide her safely to the ground, holding her umbrella to keep as much water away from her as possible. Vivian took up the length of her gown, keeping it from the water as it pooled at her feet. Looking back inside the carriage, she called out to Claire through the rain, "Now don't forget, we will be arriving at your home tomorrow at half past midday to collect you."

Claire nodded and repeated for Vivian's assurance, "Yes, half past midday, I shall be ready."

"Don't be late, I wish to arrive a bit early tomorrow."

Claire replied, "I know," rolling her eyes at the notion that she would be allowed to forget. Claire knew full well that Vivian wanted to arrive early so that she could have first pick of the bachelors who were to attend the event. The horses, now wet from the rain, stomped in the mud a bit and pulled the carriage out of the parkway.

Upon arriving back at Brookfield Manor, Forrester helped Claire down from the carriage steps. Samuel opened the door for her, and said softly, "Welcome home, Miss Stonewall." As they entered the door, Claire removed the bonnet and folded the umbrella, placing it in the container near the door typically reserved for the guests. She removed her coat, handed it to

Samuel, and then turned to him. "Do we have guests, Samuel?" Claire had nearly forgotten that she had left when Nathaniel was with her brother.

Samuel replied, "No, Miss Stonewall. Mr. Clayton departed shortly after you left. Mr. Stonewall is in the study if you have need of him. Mary is awaiting you upstairs in the baths."

"Thank you, Samuel, see that these items are returned to my room."

"Yes, Miss Stonewall," he concluded, bowing to her and gathering her items. He then made his way up the stairs to her room.

Claire walked to the study, and saw that the door was partially open. She entered the room without hesitation, knowing that her brother would have closed it if he needed privacy. There before her was her brother, leaning over the desk, quill in hand, busily writing something. "Good evening, brother," she said to him, announcing her presence. The night had crept in, even though the clouds and rain had hidden the mere fact.

"How was your trip into town?"

"It was good! Mr. Rowe had a few items for me and you will find them on the tab."

"Very good," Charles said agreeably, although it was apparent that he was busy in his current thought.

"Well, I can see that you are occupied. I will take this opportunity to go and have a bath. The recent rains are quite fierce this afternoon."

"Uh-huh," Charles retorted.

"Fine then," Claire said indignantly. "Charles, I wish to have words with you at dinner. Do not forget."

"Yes, sister, at dinner" was the best response he could muster, but at least it gave Claire an understanding that he got the message.

Claire moved from the study and out to the foyer, then continued up the stairs and down the hall, meeting up with Mary who had prepared a warm bath for her. Taking her time to relax in the tub, she conversed with Mary about the day's activities at the house. She needed to catch up on things since she had been gone. Most days, all of the staff at the home knew their responsibilities and gladly performed them. She had always had a good rapport with the staff, as they had come to love and honor the family.

After the bath, Claire began her way down to the foyer. The candles of the candelabra and chandelier had been lit. The candlelight provided enough light to see from room to room. She reached the bottom of the stairs and turned once again towards the study.

Before reaching the door, however, her brother had come out and greeted her. "I am sorry for earlier, sister, but I needed to finish that letter before I departed."

"It is fine. As long as I have you for the evening, all is well," Claire said reassuring him.

"That you have, sister," responded Charles happily. "Tell me, what news do you have from town?"

Claire began to divulge the events of the day, and her conversation with Mrs. Devereux. Vivian's interactions came up fairly regularly, not that they were asked for, but Claire thought the humor of her embarrassment was worth mentioning. They continued to talk casually throughout dinner. Charles confirmed his departure and return dates with her, which made her uneasy. The memory of the trip to London that had brought back their father in such poor health came foremost in her mind. Even though Charles had made the trip several times since, she still had her reservations.

Charles continued to comfort her as best he could, but his remorse over the loss of their father only a year ago was evident in his demeanor as well. He took extra precaution nowadays, never misjudging the importance of one's health, and the protection of others. However, Charles attempted to keep the conversation to that of more high-spirited topics. After they had finished their meal, they continued into the drawing room.

The rain was still pressing down, and it could be heard throughout the house. Charles and Claire continued to discuss the upcoming events as they rested comfortably on the couches. Charles asked Claire, "What did you think of Mr. Clayton?"

Claire blushed. "He looks like a fine gentleman." She attempted to hide her interest in Nathaniel.

Charles chuckled lightly. "I see… Well, I have it on good authority that he will be at the Devereux Ball. And from what I can gather, he is quite happy that you will also be in attendance."

"Oh really," said Claire in astonishment, doing her best to hide it from her brother. "What do you think of him, brother?"

"I really do not know much about him. He seems like a fine upstanding man, to be sure. The Clayton family is a well-known family." Claire could sense that he had some reservations, but Charles held them to himself.

"If that is your opinion of him, I must be on my best behavior. And to think, I was considering dressing the part of a circus performer at the ball this time," Claire threatened feebly.

Charles laughed. "I do not think that you could manage your way into the ball with that sort of attire."

"That may be true, brother, but it would be worth my time if I could get a laugh from you."

""Well, I hope you wear the new dress. I think it looks fabulous and you would be absolutely stunning in such a gown. I only wish that Father could have been here to see you in it." A bit of sorrow ended on Charles' tone. Claire picked up on his remembrance and comforted him.

"You know, brother, I think he will. He is still with us, in many ways. I think about him often, and although I do miss him, I see him in you. And for that I am forever grateful."

They did not speak much for the rest of the evening except for a goodnight and a hug to each other. Charles was to leave early in the morning and Claire would most likely still be sleeping when he departed. Claire headed to her bedchamber and lay upon the bed, pulling the comforter up tight as the rain continued to pour outside, the sounds of thunder far and few between. She fell asleep quite easily, despite the excitement of the day to come and the sorrow of Charles departure.

BREAKFAST
THE MORNING OF THE BALL

T HE ANNUAL DEVEREUX BALL WAS always a party of opulence and splendor that everyone looked forward to. Claire was no exception to the rule. She had high hopes of fine company, laughter, introductions, and dancing the night away until the early light of the dawn. It was common for attendees to stay and enjoy the evening's entertainment until the sun rose the next morning.

Mrs. Devereux spared no expense in the entertainment, delicacies, and drinks to be had during the extravagance. Mr. Devereux would enjoy a dance or two with one of the many young and attractive ladies who frequented their gala. Even Mrs. Devereux took the opportunity to grab a handsome gentleman from a younger generation, and with her most flirtatious grin, they would take to the dance floor. The Devereux Estate hosted some of the wealthiest families of the entire area. Occasionally, a guest or two would come in from London or some other far-off place to partake in the event.

Claire awoke with a smile upon her face. Her brother was gone to London, but she was too excited about the ball to mourn his absence. She went to the window and pulled back the heavy curtains, allowing the fullness of the morning light to enter her bedchamber. Taking a deep breath and closing her eyes, Claire felt the warmth of the sun on her face.

"Mary," she called out. A moment later, the door opened as Mary entered the room.

"Good morning, Miss Stonewall!"

"It is a grand morning, Mary," said Claire in return. "Has Lily prepared breakfast?"

"She has, Miss Stonewall, and she has been keeping it warm for you until you awoke."

Claire nodded gratefully. "Thank you, Mary," she said as she headed to the closet and gathered a casual dress from its contents. After getting dressed she headed out of her bedchamber, calling back to Mary who was about to leave the room along with her, "Mary, please prepare the dress for tonight's gala. I will need to get ready soon after breakfast."

"Yes, Miss Stonewall."

With that last request, Claire headed out of her room and down the hall, stopping short at the portrait of her parents. The anticipation of the night excited her and she smiled in her thoughts as she imagined speaking with her father. The memories of his loving adoration for her filled her spirit and she pressed a kiss into the frame before heading down the stairs.

As Claire arrived at the breakfast nook, Lily greeted her. "Good morning, Miss Stonewall."

Claire smiled. "Good morning, Lily, is everything prepared?"

"Yes, Miss Stonewall," she spoke softly as she then headed into the kitchen.

Claire sat at the table and glanced out the window. She could see a few birds as they were always the first to return. In the distance, against the tree line, she caught sight of a buck. The antlers stood out as tree branches and she felt reassured. It was a good thing, a sign of delight to come. She watched briefly as the buck turned back into the woods, and with a bounce, was gone from sight.

Lily had prepared a bit less than usual knowing that Claire would be less inclined to eat a full meal with the ball being only hours away. "Looks wonderful," Claire acknowledged aloud.

"Thank you, Miss Stonewall. When you are finished, I would like to speak with you for a moment."

Claire turned her glance to Lily. Suddenly she felt worried. "Pray tell, I have a busy schedule today."

Lily responded calmly, "I need to get some supplies from town today."

Claire exhaled a relief, for today was not the day to be having something go wrong in the household. "Yes, of course. You may ask Forrester to take you to town, I will not need his services today."

"Yes, Miss Stonewall," Lily replied before she returned to the kitchen. Lily was quite used to taking care and charge of the staff when the family was not available. Edwin had regularly charged her with the task when the children were young. Claire had only recently taken on the responsibility, but Lily was always there to help and guide her in the duties of the house. Shortly after Claire turned of age, Edwin instructed Lily to mentor her on the workings of the house.

Even though Lily was closer to Charles than to Claire, they still shared a close bond. Lily almost seemed like a second mother to both of them. Lily loved both the children, and was very proud of their accomplishments and abilities. She respected them greatly, for in her eyes, they both grew to be strong of character and a loving and honorable family.

Shortly after breakfast, Claire returned to her bedchamber to find that her new gown was freshly pressed and placed neatly upon the bed. Claire was overwhelmed as the memory of her sweet brother's thoughtful gift entered her mind. She walked up to it and lightly ran her fingers along the smooth fabric. Her thoughts were of her brother, and how he would not be present. A slight sigh escaped her, as she had forgotten about his request for her to try on the new gown before his departure. The thought of his absence seemed to creep into her mind and she pushed it away, knowing he would be returning home soon enough.

Mary had entered the room shortly after Claire and was standing behind her, ready to assist in Claire's preparations for the coming ball. Claire looked to Mary and nodded, and they began to enrobe.

THE DEVEREUX BALL

LILY, SAMUEL, AND FORRESTER WERE talking amongst themselves in the foyer when Claire reached the top of the stairs. Lily was stunned at the sight of Claire and the others turned to see her. There, at the top of the stairs, Claire smiled back at them. The warmth rose to her cheeks as she was not accustomed to their gaze. The dress was elegant and vibrant, clearly showing off Claire's natural beauty. It was a stately dress, in a yellowish-gold hue, complete with ribbon and bows along the length of the entire gown. The ruffled top was rimmed with a cream-colored lace all along its edge. Over her shoulders draped some of the fabric as if to represent a shawl. The gloves she had procured at Rowe's were made from the same fabric; they reached above her elbow and were accented with the same lace as around the dress itself.

Claire's hair was curled and pinned up, with speckles of golden pearls intertwined within the tendrils. The bonnet's rim barely covered her entire head and was more of a decoration than a functional piece. The bonnet was a cream color similar to that of the lace, and had golden ribbons that matched the color of the dress.

In Claire's hand was a small, ornate paper fan that wielded the same color and accents. Mary stood proud and beaming behind her. As Claire headed down the steps, you could catch a glimpse of her feet as they escaped the thickness of the hem of the dress. She wore a pair of slippers that would be suitable for dancing, yet matched the overall design of the dress. The light reflected from the surface of the slippers in speckled gleam until covered by the hem once again.

Unable to see the steps through the thickness of the dress, Claire reached to the side of the stairwell as she began to travel down them. She had traveled the steps many times before, but still wished to ensure her steadiness. Just as she reached the foot of the stairs, a noise came from outside the door as the carriage arrived at the household.

Samuel hesitated for a moment as he looked upon the sight of Claire, then headed out the door to see to the Hawkins family. Vivian stepped immediately out of the carriage, and came quickly to the front door. "Good afternoon, Miss Hawkins," Samuel greeted as Vivian brushed right by him and straight through the door.

As Vivian crossed the threshold, she stopped in her tracks when she saw Claire standing in all of her splendor. She stood there for a brief moment, saying nothing as if she had lost her purpose for charging into the house. Her mouth held open for a moment, and eventually turned into a smile. "Why, cousin! You look absolutely beautiful!" It seemed as though Vivian was caught by surprise, as it was rare for her to enter the home with Claire so readily prepared.

Vivian, on the other hand, was wearing a beautiful gown as well, perhaps not as well decorated as Claire's, but still very beautiful. Claire felt the warmth of her cheeks continue. "As do you, cousin." She stepped closer to Vivian with her hands out in front of her. Vivian took her hands and they kissed each other softly on the cheek.

Vivian always tried to look her best, but this time, she was much more elaborate. Vivian looked to her own gown, lifting it up and retorting, "Oh this old thing? Well, I do declare, we should be able to ensnare fine gentlemen for the both of us."

Vivian turned on the spot, and with a firm grasp on Claire's hand, she left the foyer as quickly as she had arrived.

"Yes, cousin…" Claire said before looking back to the staff and waving to them. Vivian was not to be delayed, and Claire knew her intention. "We do not want to keep the handsome gentlemen waiting, now do we?"

"No, that would just not do!" Vivian replied just before she climbed into the carriage. Claire sighed lightly, and took one last look to the staff as they watched from the porch.

Claire turned towards the carriage and caught a glimpse of her uncle and aunt looking out the window, their faces stunned to see the grandeur of Claire's gown. Vivian's brother, Michael, was also in the carriage, along with Vivian's sister, Anna Beth. Vivian took her seat next to her mother and father, and Claire entered the carriage, sitting next to Anna Beth. When they were seated, the door was closed and Claire looked to her Uncle Richard, "Good to see you, Uncle."

"And you, Miss Stonewall, you look adorable. I most certainly believe that you will be the center of discussion at tonight's gala." Richard was a proud man, though he rarely spent time divulging his efforts to his children. He was a few years younger than Edwin, and a much more solitary man. He was wearing a fine tuxedo, with long coattails and a tall hat. He had a black bow tie and a fine white shirt, pressed and clean. The suit was something he'd worn on previous occasions. His shoes were polished, but showed a slight scuff upon the surface as they were used on a regular basis.

Claire blushed slightly, turning to her aunt. "Good afternoon, Aunt Sarah." Edwin and Sarah were raised together in a caring and loving environment in which both of them learned the value of family. In their later years, they both attempted to spread that same sentiment to their own families. Since Josephine's passing, Sarah would call on the household often and ensure they were well taken care of. Claire had always felt that Sarah would do anything for her and Charles if the need arose, but at the same time would keep her distance, allowing them their independence.

"You are absolutely beautiful, Claire, your father would be so very proud of you," Sarah said genuinely, with a small tear in her eye. Sarah still mourned Edwin's passing, and Claire and Sarah were connected in that sentiment. "It has been too long since I have heard any news from Brookfield Manor. I do hope to receive a letter from you soon, with all the details!" Sarah had pestered Claire for a letter now and again, and to Claire's embarrassment, it had been a while since she had written. She regretted how long it had been.

"Yes, Aunt, I will be sure to write soon." Claire looked to Vivian who was amused that Claire was in trouble with Sarah. Claire turned her attention to Michael, who obviously could not take his eyes off Claire's gown. "Why, Cousin Michael, whatever is the matter?"

"It's just... It, umm..." choked out Michael, until he had to blink and shake his head. Anna Beth giggled, looking to her elder brother. "You, umm…" Michael continued to utter while the rest of the family began laughing at his stammering. Michael blushed. "You look nice, cousin," he said finally, trying not to show his obvious flare in cheek color. He was dressed in similar fashion to Richard, though the tuxedo he donned also included a vest and was a bit larger than he was accustomed to. Michael was not a bad-looking gentleman in his own right, just lacked a bit of confidence, and was always teased by his younger sisters about it.

"Thank you, Mr. Hawkins," Claire replied in playful respect. Claire looked down to Anna Beth, who was dressed in a fine-looking garment, abundant with frills and lace. "And what of you, Miss Anna Beth?" Claire had always called her that even in their youth. Claire thought of Anna Beth as her younger sister, more than a cousin.

Anna Beth blushed slightly, her rosy cheeks still apparent. She was just of age, and quite excited to be going to the ball. The year prior she had much less interest in the comings and goings of the gentlemen, but now that it was her turn to join society, she was quite anxious. She looked to Claire. "Oh, cousin, I am so happy to have you with us." She had looked up to Claire throughout her youth and always wanted to mimic her in her own ways. "Do you like my dress?"

Claire looked at Anna Beth's dress. It was not a formal ball gown, but a fine dress for a more active girl to wear. The light green color of the dress accentuated her eyes. She had done her best to match her attire with a pretty, light green ribbon tied within her hair, though the color of it was not quite the same. Claire looked upon her fondly. "You look vibrant, dear cousin. I am quite sure you will turn a head or two at the ball."

Anna Beth looked to Vivian with a championed expression. Vivian simply watched in return, not giving Anna Beth any satisfaction. Claire could only imagine the ways that Vivian may have ignored Anna Beth in her preparations. Sarah, on the other hand, smiled at them both during the conversation, as it was apparent that Anna Beth wanted to impress Claire with her beauty. For Sarah, this of course meant the last of her daughters was soon to be gone from the household, and that meant a quieter time in the near future. Sarah loved family, and although it seemed that her children did not share in her passion, to her it was still a loving family.

The carriage continued down the long road, passing other patrons as they walked beside it. Some dressed in fine attire, heading towards the Devereux Estate; others dressed with less grandeur, headed on their way into town. The day was late, and the afternoon was waning into the night. To Claire, it looked as though the sky itself was commanded by Mrs. Devereux, and she would not allow for rains nor clouds to dull the party. The sun was touching the horizon, and the moisture from the lands completely dried. A few early blossoms could be seen among the fields, and a smile crossed Claire's face as she looked outward from the carriage.

For the remaining journey, the conversation consisted mostly of speculation concerning the events that were to unfold and minor gossip that Claire rarely paid any attention to. Claire recognized that the gossip that circulated around the town and inhabitants rarely had any truth about it, and it made her feel quite uneasy if she did not know the facts. She would smile and nod as they traded their stories, Vivian most of all.

The carriage approached the turn for the Devereux Estate and Claire looked outward from the carriage window. She saw several young children sitting upon the stone wall that guarded the entrance to the estate, pointing their fingers at the carriages and talking amongst themselves. She could only imagine what they were expressing as the carriages rode by the gates. The road was lined with buildings tightly crammed together. She knew that the homes that lined this part of the road were intended for the families of the staff who worked at the manor, and assumed that the children lived in these houses. Her thoughts moved to the uncommon generosity of the Devereux family to provide these dwellings for the staff.

Most of the guests arrived by carriage, though some single men came by horse. As the carriage rounded the bend of the parkway, Claire saw the remnants of the sun as it ducked away under the horizon, and so started the night ball. They were intending to arrive early, but it seemed that others had the same thought. Ahead of them was another carriage, letting out its passengers until it moved away. The carriage had one last jolt as it moved forward to the entrance, and the driver jumped down from the perch.

The door opened and a hand came out, offering assistance from the carriage. Claire waited patiently for the chance to disembark. Vivian wasted no time at all and rose from her seat and left the comforts of the carriage first. Aunt Sarah was second to leave the carriage, followed by Uncle Richard. The two then checked each other's appearance and straightened themselves for the introduction. Claire followed her aunt and uncle, and upon exiting the carriage, she looked first to the manor in its entire splendor. It was well lit and ready for the gala of the night, no expense spared as usual per Mrs. Devereux's taste. The door was open, and there was already an abundance of chatter to be heard from inside. Claire straightened herself and her belongings, allowing her to be presented in a strong fashion.

Though not quite as large as Brookfield Manor, the Devereux Estate was a splendid piece of architecture. The grounds were filled with patrons, each wearing elegant attire and joyfully heading towards the entry. Claire spent a few moments looking around at all the well-dressed people, until Vivian reached for her and tugged her towards the door. The six of them gathered together, and the Hawkins family entered the home first, announced properly by the doorman. "Introducing Mr. and Mrs. Hawkins, Mr. Hawkins, Miss Hawkins, and a Miss Hawkins." Then, as a family, they moved directly towards Mr. and Mrs. Devereux and greeted them personally.

Claire took a breath, and stood tall and graceful. The doorman took a moment to take in her appearance and smiled, though he should not have. He coughed his excuse and turned to the interior of the house. "Introducing Miss Stonewall." As this announcement rang among the attendees, some turned and looked to Claire, who stood there in the doorway. Many quieted their conversations for a moment, and looked upon her in awe of her beautiful appearance. Claire took a few steps into the foyer, and greeted Mr. and Mrs. Devereux. Mrs. Devereux was especially excited and curtsied with a grand smile upon her face.

Mr. Devereux took Claire's hand and bowed slightly. "A pleasure to see you this evening, Miss Stonewall, please make yourself at home." The words felt sincere as he was a kind and gentle man.

Mrs. Devereux looked to her in fascination. "Miss Stonewall, that is a fabulous gown." She placed her hand upon her chest, feebly feigning a hint of a breathtaking event.

"It was a gift from Mr. Stonewall, who sends his regards and heartfelt regret that he will be unable to attend."

"I am sorry to hear that, Miss Stonewall. But not to worry, I am sure that your card will be filled quickly this evening. If you need rest, please come to me and I will relieve you what I can from those that approach you." Claire saw that Mrs. Devereux was quite intent on having a pleasant evening.

"That would be most advantageous, and I appreciate your generous offer. Though I do believe that you will have your own card to attend." Claire then curtsied her farewell for the moment, as she turned to Vivian and stood beside her.

The house was filled with attendees, and Vivian had already begun her scan of available bachelors. The two of them looked to Richard and Sarah and nodded. The group of them split paths and began to mingle with the others. The dancing had not yet started, as the majority of people had not yet arrived, but the musicians were already playing familiar songs.

Claire walked to the nearby table that was filled with a bountiful feast of flavor and foods. She perused the available delicacies and took a small morsel, relishing in its splendid flavor. There were fine meats, cheeses, breads, and sweets all laid out neatly on the table. As Claire looked around the room, she saw various servants dressed in white attire with black ties and shined shoes, holding trays of various drinks and appetizers. Vivian reached down and plucked a small bite-sized piece of chocolate, placing it in her mouth, and showing a clear telltale smile to Claire. Claire joined her in indulging in the sweet treat, smiling herself as it was a delicacy made specifically for this event. Enjoying the fine smoothness of the chocolate, a server came to them, offering a drink.

Vivian and Claire both took a glass and sipped from it, the joining of the flavors robust and dreamy. They looked to each other and relaxed as they both enjoyed the combination most heartily. Vivian continued to look about the room, searching through the crowd of people for her first dance partner. Claire looked to see that many of the other attendees were dressed in fine style, and few had recognized her from a distance. Occasionally, Claire's eyes would meet another of her acquaintances, and she would nod to them. A few of Edwin's friends came to Claire and gave their blessings. Some of them stayed to talk briefly, asking

Claire of her household and family, then trading tales of current events before moving on in the crowd.

Claire and Vivian traversed through the fields of people, introducing each other to their acquaintances so that neither one nor the other would be left out of the conversation. Claire relaxed a bit more, as she felt more comfortable with the large crowd. Vivian never stopped scanning the room intently, searching for her soon-to-be partner for the first dance. Vivian detested being left out of a dance. She felt that it was her time to shine and gain the favor of a potential engagement.

They continued through the rooms until Vivian stopped in her tracks. Claire recognized that she had spotted her prey. There was a tall and muscular man looking towards them, and she immediately desired to be in the forefront of his attention. Without delay, she walked towards him, tugging Claire in tow. Not knowing exactly where Vivian was headed, Claire simply attempted to keep in stride as a pretense of knowledge. Vivian weaved between the crowds of people, and stopped once again. She leaned into Claire. "Look at him," she said softly, not taking her eyes off of the man.

Claire looked around the people in an attempt to sight Vivian's intended target. Before Claire was able to speak, the man approached them both, and Claire stood watching him silently as he came forward. As it had been when they first met, Claire found herself shy and speechless in his presence. She had already known that the man who had caught Vivian's eye was attending the very event. He stopped before them and bowed graciously, looking to Claire with his debonair smile. "Good evening, Miss Stonewall, it is a privilege to see you again."

AN INTRIGUING
INTERLUDE

CLAIRE BLUSHED, FEELING THE GRASP of Vivian's hands as they strangled her arm in anguish. It was not that she intended to withhold the information from Vivian, only that the subject of his handsomeness had not been a topic of their conversation. In part, Claire felt a childish pride come over her, knowing that Vivian was a bit jealous of her acquaintance with the man. She looked to him and curtsied. "Good evening to you, Mr. Clayton, it is a pleasure to see you as well." She separated herself slightly from Vivian and pointed her out to him. "Mr. Clayton, I would like to introduce my cousin, Miss Vivian Hawkins. Miss Hawkins, this is Mr. Nathaniel Clayton."

"An absolute pleasure, Miss Hawkins." He bowed to her honorably. Vivian, in turn, stared at him in astonishment, blushing and blinking rapidly. Nathaniel's confident smile shone brightly and Claire could sense a slight humor under his expression.

"The pleasure is mine, Mr. Clayton." Vivian allowed the words to escape her lips.

"Miss Stonewall, if you would do me the honor, I would like to request the first dance this evening," Nathaniel said promptly.

Vivian stood there for a moment in shock, unable to speak. Nathaniel was quite confident in his intention and wasted no time in asking Claire to dance. Claire placed her hand to her chest lightly and looked to Vivian shyly, not quite sure what to say to her. It was rare that Claire was asked to dance before Vivian. She turned to Nathaniel and curtsied again. "It would be my honor, Mr. Clayton."

If Vivian had not pulled Claire to Nathaniel, Claire was quite certain that Vivian would have been the first one asked to dance. Nathaniel anticipated Vivian's plight and looked to the rest of the attendees. Most of the men in the house were busy in conversation. However, Nathaniel called out to one of the many gentlemen standing behind him, "Mr. Lawton!"

Without a moment's hesitation, another strapping young man came to join them. "Mr. Lawton, please allow me to introduce you to Miss Claire Stonewall and Miss Vivian Hawkins. Ladies, allow me to present to you Mr. Edward Lawton. I do recall that you were looking for a partner for the first dance, and Miss Hawkins here is readily available."

Claire was taken aback by Nathaniel's actions. Not only had he immediately taken the opportunity to ask her to dance, he quickly found a handsome young man for Vivian as well. Vivian stood there stunned for a moment before she curtsied to the newcomer. "A pleasure, Mr. Lawton."

Claire bowed her head as well. "It is a pleasure to meet you, Mr. Lawton."

Edward bowed graciously to the two of them, and then looked to Vivian. He flashed a confident grin. "It would be my honor to accompany you on the first dance of the evening, Miss Hawkins, if you would be so inclined."

Vivian, not willing to take a chance on another suitor, replied cordially, "I would, Mr. Lawton." Of course, Claire knew that she would have to explain herself later, but for the moment, Vivian's disappointment had been sated.

With a call from the ballroom announcing that the dance floor was open, the grand double doors opened wide. A large gathering of people clamored into the oversized room and took their places. The musicians were situated on a balcony overlooking the floor, standing attentively and awaiting instruction. Mrs. Devereux stood in the very center of the room and called attention to herself. She turned to the musicians and clapped her hands together to quiet the room, calling out to them, "Musicians, if you please." Then, standing on one side of the centermost part of the room, all of the women lined up beside her. Their partners, on the other side of the floor, lined up in a similar manner.

The musicians propped up their instruments and burst into a light melody. Nathaniel and Claire looked upon each other and smiled. Nathaniel, a full head taller than Claire, had to look down slightly. Stepping in tune with the music, they began their interlude. Claire watched Nathaniel as he glided along, noticing that he was an accomplished dancer. The first few moves brought them together closely, and Claire felt a flutter of nerves within her. She realized that this was the closest she had ever been to another man, outside of her family. She was both intimidated by his presence and seduced by his charm.

They traversed and interacted with various partners while the music continued, joining together every few steps as the choreographed dance commenced. Each time they traded partners, Claire noticed Nathaniel's attention was more upon her than the partner he was with at the time. When the time came for them to be near each other once again, Nathaniel took the opportunity to speak a few words to her, timing them with the dance. "I am so glad I caught you when I did." His timing was impeccable, as they parted ways just as he finished.

Claire felt challenged. It was not that it was difficult for her to focus on the dance, but now she felt the want and need to converse with him as well. When they rejoined once again within the dance, she took the opportunity to reply, "I am intrigued, Mr. Clayton. Pray tell, why would you be so inclined to catch me so early in the night?"

Nathaniel was amused. He easily kept in step with the dance as he spoke to her. The dance called for a more intimate step with their partners, and Nathaniel used it to his advantage. "For I knew that it was my one chance to have you to myself. I would have found it difficult, to be sure, if your brother were in attendance."

Claire felt the full impact of his seductive tone, but steadied her mind as best she could before responding, "Why would it be as difficult as you say if my brother were present this evening?"

"I find that your brother is a bit intimidating, and if I would have spoken then as I do now, I do not know if he would have approved of my forwardness that morning. Truly, I find myself awestruck as much now as when we first met."

Claire caught the decadent words he chose, stimulating her thoughts as she listed them in her own mind. "Delightful, awestruck, intimidating… My dear Mr. Clayton, how ever is a girl to manage with such a passionate selection of conversation? You have caught me off guard, I have not the words to express the intrigue that you have shown to me this evening."

"I dare not challenge one of your capability, but I do hope to bring you a little enjoyment to our banter."

"Mr. Clayton, I must admit, this is quite unexpected. How am I to conclude the evening if not to take up a challenge of words with you? You have my utmost attention, and now prey on my ability to keep in step with the dance, and challenge my wits to speak to you in such decorum." Claire was barely able to end the last statement before they switched partners yet again. She looked now to Nathaniel as their conversation had begun to captivate her. He was not as boisterous in his speech when they had first met, but to her own admission, neither was she.

The music continued, and throughout the dance they rejoined each other, dueled with words and banter, and separated again. Claire enjoyed herself and Nathaniel's company thoroughly as the dance continued. Claire caught a glimpse of Vivian on occasion, and although she was dancing with Edward, she could see that Vivian was not as impressed with her dance partner.

The song soon came to its end, and all of the dancers stood back in their starting positions. The partners and the onlookers broke out in cheer, for the set was completed. Nathaniel walked towards Claire and bowed gracefully. "I thank you for the dance, Miss Stonewall, and the splendid conversation. I would like to request your company on the third set as well, in order to continue our discussion and accompaniment."

Claire curtsied. "Indeed, Mr. Clayton, perhaps another dance and challenge of wits awaits us. But why wait until the third set, is anything the matter?"

"I was requested by Miss Hawkins for the next dance, but do save the latter for me."

Claire realized what had happened and agreed to save the dance for him. She was not at all surprised that Vivian took to him so fondly, Nathaniel was quite a handsome gentleman. Claire turned and headed into the crowd, searching for a good spot to watch the dancers as they moved about. She was thankful for the rest, having not expected such an encounter. It was rare for her to spend any time with a man of wit and genuine ability, a fair challenge and a delight in her mind.

Claire glimpsed a servant holding a tray of refreshments, and she charged to him. Taking a glass of wine from the tray, she then managed her way through the crowd to the edge of the room. She stood with her back to the large glass windows that lined the outer wall and felt a light breeze come in from the cool air. The musicians began to play the next session of music and she took a sip of the wine. With the crowd's attention returned to the center of the room, Claire was awarded a moment of serenity. She looked out the window and saw that the darkness had crept in while they were inside. There was enough light from the manor to shine upon the stables and horses in the short distance. Several carriages were all aligned in a row, but Claire saw none of the drivers. She contemplated for a moment before assuming that they must have entered the house. She watched the light as it flickered about the scene.

She took another sip from the glass and as she was about to turn away from the window, she noticed some movement on the grounds below. There was a horse being guided from the stables and brought forward into the light. It was an excellent horse, and she could tell in its stride that it was a pride of its owners. Its lengthy tail swished in the night air, and it tousled its mane while it strode gently passing the carriages. Claire knew that the horse would not be walking freely in the open space, but she could not see who was guiding it. She watched intently for signs of the person leading the horse. The thoughts of the horse escaping the yard on its own rushed through her mind.

Suddenly, through a break in the carriages, she could see a figure leading the horse. She drank the remaining wine in her glass and watched silently. The man's face could not be easily seen, but he was dressed in stable attire. He took a brush to the horse, and began to gently stroke it. Claire's mind focused for a moment, thinking of the man out in the twilight tending to the horse. She wondered what kind of life he must lead to spend his time working when there was a grand celebration in the home. She knew it was not her place to ponder the trials of those less fortunate, but on occasion she found herself imagining the lives they led.

She continued to watch the man as he tenderly attended to the horse. She considered that there was a purpose in his actions, but could not understand why he had chosen this particular time. In her mind, she began to ponder the thoughts of the stableman. Foremost, she wondered if he simply enjoyed his work and the company of horses over people. Then again, it could be that he was specifically instructed to tend to the horse and pay special attention to it. Either way, it was not Claire's responsibility to consider such actions, nor even to take note of them, but she found herself intrigued.

The man suddenly turned towards the home, and Claire felt his eyes upon her. She turned quickly, hoping that the man had not noticed her watching him. With a slight pause, she caught sight of Vivian, speaking to yet another fine-looking gentleman. Surprised that she allowed the thought of the stableman to entertain her thoughts for so long, she turned around as another server came strolling by with a few appetizers on a platter. Claire took one of the delicate pieces and placed it in her mouth, enjoying the taste of it. Without a glance back through the window, she stepped back into the festivities of the ball. She forced the thought of the stableman out of her mind for the remainder of the evening, and continued to indulge in the party of the night.

Although there were many eligible people worthy of Claire's attention gathered together under such opportune circumstances, Claire was not one to go about the room and open conversations in which she was not invited. Typically, in these events, she had no problem occupying herself with open conversation, because her brother or Vivian would be so dutiful in their introductions. The night was young, and besides the occasional nod to an onlooker or greeting from some past acquaintance, Claire mostly kept to herself. She spent a good portion of her time watching others and filling her own mind with stories as she would see them from a distance. This was her comfort, in such circumstances. To an outsider's point of view, it may have looked like she was alone and bored, but the truth was, Claire was quite content with herself.

At times, it did present a problem for Claire, for this event was quite different for her than most. Not only did the occasional acquaintance console her on the loss of her father, but her brother was not present and without his protective shield, she felt a bit more defenseless against the queries. It had only been a year since her father's passing, and because of that, she could sense that many of the attendees who had not seen her since wondered about her wellbeing. Occasionally, Claire was reminded of times when her father or brother had made introductions or comments, causing her to feel the loneliness creep up within her.

A NIGHT WORTH REMEMBERING

BEFORE LONG, THE THOUGHTS WERE turning sour in Claire's mind, and she had determined that she would not waste such an evening on poor thoughts. With renewed vigor and a smile upon her face, she took the few steps to Vivian and stood beside her. Vivian was giving a rather handsome gentleman her attention and did not notice Claire's presence until she bumped into her. Vivian immediately took Claire's wrist and squeezed it gently.

After Vivian had finished with her farewell to the young man, she turned to Claire. She was barely able to contain the excitement, and panted for her breath. "Oh my!" exclaimed Vivian. She pulled up a paper fan to cover her face and whispered to Claire without being seen, "Oh my, indeed!"

Claire pulled out her own paper fan and opened it so that the two of them could be seen having a private conversation, though they were laughing together more than talking. Through Vivian's intense interaction throughout the party, she had filled her dance card for the entire evening, snatching the opportunity with each and every one of the various handsome gentlemen. Her goal was to not let a single man, whom she felt worthy, slip through her grasp.

Claire did not concern herself with her dances for the evening as Vivian did, but listened intently as Vivian began to call them out among the crowd. The two of them walked arm in arm as they paraded through the rooms. It was almost time to begin the next series of dances. Claire looked towards the entry and was captivated as she saw Nathaniel standing proudly and looking in her direction. To her embarrassment, he smiled softly, as if he had been watching her like a hawk stalking its prey from above. Claire, stricken by his intense gaze, cautiously whispered to Vivian, "And there he is!"

Vivian looked in the direction of the entry. "Yes he is. And a fine catch, cousin, if ever there was one in the whole house."

"If he is such a fine catch, why are you talking to everyone else?" Claire knew that Vivian would do whatever she could to stay in the sights of a man of his stature.

"Because, sweet cousin, I already danced with him. I must tell you, Miss Stonewall, you have put a spell on the poor man. All he could talk about while we danced was you!" Vivian winked as she looked to Claire, and gave her a little push towards Nathaniel. Claire looked back, almost scowling at Vivian for not telling her what was said. She turned back to see Nathaniel standing there with his hand held out, ready and willing to usher her to the dance floor.

Claire put the fan away and took Nathaniel's hand, the rosy color from her cheeks still present as the thought of him overwhelmed her.

"We meet again, Miss Stonewall," he said to her as he flashed his familiar smile.

"Pray tell, Mr. Clayton, how was your dance with my dear sweet cousin?" Claire wanted to learn about what they discussed so desperately that she could not think of anything else to say at that moment.

Nathaniel ushered Claire towards the dance floor. "Miss Stonewall, do I detect a faint hint of jealousy in your question?"

Claire blushed once again as they reached the dance floor. The musicians collected their instruments and the crowd focused on the dancers once again. She had not imagined herself to be so curious, but the question was so abrupt that it could easily have been interpreted as such. She found herself looking upon him, not saying a word, but biting her bottom lip in fear that he had caught her in the act of doing something wrong, asking something she should not have asked.

The music began and Claire felt saved for the moment, not knowing exactly how to reply to his question. They moved along in the dance, and she broke the silence that had taken over her. "I must admit, Mr. Clayton, you do have your wits about you this night. You know exactly how to take advantage of the situation." Her curiosity of their discussion was not forgotten, but she figured it was best not to ask again and would have to wait until she could speak to Vivian in private.

Nathaniel responded with a laugh, and as they danced, the conversation turned. They battled each other with fine quips as before, enjoying each other's companionship. Claire could barely keep up with him, he had one of the most insatiable and intelligent tongues in all of her experience. At times, she struggled and had to focus her attention to do her best to be as witty and affluent. It seemed that the two of them were alone in the entire ballroom, dancing and moving through partners as if they were ghosts, not paying any attention to those they came in contact with. Their eyes rarely separated for the entire dance, and before they realized it, the music had ended.

Claire turned to Nathaniel and curtsied as she had done previously.

"If you have no objections, Miss Stonewall, I would like to request your presence for the remainder of the evening." Claire stood there beside herself. No man had ever asked her for the entire night. She had imagined that a man of his caliber would find her intolerable or boring after such a long engagement. She quickly looked around to see if she could spot Vivian, but she had no such luck. She looked to Nathaniel, unsure of what to say. "It would be a pleasure to spend the evening with you, Mr. Clayton." Claire accompanied him to the next room, allowing them both to relax and talk before the next set of dances.

The rest of the evening wore on in much the same way. Claire attended to Nathaniel and would take to the floor each dance, and their conversation continued uninterrupted. Various subjects were discussed between them, from philosophical to the more social of topics. Claire was quite intrigued by Nathaniel as the night carried on. As they danced, Claire would occasionally catch the eye of Vivian, who smiled back at her. At one point, Claire looked to see Mrs. Devereux, who was talking to another lady who was attending, speaking together in confidence, and as their eyes met, Mrs. Devereux winked.

Claire suddenly realized what had happened. She was so completely lost in the attention of Nathaniel that she had not separated from him for the entire night. Mrs. Devereux must be quite beside herself, thinking that as a matchmaker she had paired Claire and Nathaniel together. Claire looked to Nathaniel, a look of surprise on her face. For a brief moment, the thought of the possibility with him entered her mind. Surprisingly to her, she did not flinch at the thought of it; rather, she was pleased by the notion. Nathaniel may very well be the one to ask for her hand. She attempted to force the thought out of her mind in order to enjoy the remainder of the night. But it was too late, she found herself thinking more and more about his company, and was intoxicated by the thought.

Claire continued to engage in dance and conversations with Nathaniel through the rest of the night. Her attention was focused on him, and the rest of the attendees were absent from her mind. The only exception was Vivian, who occasionally came to them between sets to discuss her latest dance partner. While Vivian was talking with Claire, Nathaniel called to one of the other gentleman nearby, discussing various topics that Claire could not overhear. All throughout the night, Nathaniel showered Claire with personal attention, but allowed her to converse in private when the time came.

As the night wore on into the early morning, Mrs. Devereux was still seen on the dance floor, hand in hand with yet another younger gentleman, flirting and carrying on about the other eligible ladies who had attended. It seemed as though it were her goal to have each and every one of them paired off in the night's engagement. Claire caught the attention of Mrs. Devereux and noted the look upon her face several times, knowing that she was quite pleased with her intention for the two of them.

The time came for the last dance of the night. Claire took the opportunity to look around the room, and found Vivian with yet another new partner. She then spotted Mrs. Devereux, this time holding Mr. Devereux's hand as the dance began. Claire was reminded that it was customary for them to dance the last dance together, a sign for all those acquainted with them that this was goodnight. The song was slower than all those that preceded it, for it was reserved as a couple's dance. Nathaniel was standing beside Claire on the dance floor, holding Claire's hand, as he had been the entire evening. Their playful banter had long passed, and now they looked deeply into each other's eyes. Claire could not have imagined such a splendid evening, and found herself lost in her partner's attentive gaze.

At the conclusion of the dance, they applauded the musicians and all gathered with their parties, saying their goodbyes as they headed towards the door. The remaining carriages were prepped and ready for the last of the attendees. More than half of the attendees had already left for their homes, and the crowd was thinned quite dramatically. Nathaniel, who arrived alone to the dance, had come by horse, and stood just before Claire, sharing words with Richard and Sarah. Claire, arm and arm with Vivian, both too exhausted to speak much, made their way to the exit. Michael and Anna Beth were behind them. Anna Beth was almost completely asleep, and Michael was more carrying her to the entry than walking beside her.

Mr. and Mrs. Devereux stood at the doorway, saying their goodbyes to everyone who was leaving. One by one, each family made their way to their carriage and drove off into the early morning light. The sky, once darkened in the night, now was beginning to lighten, and Claire knew that the sun would crest over the horizon soon. The Hawkins family came to the doorway and said their goodbyes and generous thanks to Mr. and Mrs. Devereux. Nathaniel stood by them and waited patiently for Claire's exit.

Claire hugged Mrs. Devereux tightly, thanking her for the wonderful evening, and as she did, Mrs. Devereux whispered softly to her, "I shall not wait long for an update, Miss Stonewall."

"I shall be sure to keep you informed." Claire had no doubt that she wanted to know of any updates in her relationship with Nathaniel.

As Claire exited the doorway, Nathaniel reached for her hand and took her into his, carefully guiding her and Vivian to the carriage. After Vivian entered the carriage, Nathaniel took the opportunity to pull Claire aside, allowing Michael and Anna Beth to climb inside. He did not keep Claire long, but lifted her hand and placed his other hand upon hers. "Thank you for an exuberant evening, Miss Stonewall," he said softly and bowed to her gracefully.

Claire curtsied through her exhaustion and looked upon him softly. "Trust me when I tell you that this was the most wonderful night that I have ever had in all my life." She almost wanted to embrace him, but thought better of it. It seemed that he felt the same way she did. If it were not for social graces and expectations...

"May I call upon you soon?"

"I shall look forward to it."

With that, Nathaniel guided Claire to the carriage and assisted her inside. He closed the door and stepped away, watching the carriage as it headed off down the parkway. Claire looked through the window and saw him climb upon his horse and begin to trot behind them.

CHARLES' RETURN HOME

CLAIRE AWOKE SLIGHTLY, HER BODY aching as she stretched under the covers. She had slept soundly through the early morning, no doubt due to her overall exhaustion from the gala. The heavy curtains were pulled tight, shielding the room from the bright sunlight as it was late in the day. Her eyes opened fully and the thoughts of the evening swam in her mind.

She lay there in solitude for a few moments, reminiscing about the night before, and was amused as she recalled the various conversations that she'd had with Nathaniel. The dancing and bantering with him seemed to plague her mind incessantly, and now she knew that he had taken residence in her life. She eventually rose from the bed, and went to the curtains to peek through them. It was a fine day outside, and the sun was beating down upon the grounds. The snow had nearly melted away completely, and Claire was even more excited by the coming spring. A few moments passed by as she looked out of the window, and the door behind her quietly opened. Mary had poked her head into the door to see if she had risen from her somber sleep.

"Good morning, Miss Stonewall."

"Yes, Mary…" She turned and looked to Mary, taking in a deep breath. "It truly is a grand morning." Claire could not help herself, the night before had left her with such joy and happiness that it spilled into the next day. She danced her way to the closet, and began perusing the various dresses it contained. Mary opened the curtains, allowing the light to fill the room. It was uncommon for Claire to think twice about choosing her attire for the day, but after pulling out her usual garment, she returned it and selected a more ornate one. Her eagerness for Nathaniel's arrival was evident as she took the dress behind the screen.

Claire exited from behind the screen, sat herself at the dressing table, and began to run the pearl-handled brush through her tangled hair. As she sat there in front of the mirror, she started to hum one of the tunes that the musicians had played the night before. It was quite apparent that Claire had a wondrous night at the ball. As Claire finished putting her hair into place, she stepped lively from the chair and continued down the hall. She stopped briefly at the portrait of her parents and placed her kiss upon the frame, smiling, then biting her bottom lip as the thought of her romantic encounter came to the forefront of her mind. She began to pretend she was telling her parents about the prior night's event, smiling and blushing lightly as she imagined their responses.

As Claire turned, she continued to dance her way to the top of the staircase, reaching out with her hand and grasping the railing. "Well, I must say, you are bright and chipper this late afternoon," called a voice from the foot of the stairs. Claire stopped for a moment, focusing on the figure standing there and looking back at her.

"Brother!" exclaimed Claire as she bounded down the stairs. Reaching for him with open arms, she hugged him tightly and kissed him on the cheek. "I thought you were not to be home for a few more days."

Charles laughed. Catching Claire in his arms, he held her tightly as she kissed his cheek. He stood, smiling as she pulled away to her own stance. "Oh? Would you have rather I stay away and leave you to your obvious exhilaration?"

Claire blushed, turning her head slightly in embarrassment. "No!" she replied quickly. "I just am surprised to see you, is all. Happy, that is for sure, but surprised nonetheless."

"Well, I must admit, you are in a delightful state. I am glad to see you with as much enthusiasm."

"Oh, Charles, I have had the most wonderful night of my entire life."

"In that case, please do tell…"

As the two of them walked to the drawing room, Claire recounted the events of the ball. She spoke very highly of Nathaniel and the interactions they'd had throughout the night. She then described to him her thoughts of Vivian, and her reactions to Nathaniel, as well as Mrs. Devereux's plot as it flourished through the evening. Claire described the state of the manor, the music and food that were presented in detail. However, the majority of her story revolved around Nathaniel.

Charles listened intently and asked only a question or two as Claire carried on about the ball. Towards the end of her tale, he sat back in his seat and looked to her, his hands covering his face as if he were in deep thought. "So tell me, sister. How do you feel about Mr. Clayton?"

Claire stopped for a moment, and realized how apparent her emotions must have been. She took her bottom lip into her teeth, hiding her embarrassment for the moment, and thought about how she could respond to him. "Oh, Charles! I have never felt this way for another man. I find myself longing to see him again soon."

"I am so very happy for you, sister. He is a handsome gentleman, and I am sure he will call soon." He smiled and Claire could tell that he was quite sincere.

Suddenly, the words from Charles struck a chord in Claire's mind. The last request from Nathaniel entered her thoughts. She was exhausted when he mentioned his intent to call upon her, and had not thought to ask him when to expect his arrival. She had prepared herself to see Nathaniel that day, but realized that she had no idea when she would see him next.

NATHANIEL
ARRIVES FOR TEA

SAMUEL OPENED THE DOOR, AND Claire and Charles turned to see him. "A Mr. Clayton calling to see Miss Stonewall." Charles and Claire exchanged glances. There was an obvious excitement in Claire's face as Charles looked to Samuel calmly. "Show him in."

As Samuel turned around and left the room, Claire attended to her appearance. Claire caught Charles chuckling under his breath and looked to him, sticking her tongue out of her pursed lips. She knew that he had rarely seen her so intent on her outward appearance. Within moments, Samuel opened the doors once again and stepped to the side as he made way for Nathaniel.

Nathaniel was dressed properly and wore a fine suit, complete with pleated shirt and a top hat that he had tucked under his arm. "Welcome, Mr. Clayton," Charles greeted him as they bowed their hellos.

"Good morning, Mr. Stonewall." He turned to Claire who was smiling, her eyes fixed upon him. "And good morning to you, Miss Stonewall."

She bowed her head and curtsied. "Yes, a splendid morning indeed, Mr. Clayton." She was suddenly aware of the flush of warmth once again on her cheeks. Why she felt the need to blush so often was a mystery to her.

Charles watched as they said their hellos, and decisively spoke to Nathaniel. "Mr. Clayton, would you care to join us for tea? I fear the morning has all but left us this day, and I am sure that Miss Stonewall would agree that it is high time for some edible sustenance."

Nathaniel took his eyes off Claire, which seemed to be a challenge for him, and turned to Charles. "It would be an honor, Mr. Stonewall."

"Very well, I will make the necessary arrangements. Please make yourself comfortable, I will be just a few moments." Charles headed out the door to instruct the staff to make preparations for tea.

"How did you sleep, Miss Stonewall?" asked Nathaniel, allowing Claire to refocus her thoughts to his presence.

"I slept well, and you, Mr. Clayton?"

"What sleep I was able to capture will have to suffice for me. I could not stop the need to come and see you."

"Mr. Clayton, you flatter me so. I would think it more important to rest for the night. You must maintain your vigilance in the event we continue our battle of wits."

"I must declare, Miss Stonewall. You have bewitched me, for neither wake nor sleep saves me from my thoughts of you. And I, at your mercy this day, pray that you take pity on a man who can do nothing to save himself from his torment."

"Mr. Clayton, I must protest. You barely know me, nor I you for that matter. There is no reason for your mind to think of me, 'less you let your imagination take control of your thoughts."

"Ah, so it is true then?"

"I will not pretend to know what you are referring to, Mr. Clayton. What is it that is true?"

"Your intrigue and conversation are as beautiful as you are, no matter the time of day"—he paused with a light chuckle—"or lack of sleep."

"You say these things, sir, but heed not my protest!"

"Miss Stonewall, I just find myself unable to resist the temptation of your intoxicating presence and joyous conversation."

"I must admit that when I am in your company, I too find the chance to converse with you irresistible."

They sat together upon the couch, unaware of what was going on around them. Claire and Nathaniel were too focused on their conversation and their time together to pay attention to anything else. Samuel had entered the room once more and took the opportunity to grab their attention by coughing lightly. "A Miss Hawkins, calling upon Miss Stonewall."

Claire looked to Samuel, surprised to hear about her cousin's arrival. "Are we not the popular household this morning? You may show her in, Samuel." Samuel turned to fetch Vivian, and entered the drawing room with Vivian close behind him.

As Vivian entered the room, both Nathaniel and Claire stood to greet her. Charles had not yet returned so Nathaniel spoke first. "Good afternoon, Miss Hawkins," he said to her with a bow.

Vivian quickly looked to Claire, her mouth gaping open, indicating her surprise at Nathaniel's presence. Claire shot a look to Vivian who then quickly shut her mouth, looking to Nathaniel as he bowed to her. "Good afternoon to you, Mr. Clayton. It is a pleasure to see you again." Vivian curtsied and again looked back to Claire. "Please excuse my interruption. I did not know that you had company this afternoon."

"Cousin, you are welcome here any time." Claire remembered that Charles was getting tea prepared, and thought it best to properly invite Vivian since she was present. "Vivian, we were just about to have tea, would you care to join us?"

"That would be delightful, cousin. As long as I am not intruding by any means."

Claire called out to Samuel just as he was leaving the room. "Samuel, please inform Mr. Stonewall that Miss Hawkins will be joining us for tea as well."

Samuel bowed to Claire. "Yes, Miss Stonewall," he said as he turned towards the kitchen.

Claire offered her hand to the adjacent couch, inviting Vivian to sit with them, and Vivian sat comfortably upon the sofa. After a brief and awkward silence, Claire was first to offer a casual subject. "How is the family, Miss Hawkins? After last night, I do not remember who was awake and who had fallen to sleep during our travel home."

"They are still sleeping or lazing about the house, half awake. In all honesty, I was sure that I was to find you in a similar state. I am pleased to see that you are not."

"I woke not long ago myself, but to my surprise, my brother had returned home this morning. He has gone to organize our tea, but I am sure he will be back shortly."

Nathaniel chimed in, "Did you rest well, Miss Hawkins?"

"I did, sir. I do not put much faith in sleep. Wasting the day away, in my opinion. And you, Mr. Clayton, how was your night's rest?"

"Given the fact that I enjoyed a rather masterful ball last night, I slept quite soundly. It is always good to have a bit of adventure during the day to help you sleep at night."

Claire noticed the inconsistency in Nathaniel's response to Vivian. Although his reply was different than when she had asked him, Claire attributed his previous answer to the privacy that the two of them shared before Vivian arrived. She watched Nathaniel as his demeanor seemed to shift now that Vivian was with them.

Charles entered the room, and bowed to Vivian lightly. "Good afternoon, Miss Hawkins."

"Good afternoon, cousin. I am happy to see that you arrived safely from your trip to London."

Charles sat in one of the smaller couches nearby. "Tea should be ready within the hour. I do hope you do not mind waiting."

Nathaniel was first to respond. "I have already come to my most pressing appointment, and have the day to spend, as long as it suits Miss Stonewall."

Claire turned her head downward, blushing once again. Charles replied cordially, "You are welcome to stay, and the day itself looks to be turning out to be splendid."

After a few moments, Charles continued the conversation. "I was just asking Miss Stonewall to regale me with the stories of the ball. I was so unfortunate to have missed the festivities, but I am glad to hear that it was a rather engaging event."

Vivian piped up and recounted her evening to the entire group, telling various stories and spreading some of the gossip that she had heard. The four of them engaged in conversation, laughing and making comments as the stories unfolded. Time slipped by until Samuel entered the room and announced that the tea was ready.

The four of them stood and entered the dining room where a bountiful tea was set before them. The table was set for all four of them with various pastries, breads, jams, meats, and cheeses along with the tea. They arranged themselves at the table, Charles taking the head of the table, Claire and Nathaniel on one side, and Vivian on the other. The four of them continued their conversation through the meal and spent the next few hours in comfort while they sat at the table and exchanged stories.

The day moved on without their notice and the door opened once again with Samuel carrying a platter in his hands. The platter he was carrying was small and uncovered with a folded piece of parchment lying upon its surface. He walked past the table and presented the letter to Charles. Charles took the parchment from the small silver tray and spoke softly. "Thank you, Samuel." Samuel bowed his head slightly and turned back out of the dining room.

It was common for Charles to receive letters from various correspondents throughout the day. Most of the time it was business related, except for the occasional letter to Claire from her aunt. Charles opened the letter before them, and they were intrigued. If it were a business letter, then he would have opened it in the privacy of his study. Charles glanced over the contents before proceeding to read them aloud. "Mr. Charles Stonewall and Miss Claire Stonewall are hereby cordially invited to attend the Springhurst Spring Ball, held Saturday, March twenty-second at dusk. Respond if you please to Mr. Benjamin Devitt by the sixth day of March. We are looking forward especially to your attendance."

Vivian chimed in at the end of Charles' recital, "Please do say you are attending, dear cousins. I have already returned our invitation, and am quite excited that the ball is so soon."

Claire noticed Charles hesitate for a moment. As she looked to him, she saw his concern over the letter and knew that he was troubled with the announcement. She whispered lightly to him, "Brother?" Claire did not hide her questioning gaze as Charles glanced to her.

Charles looked to Vivian and nodded to her. "Yes, we will both be attending." Then he turned to Claire and spoke softly to her concern. "I would rather not subject you to another ball without a proper escort."

"Yes, brother…" Claire sighed lightly. "Thank you. Your company means so much to me."

Nathaniel waited until their conversation ended before speaking. "Yes, I have already returned my invitation as well, and will be looking forward to the event. And before any other can stake their claim to it, I would like to take this opportunity to request the first dance of the evening with you, Miss Stonewall," he said with a devilish grin. This made Claire blush and think of last night, when he occupied nearly all of her time. Claire was enthused at the thought of yet another festive ball.

"It would be a pleasure to join you, Mr. Clayton, we have had a splendid dance, and you are an accomplished partner."

They continued to talk amongst themselves for a while thereafter until Charles stood from the table. "If you would excuse me, I will take this opportunity to respond our attendance in kind," he announced before heading to his study.

"Mr. Stonewall," Vivian called out to him before he could leave the room. "If it would not be a bother, I would like to request to spend the evening here with Miss Stonewall." Vivian would occasionally request to spend the night, typically to escape the dealings with her own family. However, Claire assumed that she wanted more private time with her. It had been a while since Vivian last stayed the night, but she knew she was always welcome.

Charles looked briefly to Claire to see any sign of disapproval. "It would be splendid to have you join us for the evening, Miss Hawkins. I will make the necessary arrangements." Charles decided to take it upon himself, as it seemed that Claire had her hands full with both Vivian and Nathaniel wanting her attention.

"Thank you, brother, we shall be in the drawing room if you care to join us."

Charles continued towards the study with the letter in hand. As he left the room, they stood from the dining table and moved into the drawing room. Once there, they sat upon the couches once more and continued on with their general discussion. Claire noticed that Nathaniel was very attentive to the conversation, as if he were going to be tested on the discussion at a later time. Claire was impressed that he would also ask a related question now and again to show his genuine interest in anything that he was unfamiliar with.

A NIGHT WITH VIVIAN

THE NIGHT WAS LATE, AND darkness had covered Brookfield Manor. Much of the staff had already retired from the long day, but a few were still walking the halls. Although there were plenty of rooms available for Vivian to use, she chose to stay with Claire in her room instead. In their nightgowns and tucked under the covers of Claire's bed, they giggled and talked as they did when they were younger. The light from the candlestick shone through the thin sheet, allowing them to still see each other easily.

"Mr. Clayton seems to have a keen interest in you. Have you considered his intentions?"

"I have thought about it. He is a fine gentleman. But what makes you so certain he is interested in me?"

Vivian pretended to be awestruck. "Claire! How do you not see the very moment you are in the room with him that he cannot take his eyes off of you? He beckons to your every call, and even takes your lightest suggestion or comment with a defined interest that could not be mistaken for anything else. The way he talks about you is nearly fanatical. Have you not seen how he behaves when he is around you?"

"All right, Vivian. Yes, I have seen the way he looks at me. I am unable to say that I am not smitten by the way he makes me feel."

"I would not be surprised if he asked for your hand."

Claire quickly gawked at her comment. "My hand? Why ever do you think that he would want someone like me? We are far too different!"

"Do you honestly think he minds? He most certainly made his intentions clear enough."

"Cousin, I have no idea what you are going on about. I have my own dealings to be had, and I do not think it is wise to play fancy with such a man."

"This is me you are talking to. I have seen the way you look at him, you need not play coy with me."

"I know, Vivian. I know what you say is true, but I do not understand it. Why does he have such a keen interest in me? I am nothing special. There are far better than I to be had. What is it that he sees in me that I do not see myself? Why has he not fallen for you?"

"You have no idea the thoughts of gentlemen, and it is obvious. If he had any inkling towards me, you would not see him behave the way he does when I am around. It is as if I am not in the room at all. He is so much more attentive to you than you realize, and he is quite smitten. Though I do not know for how long. You best snatch him up while you can, before you lose your grasp on him."

Claire was beginning to feel a bit uncomfortable and attempted to change the focus of the conversation. "What about you? How many men have caught your fancy as of late? I am quite sure you have a long list of admirers who, even to this day, are at your beck and call."

"There are a few, that is for sure. But none can hold a candle to Mr. Clayton. How lucky you are, cousin, to have found such a wonderful man. I could only wish to be as lucky as you are."

"Cousin, you have nothing to worry about. You have so many admirers, you have the ability to pick and choose a man worthy of your time," comforted Claire.

"Yes, but it is not only the man that I need to be concerned with."

"Oh?" said Claire, intrigued by Vivian's response.

Claire noticed a sadness come over Vivian as she spoke softly. "This is just between us, Claire. I love my family but I often find myself wishing I were in another one. Our family is simple and lacks the graces that make it important in society. Yes, they are in society and attend the right balls, but they could be so much more than they are. With just a little effort, the Hawkins family could be considered one of the best families in the area."

"But your family is very kind and generous. In my mind, they are already a huge part of society."

"I think it's more that I feel so different from them. I want more than what we have and are. I believe we could increase our stature with just some minor adjustments."

Claire struggled to understand Vivian's desire for a different family. In her mind, the Hawkins family was well known throughout the area, and was highly respected in the community. They were considered a kind and generous family, and Claire believed that was all that mattered.

Vivian, apparently seeing Claire's hesitation, attempted to reconcile her statement and mask her true feelings. "I do love them so. Enough of that, we need to get our beauty sleep so we can look fresh in the morning for Mr. Clayton." Claire rolled her eyes and they joined in laughter. Within moments they slipped into sleep. Claire's last thoughts were of Nathaniel and dancing the night away.

The following morning, Claire woke to the brightness of the sun as it shone through the window. Vivian was already out of bed and urging her to get up. Claire knew that Vivian would not allow her out of the room with anything less than her best attire. Mary entered the room and stood by, ready to assist them in their preparations. The two of them did not talk much as they got dressed, but they enjoyed each other's company.

Claire sat at the dressing table after Vivian finished. Instead of doing her own final touches, Vivian began to work her magic. Claire simply watched as Vivian worked with her hair. As per her usual, Vivian made no small effort in making Claire look radiant for the day ahead. They embraced each other before heading out the door and into the hall.

As they approached the stairs, Vivian stopped before the portrait and waited for Claire to pay her respects to her parents. She had always known Claire's morning routine, and had never said anything about it. Claire knew Vivian understood it was something that had to be done without complaint or explanation.

Arm in arm, the two of them walked down the stairs, headed for the breakfast nook in hopes of getting a fine meal this morning. Charles peered from his study and saw that they had awakened. He left the study and greeted them. "Good morning, Claire and Miss Hawkins. At least you can call it morning. If it were not for you, Vivian, I believe it would be quite the challenge to get my sister up so early in the day." He was teasing them, and they knew it simply by his tone.

"Mr. Stonewall, do not jest your poor sister. She takes full advantage of her beauty sleep. Do you not think your sister looks absolutely radiant?" She waited for his response, knowing that he really had no choice but to agree with her.

"Absolutely!" he responded quickly and looked to Claire as the three of them walked together into the breakfast nook.

Lily noticed their entry and quickly made her way back into the kitchen to gather the morning breakfast. The three of them sat at the table and glanced out the window to the bright and sunny day.

Lily entered the small room and dressed the table with tray after tray of food, each warm and inviting. Vivian's eyes opened wide, seeing the splendor that was presented to them. She took upon her plate the most decadent of entrees available. Claire looked to Lily fondly and Lily winked before returning to the kitchen.

Each of them devoured the delicious food before them. Occasionally they would stop briefly to have a quick discussion of some random topic, or to take a drink from the tea that was provided.

"Do you have plans today, cousin?" asked Charles.

Vivian looked up from her demolished plate of food, having taken the sweetest part of each of her chosen items and enjoying them most heartedly. "Yes, cousin, I am due back at home this early afternoon and will be taking my leave shortly. Is there something that I may assist you with, or something that you need of me?"

"I only wish for you to take a letter to your father for me. I would rather not make the extra trip if you are surely returning home soon."

"I would be honored to deliver it to him on your behalf. He will have it in his hands the moment I arrive at home. Besides, you have been gracious with me enough with this meal and a fine night's sleep."

"I would hope it was a fine night, though you must have spent most of it getting yourself ready for such a simple journey." Charles paused to show a slanted smile. "You are far too well dressed for such a short distance."

Vivian retorted with a smirk, and Claire could see her concoct a suitable response. "You might want to take a good look in the mirror, Charles." Claire could not help but chuckle under her breath as she heard the playful tone in Vivian's voice. "Unlike you, I prefer to not have the appearance of having slept in the barn the night before."

Charles and Vivian broke out in laughter. Having watched the two of them banter back and forth, Claire could not help but to join them.

They spent the next few moments enjoying the conclusion of the breakfast. All of them had reached their fill for the meal, and were quite content. "Unfortunately, it is time that I returned to my own home, I am expected there shortly. If you have that letter, I will take it with me now." She wiped her face one last time, tossing the napkin lightly onto the table, and stood.

Charles and Claire both stood from the table as well. Claire walked to Vivian and took her arm. "Cousin, I shall see you on your way then."

Charles left the room for his study to collect the prewritten letter that he needed Vivian to deliver to Richard. Claire casually walked with Vivian towards the foyer. Vivian's belongings had been brought downstairs and were placed in a box for traveling. Samuel saw their approach and left to fetch Forrester and the carriage. Charles followed from the study and handed the letter to Vivian. She promptly placed the letter in her waistcoat pocket.

Charles and Vivian said their brief farewell before he returned to his study. Claire and Vivian made their way toward the carriage. Just as Vivian entered it, Claire heard a horse approaching the home. Nathaniel reared the horse next to the carriage. "Good afternoon, Miss Hawkins," he said to Vivian, seeing her as she poked her head through the carriage door.

"Good afternoon, Mr. Clayton." Vivian pulled herself back into the carriage and shot a glance to Claire. Vivian's expression was that of shock and awe, which made Claire feel a bit embarrassed.

Nathaniel came off his horse and handed the reins to Samuel. He strode to Claire, bowing before her and looking deeply into to her eyes. "Good afternoon, Miss Stonewall."

Claire blushed deeper than ever before and nearly melted on the spot. She steadied herself as she felt weakened from his overwhelming charm. "Good afternoon, Mr. Clayton."

The carriage took off down the pathway, and Claire invited Nathaniel into the home. "What brings you to Brookfield Manor this fine day?"

"Is it that you ask to confirm what you already suspect? Or have I not explained myself fully just the day before? I have come here to spend time with you, Miss Stonewall. What other glorious purpose could there ever be?" He smiled, flattering her in every way possible.

Claire looked to the house and caught a glimpse of her brother looking back at them intently through the window of his study. She turned her attention toward Nathaniel and walked with him into the foyer. His devotion to her attention was unmistakable, and Claire was beside herself with this new concept.

TIME WITH MR. CLAYTON

FOR THE NEXT FEW DAYS, Nathaniel continued to call upon Claire at her home. Each day, they spent time talking and taking walks along the grounds. They asked questions of one another, shared opinions and beliefs, and told stories of various past events. Claire was enthralled with his presence, and looked forward to each day she was able to be with him. Even Charles kept his distance from the two of them, giving them the space that was needed. Claire payed little attention to Charles' absence, focusing her attention on Nathaniel whenever he was around.

One bright and sunny day, Nathaniel arrived as he typically did, but that day they had planned to go out to town together. Claire had bestowed a stately gown for the day, as this was the first time they would be in public together since the ball. He stood in the foyer and looked upon her as she came to the top of the stairs. She looked down and gazed upon him. He was dressed in a fine suit, and ready for their engagement in town.

Claire made her way down the stairwell, and as she reached the bottom of the stairs, Nathaniel came to her. He bowed before her and spoke to her in his most charming way. "You look beautiful, Miss Stonewall."

Claire blushed, though she had been doing so less often as she was accustomed to his flattery. "Thank you, Mr. Clayton, and may I say you are quite handsome as well. I do not recall seeing that suit before."

Nathaniel looked to what he was wearing briefly and retorted, "We have not known each other long enough to reveal our entire wardrobes."

Samuel opened the door and bowed slightly as they passed over the threshold. Forrester stood there, holding the carriage door open for them. He was smiling as they approached, a grin that showed pride and a caring sentiment. "Good afternoon, Miss Stonewall, Mr. Clayton."

Nathaniel did not respond to him, instead he helped Claire into the carriage and followed her inside. The plan for the day had already been set forth, and Claire looked to Forrester as she sat down in the carriage.

The grass was almost completely covering the ground once again. The flowers and bushes showed their buds. Although it was not spring yet, much of the foliage around the grounds had begun to grow early that year. The birds were chirping and bountiful in the lands, which made Claire relax in the songs they would sing. She sat back once again in her seat and her eyes caught Nathaniel's, feeling comfort in his watchful embrace.

As the carriage began to enter Springhurst, the carriage wheels rumbled against the cobblestone roadways, and the sounds from the horses' feet got louder and more defined. Children could be seen playing along the roads, weaving in and out of patrons as they walked along. The town was a busy place, full of life.

Claire watched the patrons through the windows of the carriage. She pondered their purpose and imagined the stories behind their actions. She breathed deeply as they approached one of the few bakeries in town. The aroma from the fresh baked goods filled the surroundings, and she realized that she was hungry. They were on their way to have tea with Mr. Edward Lawton, and so she did not raise a concern to Nathaniel.

The carriage arrived at Sweetwater's tea shop. Nathaniel straightened his posture, and seemed to be quite distracted by his own thoughts. Claire assumed that he was rehearsing some story in his mind, and decided to straighten herself as well. Although they were intending to meet with a friend, Claire felt anxious as it was their first appearance in public together.

Nathaniel exited the carriage first and glanced around before straightening his coat, brushing away the signs of his recent travel. He lent out his hand and assisted Claire as she exited the carriage. The two of them took the few steps to the entry of Sweetwater's.

They were greeted by the host of the shop with a slight bow. "Mr. Clayton, good to see you this fine afternoon."

"Mr. Blackwood, good afternoon. I believe that Mr. Lawton is expecting us."

Claire stood there beside Nathaniel, watching them both and holding her tongue. She had not met the man, and did not want to seem out of place. Mr. Blackwood took them into the shop, and guided them to a table set for four people. Edward was seated at the table, along with a woman of fine stature.

Edward and his companion stood to greet them. "Mr. Clayton, may I present Miss Jane Alcorn."

Nathaniel looked towards Jane and bowed slightly. "A pleasure to make your acquaintance, Miss Alcorn. Allow me to present Miss Claire Stonewall. I am sure, Mr. Lawton, that you remember her from the Devereux Ball."

Edward bowed to Claire. "Yes, I most assuredly do. A pleasure to see you again, Miss Stonewall." Jane said nothing, but simply curtsied her greeting.

Claire curtsied her respect. "The pleasure is mine, Mr. Lawton. I take it you have recovered well from the late-night events of that evening?"

Edward relaxed a bit more as he heard Claire. "Yes, I have. I must admit that it was quite the exercise. In earnest, you and Mr. Clayton made it especially difficult to keep in stride."

Jane stayed her tongue, keeping the plastered smile upon her face. She was slightly younger than Claire, and seemingly intimidated by social grace. They sat at the table, Nathaniel took the seat next to Edward, and Claire sat between Nathaniel and Jane. Claire saw that she was shy and nervous about the meeting. Claire smiled softly to her, hoping that she would be comforted in some measure.

Nathaniel and Edward quickly began their conversation regarding various contacts and recent events. Claire pretended to listen intently to their discussion, but found no real interest in the topics of their conversation. She looked to Jane and saw that she was silent and removed from the dialogue. Instead, Jane focused on the place set before her. The tea had not yet arrived, but she was apparently admiring the décor.

Claire decided to break the ice with Jane and spoke to her gently. "How do you fair this fine day, Miss Alcorn?"

Startled, Jane started to fidget a bit with her fingers under the edge of the table, her eyes betraying that she was not accustomed to the finery. "I am well, Miss Stonewall. I thank you kindly for asking."

"I do not recall your attendance at the Devereux Ball, Miss Alcorn." On the contrary, Claire did recognize her from the Devereux Ball. However, in hopes of striking up a conversation, she played as though she had not.

Jane looked up from the table to see Claire's comforting and attentive gaze upon her. "Yes, Miss Stonewall, I was at the ball. Was it not the most extravagant one yet?"

"Indeed, Miss Alcorn." Claire leaned over to her and whispered lightly, "Though I do believe that it is a danger to be among such fine delicacies."

"Pardon me, Miss Stonewall, but what delicacies do you consider to be dangerous? I had found all of the food available at the ball more than delightful."

Claire whispered again so that only Jane would hear her response. "It was not the food that was so delicious, as much as the fine gentlemen who were abundant during the event."

Jane blushed slightly. "Ah, Miss Stonewall, I see that your notice was well warranted."

As the conversation bloomed, they began to speak more confidently with each other. The discussion grew into a wide variety of topics, both personal and general. By the time the tea arrived, they had a newfound friendship between them. Eventually, Nathaniel and Edward chimed into their discussion, and the conversation was opened to the four of them.

Claire noticed a stately woman walking towards them. She was accompanied by another lady of about the same age, both talking between themselves. She recognized one of the ladies to be Mrs. Devereux. Claire brought this to the attention of the remainder of the table, and they all stood, honoring Mrs. Devereux's attendance.

"Good afternoon, Mrs. Devereux," offered Nathaniel.

"Good afternoon, Mr. Clayton. How good it is to see you. Mr. Lawton, Miss Alcorn, Miss Stonewall. Mr. Clayton and Miss Stonewall, I would like to request your attendance at dinner this evening. I know it is short notice. If you would do me the honor of accepting, I would be most grateful."

Claire was shocked at the abruptness of the request, and after considering it briefly, she had no objection to it. Before she could answer Mrs. Devereux, Nathaniel spoke. "It would be our pleasure, Mrs. Devereux. Miss Stonewall and I are pleased that you would offer." Claire was puzzled why he was so quick to answer for her. It seemed to her that he assumed her acceptance without asking for her own response.

"Very good, we will expect to see you at dusk then. Good day to you all, enjoy your tea." Mrs. Devereux and her friend exited the shop. The four of them sat back at the table and continued their discussion as though nothing had happened.

Eventually their tea ended, they parted after stating their farewells, and Nathaniel and Claire returned to Brookfield Manor. Claire and Nathaniel were discussing the tea and sharing their opinions of Edward and Jane. They arrived at the manor to find that Charles was away from the home. Nathaniel joined Claire in the drawing room, and awaited their departure in just a few hours.

It was a surprise to Claire, for sure. She had not been invited to a dinner in such a manner before. Mrs. Devereux seemed quite adamant that she and Nathaniel attend that very evening. They arrived at the Devereux Estate at dusk and Claire took a brief look around the grounds. The estate was not dressed as immaculately as it was the night of the ball.

As the carriage drove towards the stable grounds, Claire glanced back and noticed the stableman joining Forrester on the perch as it rounded the edge of the manor. Seeing the two of them together comforted her, knowing that Forrester was not left alone. She turned to the entry once more, and the familiar doorman greeted them and welcomed them into the home. "Please wait here," he said to them before turning away. Claire looked around the room and noticed the state of the household. The interior was clean and well kept, and the decorations from the ball were removed. Something felt different to her than the night of the ball, not only due to the crowd of people who were in attendance, but something else that she could not think of.

A few thoughts ran through her mind until Claire realized what was troubling her: it was the music that echoed through the various rooms. Obviously, it was provided by the musicians for the ball, but without it, the place seemed a bit less bright. Mr. and Mrs. Devereux came through a door and walked to them, greeting them warmly. "Mr. Clayton, Miss Stonewall. Come inside, come in…" said Mrs. Devereux. She was wearing a different gown than before, but it was just as decadent. Claire smiled as she saw Mrs. Devereux reach out her two hands to grasp hers. Claire had to let go of Nathaniel's arm before accepting Mrs. Devereux's greeting.

Mr. Devereux allowed Mrs. Devereux to give her greetings before he chimed in with his own. "You look lovely as ever, Miss Stonewall." He had already greeted Nathaniel with a handshake and a grin, and the two of them were watching Mrs. Devereux lavishly greet Claire. Taking a deep breath, Claire noticed the wonderful smell of the food that was being prepared for them. "Thank you, Mr. Devereux. The food smells delightful."

Mr. and Mrs. Devereux guided them into the dining hall. Mr. Devereux held the seat out for Mrs. Devereux, and Nathaniel stood before the chair across from her. Claire walked over to the chair next to Nathaniel and Mr. Devereux coughed. He was standing next to Mrs. Devereux and holding out a chair for Claire. Claire said nothing and moved around the table to stand next to Mrs. Devereux instead. Mr. Devereux went to the head of the table and the four of them sat in their assigned seats. Moments later, two staff members came around and laid the napkins across each of their laps in succession.

The service of the dinner was more like a dance of the servants, moving in and out of each other as if in a finely choreographed performance. The four of them were uninterrupted as they began with their conversation, discussing the days since the ball and the most current gossip channels. Claire's thoughts diverged from the conversation as they began to relay the various stories of acquaintances and friends. She looked down at her plate, and noticed the delicate flavors of dessert as the final course of the meal had been served. She took her fork and played with the pastry. She had already eaten so much that evening that she had little interest in any more.

"Will you join me for a cigar, Mr. Clayton?" asked Mr. Devereux.

"Certainly," Nathaniel responded. The two men stood from the table and walked off to the distance, leaving Claire and Mrs. Devereux to their own devices.

"Will you join me in the parlor, Miss Stonewall?"

"It would be my pleasure, Mrs. Devereux."

The two of them made their way down the hall to a small room that was tucked away from the rest of the home. Claire followed her into the room and looked around. Inside the room were a few small couches covered in pillows, and flowers upon each of the tables that stood between them. There was a fireplace towards one wall, decorated on either side with windows and dark curtains. Mrs. Devereux closed the door behind them and proceeded to take a seat on one of the couches.

"We can talk freely here, Miss Stonewall. This is my private room, and we will not be disturbed." Laid upon the table was a silver platter, a tea pot, and a pair of cups. "Would you care for a spot of tea?"

Claire took a seat upon the loveseat on the other side of her. "Tea would be nice."

Mrs. Devereux poured a cup of tea and held out the serving for Claire, and Claire took it onto her lap after adding a bit of sugar to it. Mrs. Devereux proceeded to fill another serving for herself, and added a bit of cream and sugar in hers. "How are things going with the strapping Mr. Clayton?"

Claire coughed slightly, having just taken a sip of the tea. "I am sorry, Mrs. Devereux, what exactly do you wish to know?"

Mrs. Devereux casually took a sip of her tea. "From what I have heard, the two of you have not left each other's side since the ball. I was wondering if he had come to ask for your hand."

At that moment, Claire knew exactly why Mrs. Devereux had invited the two of them over for dinner. It was quite apparent that she wanted to know if her matchmaking plan had succeeded. Claire decided to respond playfully. "Why would you ever think that he would do such a thing, Mrs. Devereux?"

"I have no reason to believe otherwise, Miss Stonewall. It is no secret that you have taken to Mr. Clayton. Do you pretend to deny the claims that you have been actively accompanied by Mr. Clayton every day since the night of the ball?"

"No, I do not deny the truth. He has been most diligent in his visitations with me. Though I would not necessarily proclaim to know his intentions, he has made no mention nor given me any sign about his interest in my hand."

"Miss Stonewall, you must not pretend to be so naive in knowing his true intentions. He is just so very prominent in his actions. Look at the way he pays attention to you when you are around, his constant diligence in your comfort and wellbeing. Make no mistake, the man does care deeply for you. If he has not admitted it to you, then it is most definitely on the horizon." Mrs.

Devereux paused and raised her tea just to her lips. Before taking a sip, she smirked proudly. "Trust me, there is no doubt about his intent. Heed my advice, Miss Stonewall, you might want to consider preparing yourself for the eventuality of the moment."

Claire was lost in thought for the remainder of the evening. She paid more attention to Nathaniel and his behavior around her. The evening came to an end and they said their farewells. Claire could think of little else besides her rambling thoughts of Nathaniel's intentions. Nathaniel said very little to her, and noticed her distracted demeanor. "Miss Stonewall, is everything all right?"

"Forgive me, I am lost in thought at the moment." She looked to Nathaniel and could easily see a concern come over him.

"I understand, Miss Stonewall. I know that you are not accustomed to attending so many activities. If it would please you, we can delay any further attendance until you are comfortable."

The words that he offered seemed to rattle through her mind. She was so entrenched in her thoughts of his true intentions that the idea of additional public engagements was furthest from her mind. They reached the manor and Claire was unable to find a means to ease her thoughts. "We will see how I feel tomorrow."

Nathaniel replied in his most charming tone, "Very well, I will be by to call upon you tomorrow."

Claire exited the carriage without looking behind her and went inside. She was not sure if she wanted him to come the following day or not. She immediately headed up the stairs to her room. It was late in the day, and she found that she was more tired than usual due to the unexpected conversation with Mrs. Devereux. She reached her pillow and the thoughts of Nathaniel filled her mind as she drifted away to sleep.

A CLOSE CALL

THE SUNLIGHT WAS SHINING THROUGH the windows and illuminated the surface of a small writing desk in the drawing room. Claire looked out the window, a blank parchment lying upon the desk and a quill resting comfortably in her hand. She sat there, recollecting the last few weeks at Brookfield Manor. Most of Claire's time had been spent in the company of Nathaniel, and the various acquaintances she had come to know through him. Each day was spent attending some social event with one or more important people. Claire had very little time to herself.

Claire looked around the empty room in hopes of finding some inspiration for the letter. Nowadays, she felt more like a stranger in her own home. It was not long ago that she would spend the majority of her days reading and relaxing in that very room, traveling to the wondrous lands and far-off places that were unfolded by the stories that she read. But now that Nathaniel had come into her life, she felt compelled to present herself in the forefront of society. She dipped her pen in the ink well and wrote her introduction on the parchment.

Claire paused and looked out the window once again with a sigh. The thoughts of her father began to enter her mind. She was reminded of how she used to play hide and seek as a little girl behind the shrubs and statues. Her father would pretend that he could not find her, and at the last minute, lunge at her to pry her from her hiding place. Shrieks of laughter would then emerge from Claire's lips as she was chased around the grounds. Claire had such fond memories of spending time with her father. He was such an important figure in her life and she missed him deeply.

She remembered how she loved to see him come up the grounds and stairs from a walk or hunt. She awoke from her daydream to see two figures walking up to the house. Nathaniel and Vivian strolled up the grounds and onto the porch. Claire remembered that the two of them had decided to take a walk, while she was required to write the letter to her aunt. Seeing them come up to the house brought Claire out of her reverie with a bit of a panic. She looked down at the partially written letter and knew she had not gotten very far in her task. She dipped her pen in the ink well again and continued to write the letter. She hurriedly wrote of the weather, her recent activities with Nathaniel, the state of Brookfield Manor, and inquired after her aunt's health. By the time Nathaniel and Vivian came into the room, she was nearly done.

"Have you finished yet, Miss Stonewall?" asked Nathaniel.

"Just need to finish the last sentence and endorse it."

"Very well, the carriage should be here within moments. We will need to be on our way before the time is lost. Do hurry in your task, I do not wish to delay our business in town."

"The act of writing letters to family or friends can never be hurried, it is meant to be thoughtful and intimate so as to share those sentiments with the parties in question. I do enjoy reading a good letter, and therefore, make sure to write good letters in turn. But not to worry, Mr. Clayton, I am finished." Claire signed her name on the parchment and put her pen back in the ink well. She folded the paper and addressed it, then melted some wax onto the paper and stamped it with the family emblem.

Claire heard the carriage come up the parkway and knew that it was time to leave. She stood and left the room to meet Nathaniel and Vivian in the foyer. The carriage came to a halt in to take them into town.

Claire caught a glimpse of Charles in his study, off to the right of the entranceway. He seemed to be pouring over documents and papers that must have been important. Hearing the carriage, Charles looked up briefly to nod a goodbye to her, and smiled. He always smiled when he caught sight of Claire.

Travelling down the road, Claire found little pleasure and even less interest in the conversation that was active between Nathaniel and Vivian. It seemed to her that Nathaniel was genuinely intrigued by gossip, perhaps as equally as Vivian. And Vivian never refused the chance to spread what new, yet questionable, stories she had heard.

Claire noticed a young woman walking along the road carrying a woven basket, filled to the brim with gorgeous, vibrant flowers. She was wearing a light-blue dress accented by a bonnet and matching ribbons tied in a bow that dangled below her chin. The hem of her dress was covered in mud and dirt at least several inches from the hem.

Claire spoke. "I hope she doesn't have far to walk, I think it's going to rain soon." Vivian and Nathaniel both looked out the window toward the girl and were at odds with Claire's interruption.

"There is no need to worry yourself with her, she is probably a simple town girl. And look at that dress she is wearing. It is so plain and common. If she does not have the tenacity to keep it clean, then it would be best to let her be," Vivian retorted.

Nathaniel decided to say nothing, and just as quickly as their conversation was interrupted, they continued their discussion, ignoring the young woman. Claire continued to watch her as she stumbled along. Despite the worry and concern that she had over the young woman's trial, Claire did nothing as they continued on, passing her by.

The carriage strode into town, and stopped short of the many shops that lined the street. Vivian left the carriage first, after ensuring she had her possessions in hand. Nathaniel followed behind her, and stood at the door as he waited for Claire to exit. Claire took her time leaving the carriage. She took Nathaniel's assistance and stood by the two of them, ready to subject herself to whatever came her way. The three of them straightened their attire as Forester drove off to the stables.

The stores that lined the streets had large windows which were decorated with various wares. They looked through the windows at the various offerings provided by each of the uniquely quaint shops, and made comments as they found something worth their interest. The afternoon crowd cluttered the street and walkways. It was busier than usual, but it did not distract them from their shopping. The patrons were all dressed in their socially acceptable attire, based on their independent status within society. As the three of them moved down the street, they bid their greetings to various acquaintances. Claire noticed that Nathaniel enjoyed this portion of their travels the most. Nathaniel looked forward to the potential introduction to some high-class citizen.

Once they arrived at Mr. Rowe's Garment Store, Claire watched Nathaniel as he opened the door for Vivian and her to enter. Nathaniel's attention seemed to be on the many patrons on the street rather than the two of them entering the store. When he realized that they were inside, he briskly followed them.

"Good afternoon!" cried Mr. Rowe to the three of them as they entered the store. "I will be with you in a moment..." he said hurriedly, as he was dealing with other customers. Claire followed Vivian throughout the store, and they browsed the various articles of clothing and ribbons. Vivian occasionally made some comment on a particular item, and held it up to Claire for her response. Nathaniel offered his thoughts on the article, and if he found some interest in it, he would press it up to Claire as if she were wearing it. Claire felt as if she were a doll being dressed by the both of them, rather than a participant. Her comment was usually dismissed immediately, and they would discuss it between themselves without heeding her words. Vivian kept the two of them in constant attention, and would not allow either to be separated for long.

Claire could tell that Nathaniel was not quite himself. While Vivian was perusing a collection of various gloves and scarfs, Claire took the opportunity to whisper to him softly, "Is there anything the matter, Mr. Clayton?"

"Not at all, Miss Stonewall. It is simply that I find the search for garments of a fine woman's taste to be lost on my attention. I would normally not be privy to such consumption, but as it is Miss Hawkins' intent to be here, and her persistence ever so daunting, I chose to come along. At least it gives me a grand opportunity to see that bright shade of red within your cheeks now and again."

"Well, I will do my best to keep you entertained then. It would do neither of us any good to have you so lost in complacency. I do not think that we will be here long though, we were here just before the Devereux Ball. And I do not recall Miss Hawkins to have been keen on anything at that time either."

Vivian was quick to return to the two of them, and Claire could only assume that she was feeling left out of the conversation. "I do not think there is a new ribbon or lace that I would need in this entire village. What it is to live in such rural places. I would imagine that the stores in Paris or London would have a grand selection," Vivian interrupted.

"Oh, now, cousin! There may be more to offer in the larger cities than in our own Springhurst. However, Mr. Rowe always brings back the finest available in all of the cities. Besides, there are several things in my own possession if you care to browse my closet. Find anything that you like, and it is yours to be had."

"I do not think that we need to linger in this place any longer. If I have not seen what I need by this time, then certainly what I seek is not here."

Vivian left the store without delay, Nathaniel and Claire following her closely. Once outside the garment store, the three of them continued down the street. Several carts were lined along the street. Each of them displayed an arrangement of items for sale by the local townsfolk. The three of them joined the rest of the crowd as they browsed through the available selections. They had stopped by one of the carts and were looking through the crafts that were being offered when Claire felt a brush from a little girl as she ran by her. Claire's attention turned to the children as they were weaving in and out of the crowds of people playing some sort of game. The joy she saw in the children reminded her of how Charles and her used to play. She looked out toward the street and saw a young girl, not more than six years of age, crouched low to the ground, obviously fixated upon something near her feet.

Claire moved away from the carts to get a better view of the little girl. Attempting to see what captivated her, Claire squinted her eyes and covered her brows with her hand. She noticed a small flower had popped out from between the cobblestones on the road. Atop the flower, she could faintly make out the beating of a butterfly's wings. So delicately perched upon the fragile flower, the butterfly stayed its position as the girl looked onward, not wanting to disturb it. Claire felt a small smile as it crept upon her, in admiration of the young girl's treasured find.

Claire heard a faint but steady beat of hoofs upon the cobblestones. She turned to look down the street. The sound was getting louder by the second, and Claire was suddenly concerned. She looked briefly above the horses and noticed that the driver was nowhere to be seen. Shocked and stunned for a brief moment, she shouted clearly in a strained attempt to gather the child's attention, "Look out!"

Many of the townsfolk looked to Claire, first and foremost, not sure where exactly the call had come from. Claire took a step further into the street, but not knowing what to do, she called out to the child again. "Girl!" Her voice was loud and abrupt, but to no avail. "Look out! Runaway carriage!"

Suddenly, the crowd's attention turned to the horses that were barreling down the street, pulling an unmanned carriage behind them. The child had not moved from her position, still attentive to the butterfly that was before her. Abruptly, a man popped out from the crowd wearing a simple brown suit and coat. He was well defined and strong, and Claire did not recognize him. The stranger rushed out into the street, quickly and with voracity. Claire watched as the man ran up to the girl, and without hesitation, scooped her up into his arms, and continued across the street safely to the other side.

Claire found herself walking briskly down the street. Another man, just a bit further down the road, came out and was able to successfully grab the side of the carriage. Once he secured his footing, he grasped the reins and slowed the carriage to a halt. Claire's attention returned to the girl, attempting to ascertain her safety. The man who had grabbed her held the little girl securely and was standing her to her feet at the side of the road. His attention was focused on the little girl, ensuring that she was all right. He began to brush away the dust and dirt from the girl's dress. Claire sighed in relief, seeing the little girl standing safely and unharmed.

"Anna!" cried a woman from behind Claire as she rushed across the street. The woman knelt down to the girl and wrapped her arms around her. She looked to the girl's hero with an expression of gratitude. "Thank you, sir! Thank you so very much!" The woman continued to give high praise to the man who had just saved her daughter from certain harm. Claire stood in the middle of the street, watching the two of them in awe. The man looked to Claire and pointed to her as he exclaimed to the others, "I would not have known if it were not for the lady there!"

The woman looked behind her, still crouched and protective of her daughter. She saw Claire and expressed her thankfulness. "Thank you, lady, you have saved my little Anna." Claire could see tears as they came down the woman's cheeks.

"You are very welcome," Claire said softly, though the woman could not hear her from such a distance. Nathaniel and Vivian came up just behind Claire and looked to the scene, wondering what was going on. "Are you all right?" Claire asked the little girl, who was still a bit shaken and seemed to be confused as to what exactly had just happened.

Anna looked to Claire and smiled softly, still a bit shocked but glad to see that she was so well guarded and in her mother's arms. Nathaniel and Vivian looked to Claire. "What was that about?" asked Vivian.

"It was nothing, cousin, just an accident is all. All is well." Claire knew that neither Vivian nor Nathaniel would be interested in her involvement, and so walked with them to the side of the street.

The clouds had darkened slightly during the events that took place, and the rain began to drip from above. "We best be getting back to the manor, Miss Stonewall. It looks as though the rain has finally caught up with us." Nathaniel held out his hand, pointing down the street, urging Vivian and Claire to leave.

The three of them walked back and made their way toward the stables. Claire looked back briefly to the man who had saved the young girl. He had turned to the others who were standing behind him, several of whom patted him on his shoulder and back, obviously congratulating him on his successful rescue. Claire wondered to herself the words that were being shared and the newly found fame that the man had obtained. She turned back to find Nathaniel and Vivian discussing the state of the people of the town and their obvious annoyance with the activity. Rather than cause a scene with the two of them, she chose to not add to their conversation, regardless of how wrong she thought them to be.

Forrester had brought the carriage around and collected the three of them just before the rains began pouring heavily. There was very little conversation regarding the rescue that just took place moments ago. Vivian and Nathaniel returned to the gossip that had occupied them previously. Claire looked out the carriage window as she had always done, watching the rain as it collided with the glass. The occasional splash of water from the wheels caught her attention, as she recollected the entire event in her mind rather than listen to the discussion going on beside her.

CHARLOTTE'S ENCOUNTER

A LARGER SPLASH FROM THE WHEELS of the carriage covered the window, and Claire noticed a figure through the blurred window pane. It was the young woman they had passed on the way into town, her basket of precious flowers soaked with rain and dirtied with mud. It seemed to Claire that they may have been dropped on more than one occasion. As the carriage continued towards the figure, Claire could not take her attention away from the young woman. She watched her as she stumbled alongside the road, falling prey to the mud and rain as it poured heavily down upon her. "My heavens, we need to stop!" Claire blurted out to the rest of the carriage.

Vivian looked through the glass, saw the desperate woman, and scrunched up her face, "And do what exactly? She is a commoner, and no one to chance your own health for."

Nathaniel chimed in with a tone of disbelief, unwilling to understand Claire's reaction. "Are we to stop and help the entire village? It is raining. Do not think it is your concern, Miss Stonewall. They should have a mind about themselves to stay clear of it. Nothing for you to do in the matter. In any case, you should let her be. The sooner she gets home, the sooner she will be all right. You can no more help that woman than you can stop the rain from coming down."

"It is our responsibility to look after those who are less fortunate than ourselves, Mr. Clayton." She expected a condescending response from Vivian, but she had hoped that Nathaniel was a bit more understanding. While continuing her gaze at Nathaniel, Claire rapped her flat palm against the wall of the carriage, and suddenly they felt the halt of the horses.

Forrester jumped down from his perch and came to the door, opening it slightly to keep the rain from coming in. Claire looked to him and was glad to see that he was dressed in viable attire to protect himself from the rain. Forrester spoke clearly and attentively. "Is everything all right, Miss Stonewall?"

"Forrester, the young woman there needs our help. Gather her and bring her into the carriage!" She nodded out the window in the direction of the young woman. The once-beautiful flowers were scattered and covered in mud, trodden and ruined. The woman was lying upon the ground, having lost her footing and fallen into the mud.

Forrester shut the door and leapt over to the side of the road, getting a better footing for himself. He proceeded towards the young woman and attempted to help her to her feet. She was a small woman, of light weight and fragile frame. Forrester was able to lift her with ease and carried her gently to the carriage.

Vivian and Nathaniel sat there beside themselves, unable to comprehend what Claire was doing. She had set her mind to help this poor woman, despite their protests. Instead, they scooted themselves away from the door.

Forrester arrived carrying the young woman and Claire assisted him, sitting the young woman on the seat next to her. "Miss Stonewall, she is really weak. I fear she may be stricken ill soon, if not already." The young woman coughed hoarsely as Forester reported her condition to Claire.

"Then let us head straight to the manor with much haste! The poor woman."

"You are not to be taken seriously, cousin! We will all catch a death of cold, mark my words!"

"Cousin, if you wish to walk home from here, the door is open!" Claire said to Vivian with a fierce determination. Her voice was so strong and stern that it shocked both Vivian and Nathaniel. "Otherwise, hold your tongue and let me deal with this girl as I feel is necessary." With a quick glance to Nathaniel, Claire could tell he was not about to start an argument with her.

Claire took it upon herself to help stabilize the young woman in her seat. Claire saw a look of approval upon Forester's face as he shut the door before returning to his perch.

"She is getting mud all over the cushions! Really, Claire, do you not have a mind to keep to your own station?" Claire looked back at Vivian, who was once again silenced by her gaze. Vivian reluctantly looked downward, knowing that she was in no position to argue with Claire.

Within seconds, they continued to Brookfield Manor. As the carriage now carried the four of them down the road, Claire's focus was pinned to the health and safety of the young woman. Claire leaned in closer to her and began hearing the woman mumble, but was unable to make out what she said. "Excuse me, Miss," stated Claire gently in an attempt to gain her attention. "What is your name?"

Briefly, the woman struggled to look up to Claire, her eyes at half-mast, speaking hoarsely in nothing more than a whisper. "Charlotte." She paused and took a deeper breath, a twinge of pain evident on her face. "Charlotte Edleman," she said, clarifying her name just before collapsing once again into the corner of the carriage. Claire attempted to calm Charlotte from the obvious struggle she was under.

Just as they arrived at the manor, Forrester quickly opened the carriage door in order to check on Charlotte. Claire leaned over Forrester and motioned for Samuel to come and assist him. Samuel came quickly to the side of the carriage and awaited further instruction. "Samuel, have the maid turn down the spare bed, and lay Miss Edleman there. She is in dire need of rest and a doctor. Forrester, as soon as she is settled, I will need you to get word to the doctor. Bring him hence forth with urgency to attend to her health." Samuel and Forrester carried the woman inside. Claire, Vivian, and Nathaniel followed them in succession, shedding their wet coats in the entry. Claire watched the commotion as the servants of the house hastily attended to Charlotte's condition.

Nathaniel shook his head in disapproval and pulled Claire aside, away from the others who were nearby. He spoke his concern in confidence and out of earshot from anyone else. "What do you think your brother would say to your act of unexplained and awkward charity?"

"Mr. Clayton, I do not request your council in this matter. Do not pretend that you know my brother more than I. My brother will understand this is my doing, and I will not blame you nor Miss Vivian in its eventual discussion." She realized that the two of them differed in this matter and paused in thought for a few moments.

She left Nathaniel there as he stood quietly, and went to Vivian who was still standing in the entry. Knowing that Vivian was so knowledgeable of the gossip channels around town, she trusted in her ability to recall a name. "Edleman, I believe she said. Do you know the Edleman family, cousin?"

Vivian thought for a moment then shook her head. "No, cousin, I have not heard that name before. Perhaps it is one of the common folk at the village." Vivian was still disgusted with the fact that they were continuing with this charity. She looked over to Nathaniel with an expression of impatience upon her face. Claire could sense that Vivian was seeking Nathaniel to put a stop to this foolishness.

Claire would not give Vivian the satisfaction. She turned to Nathaniel and asked swiftly, "Mr. Clayton, do you have any knowledge of the Edleman family, or where they may reside? I would think it pertinent to notify their family of Miss Charlotte's whereabouts before concern is raised beyond repair." Claire knew that Nathaniel did not share her evident concern over Charlotte, but still had hope that she could persuade him.

Nathaniel pondered for a moment as he walked closer to the two of them. It was obvious to Claire that she had at least convinced him enough to actually think on the matter. However, after a few moments, he looked to Claire and shook his head. "I am afraid not, Miss Stonewall. I have no knowledge of the family nor their whereabouts. I think it would be best to seek out the constable and notify them of the person. The doctor may know of them, perhaps you may query him when he arrives."

Forrester had come down the stairs while the three of them were talking. He waited for the opportunity to speak, and called for their attention with a faint cough. "Miss Stonewall, I know of the Edleman family. Mr. Edleman tends to the stables near town, as well as the stables at the Devereux Estate. I would be more than happy to notify them on the way to gather the fine doctor."

Wasting no time, Vivian saw an opportunity to excuse herself from the manor. "That is settled then, I think it is past time for my return home. Mr. Clayton, if you would care to see me to Bedford Park? I believe that Miss Stonewall will have her hands full with this Miss Edleman. Forrester, you will take Mr. Clayton and I to Bedford Park before fetching the doctor and notifying the Edleman family." Vivian then reached her hand up, expecting Nathaniel to take it and guide her from the house.

Claire nodded to Forrester as he looked to her. She felt that it would be best to allow this request regardless of the outcome. Claire looked to Nathaniel for his input, still hoping to see the man she wanted him to be. Nathaniel looked to Claire, then to Vivian, and sighed. He had plans for the evening which did not include a new charity project from Claire. He leaned over to Claire and spoke softly. "Do take caution, Miss Stonewall, who knows what ailments she may be inflicted with. It would not do to see you put yourself at risk, for the sake of your own house." He then turned to Vivian and the two of them gathered their coats and headed back out to the carriage.

Claire followed behind them and watched from inside the open door as they departed. Claire was disappointed in his reaction, and she blamed Vivian for his departure. As the carriage moved out of sight, Claire turned and made her way up the stairs to see Charlotte. She reached to the top of the stairs and turned her attention to the portrait of her parents. One glance to their faces and she was reassured. She thought of the new charge she was undertaking and felt a sense of pride that her father would have bestowed upon her. She had always felt the necessity to be helpful to those less fortunate, and it was instilled upon her by her father when she was young. They had not often brought strangers into their home who were ill and found upon the roadside. However, they did allow people to call upon them in times of need, and offered them comfort and protection when warranted.

She looked down the hall, and saw a maidservant enter one of the many spare rooms in the home. She followed the maid to the room and stopped at the entry. Mary and another of the maidservants were tending to Charlotte. They were able to put Charlotte into the bed, and had just pulled the covers over her. The maidservant who was assisting Mary brought in a bowl of warm water and clean rags. Mary noticed Claire in the doorway and nodded to her. She returned her attention to Charlotte and finished tucking her into the bed. Carefully and quietly, Mary walked to her assistant and whispered a few instructions before making her way toward Claire.

"She is running a high fever and coughing deeply, Miss Stonewall. I would say it is imperative that the doctor is called straight away. She could very well need medicine that we do not have."

Claire held her hand to Mary's wrist. "I have already sent Forrester to fetch the good doctor. I am confident that he will return promptly with the doctor in tow." She then watched the maidservant as she took a damp, warm rag from the bowl, twisting out the moisture before dabbing it gently across Charlotte's forehead. "Has Miss Charlotte said anything else, Mary?"

"No, Miss Stonewall, she has not said much at all. I believe it may be too straining on her at the moment. She has barely attempted to open her eyes, either too tired or too weak to do so."

Claire sensed Mary's concern, and comforted her. "It will be all right, Mary. Forrester stated that he knew the family, and would be sending word to them. I just hope that we were in time." She paused for a moment, and watched her from the distance with concern. "The poor girl."

"Yes, Miss Stonewall." Mary did not know what more could be done for Charlotte. She stood beside Claire as the two of them continued to watch the maidservant attend to her.

Claire felt the urgency to do something more. She looked to Mary and offered her a task to perform in hopes that it would calm her down. "Mary, go down to the foyer and wait for the arrival of the doctor. He should be here soon. Show him upstairs to the room when he arrives. I will remain here in the event that she awakens."

"Yes, Miss Stonewall." Mary took a few seconds before departing down the hallway.

Claire went to the foot of the bed and watched Charlotte closely. She was a young woman of simple beauty, her hair was long and well cared for. Her face was soft and gentle, with little to no imperfections. She seemed peaceful as she lay still in the bed. Claire pressed herself to one of the bedposts, allowing it to hold her steady as she continued to watch Charlotte. Suddenly, Charlotte sat upward and broke out in a fierce, deep cough. The maidservant rushed to the bedside and supported Charlotte as she continued. Time and time again, Charlotte would rise with another fit of coughing, and then fall back to the pillows with eyes closed, continuing to breathe shallowly.

As each fit of coughing seemed worse than the previous one, Claire's concern over Charlotte increased. Claire moved from the foot of the bed, and sat upon the side opposite the attending maidservant. She carefully watched Charlotte with a sorrowful gaze, taking a moment to stroke Charlotte's arm gently. Claire could tell that she was greatly ill, for the color of her face had drained since their ride in the carriage. Charlotte's hands were icy cold to the touch and moist with sweat. Claire decided to reach for Charlotte's forehead, and felt the strong heat emanating from her skin. She knew the signs and was dispirited with regard to the fever that Charlotte must be enduring. Claire proceeded to lift the back of her hand above Charlotte's nose and mouth, and felt the shallowness of her breath as she lay there. She knew that Charlotte was lucky that they had gathered her when they did. Claire's concern deepened as the faith in her recovery was fleeting.

She was continuing to care for Charlotte when Mary returned with the doctor. Mary walked quietly into the room and placed her hand gently on her shoulder to gain her attention. Claire turned and saw the doctor standing in the doorway and motioned for Mary to take over in her stead. Then she signaled the doctor to follow her into the hallway. Once outside the room, she curtsied to the doctor. "Thank you for coming so soon, Dr. Michaels."

"My pleasure, Miss Stonewall, though I wish it were on more casual of terms. Tell me, Miss Stonewall, what have you found out from your charge?"

Claire looked briefly toward the room and ensured that they were out of earshot before continuing. "This poor girl is Miss Charlotte Edleman, so we believe. I had noticed her out in the rain, she was drenched and very weak with cough. I brought her inside to care for her, as she was stricken ill. I had Forrester gather you as soon as possible for I am concerned over her wellbeing, Dr. Michaels. She has not spoken since, and I fear for her ability to speak to her condition."

"Anything you can tell me of her symptoms, Miss Stonewall?"

"She seems to be running a strong fever, Dr. Michaels. Her forehead and chest are very hot with heat and sweat, but her palms and hands are cold and wet. She has a deep cough, though I do not claim to know to what extent. I will leave the diagnosis to you, Dr. Michaels."

"It is a good thing you collected her when you did, Miss Stonewall. I fear she may have only gotten worse if she were left on her own. Give me a few moments, and let me see what ailments have laid claim to her." The two of them quietly reentered the room. Dr. Michaels was carrying with him a black leather bag which he usually brought wherever he was needed. He placed the small bag on the bedside and reached into it, pulling out a stethoscope to listen to Charlotte's breath and heart. He turned to Claire and whispered loudly enough to be heard, but quiet enough to not disturb Charlotte, "Miss Stonewall, may your maidservant remain here to assist me?"

Claire nodded and left the room with Mary. The two of them entered the hallway, shutting the door quietly behind them. Claire saw Samuel coming up the hall to their location. Samuel stopped just before them and bowed slightly. In a whisper, he made his introduction. "A Mr. Thomas Edleman has come to call upon the state of his sister."

Claire was surprised that there would be someone here so soon to see her. "I shall see him at once, Samuel." Claire looked to Mary. "Inform me if the doctor should need anything."

Claire followed behind Samuel as he went to the foyer. She looked down from the top of the stairs and saw the man standing there, anxiously looking back at her. Claire recognized him immediately. "Sir!" It was the same man who had saved the little girl in town earlier that day. Claire continued down the stairs and looked in wonder at the stranger. She had not met the man earlier, but was astonished to see him twice in the same day. She felt the beat of her heart increase the closer she came to him. He was a very handsome man, and even though he was dressed as a commoner, he had a pride about him that was evident to Claire.

"Good afternoon, Miss Stonewall. I have heard that you have news of my younger sister, Miss Charlotte Edleman." He pulled his hat from his head and held it intently in his hands. He was concerned for Charlotte's condition, and it showed. His hat and coat were soaked from the continued downpour of rain.

Thomas was taller than her brother and more muscular in his overall frame. He was obviously a man of strength and physique. Claire curtsied before Thomas. "Mr. Edleman, your sister is being attended to by the physician at present. If you would be kind to leave your coat and hat here in the entry, I will take you to see her."

Thomas went directly to the stand and placed his hat on a hook. He took off his coat and hung it on another hook. Claire watched him intently as he did exactly as she instructed. Within moments, he turned to follow her and she was drawn to his attention. He spoke clearly and urgently. "Miss Stonewall, how is my sister? Is she all right?"

Claire awoke from her daydream and was relieved to find him as troubled as she was. She turned towards the stairwell and guided Thomas to Charlotte's room. "She is in good hands, Mr. Edleman, and is being well cared for. Miss Edleman is running a fever, I am sure the doctor will tell us more when he completes his diagnosis. Dr. Michaels arrived just shortly before you did, and was seeing to her just as I came down to greet you."

Thomas followed her diligently, anxious to see his sister. There was obviously a true sincerity in his demeanor, and Claire felt it as they walked down the hall towards the door. Claire held out her hand to halt Thomas at the doorway. She knew that she did not have nearly enough strength to stop him if he persisted, but she trusted in his character. Thomas accepted the gesture and waited patiently as Claire turned to the door. Mary was nowhere to be seen, so Claire opened the door cautiously, looking inside to see what was transpiring. Mary was inside with the other maidservant, listening intently to Dr. Michaels at the foot of the bed.

Claire paused for a moment, waiting for an opportunity to grab their attention. Dr. Michaels saw Claire at the door and held his own hand to signal a pause to their entry. Claire nodded and shut the door quietly. "The doctor will be with us in a moment, Mr. Edleman."

Thomas was restless and began to pace back and forth in the hallway. Claire watched him and guarded the door. After a few moments, Dr. Michaels came out of the room and shut the door behind him. He ushered Claire and Thomas further into the hallway.

"Dr. Michaels, this is Mr. Thomas Edleman, Miss Edleman's brother."

Dr. Michaels reached his hand out to Thomas in acceptance of their acquaintance. "A pleasure, Mr. Edleman, though I would have hoped for it to be under different circumstances."

Thomas took his hand and responded without further delay, "How is she, Dr. Michaels?"

He took a moment to consider his diagnosis. "She is very ill. I would wager she has a slight pneumonia at present. Though I do not know to what extent this illness will continue if not treated with great care. You have much thankfulness to give Miss Stonewall here. If she had not attended to the wellbeing of your sister, she would be much worse off than she is now."

"I do not know what to say, thank you both for your attention to my sister."

"For the time being, she needs as much rest as she can obtain. I do not recommend moving her unless absolutely necessary. I expect that she may be bedridden for the next week at the least. I do not expect to know more until a few days. This time is crucial to her recovery, and we will need to maintain a constant watch over her for any changes."

"Dr. Michaels, is there anything else we can do for Miss Edleman?" Claire asked with a sincerity that caused Thomas to look her in direction.

"Miss Stonewall, I have already given instruction to your maidservants, and they know what must be done. For now, she is asleep and should stay that way as best as possible. Mr. Edleman, you may go in and see her, but take heed to not wake her from her slumber. The rest she requires will help her to recover as fast as her body is able."

"If you would excuse me, thank you again." Thomas turned to the door, cautiously opening it and slipping just inside, shutting it once again as quietly as he could.

Claire watched as Thomas entered the room and then turned to Dr. Michaels. "I will escort you to the door."

As they walked down to the stairwell, Claire and Dr. Michaels talked together softly. Claire entertained the concern of the doctor as they walked, then just as they reached the portrait, the doctor looked upon Claire's parents and paused. "Miss Stonewall, your mother and father would be so very proud of the strong woman you have become. Trust in their love for you, for they loved you very much. You could not imagine the strength in their devotion to you." His reminiscence of her parents obviously brought about a strong emotion within him, which he attempted to hide from Claire.

"I know, Dr. Michaels, and I know you and Father were quite close. He always admired you, and had full faith in your abilities. His passing was unfortunate for us all, but he was so grateful for your care of him."

"He was a great man and a good friend. I miss him very much. If ever there is anything I can do for you, please let me know."

Claire looked to him fondly as a loving daughter would look to her father. "You already do us a great favor by looking after us all. I cannot thank you enough, Dr. Michaels. We will see you in a few days."

Dr. Michaels nodded and turned to the door. Forrester was already prepared with the carriage to take him anywhere he needed. There were no words necessary from Claire, for they all honored Dr. Michaels and his constant vigilance to their health and care. Claire watched until the front door was closed and took a deep breath to collect herself before she returned to Charlotte's room.

As Claire reached the room, she opened the door gently so as not to disturb the occupants. She saw that Thomas sat where she had before, holding Charlotte's hand gently. The maidservant was there with the rag, still blotting away at Charlotte's forehead. Behind Claire, Mary entered the room and whispered softly to her, "The doctor requested that we serve her a small amount of sherry to help her to sleep."

"Yes, of course, Mary, whatever they need. Miss Edleman and her brother Mr. Edleman are guests of the estate."

Mary walked to the other side of the bed, opposite from Thomas, and gave the glass of sherry to the maidservant. The maidservant reached over to Charlotte, and attempted to lift her gently from the pillows, waking her slightly.

"Miss, drink this..." the maidservant called out to Charlotte.

Charlotte woke slightly, enough to see the glass in front of her. She leaned forward, taking the glass to her lips and drinking the sherry. Feeling the alcohol as it traveled down her throat, she coughed a little and leaned back against the pillows. "Flowers… Mother…" she mumbled almost incoherently. Thomas comforted her hand and looked to her, seeing the unrest that began in her feverish state.

"Charlotte," Thomas called out to her softly, ensuring that she would recognize his voice. "I am here. There is nothing to worry." As if his voice were a healing potion, Charlotte quieted down a bit more. Her breathing became calmer and more stable than it had been since they collected her from the rain.

The maidservant returned the glass to Mary and continued to dab Charlotte's forehead. All was calm within the room, as they quietly awaited some sign of improvement. Charlotte drifted off to sleep. Mary took a breath and walked over to Claire who was standing inside the room just before the door.

"Miss Stonewall, will we be expecting Mr. Edleman to stay with us? Shall I prepare a room for him?"

Claire nodded. "Yes, Mary, prepare a room for the gentleman. I will speak with Charles when he is available."

Mary left the room and Claire walked to the maidservant and whispered to her quietly, "Go and assist Mary, I will take care of her for now." She took the rag from her and saw the concerned expression come over Thomas. Claire took the rag, dabbed it into the warm water, and wrung it out once more before leaning over and blotting Charlotte's head. Claire looked upon Charlotte tenderly.

She noticed a small strand of hair lying wet across Charlotte's face. She put the rag in her other hand and reached over to move the strand. Thomas reached over before Claire and moved the strand himself, brushing his hand lightly against Claire's in the process. Suddenly aware of the closeness of him, Claire pulled away. It was a brief touch, much like a feather's stroke, but it was enough to startle Claire and her thoughts of his presence.

Claire looked to him and caught the intensity of his expression. As their gazes locked, Thomas took the opportunity to speak to her strongly, but in a hushed tone so as not to disturb Charlotte. "I want to thank you for your extreme kindness and generosity. It is not often that someone will stop to help someone else, especially someone like my sister."

Claire was unable to escape his gaze until she looked down at her clasped hands. "You have done so much for my sister already that we cannot impose any further." He took the rag from her hand and she looked upon him once again. "I will now take care of her and burden you no longer."

Even though the words were politely spoken, Claire felt that they came across as more of an instruction than a gracious sentiment. A little taken aback, Claire slowly moved away from him, Charlotte, and the bed. She was a little hurt at the words, as all she wanted was to make sure that Charlotte was all right. Even though she was in her own house, she felt like she did not have much authority in the situation. First looking at Charlotte, then to Thomas, Claire reluctantly turned toward the door. Taking one last look inside, Claire saw Thomas had gone to the other side of the bed and begun to dunk the rag into the warm water himself. Claire closed the door quietly and entered the hall, feeling a bit defeated in her attempt to care for Charlotte herself.

She took a deep breath and headed down to the foyer. The rain continued to pour, and any hint of sunlight was hidden by the clouds outside. The servants walked around the home with their candlesticks as they lit the various rooms. The light flickered against the walls as the candles burned. She caught sight of Samuel and called out to him, "Samuel, have you seen my brother?"

"He is in his study, Miss Stonewall. Shall I retrieve him for you?"

"No, that will not be necessary. I will call upon him myself." Claire made her way to the study. The door was shut and Claire took a deep breath before holding her closed hand up to the door, ready to knock lightly upon its surface.

AMONGST STRANGERS

CLAIRE WASN'T QUITE SURE WHAT to do, having not been in this situation before. This was not a typical call of conversation and tea. She knew what to do in those situations. It was pretty easy, really: quietly sip her tea, periodically flatten her dress during silent pauses, and make idle conversation about the weather or general gossip. But this visit, if one could call it a visit, was something entirely different.

There was a man involved, a man whom she did not know, from a family she had not heard of. This was not the way to be introduced to someone new, especially of the opposite sex. Generally, in order for her to meet a new gentleman, he must be first introduced by someone else or discovered at a ball. She wasn't quite sure he was even a gentleman. His previous encounter with the carriage in town revealed that he was brave and honorable. Vivian would have known about the family if they were of proper station, or even Nathaniel, but neither of them had any recollection of the name. He was a handsome man, but she knew so very little of his character and beliefs. The thoughts burned inside Claire and, to her surprise, took an exuberant amount of effort to surmise from her limited observation of him. In the end, she contemplated why he was taking up so much of her thoughts in the first place.

It was not common practice to invite a man to stay the night, even under this circumstance. She stood, stunned, in front of the study. Ultimately relinquishing her control, she gave in to the idea that Charles had the final word. "It is up to Charles. He will know what needs to be done, and he can handle it," she whispered lightly to herself. Claire rapped her knuckles on the door, and waited for Charles' reply.

"I hear that we have a couple of visitors," Charles said as Claire entered the room.

"Yes, brother."

Charles looked to Claire with concern. He walked over to her and saw that she was quite beside herself. He placed his hand gently upon her shoulder in comfort. "Do we know who they are and where they are from, sister?"

"No. I do not know the family, although I have met both the girl and her brother. They are of the Edleman family. From what I understand, they are a common people living near the Devereux Estate. At least that is all that I have been informed of. The man is a Mr. Thomas Edleman, and it is his younger sister who we have in our charge. Her name is Miss Charlotte Edleman. Dr. Michaels requested that she remain in bed for the next week. He will be returning in a few days to check on her progress."

"Miss Charlotte and Mr. Thomas Edleman. I see. How is Miss Edleman doing now?" asked Charles sincerely.

"She has a fever, and deep congestion within her chest. She is resting well now, and in the comfort of her brother. In truth, brother, I met Mr. Edleman in town this very day. He is the savior from an incident whereby a young girl was saved from a runaway carriage."

"I have not been fully informed of the situation in town today, though I have heard a few rumors from the servants. Will you take the time to discuss the particulars with me over dinner?"

Claire simply nodded. "So much has happened today, I would barely know where to start."

"Start at the beginning. From what I can recall, the three of you went to town this early afternoon. Inform me of the events as they happened from there."

Claire then relayed the entire story to Charles as they ate their dinner. "I just could not leave her on the side of the road. How dreadful!" Claire looked to Charles and saw that he was deep in thought about the situation. She softened her gaze and asked him blankly, "Did I do something wrong, Charles?"

"No, my darling sister. You did nothing wrong. Your heart proudly outshines any thoughts to typical social expectations. And your kindness speaks volumes to your good nature."

With the immediate sense of approval, Claire felt reassured. "There is one more thing, Charles," said Claire hesitantly, feeling that she may be overstepping her abilities.

"One more thing?"

"Well, yes, in fact," responded Claire, as a slight embarrassment swept over her. "Her brother showed up some time ago and, as I said before, is with her now. However, I did not know what to offer him as far as staying here for the night. I have already informed Mary to fix him a room, but I chose not to offer it to him, thinking it would not be prudent. In all honesty, I am not quite sure what to do with him."

"I see."

"I didn't want to be so impertinent as to invite him over, but he truly does have concern for his sister. And it is getting late."

Charles let loose a light chuckle. "It is nothing to fret over. I will go up and talk to him personally."

Just as Charles stood from the table, a knock came at the door. Thomas entered the room and bowed honorably to the two of them.

"Sir, I do humbly apologize for this interruption, but I find it getting late and it is about time I bid you both goodnight. Again, I thank you for your hospitality and dutiful care of my sister. She is far better off here than she would have been at home."

Charles walked towards Thomas. "We are glad to be of assistance to your sister. Miss Charlotte Edleman, is it?"

"Yes, sir. She is currently in the care of one of your maidservants."

"Splendid. I am Charles Stonewall. My sister, whom you have already met, is Miss Claire Stonewall. May I ask your name?" Claire heard Charles' tone and knew that he was attempting to lighten the mood.

"Excuse me, sir. I did not mean to slight you in any way!"

"No slight whatsoever, just wanted to know who I was going to shake hands with."

Thomas grabbed Charles' hand, and shook it solidly as he introduced himself. "Thomas. Thomas Edleman, sir."

"Well met, Mr. Edleman. Miss Stonewall will be in charge of your sister's care while she is our guest here. You are welcome to stay here at Brookfield Manor until your sister has recovered fully."

Thomas looked shocked. The thought had apparently not occurred to him that someone of such high stature would give him a second notice, let alone take him in or offer their hospitality without a concern. "Sir, although I do greatly appreciate the gesture, I am unable to accept the offer. I fear it is time that I return to my own home to take care of the rest of my family. May I request to return tomorrow morning to check on Miss Edleman?"

"By all means. I will leave word with the doorman and the staff here to give you the freedom you need while your sister is in our care. We will look forward to your patronage tomorrow at whatever time you are able."

Thomas shook his hand and looked to both Charles and to Claire. "I bid you both a pleasant evening. My family and I humbly thank you for your gracious hospitality." He turned to the door and Samuel was standing there with his coat and hat in hand. The rains had lightened a small amount, but still showered upon the grounds. Thomas put on his coat and hat, exited the manor, and jumped onto his horse. Within moments, he was charging down the parkway on his way home, not giving a second glance to them as they watched from the comforts of the dining room.

"Well it seems to me that you have had quite the adventure today," Charles admitted to Claire as he watched Thomas ride away on his horse.

"Yes, but I do still concern myself with Miss Edleman. I hope she recovers quickly, I hate to see such a pretty young woman so ill. If you do not mind, brother, I would like to go and see to her."

"Make sure that you get some rest yourself, sister. I will be retiring for the night shortly. "

Claire made her way up the stairs and into Charlotte's room. She carefully and quietly entered the room, ensuring that she would not disturb those within. The maidservant was tending to Charlotte, and Mary was standing just at the foot of the bed, watching over her. Claire walked to Mary and whispered, "Mary, how is she doing?"

"Not much change, Miss Stonewall. Why don't you get some rest, we will watch over her during the night in shifts. We will come and get you if anything changes in her condition."

Claire placed her hand on Mary's arm. "Thank you, Mary," she said before heading to her own bedchamber for a night's rest. Her mind went over everything that had happened that day, as it was undoubtedly one of the most adventurous days she had ever experienced.

DAY ONE OF
CHARLOTTE'S INFIRMARY

CLAIRE AWOKE FROM A SOUND sleep, alert and ready for the day ahead. She went to the window and opened the curtains wide, allowing the light to fill the room. As she looked upon the grounds, she saw the green grass, as it had fully grown in. The lakes had melted and were now flowing with what she imagined to be ice-cold water. The small animals were beginning to wake from their long hibernation and scurried about the grounds. Various ripples in the pond gave some hint to the insects and fish that were feeding that morning. Leaves were sprouting on the trees and a few blossoms could be seen emerging from their buds.

Mary entered the room and called attention to Claire, pulling her away from her reverie. "Mary, how is Miss Edleman this morning?"

"She is doing better, Miss Stonewall, she is currently being attended to by Mr. Edleman."

"Mr. Edleman?"

"Yes, Miss Stonewall. Mr. Edleman came to call upon his sister just an hour ago, and has been with her ever since. He relieved the maidservant and has been diligently watching over his sister. He said that he would inform us if anything was needed."

"Very well then, thank you, Mary." Claire was quite surprised that Mr. Edleman had arrived so early that morning. She attributed his diligence to his devotion to Charlotte's health, and Claire was pleased to see such brotherly affection. She left her bedchamber and decided to leave Charlotte and Thomas alone for the moment. She went down the hall and paid her tribute to her mother's and father's portrait.

Claire continued down the stairs and briefly looked out the entry windows. There were a few early blooms in the entryway and she went directly toward the front door. Samuel greeted her on her way out and she smiled to him as she passed by.

She took her time around the lands, looking at what flowers were early to bloom, and picked a few of the most beautiful. She had decided to take a bundle to Charlotte, recollecting the flowers that she had lost the day before. Within a short period of time, she had a fairly large bouquet of beautiful spring flowers.

Claire procured a vase capable of containing the flowers and arranged the various flora within it. The smell of the flowers filled the hall as she walked by, a very pleasant aroma, she thought to herself.

As Claire reached the door to Charlotte's room, she opened it softly, and looked within. Thomas was sitting on the far side of the bed with a book in his lap. He was reading the story to his sister, speaking in a soft and low tone to not wake her. Claire watched in wonder as he read from the book. He emphasized parts of the story, and would change his voice to mimic a particular character. Claire lowered the vase to her hip as his voice was comforting to hear. Claire was instantly reminded of the times that her father would read to her when she was young, and a tear fell from her cheek.

A few moments passed before Thomas realized that Claire was standing in the doorway. Once he did, he folded the book and placed it down quickly, then rose to greet Claire properly. Claire motioned her hand to have him remain seated, but he disregarded the gesture. "Good morning, Miss Stonewall."

"Good morning, Mr. Edleman. I thought your sister would like these pretty flowers. The flowers she had in her basket yesterday were ruined." Claire placed the vase upon the bedside table.

"I believe you are correct, Miss Stonewall, she would like them very much. She and our mother love fresh flowers. My gratitude for your kind gesture."

Claire and Thomas looked at each other and an awkward silence fell between them. After a few moments, Claire attempted to open the conversation. "How is she doing this morning?"

"I am afraid that I have little knowledge to provide an accurate diagnosis, Miss Stonewall. She does seem to be cooler than her feverish state yesterday, but she has still not awoken this morning. Unfortunately, I must take my leave shortly, and I was hoping to speak with her before I depart."

"It is generally considered a good sign if her fever has been broken, Mr. Edleman. The good Dr. Michaels clearly instructed that she needed as much rest as can be afforded. I am quite assured that she will be fully recovered in due time. Though I am sorry to hear that you are leaving."

"Of course, Miss Stonewall, I thank you for your diligence and faith in her recovery. However, I must return to the Devereux Estate this morning, but I will return in good time. If she does wake from her slumber, could you inform her that I was here and will be returning soon?"

"I am sure she will be quite relieved to hear that you have been constantly by her side. I will relay your message to her in the event that she awakens from her sleep."

Thomas checked his sister once more and placed his hand upon her wrists. He leaned over the bed and pressed his lips to her forehead, depositing a kiss to her restful state. "Miss Stonewall, I appreciate your earnestness, and must excuse myself for the day as I must attend to my daily duties."

Claire was surprised that he had more pressing duties and surmised that it was due to his station. "You are free to visit Miss Edleman when you are able. We will make sure she is comfortable and well looked after."

"Again, thank you, Miss Stonewall, for your kindness to my sister. It is truly appreciated." Thomas turned around and left through the door, closing it quietly behind him.

Claire remained at Charlotte's side, making sure that she had clean water to drink, and frequently dabbed her forehead with a damp cloth. Thomas was right; Charlotte's fever was diminishing, although still present. Claire looked to the chair that he was sitting in and saw the book that he was reading from. She took it in her hand and sat in the chair. The book was familiar to her, and one that she had read on multiple occasions. She opened the book and began to read from it, keeping her voice low as to not interrupt Charlotte. It appeared to help as Charlotte's breathing settled and she seemed to be calmed.

As the day wore on, Claire continued to read to Charlotte. Every so often, she would go and check on Charlotte's fever, keeping a watchful eye upon her if she moved or showed any signs of awakening. Her voice was loud enough to hear, but not loud enough to disturb the serenity of the room. She would emphasize portions of the story just enough to show emotion when it called for it. Occasionally, she would even find herself speaking with her voice strained, mimicking what the character sounded like.

The day wore on as she was reading from the book and she lost track of time. As she was reading, a light coughing sound was heard from the doorway. Claire was startled to see that Thomas was standing there quietly, watching her as she read from the book. She stood and folded the book shut, placing it upon the bedside table. "Good afternoon, Mr. Edleman, please do come in."

She stepped away from the chair and watched as Thomas entered the room. He was well dressed, as before, and the overall presence of him gave her a bit of a chill down her spine. She did not know why he affected her so much, but she found herself wanting to straighten up and show her station when he was around.

Thomas came to Claire and stood beside her as he bowed slightly. He looked to his sister who was still sleeping calmly in bed. "How is my sister doing, Miss Stonewall?"

"Miss Edleman seems to be improving, however she still has not woken from her current sleep. Her cough has been decreasing, and her breathing has stabilized. Her fever has not returned, and is holding steadily."

"Thank you for continuing to care for my sister, Miss Stonewall."

Thomas moved passed Claire and put his hands on Charlotte's wrists. She was much cooler to the touch today, and it seemed that more life pulsed throughout her body. The color in her face was better than the ashen shade she was yesterday.

Claire took a few steps towards the foot of the bed and watched Thomas as he began to look after his sister. "I will leave you to be alone with your sister. Please call upon me if you have need of anything."

"Oh please, do not leave... Your voice is so much better than my dear brother's!" The voice came from the bed as Charlotte opened her eyes slightly, a small smile showing upon her face.

Thomas looked to her and playfully retorted, "Do not be so mean, sister!"

A bright smile appeared over Claire face, as she felt the relief of Charlotte's wellbeing.

"How are you feeling, sister? Is there anything that you need?"

"I feel a bit hungry, brother. May I have something to calm my stomach?"

Claire overheard the request and responded quickly, "Certainly, I shall have the cook get you some warm soup to help with your throat and stomach. I will leave you two and have it brought here as soon as possible." Claire left the room quickly and shut the door behind her. She was happy to see that Charlotte was doing so much better. She entered the dining room to see Charles sitting at the table patiently. At that moment, Claire realized that she had not eaten anything that day either. She was far more focused on Charlotte's wellbeing than her own.

"Brother, you should have told me that you were waiting for me!"

"I knew you were occupied with your charge and could wait until you came down."

"Thank you, Charles, that was very thoughtful of you. Though I must inform Lily that Miss Edleman has just awoken. She has requested something to eat. Let me ensure that she gets some soup to calm her hunger and that it is taken up to her shortly."

"Do you need to attend to Miss Edleman?" asked Charles sincerely.

"No, no, dear brother. Mr. Edleman is with her now, and he is more than capable of caring for his sister, apparently." Claire continued into the kitchen and within a few moments, she returned to the dining table and took a seat next to Charles.

As they were finishing up dinner, Thomas entered the room. "I apologize for interrupting your dinner, but I just wanted to bid you farewell. I will return in the morning to check on Charlotte."

"The offer still stands, Mr. Edleman. Just say the word, and you are welcome to stay the night," Charles called out to him in earnest.

"I do appreciate the offer, Mr. Stonewall, but need to tend to the rest of my family. I will call again early tomorrow. I wish you both a good evening."

"Do take care, Mr. Edleman. We will look forward to your visit tomorrow," Claire offered to him before he bowed and left the manor.

DAY TWO OF
CHARLOTTE'S INFIRMARY

CLAIRE WOKE EARLY THE NEXT morning, before the sun crested over the hills. After putting on a simple dress, she opened the door and went directly to Charlotte's room. Although Charlotte had shown improvement the day before, Claire was still worried for her.

She opened the door to the room and saw that Charlotte was still fast asleep. One of the maidservants looked to the door and stood quickly from the oversized chair. Claire signaled to the maidservant to be quiet. The maidservant nodded, having understood the signal, and Claire entered the room, closing the door quietly behind her.

Claire stepped closer to the side of the bed. Charlotte seemed to be resting comfortably. After watching Charlotte for a few moments, Claire looked to the maidservant and whispered softly, "You may go, I will look after her for a while. Get yourself some rest."

The maidservant quietly curtsied to Claire and left the room. Claire looked to the basin that was near the bedside to ensure it had enough fresh water. She took a rag from the table and rinsed it in the basin. Being sure not to wake Charlotte, Claire felt her forehead to check for any sign of a fever. The color in Charlotte's cheeks and face looked to have returned to normal. She was still warm to the touch, but it was hardly worth a concern. Claire gently blotted the damp rag on Charlotte's face and chest, being careful not to wake her.

She placed the rag back into its place, and took her seat in the chair next to the bed, keeping a close eye on Charlotte as she lay there. After a few moments of silence, Claire picked up the book that she had been reading to her the day before. She noticed that one of the pages was folded in the corner. She opened the book to the folded page and unfolded it. She looked at the pages and realized that it was a marker for the previous reader. The thought of Thomas reading to his sister entered her mind once again. Perhaps this was where Thomas had stopped reading to her before he left the night before.

She imagined Thomas sitting in the chair and reading to his dear sister as she slept. She took a few moments and found where she had left off in the story, and read silently the few pages in between. The book was one that she had read before, but she wanted to recall the various events that she had missed during Thomas' reading. Her mind still held him in the background as she read on.

Claire adjusted herself in the chair while she was reading. It was an oversized chair with a large back and soft cushions. The fire was flickering in the background, and a few crackles could be heard as it filled the room with light and warmth. Claire wedged herself into the corner of the chair and lifted her legs over the armrest, almost in a cradled position. The light of the fire reflected off the surface of the pages as she read them. She reached the page that was previously folded and folded it again so as not to lose Thomas' place in the book. Holding the book against her stomach, her eyes closed and she fell asleep once more.

The sun rose and the grounds were well lit. Charlotte's room was shielded from the sunlight with the heavy curtains drawn to a close. Claire's eyes opened slightly as she realized that she had dozed off. Her sight focused on the opposite chair in the room. She blinked a few times, and saw that Thomas was sitting there looking back at her. Taken by surprise to see him, she straightened herself quickly in the chair. The blanket fell silently to the ground around her feet. She looked to Thomas with a stunned expression, unable to find the words to say at the moment.

Thomas looked to her and raised his finger to his lips, motioning her to be quiet. She looked over to Charlotte who was still fast asleep. Claire carefully stood from her chair, and Thomas was quick to stand before her. He kneeled down and took up Claire's blanket into his hand. Claire was beside herself, unable to take her eyes off him. She watched him as the seconds that he was near her seemed to last much longer. He grinned to her, holding the blanket in his hand.

Claire handed him the book in exchange and whispered softly to him, "Your place is secured, Mr. Edleman. I will leave you to attend to your sister."

"Thank you, Miss Stonewall. You honor me and my sister, and we are forever grateful."

Claire curtsied softly, a slight blush overcoming her comfort. Without knowing what to say in return, she stepped lightly towards the door. Before leaving the room, she glanced back to see Thomas standing there, looking at her. Her discomfort intensified with his stare and she fumbled slightly, quietly closing the door behind her. Alone in the hallway, Claire leaned against the wall and stopped for a brief moment, remembering the detail of the scene within the room. Thomas standing there, watching her diligently, the firelight reflecting off of his skin and attire. Her heart was pounding heavily, and her breath was heavy. She calmed herself as best she could and continued down the hall, stopping at the portrait of her parents.

She focused her attention on the image of her father. He was standing tall behind her mother, with a genuine smile upon his face. Claire was comforted, and pressed a kiss to the frame of the portrait. Her fingers lingered upon the frame for a moment and her thoughts proceeded to commune with the images of her parents. The questions of Thomas came foremost into her thoughts. Who was this stranger she had come to know by happenstance? Why had he taken so much of her thoughts? How did he make her feel the way she did when he was present? What did it all mean? Claire did not know the answer to the questions, and it made her feel lost and confused.

Claire took a deep breath and curtsied to the portrait before heading down the stairs. She forced the thoughts out of her mind, and instead, put her focus on the day ahead. She walked to the breakfast nook and sat comfortably at the small table. As Claire looked out the windows, it did not take long for the thoughts of Thomas to find their way back into her mind.

Charles entered the room and sat down next to her. "Good morning, sister."

Claire awoke from her daydream and was startled to see Charles sitting next to her. She straightened herself and shook the thoughts away. "Yes, good morning, brother."

"How was your sleep last night?"

"It was well, thank you. And you, brother, how did you sleep last night?"

"Good enough, have you had the chance to look upon your charge this morning?"

"Yes, Miss Edleman is doing better, her brother is with her now."

Lily entered the room with a tray in her hand, calling out to the both of them, "Good morning, Mr. Stonewall, Miss Stonewall." She carefully placed the tray in the center of the table, taking the lid from it and exposing the contents therein. "Enjoy your breakfast."

"Thank you, Lily." Charles said to her as he looked over the food.

Claire suddenly realized how hungry she was. She took the serving fork in her hand and began to take various items from the tray, placing them on the plate before her. Charles poured a drink for himself, and then one for Claire. He took the serving fork in turn and collected food onto his plate as well. "What are the plans for today, Claire?"

Claire took a bite of her breakfast, and as she heard Charles, her mind was jolted to the idea that the ball was only a few days away. "I do hope that the doctor arrives soon. I believe that Miss Edleman is doing much better, though I would want his assessment before coming to any conclusion of her wellbeing. I may need to cancel my reservation to the coming ball if Dr. Michaels does not excuse her from this illness. I know that she is doing much better than was expected, but her health is of more importance."

"I am confident in your assessment of Miss Edleman and am quite sure that Dr. Michaels will agree with your prognosis. There is no need to miss the ball in either case."

"You know me well enough to know that I could not allow that to happen. I have taken Miss Edleman into my charge, and as long as she is ill, I will continue to care for her myself as best as I can."

"I have no doubt that you will do what you are able, that is not the concern that I share with you. I know how much you enjoy the opportunity to dance at these assemblies. I was not contradicting your position, simply reminding you that you do have a choice in the matter. Have you relayed your intentions to Mr. Clayton?"

For the first time since Nathaniel's departure, the thought of his absence entered Claire's mind. She was so occupied with Charlotte that she had not thought about him in the slightest until this moment. He had not appeared yesterday, although each day previously he had come to see her. A slight concern of his whereabouts entered her mind, and she pushed the thought away. "I am quite sure that Mr. Clayton will understand the position that I have acquired. To answer your question, no, I have not had the opportunity to speak with him. I have not had the privilege of his company since I took Miss Edleman into my care. I am sure he will be by soon enough and we can discuss it when he arrives."

"Besides," Claire continued, "you will be attending the Springhurst Ball regardless, will you not?" She looked to him for confirmation. It dawned on her that his attendance may be contingent on her decision. She hoped that he would attend the ball regardless, so that he could deliver her excuse.

"I will be attending the ball, sister. There is a company of fellows with whom I wish to share a word or two. I have been informed that they too will be attending the festivities at the town ball. If I am so inclined, and with some luck, there may be a few women to entertain me at the ball as well. It may even be to my benefit if you do not attend the ball, giving me the opportunity to engage in such pleasantries."

"Brother!" Claire was shocked at his playful demeanor. "How shallow of you to tease me in this way. You will do better to not unsettle me while I have duties to attend to. But nevertheless, if I am to stay here in the home, I will need you to deliver my excuses at the ball. I am sure there will be a soul or two who would share some concern about my absence. You would do me the best favor to relieve their concerns and be a good brother."

"Oh, sister, I dare not beat off the many who would question your absence. I think if you should not attend, allow them to writhe in their concerns and make up their own minds about your excuse. I am quite sure the rumors of your whereabouts would be the talk of the town for months to come."

"Charles!" Claire said aloud, gawking at him for thinking such a thing. She knew that he was teasing.

"I doubt you have anything to concern yourself about, dear sister. I would guard your honor to the most scrupulous of people."

Claire rolled her eyes. The two of them continued on with their meal and relaxed in the atmosphere of their company.

Samuel opened the door and stood at attention near the two of them as they sat at the table. He announced in proper fashion a newcomer to their home. "A Mr. Clayton here to see Miss Stonewall."

Claire looked quite surprised and turned to her brother, gulping slightly. Charles simply smiled to her in response, knowing more than he cared to admit at that moment. Claire glanced at her attire and stood from the table. "I am in no state to see him now! Look at my dress, I cannot have him see me like this." She had chosen one of her more common dresses, thinking she would have returned to dress more appropriately after taking care of Charlotte.

"Shall I ask him to wait in the parlor, Miss Stonewall?" responded Samuel.

Claire looked to Charles once more, letting loose a slight harrumph, then turned to Samuel. "No, Samuel, I will be with him presently." She wiped her lips with the napkin and placed it upon her plate. She took a step away from her chair. "Excuse me, brother."

Samuel bowed and walked back to the foyer. Claire thought to herself, as she followed behind Samuel, 'He will just have to deal with the attire. I am not to be diverted and need to be attentive to my charge!'

Claire entered the foyer just behind Samuel and looked to see Nathaniel standing there with a tall hat under his arm. He was dressed in fine attire and looking about the entryway at the various decorations. The surprise on his face could not be mistaken, and Claire was fully aware of his disdain for her chosen attire. He hid his expression and pretended to clear his throat. "Good morning, Miss Stonewall."

"Good morning, Mr. Clayton."

"Miss Stonewall, we have been invited to tea in town this afternoon. I would suggest suitable attire for the engagement."

"Oh? Unfortunately, I am unable to attend this afternoon, as I am sure you are well informed. Until Miss Edleman has been cleared of her illness, I will need to attend to her during her recovery. I am sure you have not forgotten this."

"Miss Stonewall, it is imperative that we attend this particular invitation. Mrs. Devereux insisted upon your attendance. She will not be pleased to hear of your unavailability to her request."

"Mr. Clayton, I am sure that Mrs. Devereux will understand my absence with my current duty. Please be sure to send my regards to her at tea if you wish to attend without me."

"Miss Stonewall, I am sorry to see that you will not reconsider your attendance. I will give your regards to Mrs. Devereux, though I know that she will be most assuredly disappointed that you will not beckon to her request. Whatever should I give as your excuse?"

"I have no need to falsify my excuse, Mr. Clayton. Do tell her that I have Miss Edleman in my care and she requires my attention this day. It is my duty to take care of those who are less fortunate than myself. I have no need to hide this fact from anyone worthy of my attendance."

"As you wish, Miss Stonewall, I shall deliver your excuse to Mrs. Devereux. May I inquire as to the condition of Miss Edleman?"

Claire knew that he was attempting to placate her frustration with him. She attributed his demeanor to his inexperience with Mrs. Devereux. "She is doing better, though I do believe that the doctor should appraise her condition before I make any assumptions. If you would excuse me, I must see to her and I do not wish to delay your tea with Mrs. Devereux."

Nathaniel heard the words and understood the fierce determination that Claire expressed. He reluctantly bowed in defeat, his attempt to convince her to accompany him had failed. "Then until the morrow, I do hope that Miss Edleman recovers in time for the town festivities."

Claire did not appreciate his demeanor and was struggling to forgive his attitude towards Charlotte. "It will depend on the doctor's prognosis, Mr. Clayton."

Claire watched Nathaniel through the open door as he exited the manor and left on his horse down the parkway. Claire turned to the stairwell and felt a bit awkward about the whole conversation with him. She thought that she may have been too harsh with him. She continued on her way to Charlotte's room, thinking about what she had said to him. By the time she reached the door, she had convinced herself that it was entirely her own fault and that Nathaniel was completely innocent.

She was frustrated with Nathaniel, though she knew it was not in his nature to act as she did. Her actions were not common for her station, and Nathaniel could not comprehend her desire to assist those of lesser fortune. In most cases, it was frowned upon, but she was determined to be the woman she was. She thought of it for a few more moments before she relinquished the thoughts and focused on her charge instead.

Claire took a breath and relaxed the muscles in her face, easing the tension from her frustration. She opened the door quietly and saw that Thomas was reading softly to his sister. He had not noticed Claire's entry, and was sitting in the chair closest to the bed. Claire looked over to Charlotte and saw that her eyes were closed, though she looked as though she had moved further up in the bed. Claire quietly closed the door behind her, and stood there watching the two of them.

The thoughts of Nathaniel and their conversation only moments ago drifted away. She was relieved as the sound of Thomas' quiet voice brushed away the remnants of her frustration. His voice was smooth and deep, though barely could be heard over the crackling of the fire still burning in the fireplace. Claire's mind cleared as she focused on the sound of his voice.

Claire quietly took the chair that sat opposite from Thomas. Thomas was focused on the story of the book, and did not notice her as she sat down. There was fresh water in the basin and fresh rags on the bedside table. It was apparent that the maidservants were entering and exiting the room constantly, and Claire thought it possible that Thomas had become accustomed to their interruptions.

Several hours passed by as Thomas continued to read from the book. Charlotte remained sleeping effortlessly in the bed. The maidservants would take shifts and enter the room to check on them, as if changing the guard. They cleared the rags and brought fresh water for Charlotte. They would check her condition, and then take their leave. Thomas did not lose a beat in his reading from the book. Claire made no effort to alert him to her presence. She sat comfortably in the chair and listened to the words that Thomas spoke, keeping her eyes on Charlotte and thinking of the story as Thomas portrayed it.

Eventually, Thomas came to the conclusion of the book. Claire knew the ending well, and listened to him as he read the last remaining pages. He finished the book and looked directly to Charlotte, who was still fast asleep. He stood from the chair and stretched his arms and legs before walking to the side of the bed. He leaned over her and pulled the few strands of her hair from her face, watching her diligently to ensure that she was resting comfortably. He pressed a light kiss to her forehead and Claire could see a slight smile come over Charlotte's face. Thomas stood at the bedside for a few moments before he turned to see Claire watching him.

Thomas was startled at the sight of her. Clearly he did not expect to see her sitting there so quietly. He attempted to hold his composure. "Miss Stonewall! Please excuse me, I did not notice that you entered the room." His voice was not much louder than a whisper, and Claire stood from her chair and curtsied to him. She waved him over to the other side of the room, away from his sleeping sister.

"Pay it no mind, Mr. Edleman. It was I who stole upon the chair in secret. I could not resist hearing the words from the story as you portrayed them. It was quite comforting and I had no wish to deprive your dear sister."

"She is fond of these stories, as am I, Miss Stonewall. I appreciate you for allowing me the opportunity to read from it."

"How is your sister doing, Mr. Edleman? She looks to have been asleep most of the day. Has she been awake at all today?"

"Yes, Miss Stonewall. She woke hungry shortly after you took your leave. I beg your forgiveness, for I took the liberty of asking your staff for some food. I do hope that I have not offended you in doing so."

"No, Mr. Edleman, on the contrary, it is my desire to ensure the comfort of you and your sister while you are in my home. If you have any requirement, please do not hesitate to ask. You and your sister are welcome to anything that you need while you are here."

"I have finished this wonderful book that was left here. I was wondering if there would be a chance for another that might satisfy the time. I do not wish to impose upon you in any effect."

"If you think your sister is well asleep, we may take a brief escape to the library. From there, you may find one of your choosing and bring it hither."

"You are most gracious, Miss Stonewall."

Claire turned towards the door, being careful not to stir up too much noise. Thomas followed behind her, glancing over to his sister before leaving the room. Claire led him down the stairwell towards the library. Claire opened the door widely, allowing Thomas to take in its splendor.

"Oh my…" Thomas said aloud as he entered the room. The library was filled from wall to wall with books. There were also a few long, standing bookshelves lined up in the middle of the room. Each and every space was taken by a book, with very few places to spare. Inside the room was a large fireplace, and several large armchairs with cushions laid across them. There were several candlesticks laid about the walls, and small tables next to each armchair. The tables were decorated with lace and most of them had both a candlestick and a vase filled with fresh flowers. It was a place for reading, and was elegantly decorated for that purpose. The smell of the books, wood, and fresh flowers filled the air.

"You may take what you wish from here, Mr. Edleman. I am quite sure that you will find whatever may please you and your sister among this collection."

It was apparent to Claire that Thomas was quite beside himself in the room. "This is simply incredible, Miss Stonewall. I could not imagine the number of books here, surely you have not read them all."

"No, I must admit, Mr. Edleman. There are far too many here to be fully versed. Though I have made quite a significant impact on the collection. It was a fond pastime of my father's, and mine as well. We shared many warm memories within this room, lost in the worlds that each book portrayed. May I make a suggestion?"

"Please do, Miss Stonewall. I would be lost in this room for days on end if I were endeavoring to find something specific for the moment."

Claire took a few steps down one of the aisles created by the long bookshelves, and returned briefly with a book in her hands. "This is one of my many favorites, Mr. Edleman. It is very similar to the genre that you just finished reading. I feel that you and your sister may find it quite entertaining, and yet not too exciting as to cause strife with your sister's rest."

"I thank you for your considerable recommendation, and your concern, Miss Stonewall. I must profess, I am quite surprised to have been so well looked after while we have been in your charge. You do much credit to your station, Miss Stonewall, and I dare say it would be extremely hard for us to pay back your contribution to us. We cannot thank you enough for your hospitality and your continued devotion to us. Please do let us know if ever we are trespassing on your good graces, I fear we would be too comfortable here to know otherwise."

"Speak nothing of it, Mr. Edleman. You are most welcome, and I look forward to the chance to listen to you read from this masterful work."

"I would only be so honored to have you listen, Miss Stonewall." With that sentiment, the two of them headed back to Charlotte, who was still asleep in the room. Claire took the seat furthest away from the bed, and Thomas sat comfortably next to the bed. He opened the book and began reading from the first page. Claire listened to him as he read along, attentive to his words and watching the two of them from the short distance.

DAY THREE OF
CHARLOTTE'S INFIRMARY

T HE FOLLOWING MORNING, CLAIRE AWOKE from her night's slumber. The early morning sun broke through the curtains ever so slightly. Claire opened her eyes, took a deep breath, and smiled as she thought of Thomas reading to Charlotte to comfort his sister in her sleep. Claire stood at the edge of the bed after tossing the covers away. As she stood there, stretching away the stiffness from the night's rest, she heard a rustle from outside her door. Claire quickly put on a dress and shoes, wrapped her hair loosely in a simple ribbon, and went out into the hallway.

Charlotte's door was ajar and Mary was speaking to another maidservant just in the hallway. Claire was concerned for Charlotte and walked over to see what was happening. As she arrived at the door, she looked inside to see a bright-eyed and cheerful Charlotte sitting up in the bed. A calmness came over her, as she had feared something dreadful may have occurred. Claire entered Charlotte's room and approached the side of the bed.

"Good morning, Miss Edleman! How are you feeling this early morning?"

"Good morning, Miss Stonewall. I am feeling quite well. I do apologize if I was the cause of your rising."

"No, Miss Edleman, not at all. I was already awake this morning, and came to see how you were doing. I am so glad to see that you are feeling better."

"I am, and I thank you for your concern, Miss Stonewall. I am quite hungry, however, and was wondering if I could join you for breakfast this morning."

"Unfortunately, I do not think that is wise, Miss Edleman. I am sure that Mary will see to your needs this morning. A breakfast will be brought here into the room for you. The doctor gave his strict instruction, and I only request that you heed his direction until he has been able to assess your condition."

"Yes, Miss Stonewall," said Charlotte, feeling a bit defeated.

Claire could see that Charlotte was eager to leave the bed, and felt sorry to have to keep her there. "I do apologize, Miss Edleman, I have a hard time judging the health of others. I would feel more comfortable if the good doctor gave his blessing first. I am sure you are fine, Miss Edleman, not to worry."

Charlotte looked to Claire and could see the concern on her face. She did not want to inquire as to what Claire was thinking, as it seemed to have made her quite uncomfortable. Instead, she took a deep breath, sighed, and laid her head back against the headboard. The abundance of pillows engulfed her and she looked up to the ceiling, feeling trapped in the bed once again.

Claire took a deep breath and cleared her mind, then walked around the bed, sitting in the chair that was closest to Charlotte. "Would you care for a bit more of the story, Miss Edleman?"

"That would be lovely, Miss Stonewall. Though I must confess, I am not used to such attention."

"Nonsense, Miss Edleman. I insist on your comfort," Claire said playfully. Opening the book, she began reading from the place that Thomas had stopped. Charlotte watched Claire carefully as she read from the book.

A few moments went by before Mary returned with a tray of food for Charlotte, and placed it gently upon the bed. Charlotte began to eat and Claire continued reading without a pause to the interruption. The door opened once again as Mary headed out of the room. "Good morning, Mr. Edleman," Mary said.

Charlotte heard Mary and looked up towards the doorway. Thomas was standing and looking back at her. "Brother!"

Claire stopped her reading abruptly and stood at the front of her chair. She looked to Thomas and curtsied to him.

"Good morning, sister. Good morning, Miss Stonewall. Please excuse my intrusion."

"You have not intruded, Mr. Edleman. I am glad to see you, your sister is doing quite well, as you can see."

"Indeed," replied Thomas as he walked over to Charlotte and sat lightly upon the bedside. "You have been quite rested these last few days, sister. How do you feel?"

"I am feeling quite well, brother, though I am very hungry. Would you mind?"

"Of course not, Charlotte. Please continue your meal. I am glad to see you with such an appetite, it is a good sign." Thomas looked to Claire and she could see the relief in his expression.

"I will take my leave, and you two are welcome to the comforts of my home. If you should need anything, let the servants know." Claire folded the page she was reading in the usual manner and placed the book back on the table. She left the room and shut the door behind her, allowing them some privacy.

Claire was relieved that things were working out for Charlotte. A few moments passed before she continued across the hallway and into her own room again. She changed her appearance, fully expecting to see Dr. Michaels arrive as he had promised.

She paid her respects to the portrait of her parents, and continued down the stairwell. Looking out the windows, she noticed a gathering of a coach and several people. She stopped for a moment to see if she could identify who came to their home to call upon them so early. There were three women, one older and two younger.

The door opened and Samuel ushered the three women into the home. Samuel saw Claire and announced the visitors. "A

Mrs. Martha Edleman, a Miss Helena Edleman, and a Miss Anne Edleman to call upon Miss Edleman."

Claire curtsied to the three of them as they entered the home. "Good morning, I am Miss Claire Stonewall."

Martha looked to Claire. "Miss Stonewall, such a great pleasure it is to see you this fine day. Mr. Thomas Edleman has told us so much about you, but to see you here standing before us is a true blessing. Surely, as I live and breathe, we stand before an angel of mercy. We cannot thank you enough for all that you have done for our poor Charlotte. I do not know how we will ever be able to repay your generosity and hospitality these last few days."

Anne and Helena did their best to focus their attention to Claire, but found their curiosity overwhelming. The two of them looked about the home, obviously unfamiliar with such fine furnishings. Claire watched them and could not help but to notice their countenance in detail. They were so very similar in appearance, clearly they were mirror images of each other. Claire was unable to identify Anne from Helena, and decided at that moment, that there would be no point in even the slightest attempt. It was obvious that they were identical in many ways, in both appearance and mannerisms. The two of them stood there, looking about the room, and pointed out various interests to each other. Claire continued to watch them as they giggled at their private comments to one another.

"What a fine home you have here, Miss Stonewall," continued Martha. "I must declare, what fine furnishings as well. It is so nice to be seen in such splendor, I must say." With a flick of her hand to Anne, Martha was quick to quiet and control both of them. It was obviously a well-rehearsed understanding between them. The twins straightened themselves and produced a grand smile for Claire.

"Thank you, Mrs. Edleman. If you should like, I can arrange a tour of the home," Claire offered to them, in a small attempt to please the young girls. The attention of the girls turned almost immediately to their mother. They nodded excitedly at the offer from Claire.

"You are quite gracious, Miss Stonewall. Perhaps another time, if the offer is still available. In truth, we came here to call on Charlotte. Pray tell, how she is doing?"

"She is doing quite well, though I would wait to hear the report from Dr. Michaels. He should be by soon enough to check on her. She is upstairs with Mr. Edleman as we speak. I can take you to them if it pleases you, ma'am."

"You are so kind, Miss Stonewall."

"Certainly, if you would please follow me." Claire turned to the stairwell and began to climb the steps to the room. The three of them followed Claire, looking about the home as they walked. Claire heard a small amount of giggling and whispering from the young girls as they made their way to Charlotte's room. She was surprised to be enjoying their playfulness to such an extent. She knocked on the door to the room and opened it. "Mr. Edleman, Miss Edleman, your family is here to call upon you." She stepped into the room and held the door open for the others as they came inside. Charlotte looked to the door and was excited to see them as they entered the room. Thomas stood at the foot of the chair, focusing more on Claire than his own family.

Claire caught Thomas' stare and blushed slightly before turning out of the room once more. She continued down the hall and returned to the foyer, thinking of the reunion that was transpiring in Charlotte's room. Claire reached the study and knocked lightly at the door, waiting for her brother to respond.

"Enter," said Charles from behind the closed door.

Claire entered the room, shutting the door behind her. "Mrs. Edleman, Mr. Edleman, and two of Miss Edleman's younger sisters have come calling upon Miss Edleman."

"That is quite an assembly. How is your charge feeling this day?"

"She is doing quite well, and eating a hearty breakfast. Speaking of which, have you eaten this morning's breakfast?"

"No, I have not, shall we continue to the breakfast nook?"

"Please. I am quite hungry myself, and Miss Edleman is in full company. I would think that we would be simply interfering."

Claire recalled the morning's events and reported on Charlotte's recovery. They continued their discussion while they ate, and Charles was intrigued by the whole story. Claire thought that Charles was particularly interested in this family, as well as Charlotte's condition. Even though they had taken in Charlotte, they really did not know much about the family and who they were.

Just as they finished their breakfast, Samuel came to the nook and bowed. "Dr. Michaels to call on Miss Edleman."

Claire took her napkin to her face and blotted away the remnants of food. She stood from her chair and Charles stood as well. "I shall show Dr. Michaels to Miss Edleman personally and let you know what he says, brother." Turning to the door, Claire walked behind Samuel as they returned to Dr. Michaels. Charles sat back into the chair and continued his meal.

"Good day to you, Dr. Michaels."

"A good day to you, Miss Stonewall, how are you fairing this fine day?" He was wearing his typical suit and carrying his doctor's bag. He had a pleasant disposition and always seemed to have a pleasant smile upon his face. Claire often thought that he rarely ever found a time to be something other than pleasant.

"I am well, thank you, and Miss Edleman seems to be in high spirits. Her family is with her now, shall I escort you to her?"

"Certainly, Miss Stonewall."

Claire walked with him and guided him to Charlotte's room. She knocked on the door and carefully opened it to see everyone looking back at her. Martha, Anne, Helena, and Thomas stood as she entered the room. "Dr. Michaels has arrived to check on Miss Edleman."

Dr. Michaels entered the room and looked to the grand reception that stood before him. "Dr. Michaels, may I introduce Mrs. Martha Edleman, Miss Helena Edleman, Miss Anne Edleman, and Mr. Thomas Edleman." As Claire introduced them, each bowed or curtsied their greetings to Dr. Michaels.

When she mentioned Helena, she found that she was actually mistaken and looking at Anne. This error was accepted, as they were accustomed to such instances.

Dr. Michaels nodded to them in succession as they were pointed out. "It is a pleasure to meet you all, though I wish it would have been under different circumstances. And how is the patient doing this morning?" He looked through the entourage and saw a bright-eyed and smiling Charlotte looking back at him. Everyone stepped aside, allowing him to approach the bedside without hindrance. "You are looking quite well, my dear. How are you feeling?"

"Quite well, thanks to Miss Stonewall. I feel well recovered and rested, sir," responded Charlotte, glancing briefly to Claire and then back to Dr. Michaels.

"Well, let me check on you, Miss, just to be sure." He unfolded the top of his doctor's bag and pulled out a thermometer. "Open wide."

Charlotte obliged him and opened her mouth, allowing him to place it gently under her tongue.

Dr. Michaels took out his stethoscope from his bag and placed it gently upon Charlotte's back. Occasionally he would ask her to take a deep breath, and listened intently through the device. Folding it once more, he placed it back into his bag and took the thermometer from her mouth. He held it up to the light of the fireplace, as the curtains were still pulled shut, and read its result.

"Miss Edleman looks to be fully recovered, and has my expressed permission to return home as soon as she feels ready. She is a very lucky woman, and owes her quick recovery to Miss Stonewall. If she had not tended to her when she did… I shudder to think of what may have happened."

"Oh thank you, Dr. Michaels. It is good tidings you bring to this poor woman's heart. How are we to repay you for your assistance?" asked Martha sincerely.

"Think nothing of it, Mrs. Edleman!" Claire insisted most endearingly. "I have called him to her aid, and shall take care of everything. Do not be concerned with it. It was my pleasure to assist."

Martha stood there, unable to protest to Claire. The Edlemans were not as well off as the Stonewall family, and had very little money. To afford the services of Dr. Michaels would definitely harm their financial stability. Thomas looked as though he was about to speak up on their behalf, but Claire shot him a stern look.

Claire continued, "Dr. Michaels, I will see you to the door."

Dr. Michaels picked up his bag and walked to the door, following Claire into the hallway. "Take care of yourselves, and be more careful in the future, Miss Charlotte."

"Thank you again, Dr. Michaels, your efforts are greatly appreciated," called out Thomas.

Claire and Dr. Michaels walked down the hallway. "Thank you for your help and kindness, Dr. Michaels. I am sure they are quite grateful, as am I."

"A pleasure as always, Miss Stonewall. Do be sure to take good care of yourself and your brother." Claire curtsied and watched as he left the manor.

Charles walked into the foyer and saw Claire looking out the door. "I see that I have missed Dr. Michaels. What did the good doctor have to say about Miss Edleman?"

"Miss Edleman is fully recovered, and she may depart when she feels she is ready."

"Well that is good news, and with good timing. It seems as though you will be able to attend the ball after all. I am glad she is recovered. How are you, sister?" Charles asked in return.

"I am quite pleased. I have enjoyed the company of her, though, and I do hope she fairs well when she is gone. Her family is here, and I am sure that they will be departing shortly." Claire looked upon Charles fondly. She knew that he supported her in anything that she endeavored to take on. She thought of how Thomas cared so deeply for Charlotte, and it reinforced her love for her own brother.

"I would not say I am glad, though I am satisfied with her wellbeing. It will be difficult to see them leave, it was a pleasure to have them here. Though not under such circumstances." Claire could not recall if Charles had much interaction with the family in particular. Perhaps it was simply the conversations with Claire that provided him with such comfort in their presence.

"Indeed, brother. I am relieved that she is well, but I am not pleased to see her leave. I am sure her own family is quite happy to have her return home once again."

As they stood in the foyer talking, Claire heard the two youngest siblings behind them. She looked up the stairwell to see Thomas and his two younger sisters headed on their way down the stairs. Claire turned towards them, and Charles turned as well.

Thomas spoke with a deep gratitude in his voice. "I thank you for your most generous hospitality Mr. Stonewall and Miss Stonewall. For your generosity and your care these last few days. My sister and mother will be down shortly, and we will take our leave from your home post haste. I am quite sure that you are ready for a bit of peace and quiet."

"There is no need to be in such haste, Mr. Edleman. You and your family may stay as long as you feel is necessary," Claire responded to the comment. She had thought that his impression of her had changed during Charlotte's stay.

"I apologize, Miss Stonewall. I did not mean to sound harsh. I think it would be a greater relief to my mother, to be honest, and the rest of my family, to have her return home as soon as possible."

"Mr. Edleman, I am pleased to have made your acquaintance and to have heard that your sister is doing well. I am sorry to see you leave, but I am sure that you know what is best for your family," Charles said as he reached out his hand and grasped Thomas' with a smile.

Martha and Charlotte had just begun their walk down to the rest of the group. Charlotte was wearing her clothes, which had been washed and provided back to her. Charlotte spoke kindly to Claire as she reached her. "I thank you so very much, Miss Stonewall, and I cannot find words to express my gratitude for the kindness you have given to me."

"Think nothing of it, Miss Edleman, it was fortunate that I was there to help in time. I am pleased that you have recovered and are so well cared for by your family. I do hope that you return to visit us, Miss Edleman. Come and have dinner when you are feeling well enough. It would be great to see you again."

Charlotte appeared shocked at Claire's offer. "It would be an honor."

Charles looked to Martha, and chimed in, "Of course. What a splendid idea, sister, and we insist that you bring your family as well."

Anne and Helena looked to each other and giggled gleefully. Thomas attempted to hush them but was unable to do so. Martha looked to her children, then replied to Charles, "Thank you, kind sir. We would be honored to come and join you."

"Then we will be happy to receive you," Charles said, confirming the arrangement.

"We shall be taking our leave now," Thomas said as he briefly glanced to Claire.

Claire caught his glance, and felt a small blush come over her. She curtsied, Charles bowed, and the five of them walked through the doorway. They stood on the porch, watching as the Edleman family clamored into the open carriage. Thomas turned and bowed once more to Charles and Claire before he climbed onto his horse and headed off down the parkway with his family.

Before Charles and Claire could return inside, Claire heard another carriage as it approached. The two of them turned to see it as it came towards them. It had already been a busy day at the manor, but it was still only midday. The carriage stopped before them and the door was opened.

Vivian came out of the carriage, followed shortly by Nathaniel. It was the day before the ball, and their visit was obviously for Claire's benefit. Charles turned and entered the manor, leaving Claire to greet them in the entry. Nathaniel and Vivian walked up the front steps, and Claire found herself charmed by Nathaniel simply by the sight of him. It had been a few days since they spent any time together, and being relieved of her charge, she was quite ready for the change. Nathaniel bowed and Vivian curtsied, Claire curtsying in return.

"Good day, Miss Stonewall, I see that we have come at an opportune time," Nathaniel said with relief.

Claire reached out and grasped his arm, stepping closer to him. She looked into his handsome face and uttered softly, "Yes, Mr. Clayton, it has been too long since we have had time together."

The three of them entered the home and walked casually to the drawing room. They sat upon the sofas centered in the room. Vivian sat on the one opposite from Nathaniel and Claire. The sun was high in the sky, and the light poured in through the open windows. Nathaniel turned slightly, facing Claire. "Are we safe to say that your charge is doing well then?"

"Indeed, Mr. Clayton. It was Miss Edleman you passed by just moments ago. She has been released from my care and has returned home."

"That is wonderful news. Bravo. Shall we discuss the Springhurst Ball then? I hear there is some good news, according to your dear cousin. Though she would not divulge it to me until you were present."

"I guess there is no excuse to withhold it from you now, Mr. Clayton. As you know, Mrs. Devereux is quite the prominent one in such things as matchmaking. I have simply heard just this morning that there will be several new gentlemen from out of town attending the gallantries at Springhurst. Although I have heard little of them, I am quite certain that there will be most assuredly a fine ratio of gentlemen to attract the finer ladies of the countryside."

"This is the information that you held back from me during the trip here?"

"I fully explained it to you, this was more for Miss Stonewall's benefit than your own, Mr. Clayton. Whatever should I do to tell you my meaning other than to deliver the facts?"

"Well, I am sure you have more than that to discuss openly. Or do I need to have your cousin pry the various details out of you?"

Claire said nothing, allowing them their banter back and forth. For her, their company was a necessary change of atmosphere. The topics of their conversation did little to hinder Claire's attention. Vivian took this as an actual interest in her gossip, and continued indulging them with what information she had been afforded.

The conversation went on through the rest of the day. They teased and laughed. Stories were traded and gossip flourished between them. The night fell over the manor, and they went into the dining hall and sat around the table. Charles joined them for dinner and their discussions. Joyful conversation flowed easily that evening, and the plans for the following day were set.

SPRINGHURST BALL

CLAIRE AWOKE THE NEXT MORNING knowing that her day was going to be a busy one. It was the night of the Springhurst Ball. Nathaniel and Vivian were coming to join her and Charles for the trip into town. She lay there in bed for a moment, thinking about Charlotte and Thomas and how their relationship was similar to hers and Charles'. She pushed away the covers of the bed and was ready to start her day.

Mary came into the room as Claire was getting out of bed and went to the curtains, pulling them apart widely. The light was bright as it filled the room instantly, and Claire shielded her eyes from the window. "Good morning, Mary."

"Good morning, Miss. Will you be needing a bath this afternoon?"

"I will, Mary. Is my brother awake?"

"Yes, Miss Stonewall, he is in the breakfast nook awaiting your arrival."

"Thank you, Mary." Claire dressed commonly and went down to the breakfast nook to meet with her brother. He was sitting at the table, reading a letter. She wondered how tedious his tasks of business must be to him.

"Good morning, brother."

"Good morning, Claire." Charles put the letter down and looked to her. The two of them ate their fill and reviewed the plans for the day. Charles concluded that he would be ready in time, and insisted that Claire got an early start.

"If you are in such a hurried state to be rid of me, I find no reason to sit here and entertain you!" Claire retorted playfully. She knew that he was teasing her and she left the table, heading to the bath. The warm water was steaming and the room was filled with mist, the aroma of flowers mingled with spices.

Claire stepped one foot slowly into the tub, then another. It had been a while since she indulged in such a luxury. She lay back in the bath and allowed the warm water to envelope her fully. Her mind cleared for the moment as she drifted away, feeling the warm water swirl around her body.

A few moments went by until Mary and another maidservant entered the room. Taking care of Claire, they made sure she was well relaxed and pampered. Standing from the tub, Claire felt the water dripping from her soaked body as Mary brought her a towel and robe. Dried and robed, Claire went into her bedchamber and saw the dress she had picked out earlier. It was laid out on top of the neatly covered bed, ready for Claire to begin her preparation. Mary and the maidservant followed Claire from the bath and helped her get ready for the ball.

The dress was not as fine as the one that Charles had procured for the Devereux Annual Ball. However, it was still quite elegant for a woman of her position. The full length of the dress glided above the floor. The dress was a light cream color and decorated with lace and pearls. Although the dress was far less exposing, it showed off Claire's natural beauty. Mary tended to the laces in the back of the dress, ensuring a tighter fit. The last of the ribbons were tied about the waistline.

Claire continued to the dressing table and Mary began to brush her hair. Claire's hair was pinned up in a fanciful design with fine pearls to accent the tendrils. She stood from the dressing table and slipped her feet into a pair of light-cream shoes that were suited for dancing. Claire was well prepared for the late afternoon's engagement.

As Claire reached the portrait of her parents, she stopped. She twirled around and allowed the dress to flitter about in the space around her. She looked to her parents and felt their approval before proceeding down the stairwell.

Samuel gazed upon her as she came down the stairs into the foyer. To Claire's surprise, Nathaniel and Vivian had not yet arrived to the manor. She went into the music room and sat down on the bench of the grand piano. The light from the window shone upon it as it rested near a corner of the room. She lifted the cover to expose the keys of the piano and placed her fingertips lightly to them. The highly polished ivory keys were soft and silky to the touch. She pressed down lightly on them, and the sweet sound of the piano filled the room. She began to play a song that she had known well since she was a young child. As the music continued, she softly sang the words to the familiar song. Her voice rang pure as it echoed within the room, a full and beautiful voice. She did not sing very often, but when she did, she was well applauded for her natural talent.

When the song came to an end, Claire heard a light clapping from behind her and she looked to see who was there. Charles, Nathaniel, and Vivian stood in the open door of the music room, all of whom were praising her talent. Claire blushed and stood up from the bench, turning towards the three of them, and curtsied profoundly. She walked over to them and rolled her eyes. "Yes… umm…enough!" Claire took a few steps past the three of them, then looked back to urge their departure. "Shall we go then?"

"I had no knowledge that you were such a very talented singer, Miss Stonewall. That was a beautiful performance, never have I heard such a talent in all of my life."

"It is not a talent that I dare declare to any, and protest others from exulting on my behalf, Mr. Clayton. You would do best to forget the off chance that I was on key, and neglect to mention it to anyone. I would rather be found faulty than to be gifted, in any event." She was never fond of being thought of as higher than any other person, and to have a talent so readily known by the general populous made her feel uneasy. She was not prideful in that way, but humble, always striving to find a way to better herself even if there was no fault in her ability.

The four of them continued out the front door and entered the carriage. To no surprise to Claire, Vivian was first to clamor into the carriage and take her seat. Charles followed her, and Nathaniel insisted on helping Claire into the carriage before himself. Claire thought it was odd, for she had remembered that she was normally last to take her seat. Vivian and Charles sat across from her and Nathaniel. For a brief moment, Claire looked upon Charles and Vivian, noticing how well they looked together. The idea was thrown wildly from her thoughts as the notion was quickly dismissed. Claire chuckled lightly to herself. There was no possible way that Charles would accept her. They were far too different from each other, both in personality and manner. Her gaze turned to Nathaniel as she sat next to him. Here was a man of good standing, dutiful to her, and attentive to her stature.

Claire looked out the window and watched the lands as they passed by. Her thoughts were focused on Nathaniel, and she wondered about his intention. The thoughts that he might be the one to request her hand entered her mind. She recounted the fine qualities that she knew of him, and found herself reminiscing about the times they had shared and the conversations they had exchanged. Soon, the carriage slowed and came to an eventual stop.

They arrived at the town hall where a large crowd was gathered. As they left the carriage, they looked upon the splendor of all the decorations. The streets were dressed in celebration of the assembly. The sidewalks to the main hall were littered with patrons, many of whom were wearing their finest and most impressive attire. The four of them walked up the path to the entry. Mr. Devitt, the town mayor, stood in the entry and greeted each and every guest to the event. Inside, Claire could see that the dancing was about to begin, and Vivian came to Claire and Nathaniel in eager anticipation.

"Looks as though your cousin has need to dance, would you excuse me?"

Claire nodded and watched as Nathaniel took Vivian to the dance floor and the two of them took their places among the dancers. For a brief moment, Claire watched as the dance began, standing in the crowd as Vivian and Nathaniel moved along with the music. She felt a bit out of place, and thought that perhaps the last few days had changed him in some way.

Charles stood next to Claire and the two of them looked around the room, pointing out those of importance, and those of the stories told the night before. As the two of them continued, the music came to a stop and the dance ended. Nathaniel and Vivian rejoined them, and without hesitation, Nathaniel spoke intently to Claire.

"Miss Stonewall, would you do me the honor of the next dance? It is my intention to be close to you for the remainder of the evening."

Claire nodded and took Nathaniel's hand as they proceeded to the dance floor. Within moments, the music started once again, and Claire felt the overwhelming presence of Nathaniel and his charming demeanor. "I see that you have taken kindly to Miss Hawkins."

"I have, she is a good friend and I have come to count upon her good judgement. But do not mistake my interest, Miss Stonewall. You have captured my attention in the fullest, and I have no defense at my disposal to keep me from my need of your company. You have been absent these last few days, and it has tormented me. This short time apart has felt like an eternity, and I have struggled to keep my distance from you. I yearn every morning to be with you, and I ache when I am unable to fulfill that need."

"Mr. Clayton, you do me a disfavor. I had no intention for you to be apart from me, and had no knowledge of the infliction that you received. By what manner do I deserve such attention? I had thought that Miss Hawkins would be welcomed company in my absence."

"Miss Stonewall, I do protest. I do care for Miss Hawkins, but only as a good friend. Can you truly not know my full intention? I have made no other excuse for it. Please understand that I have no other interest than to be at your side."

"Mr. Clayton..." Claire paused for a moment, feeling overwhelmed by his fierce determination. In her mind, she could not understand why he was so intent on being with her, especially after the way he had left just a few days before.

As they continued their dance, she looked into his expression and could easily see his adoration of her. They traded dance partners, flowing through the motions, similar to a river as it bends through the land. However, they maintained their focus with each other. Claire let go of her reservations, allowing the last few days of absence to be forgotten, and the two of them continued on together as if there had been no separation at all.

The night was engaging for everyone, and the assembly continued until the light of dawn crested over the hills. Many of the patrons remained until the bitter end, others had fallen to sleep in some of the comfortable furnishings that were throughout the hall. Vivian had not missed a single dance the entire evening, though she was still able to speak in such fervent capacity that Claire wondered if her energy was ever sated.

They arrived back at Brookfield Manor, and Charles and Claire went from the carriage. Nathaniel followed and grasped Claire's hand, holding her back from entering. He smiled to her softly and leaned into her ear to speak to her in a low whisper. "Expect me early evening, I have need to speak with you in urgency." He pulled away and smirked softly, as though there was some scheme in his tone.

Claire looked upon him with a slanted gaze, and wondered what he was planning. She simply nodded in response and watched as he entered the carriage once more. Claire met Charles on the porch and the two of them waved to the carriage as it departed. Claire gave Charles a hug and went to her room, ready for some semblance of sleep after the evening's exhaustive events.

NATHANIEL'S REQUEST

THE DAY MOVED ON FROM the early morning and Brookfield Manor was quiet and calm, as both Claire and Charles were fast asleep during the morning light. The sun passed into the afternoon and Claire finally opened her eyes. The thought of Nathaniel's last words woke her from her sleep. He had been vigilant in his attendance to Brookfield Manor, though had not hinted at a purpose to his visits. Claire contemplated the words he had chosen, expressing that there was some urgency to his upcoming visit.

She rolled out of bed and paced about the floor just in front of the curtains, deep in thought. She considered that it could be either an advance of his intentions, or his admission of his concerns regarding Charlotte. One of the thoughts that plagued her mind was the possibility that he was leaving. Although they were only together for a short time, she was not sure how she felt about that particular thought. Claire concluded that if it were true, then he would not have prefaced his visit the way he did.

Her mind struggled from one idea to another until the thought of his potential proposal entered her mind. "Could it be?" she mumbled aloud as the thought overcame her. There were so many others who claimed to know Nathaniel's intentions. They would profess to her how blind she was to them. The thoughts of their encounters over the past few weeks ran through her mind. She weighed each of them in the balance, attempting to discern the flaws that she felt Nathaniel had in his character. Each action that she recalled was judged and dismissed, considering the possibility that she could change him. In a vain attempt to forgo her concerns, she forced herself to believe that she loved him. She pushed away all doubts and was convinced that she would be the one to change his character for the better, and in time, he could be the man she wanted him to be. If he were to ask her, she knew what response she would give him.

She opened the curtains wide and looked upon the grounds while soaking in the sunlight. She felt invigorated by the light and prepared herself for the proposal that was surely to come. The various ways that she imagined he would propose to her played out in her mind. The words she would use to respond to him, as delicate as ever. When she was satisfied with her appearance, she looked once more into the mirror and smiled, whispering aloud, "Even Vivian would be proud of that!" Claire went into the hall and headed directly to the portrait of her parents.

She stood there looking at her father, thinking of the many times that he spoke to her regarding her mother. She compared each memory to her feelings about Nathaniel, and concluded that the match was right. There were a multitude of differences, to be sure, but she knew that she could rise to the challenge and change him. She deposited a kiss to the frame and stated openly to the portrait, "He may not be perfect, but in time he will be."

She headed down the stairway to the foyer, looking upon the grounds through the large windows as she took each step. Anxious for the evening to arrive, she slowed her descent into the foyer. Samuel stood attentively and bowed cordially to her. "Do we have any visitors this fine day, Samuel?"

"No, Miss Stonewall. Are we to be expecting any?"

"Yes, we are, Samuel. Inform me as soon as Mr. Clayton arrives, I shall be in the breakfast nook."

To her surprise, Charles was sitting at the small table when she entered the nook. He was reading a letter and a platter sat before him. The setting was for two, and she knew he was aware that she had risen from bed. "Good afternoon, dear sister, how was your sleep?"

"Restless, dear brother. I feel I may have been tossing and turning all night. How evil of Mr. Clayton to play with me in such a manner, toying with my mind so. He most assuredly better have a good purpose for torturing me. If not, he shall be reminded how devilish I can be in my swift retribution of such torment."

"Oh dear, I do say I fear for the poor man. I know how treacherous it is to be on the other side of your wrath, sister. I do hope he comes prepared, though I wonder to myself what possible means he may have to come today. It is intriguing why he would be so intent on informing you of his audience."

"Surely you do not expect me to know what you are talking about, dear brother. Nor would I have any inkling of why he would be so endeavored to torment me this way. Perhaps you should send him a letter, to warn him of the impending fate that he is to receive."

"I would, sister, but what good would that do for the poor man? He would have no defense against your wrath, even if he were so dutifully informed. I would not want to be the bearer of bad news, as I know all too well what lies at the other side of your ferocity."

Claire knew that Charles was right nonetheless. He had experienced her wrath a time or two. But it was all in jest, and Charles knew it. The two of them continued with casual conversation as they ate at the table. Lily had prepared a various selection of foods, knowing that they were more likely to arise at tea time. Claire clearly chose her favorites from the tray, as she enjoyed much of Lily's cooking. At the slightest hint of movement seen through the window, Claire would stop everything to study it. There was nothing that could distract her from her anxiety.

She took a break from her watchful gaze out the windows and Samuel entered the room. "Mr. Clayton has arrived to call on Miss Stonewall."

Claire stood from the table and wiped the remains from her mouth, then looked to her brother. "Don't you worry, sister, I will be far from earshot. I suspect that whatever the conversation leads to, I will be informed when the time comes."

Nathaniel was standing in the foyer as Samuel opened the door, and gave way to Claire as she passed by him. Nathaniel wore one of his finer suits, which Claire had commented on once before. He was pressed and clean from head to toe with no sign of his journey. He was a very attractive man and dressed to impress her. She smiled as she looked him over and her frustration with him melted away.

"Miss Stonewall, may I make a humble request to speak to you in private?"

"Certainly, Mr. Clayton. If you would follow me into the parlor." Nathaniel followed her into the parlor and shut the door behind him. Claire continued to walk to the center of the room before turning around to face him.

The room was set, the doors closed, and the two of them were together in private. Nathaniel held his head high with an impressive confidence. His purpose could not be more clear, and Claire knew immediately what was about to happen. Her heart began to beat rapidly within her chest in high anticipation of the declaration of his intentions.

"Miss Stonewall, I cannot deny my emotions any further. My mind has been intoxicated with thoughts of you since we met that fateful day in your home. I have striven to keep my distance, but I falter in each endeavor. I can no longer dismiss what my mind and soul tell me. Despite the advice of my acquaintances, I must declare my intentions forthwith." Nathaniel placed his hat upon the edge of the nearby sofa and continued his gaze at Claire. Though his speech was well rehearsed and his demeanor lacked sincerity, Claire soaked in every word and felt her own overwhelming emotion envelop her.

"There is no denying the fact that our relations would benefit most highly from a union of our two families. As such, we make a good partnership, and together we would have a strong bond. There could be no mistake of this, for there has never been so perfect a couple as you and I have been. The expectation of our union is well known and I pride myself in knowing the affections between us, for they have been foretold by many. This is nothing without your kind consideration, for if I have not won your favor, then I have failed in my duty.

"Claire, you have captivated my heart, my mind, my soul. From this there is no escape, and I find myself wanting more and envious of all those that may gain favor in your eyes. I must declare my intentions, for I would not be able to continue without doing so." Nathaniel knelt down before Claire and looked up at her. "Miss Stonewall, would you do me the greatest honor and take my hand in marriage?"

Claire had expected this moment to come, the thoughts she had mulled over had come to their fruition. There, kneeling before her, was the man she expected, in all his complications and sophistications. The words he spoke rattled through her mind, entangled with the emotions that swelled up within her. Her acknowledgement gave him strength, his confidence giving her strength. She smiled softly as a few moments passed by, and watched the anticipation grow within his expression as she stood silent before him. Finally, the words came to her, incoherent at first, now firm and clear. "Mr. Clayton, I believe you are correct. It would be a good match. And yes, I will be honored to take your hand in marriage."

"Then let us not delay any further. Is your brother at home, Miss Stonewall?" Nathaniel stood, taking her hand in his as he asked the question.

"He is, Mr. Clayton." Claire responded to him with a firm grasp of his hand.

Nathaniel turned and headed out the door, leading Claire along with him. The door to the study was open and Charles was sitting at his desk, reading. Nathaniel whispered softly to Claire, "I will be just a moment, my dearest." He let loose Claire's grasp as he walked into the study, closing the door behind him.

Claire was alone and paced before the door, waiting eagerly for Nathaniel to reappear. The thickness of the door prevented her from hearing the conversation within. She continued pacing, her hand raised to her chin as she walked to and fro, and biting her bottom lip. Her mind wondered what was taking Nathaniel so long to return to her. Seconds turned into minutes and her patience wore thin.

Several moments later she was far across the room, now irritated with the delay. Her thoughts turned and she felt the anger rise towards her brother. He had been so jovial that morning regarding her wrath. And she felt perhaps he was trying her patience willfully. She plotted and planned her revenge upon him if it were true. After what seemed like an eternity, the door cracked open. Claire stopped and turned on the spot, looking onward to the door.

Nathaniel exited the study, and it seemed as though his demeanor had changed dramatically. He looked upon her and his expression was that of disbelief. Claire was stunned and unable to comprehend what was happening. He tipped his hat to her and left the room steadily. Claire's chin dropped as he continued to stride through the room and into the foyer without a single word or glance back to her. Claire could not think of what to say or do and simply stood still in shock and disbelief.

She watched through the open window as Nathaniel climbed up on his horse. Without a second glance to her, he was gone and out of sight. She turned toward the open door to the study. Charles stood on the other side of his desk, his expression somber and steady. He expected a confrontation with her and was ready to receive it fully.

"Brother?" called out Claire. Anger began to fill her as she looked upon him. She did not know what had just happened, and the unexpected turn of events confused her. "Brother? What is happening? Where did Nathaniel go? What did you say to him?"

Charles saw the pain that she was struggling through and chose to stand tall and firm, unsure if he was going to need to rush to her or defend himself from her rage. He was ready for either event and steadied himself. "Mr. Clayton has decided to take his leave from Brookfield Manor."

"What?" Claire's disbelief was apparent in her tone. She paused briefly before accepting what she had heard. "Will he be back?"

"I am uncertain, but I do not believe so."

"How could this be? How could you send him away? My own brother, how could you do this to me? I thought you loved me so!" Claire did not wait for a response from him, the emotions overcame her. Tears welled up in her eyes, and as they ran down heavily upon her cheeks, she turned and ran from his sight. Grasping the banister in the foyer, she felt the loss of control. She gathered herself as best she could and climbed the stairs, then turned to her room and slammed the door behind her.

Charles followed Claire to her room, knocked at the door, and cracked it open without giving Claire the opportunity to deny him. His voice was somber and sorrowful. "I do love you so, that is why I had to."

Claire snapped back at him, not wanting anything from him in her state of grief. "Go away!"

Charles closed the door softly, not saying another word. His footsteps were heard as he walked down the hallway. Claire's remorse overwhelmed her and she cried heavily into her pillows.

CLAIRE'S SOLACE

CLAIRE AWOKE, LYING IN HER bed above the covers. Her pillow was moist and cold from the tears she had released. She looked about the room and noticed that there was no light coming from the crack of the curtains. The fire was lit and the crackle was the only sound heard in the room. She looked to herself and saw that she was still wearing the dress she had put on for Nathaniel's arrival. The sadness came over her again at the thought of his departure.

She walked over to the curtains and peered through the window. It was nearly dawn and the sun was working its way to the horizon. The grounds were covered in dew and everything seemed still and timeless. She closed the curtain and changed out of her dress into a nightgown before returning to her bed.

Sitting upon her bedside table was a book that she had not noticed. She picked up the book and looked at its title, recognizing it immediately. It was the book that Thomas was last reading to his sister while she was in the home. Claire sat comfortably upon her bed and opened the book. She thumbed through the pages until she found the folded corner.

She had read the book many times in the past and began to read it once more. As she read along, she imagined the various scenes as they were described. She escaped from her own sorrow, lost in the words within the pages. The fire crackled on, and the door cracked open. Claire glanced over to the door and saw Mary looking in. Mary smiled softly and closed the door once again.

Claire took comfort in Mary's attentive care, and assumed that Mary was the one who had left the book there for her. Nothing ever seemed to pass by the servants. More often than not, they knew more regarding the parties involved than most people realized. Claire continued to read the book through the morning, finishing what was an amazing tale of bravery and love.

Claire placed the book back upon the nightstand. She changed her attire and took the book with her as she went into the hall. The hall was warm and comforting, much different than it had been for several months. The temperate spring days had arrived, and the pleasant aroma of spring flowers filled the home. Claire paid her tribute to the portrait of her parents, though she did not want to spend much time before them, as her mind was avoiding the sorrow within. She instead continued down the stairwell and towards the library.

She opened the door to the library and wandered to the place where the book belonged. Gently, she put the book away and stroked the spine of it, remembering the fondness that she had for the story that was held within its pages. She perused the books contained in the library, finally stopping before one that she didn't remember quite as well. She took the book and sat upon one of the several reading chairs throughout the room.

She started to read the book, losing herself once again in another world, far beyond the one that she was in. As she fell prey to its tale, she felt her pain and remorse fade into the background. Either by design or circumstance, the security she felt with books overcame her adversity in dealing with people. It was a much-needed escape, and the stories gave her strength when she needed it the most.

The final page of the story was read, and Claire saw that the day had not yet come to a close. Her strength improved and her sorrow was sated for the moment. She put the book back on the shelf and felt the twinge of pain in her stomach. She was hungry. It dawned on her that she had not had food since the day before, and now her body was feeling the sting of it. She walked to the kitchen in hopes of not coming across her brother. She did not know what she would say if she did. Instead, she shook the thought of it from her mind and quickly made her way to Lily.

Lily saw Claire come into the kitchen and she stood quickly to greet her. "Something to eat, Miss Stonewall?"

Claire nodded, but before she could say or do anything to serve herself, Lily stepped in once more and offered her a look. "Miss Stonewall, let me take care of it. Shall I bring it to you in the library?"

Claire thought to herself, 'The servants do know more than they pretend.' Claire nodded with a smile and went through the door to return to the library. Once again, her attention was turned to her brother and she carefully but steadily moved past the study. The thought of him still angered her and she felt a deep urge to lash out at him. The questions came into her mind, and she dismissed them hastily as she opened the door to the library.

She rarely had trouble finding an interesting book to read, as there were plenty in the library. She took another book and sat back into the same chair. As she read from the book, Lily came in carrying a small platter. She placed the tray upon the nearby table and spoke in a whisper to her. "I shall be in the kitchen if you need more, Miss Stonewall."

Claire lipped to Lily 'thank you' without actually uttering a sound. Lily bowed and showed a hint of concern for Claire as she turned from the room and closed the door quietly. Claire looked to the tray and saw a sandwich and a cooled tea tenderly placed there for her. She folded the book in her lap and ate a few bites of the sandwich in the quiet serenity of the library. After placing the sandwich back upon the tray, she reopened the book and began to pick up where she had left off.

The sun dipped below the horizon and the only light within the library was lit by candles as the darkness encompassed the world outside. Claire could not even recall when the servants of the home lit the candles, too engrossed in her story to have noticed their coming and going. Claire had spent the entire day in the library left to her own means. It was no surprise to the staff that she was in such a state. In fact, Claire thought it a bit humorous how well the staff behaved knowing the turmoil she was in. She stood from the chair, swapped out the book she had for another, and made her way to her bedchamber.

The covers were already turned down for her, and several pillows were stacked upon the headboard to help support her. The sound of the fireplace crackled, as a fresh fire was lit and its light flickered throughout the room. There was a lit candlestick standing upon the bedside table, giving her plenty of light to read by.

Claire lay upon the pillows and opened the book. The night had crept in and she sat there, lost in yet another story. When she turned to the last page of the book, she closed it and placed it upon the bedside table. She blew out the light from the candle and took away several of the pillows, allowing her to lie down comfortably. The happy ending of the story was firm in her mind as she drifted off into a deep sleep.

When Claire awoke, she walked to the curtains and opened them wide, exposing the room to the fullness of the morning light. She looked upon the grounds and sky and saw that it was turning out to be a wonderful spring day. The thought of taking a walk around the grounds pleased her, and she prepared herself to do just that. It had been a while since she was able to indulge in such a task, but was looking forward to the escape from the home.

She stepped out of her bedchamber and looked down the hall, catching sight of Mary as she approached her room. Taking the few steps to the portrait, she sat in front of it and looked up to her father and mother as they stared back at her with their constant expression. Her brother's actions came to the front of her mind. She asked her father about them, in hopes of gaining some insight to the meaning of Charles' actions. The responses that she needed did not come to her, and she knew that she would have to confront him about them at some time.

Clare was still quite upset with him and could not withstand the anger and respite when she thought of him. It was still too painful of an ordeal for her at the moment. She gazed upon her father and felt the need to be wrapped in the comforts of his embrace. The weakness was still present in her emotion, and although she had done her best to cope with everything, she was still in need of support. The longing to be with her father was more prevalent now than it had been in a long time.

She stood up and pressed a kiss to the frame of the portrait, giving her fond thoughts of her father their due. Claire then headed into the breakfast area, avoiding her brother, for she thought that it would be better for the both of them if they kept to themselves. She reached the breakfast nook and sighed slightly in relief as Charles was nowhere to be seen. She opened the kitchen door and looked within. Lily was working diligently on some sort of preparations as she normally was.

"Did you have a good sleep, Miss Stonewall?"

"I did. I will be heading out shortly, Lily. I plan on taking a walk around the grounds today."

"Oh? Very well. Here…" Lily reached over and grabbed a small plate, putting a few things upon it and handing it to Claire. "A quick breakfast to give you some strength, Miss."

"Thank you, Lily. If Mr. Stonewall asks, you may let him know I went about the grounds and not to come after me."

As Claire was leaving the kitchen, she could not help but notice that Lily was a little sad and concerned. She sat at the breakfast table and ate the small meal that Lily had given to her. She looked out the windows and saw the birds and animals as they moved about in the spring air.

Lily was fond of the siblings, and it was well known to them both. She had been there prior to Josephine's passing and helped to care for them when they were young. Lily loved them more than she ought, and her reaction was not surprising when Claire thought about her in that way.

Claire finished her plate and stood from the table to begin her journey. She passed by the study and watched the door to ensure that she was unnoticed. She reached the foyer and Samuel opened the door for her. "It is a beautiful morning, Miss Stonewall. Will you be requiring the carriage?"

"No, Samuel, I will be about the grounds this morning. I will be back before long."

"Very well, Miss Stonewall. Have a pleasant journey."

Claire stepped out onto the porch and looked outward, glancing about the estate. She took a deep breath of fresh air and sweet aroma. It was a warm spring day, the sun was shining upon the grounds, and many creatures both big and small moved about the abundant foliage. She walked through the trees, over the small hills, and out of sight of the manor. The hills continued, one after another, with patches of trees in the distance.

There was comfort for her in the solitude, making the world expand before her and feel as though her troubles were much less important than they were. Her thoughts of her brother and the situation she found herself in drifted away the further she was from the manor. She could not remember if she had gone this way before, and she saw a slight sparkle only a short distance away. There was a body of water that she had not encountered before, and she continued in its direction. She felt the curiosity grow within her as she walked closer to the glimmering reflection, intrigued with the potential of a new place to call her own.

She eventually reached her destination and found herself in front of a pond hidden between the hills and trees. Claire walked along the edge of the water. The pond was a little larger than the one that sat in the front of her bedchamber windows. It was centered within a pocket of trees and she came through the only open space between them. It was not maintained and groomed like the ponds at the manor, and she enjoyed the thought that it might be a private place that few ever ventured to.

As she walked upon the edge of the pond, she eventually came to an idyllic spot in which to take a break. There were a few rocks lying upon the beach of the pond and she walked up to one of the larger ones. Bending over to pick it up, she lifted it with one hand, though quickly realized that it was heavier than it looked. She looked out over the water and threw the rock as far as she could. The rock splashed heavily in the water. The splash rose into the air and the once-calm surface had rolling ripples spreading outward. She felt a sudden release of her emotions. A few tears escaped from her well-constructed façade and fell from her cheeks.

She took a step backward and smiled softly. The strength returned to her once again as if some weight had been lifted. The ripples splashed lightly upon the shoreline and Claire stood still, watching the way the sun reflected off the movement of the water.

"Now that was quite a splash, Miss Stonewall," said a voice from behind her. It was a masculine voice, strong and deep. And to make matters worse, it was someone who knew her name.

She turned around cautiously to see Thomas sitting on the ground comfortably between two large roots. His back was against the trunk of the tree and it seemed to act as a natural chair. He had a book in his hand with one finger holding his place between the pages. His eyes were fixated on her and she could not stop returning his gaze. He smiled fondly at her and she felt the rush of heat come to her cheeks. The depth of his gaze seemed to steal their way into her mind and she could not escape his attention.

Thomas stood from his comfort and brushed away the leaves and grass that had collected upon his attire. He took a step toward her before bowing to her. He stopped as he caught the glimmer of her tears in the afternoon light. The expression on his face changed to a true concern for her state. He reached into his pocket and offered her his handkerchief. "I'm awfully sorry to startle you, Miss Stonewall. Here, take this."

Claire looked briefly to the handkerchief and stepped closer to him. She curtsied and then refused his gesture. It was not uncommon for her to be presented with one, and she noticed that his was simpler than the ones she had seen before. She coughed slightly and gathered her composure. "I was the one who interrupted your time here, Mr. Edleman. I shall go now and leave you to your reading."

"Miss Stonewall, please. You do not have to go unless you want to. I have no special rights to this place and I am more than willing to share it with you. If you would be so kind as to favor me with your unexpected company."

"It really is quite lovely. I have never seen it before. Do you come to this place often, Mr. Edleman?" Determined to clear her mind of her distressed state, Claire sought to indulge in this chance meeting. His lack of involvement allowed her to push the troubled thoughts aside for the moment.

"I come here when I can, Miss Stonewall. Especially when I feel the need to get away from the day-to-day activities. Though I would not expect you to have needs for such a place."

"Oh, is that so, Mr. Edleman? I hate to ruin your keen understanding of what I do or do not need. But I regretfully announce that you are quite mistaken, for I too need a place to get away once in a while. Especially with recent events that have caused me such pain, I will have you know. Do not be so quick to judge me, simply because of my station."

Claire watched as the obvious fear overcame him. He was at a loss and she had taken him by surprise. She did not intend on being mean, but she'd had enough of his temperament toward her and was now forced to take action against it.

"I am… Um… Do forgive me, Miss Stonewall. I did not mean anything by it. I…I am afraid you have me at a loss, and I find myself faltering in my efforts of redeeming myself."

"Do not fret, Mr. Edleman. I hold you to no fault of your own. I know that society is what it is, and in all honestly, I have little charity for it. I would much rather allow us to behave like normal people, regardless of station, and allow ourselves to be simply just. If you find this uncomfortable, then we can continue to have less than stimulating company in the near future and say our goodbyes, as is socially acceptable."

"Well, Miss Stonewall, since you put it so delicately, I guess I have little choice."

Claire was immediately confused by his statement. She had hoped that he would be more comfortable around her and felt that perhaps she was not clear enough. As she opened her mouth to speak, she could not think of what to say. She had no idea what he meant by the comment and the more she thought about it, the more she struggled.

Thomas casually took his seat at the foot of the tree once again. "And how are you today, Claire? If you do not mind me calling you Claire."

Claire blinked a few times as she heard his playful tone. Outside of family, no one was ever referred to by their first name alone. This idea was new for her and she liked the thought of it. Having had enough of her family at present, she considered that this would make it easier for her to deal with her current issues. "No, Thomas, I do not mind in the slightest. Though I would appreciate it if you and I could keep it between us. It would be quite a spectacle if this were to be known in a more public setting. And to find the means to explain our mutual arrangement would be quite a chore."

"Indeed it would be difficult, even for our families. So it is agreed then. We will share this place, and it will be our escape from the trials of our day-to-day."

"Agreed, Thomas. Our shared escape. How is your sister doing? I have wondered about her full recovery."

"She is quite well, thanks to you. You took such great care of her, and for that we are all very thankful. We were wondering if you would be interested in joining us for tea sometime."

"That I would, Thomas. Would you be free tomorrow? I have no other prior engagements and would cherish the opportunity."

"It would be an honor, Claire. My sister has not stopped talking about you and can hardly wait to see you again."

"She is endearing, Thomas. You should be quite proud of her."

"Yes, I am."

The day began to show its lateness as the sun began to darken over the hills. Claire looked toward the water and then back to Thomas. "I must be on my way. I have to walk back to the manor, and I don't care to be too late in the day."

"If you need a companion, I would gladly walk you home, Claire." Thomas stood immediately and assisted her from her seat at the base of the tree.

"No, it is not necessary, Thomas. I do appreciate the offer, sincerely. It would bring too many questions and I am at my wit's end already with everything that has happened recently. I would rather our chance meeting be left in secret, if you don't mind."

"As you wish, Miss Stonewall."

"Have a safe trip home, Mr. Edleman. I look forward to tea tomorrow, and please, make no special accommodations for my attendance."

"I will make no mention of our meeting here, Miss Stonewall, but as for the arrangements tomorrow, I will have little say in that matter. My family will do all that is in their ability to make your visit the most enjoyable it can be. Though I have found, more often than not, that it may well be to their own undoing."

"Very well, Mr. Edleman. Good day to you."

"Until tomorrow then, Miss Stonewall."

Claire walked over the hill and left the pond behind her. She looked back and smiled at the time that she shared with Thomas. It was lucky that she was able to share in his company, and it provided her the chance to talk to someone when she most needed it. A newfound place to escape the troubles at home, and the chance to be accompanied by a new friend. When she arrived back at the manor, she looked back one last time to remember the unexpected delight she shared on a beautiful spring afternoon.

Samuel opened the door for her when she arrived. As she reentered the manor, she turned about to speak with him. "Samuel, is my brother about?"

"Yes, Miss, I believe he is in his study."

"Thank you."

Claire walked into the house and up the stairs. As she passed the portrait of her parents, she looked upon it fondly. She went into her bedchamber and emerged with fresh attire. She came across the portrait one more time and thought of Thomas and Charles. Charles loved her very much, and she knew it. Thomas loved Charlotte in much the same way. The two of them were similar in their love and devotion to family. Then a thought came to her as strong as ever. Charles would do anything for her, even if it meant his own undoing. Just like Thomas would do for his family. She stopped in her tracks as the notion came to her mind, clear as any thought that she had ever had: 'Charles could never hurt me in that way.'

Claire looked into her father's eyes, and saw the love that was expressed so easily through the painting. He loved her mother, in every possible way, even to his death. Claire thought for a moment about Nathaniel, and what she was hoping she could change in him. Charles could not know about her intentions of changing him. Perhaps Charles saw the flaws that Claire did, and denied Nathaniel's request because of the indifference that he suspected. He could not have known her attachment to him, and the purpose that she had in accepting the proposal.

She continued to look upon her father's portrait, and through his expression she remembered the love and lessons that he often taught to the both of them. He had raised them to love and honor family above all else. He instilled patience, compassion, and love within both of them. The image of Nathaniel's departure entered her mind, how he had left without a word to her. His cavalier attitude as he tipped his hat to her on his way from the manor. His actions had spoken volumes to his true emotion. She could not have expected that sort of response, especially from someone who had pronounced his love so eloquently only moments before. He had made no attempt to return to her, he departed the manor without challenge and without hesitation.

Her father's gaze was upon her, steady, strong. Full of life, love, and compassion. She knew that her brother could not be the agent of her torment. Nathaniel had shown Claire on multiple occasions that he had both the tenacity and capability to be so callous. He had pronounced his love and devotion to her moments before departing from her presence without remorse or regret. He had done nothing to fight for her affection, and departed from her presence without a second glance. She felt as though she'd been deceived in the worst of ways by the traitorous man. If it had not been for the gallant effort of her brother, the trials she could have been faced with for the rest of her days sent chills down her spine.

Claire realized she had focused all of her persecution upon her loving brother. He had played his part, and she shunned him. Charles had always been her defender, her greatest champion. And here she was making him out to be the villain in the misery that she endured. He had only done what he felt was necessary to protect her. He was always there for her, even though she rarely paid the tribute for it. She recalled the last words that Charles had said to her, the ones that he spoke through the crack of the door to her as she dismissed him without a second thought. So lost in the tragedy that was before her that she could not excuse his actions. She glanced at her father's eyes, and felt a sense of gratitude and love sweep over her. The time had come for her to lift the veil of her emotions, and to finally acknowledge her brother for his unwavering devotion.

CHARLES' FORGIVENESS

CLAIRE HAD NO EXCUSE FOR her actions toward Charles. She was lost and confused, hurt and broken, and although these feelings were so strong for so long, they did not justify her actions toward him. She took a deep breath and continued down to the study, determined to make amends with Charles. The door to the study was shut, and she thought for a moment of what she would say. She wrapped her knuckles lightly upon the surface of the door. Without hesitation, her brother's voice came from the other side. "Come in."

Claire grasped the handle of the door and carefully turned it, unsure of what to expect in the interior of the study. She cautiously peeked inside to see if Charles was looking towards her. When Claire emerged from the doorway, he stood, attentive and eager. "Claire, please, do come in!"

"Good evening, brother, how was your day?"

"Good evening, sister. My day was quite busy, having to write these many notices."

Claire looked to the desk and saw the stack of letters. She took a step forward and placed her hand upon them to measure the labor it must have taken. "Oh my! Please tell me you have time to have supper with me."

"I would be delighted, sister, I need the distraction in more ways than you know." The sound of surprise was in his tone.

"Shall we head to the dining room then?"

"By all means. How was your day, sister?"

"It was enlightening." Claire briefly recounted her interactions with Thomas that afternoon as they walked silently together into the dining room and sat down at the table.

"It seems as though you have had quite the day."

"I did, brother. However, it is not a matter I wish to discuss in any great detail." She did not know exactly how he would react to the situation she found herself in, and felt it better to keep the details of the encounter to herself.

"Well, if you ever want to discuss it with me, you know I am always here for you," Charles replied, taking the opportunity to remind her of his devotion to her.

"I know, Charles, I know…" Claire said remorsefully. She was determined to end the hardship between them. "Forgive me, brother, I reacted before I thought."

"All is well, Claire. What greater purpose does family serve?" Claire heard his response, and knew he did not expect an answer. With his sentiment, the matter was settled between them. Claire could feel their bond renewed. Her burden lifted and she was relieved.

Claire and Charles looked upon each other and continued their conversation over their dinner. They discussed the events that had taken place since Nathaniel's departure and various other topics. Charles did not mention Nathaniel during their conversation, and Claire avoided the topic, feeling that she was not yet ready for that particular discussion.

Course after course they consumed, breaking up the conversation as they took pleasure in each presentation of the meal. Eventually, they were presented with a freshly made peach pie topped with whipped cream. Charles and Claire were excited to see the delicacy before them. They knew that Lily was especially skilled at making pies of various types. Both Charles and Claire shared a love for her peach pie most of all.

"Claire, have you been reading any new books recently?"

Claire thought for a moment. It was no surprise to her that Charles was keeping track of her from a distance, and had noticed her return to reading in the library. "No, actually. Perhaps I could make a trip into town tomorrow and see if anything of interest is available at Mr. Dodd's shop."

"I think it would be good to go out for a bit, enjoy the fresh air. I know how much you love this time of the year. Perhaps Miss Hawkins would be interested in accompanying you?"

Claire stopped for a moment. She had almost completely ignored Vivian in her distress. "You are quite right! I will call on her tomorrow and we will head into town together. What a splendid idea, brother, thank you."

Claire assumed that Vivian would already be abreast of the situation with Nathaniel. It was unlike Vivian to not come and see her during such a trying period. Vivian's absence made Claire curious to a multitude of misguided thoughts. Claire feared that some sort of tragedy may have stricken the family. She quickly dismissed the thought, knowing that they would have been dutifully informed if it were the case.

At the end of the meal, Claire stood from her chair, and Charles stood with her. She took the few steps and wrapped her arms around him, giving Charles a large hug and a kiss upon his cheek. She pulled away and looked to him with a loving expression. "I am so lucky to have such a loving brother. Thank you, Charles, I have no way to express what you mean to me."

"You deserve so much more than I can offer, Claire. I only hope that our father is pleased with me."

The thought of their father entered Claire's mind. She saw so much of him in her brother. She placed her hand softly on Charles' face and looked upon him with a somber understanding. "He most certainly is, brother, and I know he would be ever so proud of you."

They smiled to each other as they felt their bond heal. Claire turned and went to her bedchamber for a full night's rest. Her heart was filled with the love from her family, and she knew that everything was going to be all right. Her strength had returned to her, and she felt assured in who she was once again.

VIVIAN'S ABSENTEEISM

THE FOLLOWING MORNING, CLAIRE AWOKE from her slumber with renewed purpose and intention. The thought of Vivian's lack of visit weighed heavily on her mind as she prepared herself for the journey into town. Mary entered the room and looked to see that Claire was already preparing for her day's trip. Claire looked to her briefly. "Mary, let Forrester know I have need of the carriage, as I will be going into town by way of Bedford Park."

"Yes, Miss. Should I inform Lily of your impending travel as well?"

"I will be leaving after breakfast, Mary."

Mary curtsied and turned herself from the room. Claire finished her preparations and ensured that she was suitable to Vivian's taste before heading down the hallway. She made her way to the study first and saw that Charles was not within. Claire went onward to the breakfast nook, where she saw Charles seated at the small table. He was looking out of the open window as she entered the room. "Good morning, brother."

"Good morning, you look fine today."

"Thank you, I will be using the carriage this morning. I think I will try to catch Vivian before she has had a chance to go into town herself."

"A splendid plan, sister. I will be in my study as per the usual. There is much that I have to do before my trip into London. Though I doubt that I would be of much use to you in picking out a suitable novel. I have such poor taste in literature." It was a relief to him that their lives had returned to a somewhat normal state. Claire knew that he would struggle during his trip if things were awry at home.

"Is there anything in town that you need, brother?"

"I do appreciate the offer, but everything is in order. I do not believe there is anything that I need."

"There is little reason for me to return to town again before you depart. You may want to regard the offer as your last chance."

"Thank you, sister, but I think I will manage satisfactorily."

Claire finished the last of her breakfast and stood from the table. She looked to Charles with a humble expression, knowing how deeply he cared for her. "I will take my leave then."

"Good luck in finding a new novel. Give my kind regards to Mr. Dodd."

Claire journeyed to the foyer and pulled on her gloves and took a parasol. Forrester was standing beside the carriage, holding the door open for her. They were on their way to Bedford Park within moments. Claire looked out the window of the carriage toward the study. She glanced back to the window of the study and saw Charles watching her as she departed.

It was not long before the carriage stopped at the entry of Bedford Park. Claire took Forrester's assistance as she exited the carriage. She looked to the entry and saw the doorman standing attentively at her arrival. She straightened her dress and called to him, "Inform Miss Hawkins that I have come to see her."

"I am sorry, Miss Stonewall, Miss Hawkins is not available at present."

Claire's plan had faltered and she was caught off guard. It was uncommon that Vivian was not available at this hour, and the response from the doorman made Claire a bit uncomfortable. "Is Mrs. Hawkins at home?"

"No, ma'am. Mr. and Mrs. Hawkins went to visit in Derbyshire last evening."

"I do say, this is quite inconvenient. Where might I find Miss Hawkins then?"

"I cannot say, ma'am." His stance was still firm, but Claire could see he was holding back some information.

"I see. Inform Miss Hawkins that I came to call upon her." Claire peeked around the doorman in a vain attempt to look through the doors and windows.

"Yes, Miss Stonewall."

Claire returned to the carriage, defeated in her attempts of gaining access to the home. Forrester opened the door for her and assisted her into the carriage. "Forrester, let us continue on to town, perhaps we may come across Miss Hawkins there."

"Yes, Miss."

Claire looked through the window of the carriage to the doorman and noticed that his expression was quite disgruntled. She could not understand why she was turned away so quickly, but she knew there was something amiss. The carriage began its way to town and Claire looked to the windows of the upper floors of the estate.

For a brief moment, Claire caught a silhouette of Vivian mostly hidden by the curtains. As she looked on, she could see that Vivian was looking back at her. Immediately, she knew why the doorman seemed to be so uncomfortable with her. Vivian was home, but had no intention of paying any attendance to Claire. The carriage continued out from the parkway of Bedford Park. The image of Vivian standing in the window stayed strong in Claire's mind. Claire struggled to comprehend a reason why she would be so unwelcome to call upon her.

It was not uncommon for her aunt and uncle to visit in Derbyshire. Richard had family in those parts and Sarah was always encouraging him to spend time with them, along with the rest of their family. Vivian, however, rarely endured such travels. She had made it perfectly clear to her mother and father that she had no interest in extricating herself further from society. Reluctantly, Sarah and Richard allowed her to remain at the estate during their excursions.

Even these circumstances did not provide the reason for Vivian to not allow Claire to call upon her. Vivian was not one to deny the pleasure of pressing upon Claire the importance of gossip and social endeavors. Claire's plan to involve Vivian in her journey to town was nothing more than a fleeting hope for comfort.

The questions continued to fill her mind with doubt: 'Why would she not see me? Why was she acting so secretively? She surely knows about Nathaniel!' The carriage continued down the road to town as the questions burned in Claire's mind. The route felt much longer than it ever had before.

Claire felt utterly alone. She had hoped to spend some time with her cousin during her trip into town. She could easily handle herself on her own accord, but she was in need of a companion. Being alone only made the journey that much more laborious.

The carriage wheels clattered along the cobblestone roads of town. Claire looked out the window, but her mind was still occupied with the thoughts of her loneliness. The carriage came to a stop before the shopping district. The door was opened by Forrester and Claire hesitated in her exit. She was unsure if she wanted to expose herself without escort to the trials of society. Forrester said nothing and waited for her patiently.

IN TOWN

I S EVERYTHING ALL RIGHT, MISS?"
"Yes, Forrester. I was only contemplating where I wanted to go first."

Claire took Forrester's assistance as she exited the carriage and stood upon the nearby sidewalk. Forrester replied, "Very well. I shall be in the stable house if you need my assistance."

"Thank you, Forrester. I shall be a while. You may come to Mr. Dodd's store to pick up anything that I may find within."

The town's sidewalks were as crowded as usual, with all of the trade stalls and commotion as the owners advertised their wares.

Claire continued down the road and caught the sight of a couple of her recent acquaintances, both of whom were talking between themselves and looking directly towards her. Suddenly, Claire felt uncomfortable as she could see that they were discussing her. They had not acknowledged her and yet maintained their stare in her direction. Out of habit, Claire turned to speak to the person beside her. She was just about to say something when she remembered that she was alone. She was so accustomed to being with someone while in town that she began to feel threatened by the onlookers.

She neared the door to Rowe's and hid within its comfort. The bell from the door had signaled her entry, and within a few seconds, her arrival was announced above the patrons. "Good afternoon, Miss Stonewall! I will be with you in just a few moments."

Claire was the center of attention. The focus from the people on the street now paled in comparison to the patrons of the shop. She attempted to calm herself as she looked upon the faces of the room, all of which paused their conversations and looked in her direction. She turned her back to them and placed her parasol upon the rack next to the door, attempting to dismiss any attentive stare that was upon her. She turned into the store and began to peruse the various dresses, hiding from the sight of the other patrons.

She was well hidden from view within the dresses, and the patrons resumed their conversations. She felt the stress of her nerves as they rattled within her, trapped in a bad dream, unable to wake. Claire forced the feelings aside as best she could, focusing on the items at her fingertips and ignoring the sounds of the others.

Claire found a particular interest in a fine blue dress. She took it from the hanger and placed the dress against her chest to help her imagine how it would look upon her. Her eyes caught the sight of Mrs. Devereux only a short distance away. Mrs. Devereux was speaking with a Mrs. Thornton, whom Claire had met once or twice before. It was well known that Mrs. Devereux and Mrs. Thornton were close friends. As Claire looked on to Mrs. Devereux, the desire for company pressed hard within her. She took the dress with her and began to head over to Mrs. Devereux.

"Yes, and Mr. Clayton was quite adamant about what had happened. It appears that he was quite rudely dismissed by her and her brother, despite his honorable intentions." Claire stopped in her tracks, overhearing the conversation. She did not recognize the woman who was speaking.

"How so?" said another voice just within earshot of Claire. They had not noticed her closeness to them and continued openly in their conversation. Claire was determined to find out more.

"Well, Mr. Clayton claims to have been thrown out of the home due to his status, and social standing. I do not know what came over Miss Stonewall, but it is rumored that she dismissed his proposal with little effort or hindrance. Per Mr. Clayton, Miss Stonewall was clear in that her intention was to be only with a man of higher standing in society and wealthier inheritance. That she had no regard for his sincerity, and that he was beneath her in every way."

"Say it is not so, the Stonewall family has always been honorable and gracious. How could it be that a young woman with such fine breeding would belittle her family's name with such a disgrace? What of her brother, Mr. Stonewall, surely he had stepped in for her behavior?"

"Quite the opposite, I heard. It would have been better if he had stepped in. But from what I have been told, Mr. Stonewall was the instigator to her dismissal of Mr. Clayton. It is well known that he was instrumental, if not the true reason behind their companionship. Having become aware of the lack of propriety rumored about Mr. Clayton, Mr. Stonewall insisted and corrupted Miss Stonewall to ensure the timely demise of Mr. Clayton's intent."

Claire had no idea where the information came from, nor who the two were who were speaking. She looked about the room and saw that most of the patrons were now looking at her and speaking in hushed tones. She knew now what they were talking about, and fear took hold of her. Mrs. Devereux and Mrs. Thornton had begun their exit out the door of the shop.

Claire quickly put the dress back upon the rack and rushed to the door. She gathered her parasol and opened the door, hoping to catch Mrs. Devereux before she was lost to her. The door swung open and Claire was faced with a great gathering of onlookers. Claire was exposed to the ridicule and had no defense in her solace. The threat of the crowd grew fervently in her mind. She was about to break down right then and there, until she heard something she did not expect.

"Miss Stonewall!" called out a familiar voice from only steps away from the door. Claire turned and saw Charlotte walking towards her with a bright smile upon her face. She was wearing a fine dress and bonnet, complete with ribbons and gloves. The dress was quite elegant for her station and she wore it proudly.

"Good morning, Miss Edleman!" Charlotte appeared to be the savior that Claire so desperately needed. The odd chance of meeting her at that moment could not have been rehearsed, and Claire was grateful for the stroke of luck in her time of need.

"Good morning!"

"What brings you to town, Miss Edleman?"

"I am headed to Mr. Dodd's to find a new book for my brother. He has been in need of something new ever since we left your home. I am afraid that you spoiled the poor man when you showed him your grand collection."

"I must say, this is a chance meeting. Would you care for some company to the store? As a matter of fact, I was just on my way to Mr. Dodd's myself."

"I would be absolutely delighted to have you with me, Miss Stonewall!"

Together, the two of them headed down the street to Mr. Dodd's store. Claire felt relieved that she now had a companion to shield her from the crowd. The loneliness and concerns of others soon abandoned her thoughts as the two of them traveled together. "How is your brother, Miss Edleman?"

"He is quite well, Miss Stonewall. We are all looking forward to your visit this afternoon."

Claire's eyes widened. She had completely forgotten the plans for that afternoon. She collected her thoughts and determined that it was more than luck that Charlotte came by. "Yes, though I hope you did not make any special preparations on my account."

"No, no, nothing like that, Miss Stonewall," said Charlotte as her cheeks began to turn quite red all of a sudden. Claire saw that she was not being truthful in the matter. She shook her head as they reached the door of Mr. Dodd's. Claire opened the door for Charlotte and took a quick glance to the various patrons among the street. Most had continued about their day, but there were still a few glances from various people, and Claire was happy to have Charlotte's company.

"Good afternoon, Miss Stonewall, Miss Edleman. Welcome to my shop. If you have need to find something particular, I shall strive to assist you." Mr. Dodd stood from his chair with an open book in his hand. He was looking to them both as they entered the store. He wore a suitable vest and a ruffled shirt. His hair was pulled back behind his head in a bow and he smiled widely to the two of them, pushing the wrinkles of his age away and baring his worn teeth. He was an elderly man and was delighted by the patrons who came into his store, as they must have had a common thread in reading.

"Thank you, Mr. Dodd," responded Claire with a curtsy. Charlotte curtsied as well.

"Come, let us see what new adventures await." Charlotte blushed lightly as she noticed the playfulness in Claire's tone. The two of them went into the store and began to peruse the various books organized so diligently throughout the store. There were nearly as many books as in Claire's library. The topics ranged from romantic novels to adventure stories. There were even a few knowledge books that were available for those who felt the need to study.

Claire looked back briefly to Mr. Dodd who had returned to his current book. She thought to herself how he came to his store each day and would read book after book from his collection. He surely had a vast knowledge, being versed in so many authoritative works. She walked to the counter and called to his attention. "Mr. Dodd, perhaps you would be so kind as to suggest a new book?"

"Certainly, Miss Stonewall. Is there something in particular that you are looking for? Romance, adventure, or perhaps a mystery? Or perhaps you would be interested in all three?"

"You know how you entice me so vibrantly, Mr. Dodd. Of all the books you have recommended to me, each and every one held me quite enthralled. I never know what to expect when you give your opinion so vividly. You have such wonderful taste in novels that I would be hard pressed to find any of your suggestions not worthy of my time."

"I know just the thing, Miss Stonewall. I procured a copy in my hopes that you might be by to see me. I have read it myself, and after doing so, I immediately thought of you. I knew that you would be most enthused over it. Give me just a moment, and allow me to retrieve it."

"Pray tell, what is this book about, Mr. Dodd?"

"Oh, Miss Stonewall, it is a book of both intrigue and passion. There is adventure, romance, drama, and a bit about a horse that I think you will find particularly interesting. But I dare not give away the story, and know that you will find it most enjoyable."

"If you recommend it, then I have no objection at all. Might I also inquire a fond suggestion for my dear friend Miss Edleman?"

"Of course, Miss Stonewall. I will have you know that there was a particular book that she was interested in not but a few weeks back, and was unable to spend the coin for it. It is a very good book, and she showed great interest, but it is a more difficult selection to obtain as it is quite rare. I still have a copy of it, I can bring it to you if you like."

Claire nodded and Mr. Dodd left to procure the books he had recommended. Each time he suggested a book to her, it was more fascinating than she expected. She looked behind her and saw that Charlotte was still busy browsing the books on the various shelves. Charlotte had not heard their conversation.

Claire looked to the book that Mr. Dodd was reading when they arrived at the store. She opened it to its first page and read it. Mr. Dodd returned carrying a few books. He placed them upon the counter where Claire was perusing his latest reading with interest. "That is a particularly interesting book, though it is my first reading. If you would like, I have several copies available. I must admit however, I have no recommendation for it, having not yet finished it myself."

Claire closed the book and returned it to the counter, careful not to lose his marker. "I would be interested in your opinion of it when you have finished. For now, I think it would be better to go with your recommendations. I am sure that you will be most forward with your advice when the time is right."

Mr. Dodd looked to her with concern on his face, an expression that Claire rarely ever saw from him. Apparently worried, he leaned closer to Clare. Though their meetings were always professional, they shared a kinship brought on by their passion for reading. "My dear Miss Stonewall," he began to say to her in a hushed tone, "I know that you have heard various stories that are spreading about the town, in relation to a certain Mr. Clayton and yourself. Keep it well in your mind that these stories are a fiction to hide the truth and benefit their source. Do not give in to them more than their due worth. I know you well enough to know that many of the stories are not true, and after the gossip has been spread far enough, they will forget their transgressions. Just keep faith that the truth will be exposed soon enough, and all will be well. I am sorry for what has happened, whatever it is. But not to worry, good tidings come to those who have the virtue to wait for them."

Claire stood there, her hand firmly within Mr. Dodd's grasp. She had just overheard a portion of the stories being told, but knew it was not her place to ask the details from Mr. Dodd. Claire was startled by his sentiment. He had shown her his true concern and seemed confident in his advice to her. Claire softly replied to him, "Thank you, Mr. Dodd."

Mr. Dodd individually wrapped each of the books he brought for her in brown paper. Then he tied a string around each one, tying it off in a fashionable bow. He handed both of the books to her. "The larger one is for Miss Edleman."

It was good timing as Charlotte came walking toward them. "Did you find anything of interest, Miss Edleman?"

"No, Miss Stonewall. It seems as though the book I was interested in is no longer available. I believe that it is near time to return home for tea."

Claire smirked slyly, thinking that the book she was interested in was firmly in her hand. "Very well, let us go and find Forrester. Would you like to accompany me to your home?"

"Yes, please, Miss Stonewall. I would be really happy for the company."

"Good day, Miss Stonewall, Miss Edleman."

"Good day, Mr. Dodd," responded Claire. The two of them left the store and walked toward the stable houses. Claire saw Forrester standing at the end of the street. She raised her hand to him and he quickly left the open street to gather the carriage. Within moments, he arrived at their side, holding the door open to them.

"To the Edlemans' residence, Forrester."

"Yes, Miss."

Claire and Charlotte were alone in the carriage as it started off down the road. Claire looked down to the two packages before her and placed them into her lap gently. Charlotte sat opposite from her and watched her happily. Excitement was in the air, as Claire was looking forward to enjoying the company of the Edleman family.

TEA WITH
THE EDLEMANS

CLAIRE GLANCED OUT THE CARRIAGE window on their way to the Edlemans' home. She soon recognized where they were and turned to Charlotte. "I do declare, Miss Edleman. We are very near the Devereux Estate. Are you familiar with the Devereux family?"

"Yes, Miss Stonewall. The Devereuxes are fond cousins of our family. They have been quite gracious in our time of need, and we are indebted to them for their contributions to us."

"I see," Claire said softly. There was a softness in Charlotte's tone that showed great respect for the Devereux family, though Claire could tell that there was some history along with her response. It appeared to be a sore subject for her to discuss and Claire decided that it was best not to press for more information.

Charlotte fumbled with the seam of her gloves quietly in the carriage. "In truth, Miss Stonewall, we owe much to the Devereux family. A few years ago, our father passed on. What little fortune we had was enough to pay the various debts that he incurred, but little remained for the rest of us.

"My eldest brother, William, well he…he took the rest of what was left, and gambled it away. His intention, although honorable, was not well thought out. Nevertheless, he disappeared, leaving us stranded with no money and a larger debt than we could sustain. We lost everything."

Claire could hear the tears from Charlotte in her voice. Before Claire could stop her from continuing her story, Charlotte began to speak again, "We would be ruined, completely and irrevocably, if it were not for the Devereux family. They have offered us a home on their estate. It is small and crowded, but it is home. My brother, Mr. Thomas Edleman, whom you well know, works with the Devereux horses and stables in an offer to repay their generosity. It was what our father had done before, and Thomas is so very similar to our father. Our mother, Mrs. Martha Edleman, well…she helps with maintaining the Devereux Estate, along with my younger sisters who do their part as well. Jonathan Edleman, my youngest brother, is intrigued and passionately interested in the farming aspect of daily life, and therefore he has become an assistant farmhand for the Devereux Estate. He has the most enthusiastic desire to share his knowledge with everyone he meets, regardless of their willingness to listen."

Claire could tell that it was difficult for Charlotte to discuss her family's history. She quietly listened to Charlotte, withstanding the desire to ask any questions to her. "Do not worry, Miss Edleman, I am quite at peace knowing that which you just explained. It bothers me not, to be in such excellent company. I am sure things will work out for the best in due time, do not lose faith."

"You are too kind, Miss Stonewall. I am just glad to have made your acquaintance."

"Acquaintance? My dear Miss Edleman, I do hope you accept me as more of a friend than a simple acquaintance. I do not take our friendship with such lightness, and look forward to the adventures that we will most assuredly share in our companionship."

"Friend? Oh, Miss Stonewall, you could not imagine how much I would enjoy this. You are such an inspiration, to be your friend would thrill me to no end."

"Trust me when I tell you that it is my honor to be in your friendship." The carriage made a turn off the main road and passed through a low stone wall. Claire looked out the window and saw the small cottage. She looked to Charlotte for confirmation that it was their home, and saw that she was still in awe of their newfound friendship.

They slowed at the entrance to the cottage and Thomas stood there waiting for them. Forrester helped Charlotte out of the carriage and Thomas came to greet her in the parkway. To Claire's surprise, it was Thomas who assisted her from the carriage. His hand was strong and comforting, and for a brief moment, she was lost in her sight of him. Claire clenched Charlotte's wrapped book in her other hand as she felt her grasp about to give way.

"It is good to see you again, Mr. Edleman."

"The pleasure is all mine, Miss Stonewall. Welcome to our simple home, I do hope you find yourself comfortable. If there is anything that you need, please do not hesitate to ask."

"Thank you, Mr. Edleman, I appreciate your offer." Her cheeks reddened and she hoped that he did not notice. Unfortunately, he was not the only one in attendance. Charlotte caught sight of the color of her cheeks and smiled. Claire assumed that the entire family was standing in the doorway, as she saw even the young boy with them.

"Miss Stonewall, may I present my mother, Mrs. Martha Edleman."

"Good afternoon, Mrs. Edleman, a pleasure to see you again."

"These two are the twins, Miss Anne and Miss Helena."

"Good afternoon to you both. You look charming this afternoon." As Claire looked at them she could see the playfulness hidden behind their expressions and felt a sense of fondness for them both.

"And this young man here is Mr. Jonathan, my youngest brother."

"A pleasure to meet you, Miss Stonewall." He bowed so graciously before her, as if it were a well-practiced performance.

Claire could barely hold back a laugh as she saw him bow. She curtsied to him as well, sharing in his overemphasized enthusiasm. "Indeed, kind sir. I am honored by your most gracious accompaniment. Might I say, if it is not too bold, you are quite handsome and such an admirable man." The twins giggled, and Claire could imagine that they had instilled Jonathan with some encouragement for their own enjoyment. Martha tugged at Helena, and the two girls straightened themselves appropriately. They reminded Claire of herself, when she was a young girl, and the teasing that she and Charles had similarly done.

"Please come inside, Miss Stonewall, tea will be ready shortly," Martha offered to Claire. The words worked on the children first and foremost as their excuse to return into the home. The twins and Jonathan entered the home almost immediately and Martha followed behind them, quickly disappearing from sight.

Claire still stood next to Thomas and whispered just loud enough that he would hear her tone, "I told you to not make any special arrangements to my attendance, Mr. Edleman."

"It was not as if I had a choice. I passed your sentiments to make them known, but cannot be held accountable if they choose not to follow your instructions."

Claire shook her head and walked into the humble home, followed by Charlotte and Thomas. As Claire entered the home, she was not surprised at its condition. It was well cleaned and yet had a clutter about it, as if the walls could not contain the contents and the family. It was a small home and it was understood that the children would be sharing their bedchambers to some extent. From the entry, the sudden break from the door led into a hall and a staircase. To the left was another hallway, and the right opened up into a small room.

Charlotte led the way and entered the room on the right. Claire followed her and Thomas was just behind. As they entered the room, Charlotte took off her hat and hung it on the rack near the doorway. Claire followed suit, and placed her hat on the rack as well. She held tightly to the package she brought in from the carriage, but did her best to not draw attention to it.

Claire noticed that Charlotte watched her diligently. "It is so nice to see you, Miss Stonewall. I can never repay your generosity and kindness. I am sorry, it's just..."

Claire interrupted her. "Miss Charlotte, speak no more of this matter. I do understand, and I am so grateful to have met you and your family. There is no more to be said, as I am quite pleased to be in your company. Let us continue as if we are and always have been good friends."

A sudden break in the formalities was made by the youngest as he ran past them, chasing one of the twins throughout the house. Claire watched with glee as the three of them continued to rouse each other. Martha was in the other room, calling out to the three of them in a vain attempt to control them. The playfulness of the children made Claire feel more relaxed and at peace.

Thomas opened his hand to the contents of the room. There was a couch and several sitting chairs arranged in the center of the room. Several decorative pillows lay upon them and a few curios were scattered about the table surfaces nearby. There was a fireplace along the furthest wall, and several books lined the mantle. "Make yourself comfortable, Miss Stonewall."

Claire strode over to the couch and sat down, holding the package in her lap, and Charlotte sat beside her. Thomas took a seat across from them and sat comfortably in one of the chairs. As he sat there, he began to massage his hand tenderly. Claire noticed his injury, and was surprised that he had hidden it so well. She looked to him curiously but said nothing, thinking that he would say something if he wanted to.

The younger children continued to chase one another despite their mother's attempts at putting an end to it. She burst out a call to them once in a while from behind one of the walls, and though it stopped them for a moment, it was not long until they started back up again. Claire wondered at the insurmountable effort that Martha had employed to maintain a calm house. Claire looked down to her lap and handed the package that she had to Charlotte. "For you, Miss Edleman. A token of our friendship, and a gift for your house."

Thomas looked up from his attended injury to see Claire handing Charlotte a wrapped package. Claire watched as

Charlotte first looked to Thomas questioningly. Thomas looked back to her and nodded with a smile.

Charlotte returned her attention to Claire and responded with hesitation. "Miss Stonewall, you have done so much for me already."

"It is my pleasure, Miss Edleman. Please allow me this gesture of our continued friendship."

The packaging did little to hide its contents. It was quite obvious that it was a book. Charlotte still held it cautiously within her hands, feeling the wrapping gently with her fingertips.

"Do not leave us in such anticipation, Miss Edleman. Open it and see what it is."

Charlotte acquiesced and pulled on the strings of the package, untying the string that held it shut and placing it next to her. Then she unfolded the paper around the book, exposing its cover to her. Charlotte recognized the book immediately. Thomas saw the book and smiled, knowing what it was. Claire was intrigued by their reaction to it.

"How ever did you know, Miss Stonewall?"

"Mr. Dodd. He was very forthcoming with your desire for this book and he procured it for me as you were browsing his collection."

"I…I…I do not know what to say Miss Stonewall. I have not thought that a gift as important as this was required. My sincere apologies for not having the sense to offer you anything in return."

"Your friendship is gift enough for me, Miss Edleman. Trouble yourself for nothing more." She placed her hand upon Charlotte's. Charlotte looked up to Claire and a tear fell down her cheek. Claire wondered why the book was so emotional for her.

Martha came into the room and announced to the three of them, "Tea is ready in the dining room." She looked to Charlotte and noticed her distressed state. "Is everything all right, Charlotte?" She glanced down as she stepped closer to her and saw the book lying in her lap. Martha placed her hand to her chest and gasped as if she were shocked in some manner. "Oh my good lord, could it be?"

Claire heard the response from Martha and it made her even more curious to the meaning behind the book. A fear came over her, considering the possibility that she had done something wrong. She turned to look at Thomas who was also in some distress over the book. It was something more meaningful than Claire had expected.

Thomas caught Claire's expression and placed a finger to his lips to hush her. Claire did not ask about it then, instead she planned to inquire about it in more private company with Thomas. Claire stood from the couch, and Thomas and Charlotte stood as well. Martha led them into the dining room and they took their appropriate seats around the table. Thomas took the head of the table, as his mother sat to his left. Claire sat to the right of him, and Charlotte sat immediately next to her. There were barely enough seats for all of them to be at the table.

The twins entered the dining room, their dresses a bit tousled from their encounter with Jonathan. Helena and Anna sat beside each other, next to Martha. Jonathan came in last and sat next to Charlotte, on the opposite side of the twins. Their play was still apparent on their expressions as they shot looks at each other from across the table.

The table was nicely decorated with fine linen. The tea was located in the middle of the table, dressed on either side with breads and cheeses. There was some sliced meat in small quantity near the bread. It was not a typical tea that Claire was used to, but due to their financial situation, she was sure that it was more elaborate than they were accustomed to. "The table looks wonderful, Mrs. Edleman. I thank you for such finery."

"Thank you, Miss Stonewall, I do hope that you enjoy."

Thomas began first, and took bread from the plate and a couple pieces of the meat. Then, as he placed the items on his plate, the others followed suit and began to plate themselves as best they could. "How is your brother, Miss Stonewall?"

"Mr. Stonewall is well, thank you for asking. He will be headed to London soon, and I hope to see him return before Anna

Beth Hawkins' Debutante Ball." The conversation was started and Martha joined in, asking all sorts of questions regarding the upcoming ball. They laughed and talked all through the remainder of the tea. Thomas, Martha, Charlotte, and Claire were the last remaining at the table. The youngest were quickly off and enjoying their playtime.

"Would you care to join me on a tour of the grounds?" Thomas said to Claire as the conversation had come to an end.

"I would be honored, Mr. Edleman." The two of them stood from the table and headed out of the room. Martha and Charlotte began to clear the table of dirty dishes and other remnants. Claire glanced back to the two of them as she followed Thomas out of the home.

Thomas and Claire walked about the grounds. "I do apologize for my sister's reaction earlier, Claire."

Claire looked down to her hands and fiddled slightly. She noticed that he chose to call her by her first name in private. "No, Thomas, it is I who must apologize. I did not mean to cause any harm or suffering from the gift. I did not know that it would have caused such turmoil."

"No, Claire, you misunderstood her reaction. The book that you procured was of a special fondness to Miss Charlotte. More than you would be able to know. It was a strong part of her history with our father, as was it also a reminder of a time when we were all younger. He would read from that book to all of us, and it had the greatest effect on Charlotte's childhood. When he passed on, the book was Charlotte's most treasured possession. When we were forced to move here, it was realized that the book was lost. It is my belief that my elder brother William took it, along with several other treasures from the home, in an attempt to settle his debts.

"I have been unable to determine the actual course of the items that were lost in those days. Nor have I been able to locate my brother. The last that I have heard rumored of him was that he was gone to the north, and we have not seen nor heard of him in many months."

Claire decided it was best not to bring up such sorrowed tales and instead inquired about his injury. "Are you all right, Thomas? I noticed you tending to your hand."

"It is nothing to be worried about, just a bruising. Though, I do wonder, Claire…"

They continued walking about the Devereux lands. In the distance, Claire could see the estate in which the Devereux family resided. Thomas looked towards the estate, then continued their walk around the cottage where his family resided.

"What is it, Thomas?"

"I am not sure if you have heard much of the rumors that have been industriously circulated throughout the townsfolk. I feel that you ought to know what is being said on your behalf, and what is being reported. It brings me much sadness to reveal to you what I know. But please, allow me this moment to recollect all that I have heard and seen over the last few days.

"Claire, you must not believe the stories that are reported about you or your brother. They have no merit, and I firmly do believe that they are being circulated in attempts to cover the truth of the matter. A very scrupulous Mr. Clayton is one of the contributors, if not the sole architect of the reports, and has little to nothing to support his indiscriminate claims." Thomas paused for a moment to see Claire's reaction.

"It is common knowledge amongst the townspeople that Mr. Clayton was intent on asking for your hand. He personally had made several mentions of the fact and it was no surprise to anyone that they had seen the two of you together. What was made clear in the last few days was that he did in fact make a proposal to be engaged with you. What followed is the incredulous story that he has impressed upon the willing listener." Thomas paused again to ensure that Claire was ready to hear what he had to say.

"Mr. Clayton claimed that when he professed his love and devotion to you, you shunned him away due to his state and fortune. Making quite clear that you and Mr. Stonewall had not the slightest interest in his proposal, but that your only purpose was to gain access to his family's meager fortune and business interests. That you prized fortune over love and devotion, and that you and Mr. Stonewall are the cause of his abrupt dismissal from Brookfield Manor."

Claire struggled to hold back the expression from her face. Nathaniel's reason for such disdain was beyond her. She trusted Thomas and yet felt the need to defend Nathaniel, even though she had no reason to.

"Though I strive to comprehend that he was working alone, it may cause you great pain to hear of his probable accomplice. I do not take any benefit in telling you this, in fact, I am quite ashamed that it is I who must come forward to you. It is imperative that you are aware of such things though, and I hope that you do not think ill of me for being the messenger in such dire times."

Thomas stopped and looked to Claire, and took her covered hands into his own, holding them tightly in order to give some sense of comfort and stability before he spoke. "Miss Vivian Hawkins."

Claire was stunned that he would be so bold as to mention Vivian in this manner. Her jaw dropped and she faintly attempted to withdraw her hands from his grasp. The ground seemed to fall away beneath her and cause her to lose her balance. Despite Vivian's capability, Claire could not understand why she would direct such actions at her. The tears welled up in her eyes and her thoughts filled with disbelief. She looked to Thomas and wondered if it were some attempt to drive her away from him.

"I could not believe it myself when I heard the news. I rushed out into town and looked upon the faces of both Miss Hawkins and Mr. Clayton as they were together in town this very morning. It seems as though they have come into each other's favor and their plans to ruin you are most prevalent on their agenda."

Claire shook her head fervently in denial of what she had heard. The tears streamed down her face and she could not hold them back any longer. She pulled away from Thomas and ran to the front of the house. Forrester had seen her and charged to her to discover what had happened. As he reached her, Claire called out to him in a broken voice, "Home, Forrester, now."

Forrester did not hesitate, and went straight to the carriage and opened the door for her. Claire looked out the window of the carriage and saw Thomas standing there alone, watching from the distance. She saw his face clearly and was lost in his confession to her. She could not withstand the pain that she was going through and she needed to be alone.

CHARLES' TRIP

CLAIRE BARELY MOVED WHILE SHE rode in the carriage all the way to Brookfield Manor. Her eyes flooded with tears as they ran fervently down her cheeks. The sky faded into darkness as they finally pulled into the parkway. She stumbled out of the carriage without assistance from Forester, not giving him the time to collect her. She made her way to the entry before collapsing in tears. Samuel came to her aid and helped her to her feet once again. She went directly to her room and shut the door behind her. The safety of her bedchamber allowed her to recoil in her distress.

A light knocking came from the other side of the door, as Charles had heard her distress. "Are you all right, sister?"

Claire wiped the tears from her face, opened the door lightly, and looked to Charles. Charles wrapped his arms around her and secured her tightly. Claire held him in return and submerged her face into the nape of his neck. The tears still fell against him, but he did not complain. He softly hushed her and attempted to calm her down. "Everything will be all right, Claire."

"I am not sure it will, brother, how could it be?" She stood before him, her eyes red and puffy with tears. She went to the bed and lay above the covers. Charles watched her intently and sat upon the edge of the bed.

"Tell me, sister, what is the matter? What has happened?"

Claire had calmed down a little and the tears were far less frequent. Charles brushed away the tears from her face, his concern evident in his manner. "I am afraid that we are ruined, brother."

"Ruined? I do not think that it would be easily said nor done. You are the pride and joy of the family and there is no doubt in your character. How, may I ask, is it that we are ruined?"

Claire rolled her eyes lightly and closed them, allowing the tears to run down her cheeks as she swallowed hard. "Brother, I fear that Mr. Clayton is determined to make it so," she said to Charles with her eyes closed, unable to consider looking at him as she spoke.

"I do not think that the man has the capacity to incur such a wrath upon us, sister. Tell me, what have you heard?"

Claire shook her head, and Charles knew that it was too difficult for her to speak of it. He interjected before she struggled any further. "Do not worry yourself about it, Claire. The truth is always stronger than anything that can be rumored. You are stronger than you know, and those who know our family will most assuredly defend us with their own honor."

The following morning shone brightly through the crack in the curtains. Claire opened her eyes to the light that was filling the room. She had slept the entire night, fully dressed and laid upon her comforter. She attributed her sleep to the emotional trials that she had experienced recently. She stood from the bed and wandered over to the window, peeking out over the lands as the sun was beating its morning rays upon it. The words spoken by her brother the night before echoed in her mind and she smiled, knowing that he was right. Still upset and hurt by what had happened, she took a deep breath and thought of the wisdom that her brother shared with her.

Taking her time to get dressed for the day ahead, Claire changed into a simple dress and slid on a pair of slippers. She had no intention of dealing with company today and did not want to see anyone else besides her brother. She left her bedchamber in thought and looked down the hall. It was surprising to her that Mary had not yet arrived, as she had every morning. She shrugged it off and headed down the hallway, leaving the door to her bedchamber open. She sat comfortably before the portrait of her parents and apprised them of the entirety of her experience the day before, including the words that Charles had shared with her.

She looked in awe at their expressions in the portrait. She knew that she was having the conversation alone, and that an answer from either of them was not going to come. All she had was the love and devotion that they expressed in that constant state, as it was captured by the artist who painted them. But the memories that she shared with her father gave her comfort. She stood before them and deposited a kiss to the frame as she always had done. She left the portrait and made her way down the stairwell and through the foyer.

Claire was just about to reach for the door of the study when she heard voices coming from within. The door was cracked open and she could hear the conversation as long as she was near the doorframe and quiet. She leaned cautiously against the doorframe and listened intently for a chance to interrupt. Lily was speaking to Charles, and it seemed as though she was speaking to her brother in confidence.

"Mr. Stonewall, I do not know the full story. I have only been abreast of bits and pieces that I have heard rumored by the other servants. I really do not know much."

"Miss Stanton, I am fully aware that the servants know more of what's going on than anyone else could ever lay claim to. So, please, do tell me what you have learned." Charles had a lightness to his voice that could not be mistaken for anything other than the trust he had in Lily's thoughts. Claire had personally observed this behavior between them on previous occasions.

Claire thought better than to interrupt, and continued to listen through the door. She was intrigued to hear what Lily knew. Lily's voice saddened, and Claire knew that she was not happy with what she had to report. "Mr. Clayton, whom you well know, has been most diligent in attempting to scrape together his own misfortunes and is purposefully redirecting any of his shortcomings to Miss Stonewall. However, he has been careless in his attempts, and many people are now coming to realize the deception that he has concocted. I dare say that it will do him more harm than good to continue to profess such contradictions. He has most deliberately attempted to taint the good Miss Stonewall and yourself, sir, of good standing and character. Though he had been so easily beguiling in the start of his story, Mr. Clayton has failed to provide adequate proof and consistency in his accusations.

"It was announced that he did make clear his intentions of taking Miss Stonewall into his possession, and proposed to her a most prosperous union of their love. However, he changed the decision of Miss Stonewall to say that she promptly rejected his proposal, and most impressively claimed that it was his inferiority that would keep him from her.

"Mr. Clayton went beyond that of Miss Stonewall's involvement and even attempted to implicate yourself, sir. In means of deliberating your instruction to Miss Stonewall's rejection regarding the proposal and that you only strive to allow your sister to marry those who are financially acceptable. Although, to his dismay, I do believe that many individuals discussing such rumors dismissed them almost immediately, thus exposing the flaws of his own character.

"It has just now come to my understanding that Mr. Clayton felt the reaction of society to his dissatisfaction, and left in quite a hurried state. There is no word on where he is, nor what his current condition is. He has so damaged his own character to the point of disbelief, and many good people have distanced themselves from him."

Lily stopped her story and the room was quiet for a few moments. Claire could imagine Charles' inability to fathom all that he had heard. She did not have the heart to speak to him in this detail and she was relieved that Lily was able to do it for her. Her confirmation of Thomas' story to her was given in full effect and tugged at Claire's heart. She remembered how he stood there in the distance as she rode away the day before. And the thought of how she treated him weighed heavily on her mind. But she wanted to hear Charles once again, knowing that he would not tolerate such behavior nor slander of the family name.

"Does Miss Stonewall know all of what you have said, Miss Stanton?"

"I do not believe so, Mr. Stonewall. Though it might be the reason why she came home in such a distressed state yesterday."

"Unfortunate timing as ever it could be. I leave for London this very morning. To have such wild stories being circulated and smearing the family name, not to mention the attempt to degrade the character and honor of Claire and myself. I do not know what it is that can be done to stop such foolish accusations."

"Pay it no mind, Mr. Stonewall, surely you must know that your good standing and character are too strong to be subjected to such wild fantasies. Mr. Clayton will be his own undoing, even now, as he is in hiding, his own reputation is falling short and his exposure will come in due time. In fact, Mr. Stonewall, Mary has just returned from town and claimed to overhear laughter at Mr. Clayton's story, being ridiculed by his own absence."

Claire thought it would be a good time to announce her attendance and knocked lightly. After a brief rustling behind the door, Charles called out, "Come in."

Claire opened the door and saw Charles and Lily standing within. "Good morning, brother, Lily."

"Good morning, sister, how did you sleep last night?"

Lily was very intuitive and knew that Claire had listened in to the conversation, though she smirked lightly, not knowing to what extent. She bowed graciously to Claire and asked, "Would you care for some breakfast this morning, Miss?"

Claire knew that Lily was onto her, but paid it no mind. "Yes, Lily, I am quite hungry in fact."

"Very well, if you would excuse me." Lily looked to Charles who nodded to her before she curtsied to Claire and left the room.

"Quite unrested I fear, brother. Are you still headed out to London?"

"Yes unfortunately, sister. I am truly sorry but it cannot be postponed any longer. Although recent events have consumed my attention, it is imperative that I take my leave this morning." Charles looked to Claire and saw the desperation in her face. He walked around the desk and took her hands into his own, comforting her. "Do not be troubled, sister. I know that things may seem dark at present. But do not give them reason to. You have nothing to fear but the worry and regret that invades your heart. You are of such strong character, our father would be so very proud of the woman you have become, as I am. All will be well in good time." He lifted his hand behind her head, tilted it downward, and placed a kiss to her forehead. "Now come, let us get something to eat. I would enjoy having your company before I leave."

They went to the breakfast nook and took their seats at the small table. Claire's mind struggled with understanding just how things would be all right. Her spirit clung tightly to his comforting words, hoping that his confidence would give her enough strength to last throughout his absence. She remembered what Lily had said about Nathaniel's disappearance and wondered if it would not be the same for Charles if he were to leave under such circumstances.

The breakfast was served to them as they sat at the table. Charles was concerned for Claire and her ability to cope with his departure. He casually spoke, in an obvious means to inquire about her condition. "It looks to be turning out to be a fine day. What plans do you have for today, sister?"

"I think I shall head out for a walk after you depart, brother. I believe that this weather is long overdue and I want to take the time to enjoy it fully." She had understood his intention and responded calmly, despite the anguish within her.

"I was lucky enough to see a flurry of wildlife this morning from my study. Please take care of yourself while I am gone.

I would be most unhappy to find that you were under any discomfort while I was away."

"I will, brother. Do not trouble yourself over me, you know that I am capable of taking care of myself."

"I know you are, sister. You have always done remarkably so. But do not make light of my concerns for you while I am gone. I will not be available to return until Anna Beth's ball."

"That long? Can you not make it before then? I would not want to travel to the ball on my own."

"Unfortunately, no. I wish I could return sooner. I am sure that you will be able to accompany Miss Hawkins to the ball, or her family at that time."

"Yes, I do hope so."

Only then was Claire reminded of Vivian's reclusion and Thomas' accusation of her involvement with Nathaniel's plot. It was so very much unlike her cousin to deny her entry to the home. Vivian's behavior, along with the claims that Thomas expressed the night before, caused Claire even more concern. She thought of Vivian's actions in more detail and turned her focus away from her brother.

"Is there something the matter, Claire?"

"No, no." Claire attempted to hide her obvious concerns, but Charles did not seem fooled by her dismissal. "I do not know in all honesty, brother. When I called upon her yesterday, Vivian was unavailable. Though when I was dismissed from the premises, I glanced to the window and could not have been mistaken about seeing Miss Hawkins looking down upon me as I went away. It is not like her to have been so reclusive, and I do not know what to think of it."

Charles took a moment to drink another sip of his coffee, having not known about Vivian's actions. "Perhaps she was taken ill, Claire. She may simply be protecting you from her infirmity. I am sure there is a valid explanation for her behavior."

"I am sure that explains it, brother. I shall call upon her again in due time, or she may come here when she is feeling better.

Not to worry." Claire was not convinced that the issue was that simple. There was more to the story than she cared to admit, but in either case, she did not want to worry Charles.

Samuel walked through the door and bowed slightly. "Mr. Forrester is ready for you, Mr. Stonewall."

"Very well, I will be there shortly."

Samuel left the breakfast nook towards the foyer once again. It was time for Charles' departure. Claire knew that Charles would stay with her if he had the choice, but he had already expressed his need to leave.

"I will be back before you realize, Claire. Do take care of yourself while I am gone."

"Be safe, brother, I shall be awaiting your return."

Charles stood from the table and they looked at each other. Their expressions of the love they shared were evident and no words needed stating to confirm it. Claire remained at the table as she watched Charles leave the room. She could see the carriage through the window and watched as it departed down the parkway. She felt the loneliness settle upon her as she was now alone, distanced from society and family.

KNIGHT IN
SHINING ARMOR

CLAIRE SAT AT THE BREAKFAST table thinking of the times that her father would go to London, and how she had missed him when he was gone. Now that her brother assumed the responsibilities of their father, she missed him just as much. The days ahead were going to be a trial for her, and she knew that there was little she could do about it. Lily came into the room and saw her as she sat there staring out the window.

"Is there anything else I can get for you, Miss?"

"No, Lily, though I do appreciate your concern. I will be fine. I think I will be taking a walk here shortly. Thank you for the breakfast."

"You are most welcome, Miss. If you have need of anything else, let me know."

Claire stood from the table and left the room. The thought of going into town or finding any company was not something that she wanted to endure. She felt more the need to be alone and escape from what was going on around her. Claire went into the library and took a book from the available selection. Without thinking about her destination, she headed to the entry to leave the manor behind.

Samuel bowed. "Will you be needing the carriage, Miss Stonewall?"

"No, I will be out on a walk. I shall return before nightfall."

"Do take care, Miss Stonewall. And have a pleasant journey."

She stepped through the doorway and looked about the grounds. The warmth from the sun comforted her and she walked down the parkway with her book in hand. She wanted a place that she could sit and read her book, somewhere away from the thoughts of her plight. She watched the birds and butterflies as they bounded around freely within the slight breeze and then gathered together in the various foliage before her. As she broke over the hilltop, she saw the pond where she and Thomas had met. In that moment, she felt comforted as her thoughts turned to the time she had spent with him.

Claire continued towards the pond and saw the reflection of light from its surface. The pond was just as she had remembered it and she walked along its shore. She turned to the tree where they had met, and felt her solace deepen. Thomas was not there, and despite her want for seclusion, she felt disheartened. She took a seat at the base of the tree, allowing its large roots to comfort her, and placed the book in her lap. The serenity of the pond relaxed her and she felt comforted by the company of nature as it shielded her.

She glanced down briefly and noticed a piece of parchment laid gently upon one of the tree's large roots. It was folded and held in place by a small stone. Her curiosity rose and she carefully took the parchment and looked at it closely. To her surprise, it was addressed to her, and she looked around fervently to see if anyone was looking. This was a place that she had shared with Thomas only, and did not know how anyone else could have found out about it.

Claire carefully looked at the penmanship of the letter and could not recognize the writing. The back of the letter was stamped with an unfamiliar seal that was unbroken. It was clear to her that the letter was deliberately placed there for her, and it was undisturbed by anyone until that moment. Claire opened the letter gently and read its contents. As she read the letter, her lips moved and formed the shapes of the words within it, but she did not read them aloud.

Dear Miss Stonewall,

I do not take pride in the fact that I have caused you pain; it was not my intention. I do hope that you will forgive me if I have wronged you in any way. I had thought it would be best to inform you of the transgressions that were put against you rather than leave you wandering in the dark as it had been so apparent. I know that it must pain you to discuss such matters, and I fear that you may have regrets for my actions.

Please know that I personally hold you and your family in the highest respect and honor. You have done nothing but shown great kindness to my family and we are forever grateful to have received your patronage.

May this rock placed upon this note give you some comfort. As you thrust it into the pond, it should make quite a splash to satisfy your frustration. I am sure that you are quite alone and in the privacy of your own endeavor, so do allow the action to help relieve you of your pain.

Your humble servant,
Mr. Thomas Edleman

The thought of the last moments that they shared together came quickly to her mind. She realized at that moment that her parting with him had left him confused and startled. His attention to her was as a dear friend, and she had callously treated his faithfulness. The circumstances that he must have gone through to deliver such information was more deserving than her response indicated.

Claire folded the letter and placed it within her dress. She took the rock that held the note in place and walked the few steps to the edge of the pond. The water was calm and motionless, and she thrust the rock as hard as she could. The water splashed high and wide as the rock broke the calm surface. The vigorous ripples spread across the pond slowly and steadily, reaching clear to the shoreline. She thought for a moment as she watched the reaction of the pond to the rock she had thrown. As if a voice were speaking to her, she heard the sound of her own thoughts. 'So simple to make such waves in otherwise calm waters.'

Within a few moments, the ripples calmed down and the pond returned to the peace it had before she disrupted it. As she watched the water return to its peaceful state, she felt the anguish within her begin to fade slightly. 'So too are the waves that I find within myself.'

Claire returned to the tree and her mind was at ease with the thoughts of such a simple act. She sat comfortably at the base of the tree and picked up the book that she had brought with her. She read from the beginning of the book and felt the escape into the lands that it described, her concerns fading away as she lost herself in the story. Time passed more quickly than Claire had intended, and as the sky was darkened into its amber blanket, she realized that it was well past time for her to head home.

Claire stood quickly and brushed off the leaves from her seat upon the ground. She looked to the pond and saw the amber reflection glow from its surface. She wanted to stay and admire the view, but felt the need to return home before night fell upon the grounds. The light continued to fail around her and she quickened her pace to reach the manor before dark.

She had not realized that she had travelled so far to reach the pond. She hiked over ridge after ridge with no sign of Brookfield Manor. She had nearly broken into a sprint when she reached over the last ridge and saw the manor clearly in the darkness of the night. The lights of the parkway were lit and the massive windows emitted a glow bright enough to light up the immediate surroundings. It was as if the home itself were a beacon of hope and warmth, welcoming any who traveled towards it. Claire's heart swooned as the love that she had for her home overflowed.

To her it was not just stone and mortar, but the manor had a soul of its own, and it breathed life into its inhabitants.

Clair approached the entry to the manor and saw that Samuel had not moved as he continued to stand there. She could see a relief come over him as she reached the steps. He stood attentively and opened the door for her. She knew that he was concerned for her and was reminded how much the staff cared for the family, more than was expected of them. "Did you worry, Samuel?"

Samuel knew that his guise was well exposed. "Yes, ma'am. I must admit, you did give me a bit of worry."

"Yes, I did lose track of the day. But not to worry, I had not traveled far enough to cause any great concern."

Claire continued into the foyer and Samuel closed the door behind them. "Did we have any visitors today, Samuel?"

"No, Miss, we have had no company today. Miss Keane returned just a few moments ago, having had to go to town for Miss Stanton."

"Thank you, Samuel, for your kindness and your obvious concern."

Claire continued down the hall and into the library, placing the book back into its place on the shelf. She felt the ridges of its leathered covering and her mind slipped into the thought of its existence. The care and devotion that it must have taken for the book to come into the world. It was not only the work of the writer in which the book was derived, but the work of others that ultimately brought it to its current place among her family's collection. Stepping away, she looked upon the numerous books and their uniqueness within the library. The thought overwhelmed her for a moment considering not only the collection, but the symbol of knowledge that it represented.

Claire returned to the foyer expecting to see Samuel and was surprised that he had left. She did not concern herself about his whereabouts, but continued on her way towards the kitchen. She assumed that Samuel was tending to some task that needed his attention at that time. The sudden sting of hunger was felt and she headed to the dining room. The table was set, but there was no food upon it. It was quite late for dinner, and she continued to the kitchen to find something to eat.

Claire reached the door to the kitchen and before she could open it, she heard Mary talking behind the door. She assumed that Mary was talking with Lily, perhaps about her trip into town that Samuel mentioned when Claire arrived. "Mary! Enough with your games, what have you heard?" said Lily impatiently. Claire paused at the door, curious about the conversation they were having.

"You know about Mr. Clayton and Miss Claire, don't you? And how we were all fooled with his impressive proposal to claim her hand? Well, that is not the half of it. More has been developed than I dare say, even more than you would care to hear."

"Go on, Mary, don't leave me in the shadows, you know how I protest against secrets in this house. Especially when they concern Miss Claire and Mr. Charles," Lily spoke firmly. Claire considered her predicament, and felt the conflict within her. She knew that it was not proper to listen through the doorway, but her curiosity was heightened and she felt that she could not pull herself away. She let go of the door handle, but before she could step away from the door, Mary continued.

"In town, I had the opportunity to find out exactly what happened only a few short days ago. The entire village was all abreast of the situation that took place between them, and it seems that it was being crudely circulated with a malicious attempt to blame the Stonewalls."

"Whatever do you mean, Mary?"

"I have heard that it was explicitly Mr. Clayton who was the source of the report. He claims to have been rejected by Miss Stonewall, and then shunned from the property by Mr. Stonewall. We know this to be a scandalous falsehood, and I have already made it perfectly clear to them that it was Mr. Clayton who left on his own accord with not a word to either of them. And that he had chosen of his own account not to return hence, regardless of his professed interest in Miss Stonewall." Claire took a quiet breath and was even more intrigued than before. She had already learned of the deceit made by Nathaniel when she spoke with Thomas, but she wanted to know if there was any new development.

"From what I understand, that very morning before Miss Stonewall went to the village, Mr. Clayton was seen about town with none other than Miss Vivian Hawkins!"

"It would not be offensive in the least to see that Mr. Clayton and Miss Hawkins are of some companionship. The two of them have been here together with Miss Stonewall these many days. Certainly there is no meaning in their accompanying each other when in town."

"I had assumed the same as you Lily, and professed as much to my informant. However, I was surprised to hear the detail in their accompaniment. Their attendance together in town would not be an issue, if it were not for the lack of space between them. Mr. Clayton and Miss Hawkins were hand in hand. It was so obvious of their affections that it was impossible to think anything less of their companionship."

"Mr. Clayton and Miss Vivian?"

"Yes, and there was no mistaking their display of such fellowship. But, Lily, that is only half of what I have come to tell you."

Claire was stunned, the memory of Vivian's dismissal of her now in the forefront of her mind. She felt her knees weaken and her breath lost. She could not tear herself away from the conversation, but leaned against the wall to stabilize herself. It dawned on her that Vivian denied her visit due to Nathaniel. The thought of them together burned inside her, and although she knew that Nathaniel was no longer a part of her future, Vivian's taking to him felt like a betrayal.

"That morning, Mr. Clayton and Miss Hawkins stood together on the side of the street. They were abruptly interrupted by a man, who took great offense to Mr. Clayton and made well known his disgust." Mary continued her story, intentionally leaving out the name of the man. Claire's curiosity was at its peak, and she wanted to know exactly what happened. She leaned closer to the door to hear clearly if it were to be whispered between them.

"The man called out to Mr. Clayton in an unmistakable outrage. Claiming his disgust of Mr. Clayton's actions and standing in such a manner that Miss Hawkins stepped away from the two of them. Imagine that any bystander who was watching intently at their argument would not be mistaken in what was going to happen." Mary waited for Lily to respond to the story as it unfolded. Claire felt the buildup of the emotion as Mary had intended, imagining the figure standing tall and strong against Nathaniel. She bit her bottom lip, not wanting to break the silence that she had been so diligently keeping.

"Go on, Mary, tell me what happened!"

"The man called out in a fit of rage, 'You are no gentleman!' Then, within moments, and with a closed fist, he thrust a sturdy swing at Mr. Clayton which struck him firmly in the face. Mr. Clayton lost his footing and fell to the floor, and the man stood over him for a few moments. From what I understand, the constable stood on the sidelines waiting for the next move. Miss Hawkins stood at the side of the carriage, looking onward. For what seemed like an eternity, the man simply stood over Mr. Clayton. But, Mr. Clayton did not move but to cover his face as the blood came trickling from his nose." Mary paused again. Claire was beside herself in disbelief. She imagined the sight that Mary described in her dramatic tale and could only wait to see if there was more. The man was standing strong over Nathaniel, and she did not know what she would do if she were watching from the short distance.

"There was not a retaliation from Mr. Clayton, not a sound from him, not a movement. The man turned his back to the both of them and walked away. Miss Hawkins ran to Mr. Clayton's aid after the assailant had left and helped him into the carriage. The two of them were last seen heading towards Bedford Park."

"Who was he, Mary? Who was the man who struck Mr. Clayton?"

Mary was obviously enjoying the fact that she withheld the name of the man to Lily. "None other than Mr. Thomas

Edleman!" Mary announced his name with a definitive and cautious clarity. Claire felt her heart sink within her. The pain of hunger that had brought her to the door subsided with the news that she had just overheard. Claire slowly walked away from the kitchen, no longer interested in eating anything at that moment.

As she continued through the next room, she recalled the thoughts of her visit with the Edlemans earlier that day. Everything began to make sense to her now. Vivian's dismissal, Thomas' injured hand, even the multitude of people discussing in confidence while Claire was in town. Claire continued walking to her bedchamber. The thoughts of what had happened unfolded before her, swelling in her mind. She blindly changed her clothes and clambered into bed, unable to focus on anything but the answers that came rushing to her. All that she could do was play out each memory with new understanding and realize how mistaken she had been in her assumptions.

The night enveloped Brookfield Manor and Claire lay there in the bed, comforted by the fire burning in the fireplace. The unwanted attention from the townsfolk weighed heavily upon her chest as the tears began to fall from her watery eyes. She continued to imagine the scene that took place in town, analyzing each and every moment over and over in her head. She came to the realization that Thomas was defending her honor, and his words to her were intended to comfort her. If she would have known at the time she visited with the family, she wondered if she would have reacted differently.

There, in her mind's eye, stood before her a knight in all his shining glory, having defended her from the evil that was out to destroy her. She imagined Thomas as if he had just slain a dragon and championed her honor, similar to the heroes in the many adventurous tales she had read over the years. The night crept over her and she fell asleep with the thought of him standing watchfully as he protected her.

IDENTIFYING WITH THOMAS

THE FOLLOWING MORNING, CLAIRE FELT rested and refreshed, more so than she had in a long while. Curious as to why she felt this way, she concluded that it was due to a good night's rest. Perhaps it was the last fleeting thoughts of Thomas and his protection that comforted her throughout the night. The thought of him once again in her mind was pleasing to her.

Although she knew that he would not accept her appreciation for his gallantry, she considered how she could show him her gratitude. She pulled away the covers of her bed and made herself ready. Before she left her bedchamber, she devised a plan to express her admiration for his actions. She thought of the pond, their common place. The place where they let themselves feel free and escape the confines of social grace and etiquette. The stage was set in her plan, and she continued to prepare herself for the journey.

She turned from the dressing wall to see Mary standing just inside the door. Claire froze on the spot. A desperation had overcome her. The guilt of eavesdropping the night before had taken hold immediately on her demeanor. She felt the need to apologize for her actions, but was also torn, not wishing to have to explain herself. Mary looked upon her, seeming to question the expression on her face. This made Claire feel even more uncomfortable than she already was.

"Good morning, Miss Stonewall."

"Good morning, Mary."

Mary looked to Claire with a suspicious gaze. Claire woke from her motionless state and attempted to cover it up as best as she could. "Mary, has Lily prepared a breakfast this morning? I am quite famished, having had no dinner before falling asleep."

"Yes, Miss. Miss Stanton has prepared your breakfast, and it is awaiting you in the breakfast nook."

"Thank you, Mary." Claire briskly walked out of the bedchamber and into the hall. She knew that she could not stay in Mary's presence without giving in and confessing everything to her. Claire felt worse about the deception that she was now guilty of hiding from Mary. She continued down the hall and stopped at the portrait of her mother and father. The thoughts of her deception subsided and she focused on Thomas and his chivalry. Claire looked to her father's expression and felt his strength fill her. Her plan to meet with Thomas was the right choice and she knew that there was nothing that would deter her. She deposited her kiss to the frame and went to the breakfast nook to partake in the meal that she needed so badly.

It was apparent to Claire that Lily was well informed of her hunger. The aroma from the breakfast filled the room as it was presented in its entire splendor. Claire's hunger increased dramatically at the sight and smell of the delicious food. She took her place at the table and pulled various selections onto her plate. Her hunger took over, and she dispensed with the delicacies of manner and ate in what she would imagine to be a barbaric fashion. After eating her fill, she felt the enjoyment of having a full stomach once again.

She rested for a few moments and watched the world outside the windows. The light songs of the birds flitting about called to her to join them. It was time for her to put her plan into action. She stood from the table and walked to the library, gathering a book to take with her in the event that she needed to wait for him.

She came across one of her father's favorite stories and plucked it from the shelf. Before leaving the library, she glanced at the small desk within the room. She placed the book upon its surface and sat at the small chair in front of it. Reaching into the drawers of the desk, Claire took out a piece of parchment, a quill, and a small bottle of ink, placing them neatly on the desk. Claire took the quill in her hand, dipped the tip into the ink, and scraped off the excess. She placed the quill to the parchment and began to write.

Dear Mr. Thomas Edleman,

The stone did in fact serve its purpose, and you have given me more than I deserve. I must admit my eternal gratitude for such a release that you so graciously awarded me. Do allow me to return the gesture, and although this offering is not that of a stone intended to be tossed into the water, perhaps it could provide you with strength and comfort in a time of need.

It was a particular favorite of my father's and of my own. I hope you find it as entertaining and uplifting as I have. Knowing that you are as accomplished a reader of such stories, I am sure that you will find this to your liking.

As to the events of which I left your side the other day, I must plead for your benevolent exoneration. The incivility of my actions was unacceptable, and I can only now humbly request your passionate clemency. You and your family did not deserve such a contemptible transaction as my sudden departure must have yielded in its wake. Please convey my most respectful admiration to your family, and afford them the knowledge that I hold them in the highest esteem.

Sincerest regards,
Miss Claire Stonewall

Claire folded up the piece of parchment carefully, then placed it face down upon the desk. In the drawer was a box of matches, which she took out, and she struck one to start a flame. Claire lit the candle upon the desk, and blew out the match. She pulled out a wax stick and a bronze seal, holding the wax near the candle. The wax melted as it began to heat up. Claire pressed the warm wax into the fold of the parchment, and then pressed the seal into it, leaving behind an engraved emblem of her family's heritage.

Claire blew on the wax seal to ensure that it solidified, then blew out the candle she had lit upon the desk. The letter was slipped behind the cover of the book, keeping it safe and easily retrieved. Satisfied with her endeavor, Claire took the book in hand and headed out of the library. The book she had taken with her the day before lay upon one of the small tables, and she picked it up as she left.

She was now prepared to meet with Thomas, and collected her hat before leaving through the entry door. She informed Samuel of her plan to return before nightfall. Samuel gave her a concerned look, for it was not the first time that she had wandered off, and it left him a bit uneasy. Claire comforted him gently before leaving.

Claire walked briskly to the pond, determined to find Thomas there waiting for her. As she reached the top of the hill that hid the location of the pond, she searched intently for any sign of him. To her disappointment, Thomas was nowhere to be found when she arrived. Claire stood there in her thwarted state, but realized shortly thereafter that Thomas had no knowledge of her intention to meet with him. How would he have known to meet her there when she had sent no word to him? Claire laughed at herself for her disappointed expectations. It was not as if Thomas could read her mind.

Looking upon their favorite sitting place, she took the books to the nearby root that served as their table. Claire placed the two books upon it, carefully balancing them so that they would not fall into the dirt. Claire searched the ground, looking for a stone to throw. Finding a small one of ragged shape, though with a bit of weight to it, she picked it from the soil and went to the edge of the pond. She tossed the stone into the water sideways, hoping in some small part to see it skip along the top of the water's surface. The rock itself hit the water, and with a splash, it sunk into the pond with haste.

She shrugged off her failure, thinking that she would probably never figure it out on her own. She looked around briefly to see if perhaps Thomas had arrived, then walked back to the tree where the books were left. She took the seat at the base of the tree and opened the book that she had brought to read as she awaited him. Her fingers unfolded the page where she had left off and she began to read from the pages.

She was quite engrossed in the story as she read page after page. The large breakfast she had consumed that morning had made her quite tired. She looked about the grounds, and seeing no sign of Thomas, decided that she would close her eyes and rest a bit as she waited. Before she realized it, she was fast asleep. Her dreams continued her escape to the lands of fantasy and adventure.

Her eyes opened after what seemed to her to be a brief instant in which she had fallen asleep. It was late in the day and the sun had just touched the horizon. Claire realized she had been asleep for several hours. She stood from her seat in a state of panic, and the book that she was reading fell swiftly to the ground.

Claire picked up the book and brushed off the leaves and twigs that it collected. Then, brushing the debris from her clothing as well, she glanced to the location where she had placed the book and note for Thomas. To her surprise, both were missing from the place she had delicately put them. She looked around to see if she could spot them, and to her disappointment, they were nowhere to be found. Claire looked to the light as the sun was steadily declining. Having made a clear promise to return to the manor in good time, she felt the need to delay her search for them until the morning light. She rushed back to the manor as quickly as she could.

The sun was midway down the horizon and the light still covered the ground as she arrived at the manor. Samuel caught sight of her haste and smiled, apparently seeing her desperation to make it home by the time she had promised him. She was grateful to have reached the manor in the light of the day, but distressed about the book and note that she had left for Thomas. Her plan had come to a bitter end. She did not gain his attention, nor was she able to provide him the favor. Instead, she had lost her father's favorite story and had no idea what happened while she was asleep.

She placed the book on a nearby table in the entry and removed her hat. She then proceeded into the dining room to have dinner. She sat at her normal seat and looked to the head of the table, the thought of her brother's absence coming to her mind. She missed his company, and assured herself that he would be returning soon. Anna Beth's ball was only a few days away, and he had promised his return by then.

One of the standing servants left to inform Lily of her attendance. Another came and poured her some wine for her supper. Claire looked out the window as her dinner arrived and conversation was absent. She thought about Thomas and her defeated attempt at meeting with him that day. She considered that perhaps her demeanor towards him had pushed him further away than she anticipated. She sat there eating alone in a somber mood with only her thoughts to keep her company. The many transgressions she had incurred and the contempt that he must have for her were the focus of her attention.

The servants left her to her thoughts and did not intrude upon her during her dinner. Claire felt more alone than ever. She missed her brother's company desperately and hoped that he would return soon. She finished her dinner and headed to the upper floor. She was glad to see Mary as she entered the hallway of her bedchamber. The idea of having some interaction with her helped to ease her state of mind.

"Mary, I think it is time for me to have a bath. Please prepare one for me, I will be there shortly."

"Yes, Miss," replied Mary before she turned toward the bathroom and began preparations.

Claire took her time heading to the bathroom. She looked along the portraits of the hall and stopped briefly at her parent's portrait, depositing her kiss upon the frame. The portraits were mostly of her family's ancestry. Most of them she had never met before, but she remembered a time when her father explained who they were. She reached her bedchamber and changed her dress to head to the bath.

The warmth of the water caused a thick, misty air to encompass the room. Claire slipped into the water as it began to swirl around her and relax her body as well as her mind. The fragrances used in the bath were thick and strong, and she felt as if they were being absorbed directly through her skin. For several moments, she lay in quiet serenity within the bath, enjoying the comfort as it washed away her undue stress.

The night crept in, and Claire finally stepped from the bath, drying off her dampened skin. She placed the simple gown over her once more and stepped towards the door. Opening the bathroom door, she was greeted with the coolness of the air within the hallway as it rushed towards her. Claire walked steadily into her room and slipped herself under the covers of her bed. Lying upon the bedside table was the book that she had placed in the foyer when she had arrived home. Mary must have retrieved it for her and brought it to her room. Claire opened the book, reading where she remembered that she left off that afternoon. Before long, Claire was once again fast asleep.

The following morning came and Claire awoke with renewed purpose and determination. Her mind was troubled over the potential loss of the book that she had intended for Thomas. She picked up the book she had been reading when she fell asleep, and left the bedchamber in haste. Claire stopped briefly at the portrait, not spending her normal stay at its base. She quickly touched upon the frame and headed down the stairs. As she went to the foyer, she thought for a brief moment, and decided it would be best to grab some small measure of a meal before she left the premises.

Claire went into the breakfast nook, then knocked on the kitchen door before opening it. Lily was there, working diligently in the kitchen. "Good morning, Miss Stonewall, is there something the matter?"

"I am in need of a small breakfast, something I may travel with. It is imperative that I be on my way."

Lily responded quickly, seeing the haste that Claire was in, and turned to the other table, taking a handkerchief and loading it with a few muffins and some cheeses. She folded it and tied it off, handing it back to Claire.

"Thank you, Lily." Claire took the breakfast and bounded back out the kitchen door towards the foyer. Samuel saw her haste and opened the door for her before she had the opportunity to reach him.

"Good morning, Miss Stonewall."

"Good morning, Samuel. I shall be back post haste, do not fret." Claire continued her pace through the doorway and off in the usual direction. Looking back to the door, Claire saw Samuel watching her as she headed off into the distance. It was more important to her that she find the book than anything else that morning.

As Claire rounded the hilltop and looked upon the pond, her eyes dashed over to the tree where she had met Thomas that fateful day. Her feet were getting heavy and her breathing was difficult. As she moved closer to the pond, she slowed her pace, feeling her destination close at hand. Just as she was catching her breath, she looked to the nook of the tree and she saw something she did not expect.

Just above the root that rose above the surface of the ground, Claire made out the shape and texture of a well-scuffed boot. Her pace slowed to a nervous state, concerned who might be sitting at her spot, and whether or not they had come across her book. She carefully took a wide berth to the tree, keeping a safe distance from it as she walked around nearer to the pond. Her eyes carefully studied the features of the person sitting at the base of the tree. As she turned and focused harder on the figure shrouded in the shadow of the tree, she saw that the man was wearing a hat and it made his facial features difficult to discern. Claire inched forward, and saw that the man was reading from a book that looked quite similar to the one that she had left for Thomas.

Claire stopped for a moment and looked more intently at the person sitting there, who was surely unaware of her presence. He was a well-built and strong man, his clothes were tattered slightly, and she could tell he was a working hand, though his attire was of better quality than a servant's. She looked intently and began to inch closer and closer to the man. Suddenly, and without intention, a quick and loud snap was heard from beneath her foot. She had stepped on a twig that broke with her weight upon it.

The sound roused the man to look up from his reading, and he looked to see what made the noise. To Claire's relief, she saw his face once again and immediately recognized him. It was Thomas, he was reading the book that she had left for him. Though now caught unsuspecting, Claire found herself in a quandary. She had lost all thought of the words she wished to express the day before, and stood there smiling in awkward silence.

Thomas stood from the spot and looked upon her face. He closed the book on his finger in order to hold the place within its pages. Taking his free hand, he brushed off the twigs and leaves that collected on his suit. Then he took a couple of steps towards Claire, speaking in a calm and relaxed voice. "Good morning, Miss Stonewall." His words encompassed Claire's head like a warm welcoming comfort that she had not experienced before.

Claire's heart beat heavily, her mind had emptied at his sight, and she found herself dumbfounded in his presence. A couple of moments passed by as Thomas stood before her. Claire took a half step back, and after what felt to her like an eternity, she finally took a breath. Her eyes stayed focused on him, and she felt the dryness of the air in her throat. She dared not blink, in fear that the vision of him would be swiped away from her. Eventually, she caught her silence, and cleared her throat lightly. "Forgive me, good morning, Mr. Edleman. It is good to see you."

"The pleasure is all mine, Miss Stonewall."

Claire watched him intently, trying to manage the range of emotions running rampant within her. Thomas smiled to her and she in turn felt the strength fade from her knees. The brief silence between them was broken as Thomas continued, "I want to thank you for the lending of your book, Miss Stonewall. I have not the willpower to put it down since I began its tale yesterday."

"Yesterday?"

"Yes. I came by yesterday, and saw you sitting here. At first, I had the thought that you were entranced in the authoritative works that you had in your possession. Though after coming closer, I recognized that you had fallen into a graceful slumber. As I reached the book lying precariously next to you, I saw the note that you had left for me."

Claire began to feel embarrassed. She had not thought of his reaction and hoped that he would not have read more into it than she intended. Though in her own mind, she began to question her intentions with the letter in its entirety. Claire lightly bit the bottom of her lip and looked downward to the ground as she stood before him.

"Did you not see the flower that I had put in its place, letting you know that I was here?"

Claire blinked several times, thinking heavily on the time that she had awoken. It did not occur to her at the time that he may have not had the ability to leave her a note in return. Instead, she had brushed away all of the leaves and twigs, and perhaps in the process wiped away the evidence that he had left for her. "No, Mr. Edleman, I fear I may have swept it away when I awoke, for it was late in the day. In all honesty, I was afraid that it may have been lost. It is such a precious treasure that I was frantic to ensure its safety."

Thomas held up the book so that Claire could see it safely in his possession. "It is here, Miss Stonewall, would you care for its prompt return? Or, would it be possible for me to finish its contents before I deliver it back to its rightful owner?"

"No, please, Mr. Edleman. I intended for you to read it, in hopes that you would find it as endearing as I have."

"Very well. Though I dare say that I will be done with it soon enough. Like I have said, I have not had the strength of will to put it down as of yet. It is a fascinating contribution of the written word. Would you care to join me in my morning's read, Miss Stonewall?"

Claire curtsied slightly to him, looking in the direction he was guiding her. Her book in hand, she went to the tree and sat down before him. Thomas took a seat next to her, his back leaning against the root that served once as a table for Claire. The two of them looked over the water and took in the splendor of the morning light and wildlife. Suddenly, Claire was reminded of the breakfast that Lily prepared for her and she took it into her lap, opening its contents so that Thomas could see as well.

"Mr. Edleman, would you care to join me in this humble breakfast? I have not had the opportunity to eat this morning, and I would not feel comfortable eating in front of you without your inclusion."

Thomas looked to the little bits of food that were presented. He nodded. "I will join you, though I have already eaten this morning. But if it will allow you to be more comfortable, I will accept your most gracious invitation."

"Thank you, Mr. Edleman, perhaps you would be so kind as to tell me of your family. I do hope things are well at home." Claire placed the handkerchief flat upon the ground, then laid out the food upon it as a miniature picnic set before them.

Thomas watched as Claire prepared the food between them, his tone reflected his gratefulness for her concern of his family. "All is well as could be. Mrs. Edleman continues her work with the twins in the Devereux Estate as they do each day. Jonathan is well versed in the life of a farmer and is quite enthusiastic at his chosen profession as always. Miss Edleman is doing her best to keep the remainder of the house in order. I am busy, as you well know, especially with the last few months' activities. It seems my time is more limited than I wish to admit."

"Oh, I do hope that you find the time to relax once in a while. It must be quite a chore, the Devereux family is fortunate to have you to assist them. Do you ever think of leaving their estate and taking on less work in order to care for your family?" Claire realized what she asked, but only after saying it aloud. She did not mean to be inconsiderate, nor disrespectful of the Devereux family.

"Miss Stonewall, I do not take trials in my endeavors. I enjoy the work that I do. We are very blessed to have such wonderful patronage in the Devereux Estate. For my work specifically, if it were not for the love of the work that I do, you can be assured that I would not be so fortunate."

"I do not understand, Mr. Edleman. I would think toiling and tending to horses to be a challenging and difficult endeavor. It would not be the life of a gentleman, being more of a responsibility for the servants of the house."

Thomas shook his head and looked to her. Claire caught his gaze and felt the sting of her own words sink within her. She had hoped to make light conversation, but in turn found herself at the wrong end of what was turning out to be a heated discussion. Not quite sure how Thomas would respond, Claire began to straighten up, but before she could apologize, Thomas responded to her badgering.

"What more pleasure is there in life than to feel the pride of accomplishment? It does not matter if you are planting fields or gardens, cooking or cleaning, farming or any purposeful work. The rewards of hard work and determination always provide the feeling of fulfillment, joy, and pride. Without these things, all life becomes is a meaningless drudgery of continuance. I know that you have been brought up as a lady, Miss Stonewall. And to that end I do not deny you your presence, nor existence. I only claim that the life that you have, as well as the lives of many around you, would be enriched beyond your comprehension if you were to claim some sense of pride of work."

Claire sat there stunned and shocked that Thomas was so blunt with her. She had not intended for it to work out that way, and it began to tear into her that she may have caused him some pain or ill temper. "I did not mean…" Claire uttered aloud, but could not finish her statement before Thomas stood up and brushed the leaves and twigs from his suit.

"I bid you good day, Miss," he said to her with a bow and turned from the spot and walked off into the distance. Claire sat there by herself. She had felt the pain of loneliness before, but she felt it even more so now. She packed up the remaining food and tied off the handkerchief. Her interest in reading was lost and she headed to the manor once again.

As Claire walked over the grass and hills, her mind went over and over the conversation with Thomas, and her regret deepened with every step. Tears began to fill her eyes. She was attempting to make an impression upon him, and instead, she shunned him away even further with her words. She felt the first of tears drip down her cheek and she looked up and gritted her teeth in agony. With each step, it seemed to take longer to reach the house. Before she could resist, she was angry with herself for her behavior. The sky darkened above her and the clouds began to hide the sun from sight. The winds picked up slightly, and a crisp scent was in the air. Claire could tell that it was about to rain and was determined to reach the house before it fell.

Claire took the few steps up to the doorway, just as the rain began to patter upon the rocks of the parkway. Samuel opened the door for her and ushered her inside. "Welcome home, Miss Stonewall."

Claire said nothing, but simply went into the common room, placing the book upon the table and the package of food on top of the book. She took the few steps to the piano and began to play. Her mind continued to burn over the discussion that she had with Thomas just a few moments ago, the rage within her still present, but subsiding slightly. She knew he was right to speak such sentiments to her, for she had seen the way the upper class lived. Although she felt that she was different than most, in reflection, she did little to prove this to herself or anybody else. Then, as the tune of the music filled her ears, her fingers moving carelessly over the keys, the thought came to her. Perhaps she should do more than she ever had done in the past.

PRIDE OF WORK

I T WAS STILL EARLY IN the evening and Claire sat at the piano bench, playing a lovely tune. The sounds echoed from the walls of the music room, and although Claire's mind was distracted, the music flowed easily and pleasantly from her fingertips. As Claire sat there effortlessly playing the piano, she pondered the meaning of Thomas' words to her, and just how she could overcome the struggle that he presented to her. Suddenly, she stopped playing, and remembered just how curious she was with Lily and her ability to prepare such wonderful meals for them. A sudden thought came to her as she recognized the enjoyment she always had at the dining table. She could learn to cook.

Claire stood from the piano bench and went towards the door. She looked to the table and saw that the package of food and book had been moved. She attributed the disappearance of the items to one of the servants, taking the items and putting them away. With a renewed determination, she crossed into the foyer, and then through the dining hall. She would assist in the meal this very evening, she thought. Her pace quickened, though not quick enough to be considered a run. She did not want to delay her newfound purpose. As she entered the breakfast nook, she turned immediately towards the kitchen door and opened it without pause.

"Lily, I request to assist you in preparing the meal for this evening!" exclaimed Claire without looking to see if Lily was in the room.

The aroma of food within the kitchen was strong. Lily had already been working diligently on the meal. Although there was no company to provide for dinner, there was an abundance of food. Claire pondered for a moment, looking to the bountiful meal that was being prepared. She realized that Lily did not prepare meals only for her and Charles, but for the rest of the staff as well.

Claire looked about the room as the smell of the dinner that Lily was preparing overcame her senses. Lily was standing in front of a large pot, a long wooden spoon in her hand, and her eyes fixed in Claire's direction. She looked stunned as her gaze was locked in place. After a few seconds of waiting, Lily's expression softened in acknowledgement. Claire figured that Lily was regaining her senses from the outburst.

"I…" started Lily. "I, um." She stood there holding the spoon, her body stiff. The steam coming from the various pots and pans seemed to be the only movement in the room. She placed the spoon down upon the table near the stove and looked around the kitchen. "Very well, Miss Stonewall."

Claire stood in the doorway and watched as Lily went about the kitchen. She took a cutting board and a knife, and placed them upon the nearest counter. Then, Lily took a few carrots and brought them to the cutting board. "Miss Stonewall, I must admit that your request is uncommon, to be honest. But if you wish to assist me in this endeavor, then I would be grateful if you would peel and cut these carrots for the stew that I am preparing."

"I would be much obliged to assist you, Lily. Though I must admit that I am not familiar with peeling and cutting carrots. Could you demonstrate what needs to be done with them?"

"Certainly, Miss. It is not that difficult to do, just you see." Lily took the knife in her hand and carefully showed Claire how to peel the carrot, then brushing the skins away, she sliced the carrot into evenly sized pieces quickly and effortlessly. When she was finished, she placed the knife down upon the cutting board and looked to Claire. "Now, go ahead and peel the rest of them and then cut them into similar pieces for the stew."

Claire had watched Lily carefully and it looked to her to be an easy task. She took one of the carrots into her hand and the knife in the other. Taking a deep breath to calm herself, she attempted to wield the knife as Lily had shown her. The knife was more difficult to hold than Claire had imagined. With determination and the will to figure it out, she continued haphazardly trimming the skin from the carrot. After what seemed like a long and tedious endeavor, she began to slice the carrot into variously sized pieces. Her movements with the knife were deliberate and slow as she chopped the carrot. When she finished, she briefly compared her result to the one that Lily had done. Her final product was not nearly as neat and consistent as Lily's, but she was determined to continue. She took the next carrot and began trimming it as well, trying to remember exactly how Lily had done it before.

Time wore on in the kitchen, and Lily was moving about from place to place, leaving Claire to attend to her task. Claire noticed her ineptitude in this endeavor and attempted to find ways to increase her productivity. In the time it took her to cut three of the carrots, Lily managed to complete several of the other tasks. Determined to improve herself, Claire continued to cut the remaining carrots, watching her progress as she went along.

Claire began to feel a bit of frustration, having only done a few carrots, none with the precision and consistency that Lily had shown her. The carrots themselves were uneven, all with varying sizes and thickness. She was nervous to admit to her faults, but called out to Lily for confirmation of her efforts. "Am I doing this correctly, Lily?"

"That is good enough, Miss Stonewall. Would you like me to finish the task?"

"No, Lily, I will finish this task. I am just seeking your confirmation that these are done properly." Claire continued to cut the carrots, slicing a piece away and then cutting it as she had with the first. Lily, on the other hand, continued to move about the kitchen, performing a multitude of tasks behind her. Her hands began to cramp up from holding the carrots and the knife. She was getting tired, and was amazed to find the amount of work that needed to be done for a single meal. She had a new appreciation for Lily and the work that she did for them.

The back door opened briskly and the silence within the kitchen was broken. Mary called out to the room, "What is taking so long, Lily, dinner was supposed…"

Mary stopped as soon as she saw her working in the kitchen. Whether it was by Lily's intervention or Mary's own accord, Claire could not tell. She felt a bit embarrassed that she was the cause in the delay, and focused herself to finish the task as quickly as possible. Mary and Lily spoke briefly in such a hushed tone that Claire could not understand what the conversation was about.

Claire heard the door shut and Lily continued her way about the kitchen. Lily was behind her as she made the last cut. "That is good enough, Miss Stonewall, I will continue from here. The meal will be ready shortly, perhaps it would be a good time to ready yourself?"

Claire brushed the peelings from her dress and left the kitchen. Her hands felt sore from wielding the knife. Lily had performed the demonstration so efficiently that it made the task seem easy. It turned out to be more of a challenge to her, but she was not discouraged. Moments after she sat down at the dining table, the servants presented her with a glass of wine.

Claire enjoyed the presentation of each course as the dinner began. She paid more attention to the amount of effort that she imagined each dish required. There was much that she took for granted, and to her, the staff deserved high praise for such excellence. The meal was a masterful piece of artistry that Claire had always enjoyed thoroughly, but it was only now that she could understand the amount of work and practice that it must take to prepare such a meal.

Through the course of the meal, the stew came to her and she was delighted. The thought that she made some contribution to it, however small, gave her a sense of accomplishment. Taking a spoonful of the stew, she included a carrot of her own chopping. As she savored the taste of the stew, she felt the carrot was firmer than she had remembered. The remaining items in the stew were savory and the carrots stood out from the rest. To Claire's dismay, she noticed that the irregularity of her chopping was directly affecting the consistency of their presence in the stew itself. She hoped that the staff would not recognize her involvement, and her sense of accomplishment diminished. The stew was delightful in any case, thanks to Lily's advanced abilities.

Claire finished the meal and felt quite full and content. There were many courses that she did not contribute to, and she felt the need to push herself to do better. She had begun her training, and as she had learned from her father a long time ago, she knew that practice and patience were the key to accomplishing her dreams. This is what Thomas meant when he spoke to her earlier that same day. The pride in work that she had never known. It was not that different from when she would partake in some charitable contribution once in a while. The feeling of accomplishment and pride that she felt in doing such a simple task allowed her to see where Thomas was coming from. For the first time, she had a deeper appreciation for those who put their effort into their profession.

Claire looked out of the window and watched the dim flickering light rebound off the grounds. Her mind focused on the thought of Thomas and their encounter a short while ago. He was right to talk to her in such a way, and she now understood his position, and felt the sting of her own ignorance. She left to her bedchamber, full and satisfied in more ways than she could have imagined. Reaching her bed, she fell to sleep with the thoughts of a fulfilling day in her mind. Her dreams began with the thought of one day proving to Thomas that she had mastered cooking.

SKIPPING STONES

THE FOLLOWING MORNING, CLAIRE OPENED her eyes refreshed and full of energy. She changed from her nightgown and noticed when Mary entered the room. She peeked her head out from the side of the dressing screen and greeted her. "Good morning, Mary!"

"Good morning, Miss," replied Mary, noting her energetic enthusiasm.

Claire left the room with a light step, as if she were a child ready for the next day to spend playing. Her heart and mind filled with joyous exuberance, well over that which she had expected. She looked upon her father's expression in the portrait and imagined regaling him with the events of the previous day. Although she could only assume what his response would have been, she felt a warmth of understanding and happiness from him. He was always proud and understanding of her, and she knew that he would still be. She deposited her kiss to the frame and continued down to the kitchen to meet her next challenge.

Claire knocked lightly at the door before opening it and peeking her head inside to catch a glimpse of Lily. "Good morning, Lily!"

"Good morning, Miss. How was your night's rest?"

"Very good, Lily, and yours?"

"Well enough, though to be honest, I would much rather have your enthusiasm this morning."

"Is there anything that I may assist you with this morning?"

"I thought as much, Miss. I have some breads this morning that need cutting, and if you desire something more, you may also assist me in preparing some eggs."

Claire's eyes lit with excitement hearing that Lily was offering her to cook. "Oh, that would be wonderful, Lily." She entered the kitchen dutifully, listening to Lily as she instructed her, and did the best she could to follow her advice. It was no secret that Claire was determined to improve her skills in the kitchen. Lily encouraged Claire as best she could and advised her as she progressed. At the conclusion of the preparations, Claire entered into the breakfast nook and awaited the meal with great anticipation. She took some of the eggs she assisted with, as well as a few of the unevenly cut pieces of bread. She felt even more accomplished than she had the night before, and hoped that her experience and understanding of the skill was improving.

Looking outside the windows of the breakfast nook, Claire saw the warmth of the spring day as it graced the landscape. She felt the need to return to the pond and declare her skill to Thomas. She went to the library, retrieved the book she was reading the day before, and left through the foyer. Her step was still light and cheerful, and she was looking upon the pond in no time at all. Walking to the tree, she felt as if it were waiting for her to join it. Sitting comfortably at its base, she looked over the water and opened her book.

Claire sat there reading the book for a few moments, but had a difficult time focusing on the story. She closed the book and figured that she was too excited to sit still and read comfortably. She stood from the base of the tree and placed the book upon the root, then brushed off the leaves and twigs that had collected upon her dress. Walking over to the edge of the water, she looked at the rocks that were littered along the edge of the pond. She picked one of the polished ones and tossed it lightly in her hand. With a bit of a smirk, she threw the rock into the water and anticipated the splash as the stone broke the water's surface.

She watched as she threw another rock as before, hearing the plunk of the water as the rock splashed. Suddenly, with a bit of a startle, she heard a voice come from behind her.

"You would not be angry, would you, Miss Stonewall?"

The surprise of Thomas' voice caught her unawares, and for a brief moment, she stood there petrified, biting her bottom lip in an attempt to hide her enthusiasm. She turned to see Thomas smiling from a short distance away. She looked intently at him, taking in the awe of his presence before she responded. "You startled me, Mr. Edleman."

"I do apologize, Miss Stonewall. I assure you it was not my intention and was unconsciously done. Is everything all right?"

"Yes, Mr. Edleman. Everything is quite all right. I find myself unable to sit still this morning. So I thought the pleasure of tossing a few stones into the pond might placate my restlessness."

"Ah, permit me to join you then." He took the few steps to be beside her and then looked to the ground. He reached down and plucked a rock from the ground and tossed it aside, seeing one more to his liking. He then brushed off the dirt from the rock and placed it carefully within his hand. With a flick of his wrist, he spun the rock into the pond. Claire watched as the rock seemed to dance over the top of the water. It skipped over the surface several times before sinking on the far side of the pond. Claire was amazed, she had never seen someone do that before.

Claire jumped slightly from the ground in her excitement. "Oh, let me try." Bending over to grab a rock, she chose the first that she reached and flung it into the water. The rock hit the surface at an angle and sank quickly, not bouncing from the surface like she had hoped. Her smile diminished and she looked to Thomas inquisitively.

"Do not fret, Miss Stonewall. You would be astounded with what can be accomplished with just a small amount of knowledge and practice." He reached over and chose a more suitable rock, brushed it off, and handed it to Claire. "If you will permit me, Miss Stonewall?"

Claire nodded and Thomas stepped closer to her. He placed his hand upon hers and she felt the need to breathe in sharply. The touch of his hand upon hers sent a shiver down her spine. Her mind was lost in bewilderment for a moment as she watched their hands together. The single moment seemed to last longer than any she had ever known. Thomas positioned the rock in her hand and folded her fingers around it. Her hand was like clay being sculpted by a masterful artist.

"There, now throw this stone with your wrist. Keep it level with the ground and you should see it skip along the water's surface," he said softly to her ear. His voice was low and soothing to her as it echoed softly through her mind.

Thomas stepped away from her, watching as she stepped into the throw. The rock surely left Claire's hand swiftly. As it hit the surface of the water, it bounced and raised slightly. Claire watched the rock as it seemed to glide through the air and skip over the water. Once, twice, three times it bounded from the surface, and Claire felt the thrill grow within her. The warmth within her blossomed as she watched the stone finally sink into the water. She turned to Thomas and smiled widely, her eyes bright with excitement.

"You see, Miss Stonewall, with a little practice and a steady hand, you can accomplish many things."

The two of them continued to skip stones across the pond, not saying much between them. They watched the rocks and laughed together at their successes and failures. The afternoon continued, and the two of them found themselves quite engrossed in the pleasure of each other's company. Thomas eventually stopped and looked fondly to Claire, watching her as she continued to play. Claire turned and saw him standing there looking upon her, and she felt the rush of warmth come to her cheeks.

"Unfortunately, Miss Stonewall, I must bid you a good day."

Claire was saddened at the announcement of his departure. "Will I see you again tomorrow, Mr. Edleman?"

"Yes, Miss Stonewall, I would be happy to call upon you tomorrow. Shall we meet here about the same time?"

Claire nodded excitedly.

"Until tomorrow then," Thomas said with a bow.

Claire curtsied. "Until tomorrow." Claire watched Thomas as he walked through the trees and off towards the Devereux Estate. She took a deep breath and went to the tree and collected her book before she returned to the manor. The light shone brightly in the sky, and the grounds were littered with fluttering butterflies and wildlife. Claire was energetic and confident when she finally reached the entry to the manor.

Samuel stood attentively at the door, ready to serve her whatever she needed. "Samuel, have Forrester bring the carriage, I wish to go to town this afternoon."

"Yes, Miss." He left her in the doorway and walked directly to the stables.

Claire went to her bedchamber and changed her attire for her arrival into town. She returned to the foyer wearing a green dress. The sleeves were just elbow length and a small bit of pale green lace decorated its borders. She had put her hair into a bun, and was wearing a hat trimmed with translucent ribbons with the same green-tinted borders.

She exited the manor and saw that Forrester was standing attentively at the side of the carriage, holding the door open for her. His gloved hand was open to her, ready to assist her into the carriage easily. Claire climbed into the carriage and sat comfortably. The journey into town began within moments.

CHARLOTTE'S INVITATION

THE CARRIAGE ARRIVED IN TOWN and stopped along the road. Claire took Forrester's hand as he helped her from the carriage, and straightened her dress. The street was crowded with various stalls, selling their wares to the passersby. There were quite a few people gathered in town that day, and Claire felt a bit of a relief. Her fears about going into town were gone, and she did not feel the need to hide from society. She did not know if it was due to her understanding of the recent gossip, or the confidence that Thomas instilled upon her. In either case, she was comfortable to walk the street without an escort.

"I do not expect to be long, Forrester."

Forrester closed the door and climbed to his perch to take the carriage around the corner to the stables. Claire watched the carriage as it disappeared from view, then walked to Mr. Dodd's shop, weaving through the patrons as she passed by. The thoughts and stories of their purpose in town that afternoon ran through her mind. The children were playing as they usually did and the sight of them brought a smile to her face.

Claire reached Mr. Dodd's shop and looked briefly through the window before grasping the handle of the door. It seemed quiet inside and Mr. Dodd was sitting at the counter, his back turned to the street. Claire could see that he was leaning over a book, intently reading. The bell chimed, announcing Claire's arrival into the store. Mr. Dodd turned to see Claire and stood with a wide smile upon his face. "Good afternoon, Miss Stonewall. It is a pleasure to see you today."

"Good afternoon, Mr. Dodd. And I am grateful to be seen, thank you. Do you have anything interesting for me today?"

Mr. Dodd held up a single finger and winked to her. He stood from his seat and placed a marker into the book to hold his place as he closed it. He walked to the back door of the store and disappeared from view. Claire perused the collection of books that were arranged on the small tables. Mr. Dodd usually kept his newest and notable books on the tables near the front of the store, giving patrons a chance of seeing something of interest.

Claire picked up a leather-bound book and ran her gloved fingers over the lettering of the book's title. Then, opening it gently, she began to read the first couple of pages. It was her means of identifying the book to see if it was of some interest to her. She put the book back into its place, having not felt the attraction to the work it contained. One after another, she read a book's title, and then decided to read the first few pages.

Mr. Dodd opened the back door once again and walked towards Claire. Claire folded the book she had picked up and held it as she turned to see him. He was carrying a loosely wrapped book, and he seemed to treat it as if the book were both delicate and precious. When he reached Claire, he held out the book in one hand and uncovered its loose wrapping with the other. Claire's eyes widened as she saw the cover to the book. The book was masterfully engraved, and the cover was artistic and purposeful. It was by far one of the most ornate designs that she had seen. She placed her gloved fingers over the title on the cover and felt the engraving of the letters that were pressed into it.

Mr. Dodd watched her delicately handle the book. As she examined it, he began to describe its procurement. "Miss Stonewall, this book was actually acquired by a pleasant happenstance. It is a long-told story, though there were few in publication. The book itself came from a small bookshop in London, and I was quite happy to come across it. The merchant there told me that the book was collected from an estate that had been passed down through the generations. He was not familiar with the author, but I am sure that you would appreciate its worth."

Claire took the book from him gently and opened it carefully. Based on the delicate and precise lettering laid in the book, she could easily identify that it was one of the earliest prints that she had seen. Many of the pages were handcrafted and designed with particular flare and decoration. "Indeed, this is a rare book, Mr. Dodd. How did you manage to obtain it?"

"The merchant in London was not overly concerned with its origin, and I am surprised that he was able to part with such an art for so little a price. When I discovered it, I immediately considered you and purchased it from him in hopes that you would be honored to acquire it. I know that you, of all patrons, will give this piece of mastership a proper home and the respect that it deserves."

"Yes, Mr. Dodd. You are so very thoughtful. Thank you." She held the book out for Mr. Dodd. He took it back from her and looked down to the book that she had tucked beneath her arm.

"Would you care for that book as well, Miss Stonewall? It is a very good book, full of love and adventure."

"I would in fact, thank you again, Mr. Dodd." She had not intended to purchase such grandeur, but could not believe the luck she had in her choice to shop that day. Mr. Dodd took the two books to the counter and wrapped them individually. The elder of the two was wrapped multiple times in an attempt to protect its more delicate construction. When finished, he held out the two books to Claire.

"Thank you, Mr. Dodd. Have a most wondrous day!"

"You are most welcome, Miss Stonewall. I look forward to the chance to see you again." Mr. Dodd bowed slightly to her. Claire curtsied and left the shop, quite happy with the books that she acquired. She continued down the street toward the edge of town, having felt secured in her endeavor that afternoon. After watching a young boy being chased by an even younger girl, Claire turned to see a familiar face walking in her direction. "Miss Edleman!"

"Miss Stonewall! It seems that it's been so long since we have spoken. I see that you truly have an affinity for the written word."

"Yes, it does seem as if it were a long time. How is your family? I do so very much miss their cheerfulness." Claire was not sure if Thomas had spoken to Charlotte about their encounters over the last few days. She was curious to see if Charlotte had any knowledge of them, and waited in anticipation of some excuse in the event of having to explain herself.

"The family is well, Miss Stonewall. You are too kind to ask. What of yourself, are you well?"

"I am quite well, in fact. I was just leaving from Mr. Dodd's bookshop."

"I can see that, Miss Stonewall. It seems that both you and Thomas share a passion for book reading. I have never seen him so intent in reading. Especially over the last few days."

Claire half expected Charlotte to mention their plausible connection. In her haste to evade the topic, she quickly changed the subject. "What brings you to Springhurst, Miss Edleman?"

"I was on my way to peruse the available ribbons at Mr. Rowe's. I had heard that there were some new fashions brought earlier this week from London. And I could use the distraction from the house, in all honesty."

"Would you care for some company? I would be pleased to travel with you, as long as you have no objection."

Charlotte seemed to jump at the opportunity, obviously surprised that Claire would offer her company to her. They walked together down the street towards Mr. Rowe's Garment Store.

"My brother reads so much. I sometimes catch him at night next to the oil lamp trying to read as much as he can. I even interrupted him one time to ensure that he got his proper sleep.

He dismissed it, of course, and sent me away to sleep myself. I believe he has been reading even more these last few days. I really do not know what has come over him, to be so persistent in his reading."

"What about you, Miss Edleman? Do you read much yourself?"

"Not as much as I should, I must admit. I am not that good of a reader. Not to say that I cannot read, of course. I only find life so much more diverting. Having to care for the house occupies the majority of my time, and I find myself wanting to leave the house when I do have the chance. Not that reading cannot be done outside, it just does not suit me is all." Charlotte's attitude dimmed slightly and Claire could tell that she was saddened a bit.

Claire looked briefly to Charlotte as they walked down the street. "Is there something the matter, Miss Edleman?"

"No, nothing, Miss Stonewall. Everything is as it should be."

"Please, Miss Edleman, there is no need to withhold your feelings from me. You are a dear friend and I can see the discomfort as plain as the light that shines on your face." Claire placed her hand upon Charlotte's forearm, just below the elbow.

"I do apologize, Miss Stonewall. Please forgive me. I do love pretty things, but I know that I will never be able to afford them. I do not know why I torture myself by browsing such extravagant items. Only to know that there is little that I can own and even less that I can procure. It is truly a self-inflicted misery that I find most unceasing." Charlotte finished and looked to the ground in her expressed humility.

"Oh?" Claire said in surprise. She had not expected such a detailed confession. Now that Charlotte had confessed her sorrow in full, Claire felt uneasy for forcing it from her. "Well," Claire continued, in thought for a moment, "I think perhaps you need an escape from your usual tasks, Miss Edleman. I am sure that you will be attending Miss Hawkins' Ball, will you not?" The thought had just occurred to Claire, and the idea of a plan took form in her mind.

"No, Miss Stonewall. I am not in favor with the Hawkins family. Nor do I have the pleasure of being in favor with the ladies of higher class than I. I do not believe that I would be accepted in such a grand assembly. I have never been to such an event, and although I have always wanted to partake in such fineries, I do not believe that one of my status should pretend to hope."

Claire knew that Charlotte was correct in her statement. It was always a situation of invitation, and those who were invited rarely ever included the lower class. As she stood there holding the handle of the door in one hand and the books in the other, she looked to Charlotte. Charlotte's head was down and away from her, and it saddened Claire deeply. Claire's planning continued to unfold, and although she was unsure how she would accomplish such a feat, she felt the desire rise within her.

"I am sorry to hear such a plight, Miss Edleman. I ask your forgiveness if I have made you uncomfortable, it was not intentional. But I do not think that you should give up hope. You are a gorgeous, young woman and trust that your fate is only limited to your dreams. You are still young, and you have many days before you to be so withdrawn." Claire paused for a moment and waited for Charlotte to enter the shop. "In fact, Miss Edleman, I was wondering if you would be so kind as to join me for tea tomorrow afternoon. I do miss your company greatly, and would be pleased to have you at Brookfield Manor."

Claire saw the immediate change in Charlotte's emotion. The plan had not taken its full shape, however there was little choice in her mind. It was not whether her plan would come to fruition, but more of a design that she felt needed to be explored.

"I would be delighted to join you, Miss Stonewall," said Charlotte, who was still a bit shocked at the offer.

Claire entered the shop behind Charlotte, and the two of them began to peruse the various ribbons on display. Claire watched Charlotte, though her mind was preoccupied with the plans she had concocted. "I will have the carriage collect you tomorrow then, Miss Edleman. I look forward to spending the afternoon with you and I am quite sure that we will have a grand time."

It was apparent that Charlotte was greatly appreciative of Claire's invitation to tea. They left Mr. Rowe's and walked down the street towards the edge of town. Forrester arrived with the carriage, having seen them approach the area.

"Would you care for an escort home, Miss Edleman?"

"No, but thank you, Miss Stonewall, I think I prefer to walk."

"Very well then, Miss Edleman, until tomorrow."

"Until tomorrow," Charlotte responded with a curtsy.

Claire curtsied as well, and then turned to Forrester who was now standing at the side of the carriage, ready to assist her inside. She took his hand and sat at the nearest seat to look upon Charlotte as Forrester shut the door. Within moments, the carriage was on its way down the street. She was still working out the details of her plan when they arrived at the manor.

Claire handed the books over to Samuel as she entered the manor and continued to her bedchamber to change into a more comfortable dress. She then returned to the foyer before heading to the kitchen. The plans still occupied her mind, but she was determined to continue her efforts in cooking. She knocked lightly at the door before entering, and saw that Lily was already prepared for her arrival.

Lily greeted Claire and began to explain the various tasks that she had set aside for her. Within moments, Claire was diligently cutting vegetables and peeling potatoes as Lily had instructed her to do. Claire reported to Lily the intention of having tea with Charlotte. Lily responded with encouragement, showing her happiness for Claire to have some company after such an absence. It had not occurred to Claire that it had been so long since she had company until that moment. She was sure that her plan was the right one, and eagerly looked forward to her visit with Charlotte.

Claire finished her tasks in the kitchen and sat at the dining table. The meal that she assisted with was presented before her, and her mind explored various methods in which she would announce her idea to Charlotte that next day. Being that they had little exposure between each other, she thought it best to approach Thomas and seek his guidance in the morning before the tea. She finished her meal and headed up the stairwell to her bedchamber. She figured that it would be best to get an early start for the following day.

CLAIRE'S UNORTHODOX REBELLION

T HE FOLLOWING MORNING, CLAIRE WOKE, anxiously wanting to put her plan into action. She knew that the day was going to be busy and briskly got prepared to start. In hopes of finding Thomas at the pond, she dressed in a simple gown. Her thought was to return in time to change after meeting with him that morning. She went down the hall and stopped before the portrait of her parents.

Standing before the portrait, she went over her plans for the day, seeking approval from her father. There was possibly some conflict from society that could result, but she remembered the words of her brother. She pressed a kiss to the frame of the portrait, feeling the love and understanding of her father.

Claire went down to the breakfast nook and entered the kitchen, finding Lily there as she did the night before. Claire assisted Lily in preparing the morning's breakfast. She talked openly with Lily regarding the tea that afternoon, ensuring that she had every angle of her plan worked out. Lily took the order without complaint and understood that Claire would not participate in the preparation. When breakfast was completed, Claire sat down at the small table in the nook and ate quickly.

Claire finished her breakfast and quickly left the manor in order to meet Thomas as she had planned. She did not take anything with her to occupy her time, as she was not planning on staying long. She wondered if Charlotte would have informed him of their tea that afternoon, and whether or not he would be there as they had discussed. When she arrived at the pond, she looked around eagerly to find him and was happy to see him sitting at the base of the tree reading. Immediately, Charlotte's comment on him reading more than he had before came presently into her thoughts.

Claire walked over to Thomas, and without waiting for his reaction to her presence, she announced herself. "Good morning, Mr. Edleman."

"Good morning, Miss Stonewall. I was not quite sure if I was going to have the pleasure of your company this morning."

"I did make the appointment to meet with you today, did I not?"

"You did, Miss Stonewall. Though I was not sure if you were able to keep such an appointment after offering to have tea with my sister."

"Of course, Mr. Edleman, and I am glad that you still came to meet with me. It is unfortunate that I do not have as much time as I originally had intended. I hope that you forgive me for leaving in due haste. I must ask you something of importance, and hope that you do forgive me for being so abrupt."

Thomas stood before Claire and folded the book on his finger to keep his place in the story. He looked to her and nodded, waiting patiently for Claire to continue.

"I plan on asking Miss Edleman to accompany me to Anna Beth Hawkins' Debutante Ball tomorrow evening. Your dear sister clearly explained that she has not had the pleasure of attending such an assembly. I would very much like to provide her the means of attendance. In your opinion, would she be pleased to have such an invitation?

"I do not believe that it would be of any consequence as Miss Hawkins is my close cousin, and I am surely entitled to bring an accomplice of my own choosing. I believe that she would enjoy the treasures of having such an invitation most emphatically.

Though I am concerned if she would be comfortable in such surroundings, being that she has little knowledge of those who will be in attendance. However, having my confidence beside her would surely secure her ability to experience the assembly in its fullest extent."

Thomas seemed to think about it for a few moments and paused to ensure that Claire was finished. "Yes, Miss Stonewall, I am sure that my sister would be most delighted to receive your invitation. I do not believe that she would expect it in any wildest imagination, and would be enthusiastically inclined to accept such a wondrous adventure."

Claire was pleased at his response, but felt the need to address any concerns in the matter. "I do hope that you are willing to accept the consequences of her attendance. I know that the social community can be quite abrasive and condescending at times. Though I do not believe for an instant that your sister is any less worthy than many who would be in attendance of the event." Claire's thoughts recalled the treatment that Charlotte had received from Vivian the one time that they were introduced.

Thomas stood there with a slight wickedness about him. Realizing her plan in the fullest, he offered his comfort to her concerns. "Indeed it would be a discussion of great interest to specific parties. But I believe that would be more of a declaration and acceptance of Charlotte. As for the potential retaliation by society, I think that we are strong enough in our own name to dispute any plausible defamation. Do not fret, Miss Stonewall, our family is well protected from such slander." Thomas stood there, confident and strong. Claire knew without a doubt that he had full faith in her, and her concern was sated.

"Then I will discuss it with Charlotte in the fullest intent. I do wish you a good day, Mr. Edleman, and thank you for your understanding." With this, Claire curtsied and watched Thomas bow before she walked back to the manor. She stopped after taking only a few steps and turned her attention to him once again. "Will you be in attendance at the ball, Mr. Edleman?"

"I shall, but not to the degree that you and my sister will be. I will be tending to the carriages and horses as Mr. Hawkins has requested of me. With the pure number of those in attendance, I am quite sure to be there to assist in the needs of the staff."

"Then I shall hope to see you in some small degree. Until tomorrow, Mr. Edleman."

"Until tomorrow, Miss Stonewall."

Claire turned and continued her way to the manor. She thought of how Thomas was going to work the stables, and felt saddened that he was not going to be present as an attendee. Even knowing that he was to work at the event, she looked forward to spending some time with him in at least some small part. As she reached the hill, she saw Forrester attending the horses, and went to speak with him directly. She told Forester to retrieve Charlotte for tea that afternoon and retired into the house to prepare for her arrival.

Claire went inside and sought out Mary to accompany her to her bedchamber. As the two of them entered the room, Claire announced her intentions of asking Charlotte to the ball. She notified Mary of her plan for the two of them to try on various dresses for the event. Mary nodded, offering to get another one of the servants to assist her in the endeavor.

Before long, the day came to its height, and Claire knew that Forrester would soon arrive with Charlotte. She went down to the dining table and saw that it was well prepared for the tea that afternoon, with two specific settings made for her and Charlotte. She heard the sound of hoofs pounding against the rocks outside and went to the window to gaze on the carriage as it approached. Seeing Charlotte helped out of the carriage door, Claire headed to the foyer to greet her.

As the door opened, Charlotte stood there in what Claire imagined was her best dress. Claire curtsied to Charlotte. Charlotte, in turn, curtsied as well. Claire went to her and grasped her hands. "How do you do this fine day, Miss Edleman?"

"I am well, Miss Stonewall. I cannot thank you enough for inviting me this afternoon. You have been so very kind to me."

"Think nothing of it, Miss Edleman. I am only too happy to have you in my company. Come, let us go to the dining room and enjoy this wondrous afternoon. I must confess my apology for having left in such a state when I visited your home last. It was by no means meant as a dislike for your household. I was only made abreast of a situation that needed my immediate attention." Claire guided Charlotte into the dining hall and the two of them sat beside each other at the table.

The attending servants reached over the two of them and placed their napkins in their respective laps. Then they stepped back to allow another servant to serve the two of them tea. Starting with Claire, he poured her a cup of warm tea, then one for Charlotte. The procession of their movement was an extremely well-practiced choreography. Charlotte could hardly contain herself with the splendor as it was presented to her. Claire enjoyed watching as Charlotte absorbed the grandeur of the procession.

"I had the premonition that you would enjoy the taste of a finer serving than you are accustomed to. But do not fret, Miss Edleman, today you are with good company and you do not need to hold yourself to any discerning etiquette or ceremony. Just enjoy the experience, for you are far more worth the indulgence than you may have come to expect."

Claire hoped to prove her sentiments to Charlotte from the day before. Claire knew that Charlotte could not have expected anything like what she was being exposed to. Without speaking the words directly, Claire could see the gratitude in Charlotte's expression.

The tea progressed further and they chatted about Charlotte's family, regaled each other with happy stories of past situations, and laughed as they unfolded. Charlotte appeared to be attempting her best to keep herself within the manners that would be expected of someone of high stature. Despite Claire's release of responsibility in the matter, Claire saw that Charlotte enjoyed portraying a woman with all the social graces of elevated rank. Watching how Charlotte behaved, her confidence grew as she imagined her plan coming to fruition. She continued to watch Charlotte as she enjoyed each of the various foods presented to her. Charlotte's excitement seemed to wane a bit as she reached her consumable limit.

The tea was about to come to its close, and Claire thought that the moment had come to reveal her plan in its entirety. Taking a final sip from the cup in front of her, Claire looked to Charlotte and took a sharp breath. She straightened herself and acted more to the expectation of a woman of her rank. Charlotte looked to Claire curiously. "Miss Edleman, I am so very glad you have enjoyed the tea. It has been some time since I have had any company. I have a favor to ask, if you would be so kind as to give me the honor." Claire paused to give her announcement a more dramatic effect. "If it would not be of much inconvenience to you, I was wondering if you would accompany me to Anna Beth Hawkins' Debutante Ball tomorrow night."

Charlotte had reached for a final scone and had a buttered knife in the opposite hand. She was completely still and in utter shock, unable to comprehend the fact that she was so cordially invited to such an event. Claire watched as Charlotte sat there with scone and butter in hand for several moments. As the butter fell from the knife and hit the plate, Claire giggled lightly under her breath. Charlotte woke from her stunned state and placed the scone and knife down slowly. "Pardon me, Miss Stonewall? Did you ask me if I would accompany you to the ball tomorrow night?"

Claire knew that her request would be doubted, but to further her intent, she responded nonchalantly, "I did, Miss Charlotte. I would consider it a great honor to have you come with me, you are a dear friend and I believe you to be entitled to join me. There will be far too many fine gentlemen who would be most happy to make your acquaintance. Though I am sure it would be of no consequence to you either way. However, the festivities are soon at hand and I would hope that you would kindly accept this invitation.

"I must first relinquish to you some insight to the challenges that may be presented if you do choose to accept, Miss Edleman.

Know that if you do decide to accompany me, it may not be that enjoyable. You will be new to the society and far less expected to be in attendance by many who will be present. I hate to admit it, but knowing few at the assembly may undermine your ability to find a suitable partner during the event. In truth, the two of us would most likely be the gossip of everyone in attendance for the evening. But I am confident that you would turn more than one head if you were to attend, and that in itself is worth mentioning."

"What about you, Miss Stonewall, will this not slight your reputation in some extent?"

"True, it is possible, but I have little investment in such gossip. It has never been anything for my concern. Besides, with all that has happened to me in the last few weeks, the fortitude of my reputation has already sustained an attempted slight by a certain gentleman. These last few weeks I have found that I pity even more those who think less than that which I am. Furthermore, you have never been to a ball and you deserve the right and opportunity of the experience. They are quite lovely and can be quite entertaining to those fortunate to be in attendance."

"Well, Miss Stonewall, if you are up to the challenge, then so am I."

Charlotte smiled widely and Claire joined her in laughter. The plan had begun, and the two of them were ready for the challenge. They talked about how they imagined certain attendees would react, and even began to playact using mimicked voices. Claire knew that Charlotte was a good friend, and the time that they shared at the table after tea proved it thoroughly. Claire was quite happy to have Charlotte in her life.

"Oh, Miss Stonewall, what am I to wear? This ratty old thing is the finest in my wardrobe. I have no means of obtaining new ribbons and a dress for the event. Especially with the event being tomorrow night. I surely cannot be seen at such an event wearing this!"

"Miss Edleman, you have nothing to worry about. I have already made the arrangements. In fact, if you would, accompany me to my bedchamber and we can see if there is something that you find to your liking."

It appeared to Claire that Charlotte's fear turned to excitement at the mention of wearing one of her fine dresses. The two of them went up the stairs to Claire's room for the remainder of the afternoon. Charlotte tried on dress after dress with Mary, Claire, and another maidservant helping her to find what she most adored. Once Charlotte settled on a dress for the ball, Claire sought out a similar color and fashion in order to complement her. They agreed on the attire and returned to their original clothes.

The two of them returned to the hall, walking side by side as they headed for the entry. The night had crept in as they were exploring the various contents of Claire's closet, and it was past the time that Charlotte was to return home.

"Miss Edleman, I will send Forrester to collect you in the early afternoon tomorrow. Be ready so that you can get prepared here with me at the manor. And do not forget to inform Mrs. Edleman that you will not be returning tomorrow night, as you will be my guest for the entire evening."

"But, Miss Stonewall, that would not be necessary. I am quite sure that I could return home in the early morning. You do not need to make such arrangements on my account."

"Nonsense, Miss Edleman, I will not allow you to return home at that hour. It may be far too late in the evening to do so, if not the late hours of the morning. Having you here with me will allow you to recover from what I am sure is going to be a grand night. I insist on the matter, and you will not deter me from it."

Charlotte wrapped her arms around Claire, holding her tightly. Claire returned the gesture, knowing how much their companionship had blossomed. They surely were going to be friends for a long time to come. They said their goodbyes and Claire watched as she made her way into the carriage for her journey home. Her plan had succeeded, and she was confident in the results of the coming event.

CHARLES' RETURN

THE CARRIAGE LEFT THE PARKWAY, carrying within it a most excited and overwhelmed Charlotte. Claire stood at the doorway for a few moments, watching the carriage as it left the premises and relishing in the delight of her plan as it unfolded. She was comforted by the fact that Charlotte would be accompanying her to the ball. Moreover, she thought of the advantage of having Charlotte nearby in the event that Vivian and Nathaniel were too much to bear on her own. Claire took a deep relaxing breath and headed inside, passing by Samuel through the open door.

"Was that Miss Edleman, Claire?" Claire stopped in her tracks. She turned to see Charles standing in the doorway of the drawing room.

"Charles!" exclaimed Claire as she ran towards him. She leapt into his embrace, holding him tightly in her arms. "When did you arrive? I was unaware that you would be home today!"

"Of course I am home, I told you that I would be home in time for the ball. Just in time, I should say. For a moment, I was not sure if I would make it."

"Oh, Charles, I have missed you so much!" cried Claire, overjoyed at his being safe and home at last.

"I can see that, sister, but I do not find it enough to be so tearful. I missed you as well. Not to worry, I am home now." Charles tenderly brushed the tears from her face.

Claire had forgotten his arrival that day. With everything that had happened to her over the course of his absence, she could hardly believe that he was there. The two of them went into the dining hall and sat comfortably at the table.

"Tell me, sister, was that Miss Edleman?"

Claire swallowed hard. She realized that the entire plan that she had arranged was completely unknown to Charles. "Umm." She took a deep breath and knew that Charles could easily pick up on the fact that she was up to something. "Yes, Charles, it was. I invited her over for tea this afternoon."

"What are you planning, Claire? You know full well that you cannot hide your mischievous intentions from me."

Claire blushed heartily. She knew that she was discovered and had no choice but to divulge her complete intentions. After a long description of the events that she recalled to him, Claire finished with her newest intention with Charlotte. "So I have decided to invite Miss Edleman to accompany me to the ball. I do hope that you find this agreeable, brother."

Charles was quite taken aback by what he had heard, and after a few moments of reflection, he looked to Claire. "Of course, dear sister. If you feel it is important to have her there with you, then there is no reason why she should not be in attendance. If there are any who dare to challenge her, I will honorably stand to her defense. Not to worry, Claire, all is well."

The servants began to deliver the drinks and first courses of dinner. Claire had intended to help Lily in the kitchen that evening and felt disappointed that she was unable to assist her. Lily came out with the first serving of soup and Claire took the opportunity to apologize, not realizing that Charles would be able to hear their discussion easily. "Lily, I do apologize that I did not help you this evening. I hope that you can forgive me."

Lily looked nervous, not knowing exactly what to do or what to say. "No worries, Miss Stonewall. Your brother is here."

Claire realized that she did more harm than good in her discussion with Lily. She blushed, feeling ashamed that she had placed Lily in such a situation. Charles sipped his soup and pretended to ignore the conversation. He changed the subject and began asking Claire of her reading and general information regarding any activity in town. Claire knew that her involvement in the kitchen would have to be explained later. She was relieved of the interrogation for the moment, and delightfully reported what she could.

The two of them continued to discuss Charles' trip and Claire's adventures during the course of the meal. Claire intentionally left out the portions of her meetings with Thomas and learning to cook under Lily's tutelage. Although Claire knew that Charles would see through her veiled attempt to hide certain things from the discussion, she also knew that he was patient enough to give her the time she needed. The night crept in and Claire began to feel her energy wane. It was time for her to retire for the night.

Excusing herself from the dinner table, she wished Charles a good night. She slowly made her way to her bedchamber and fell asleep promptly. Her mind continued to dream of the upcoming activities, and she found her dreams vivid and provoking.

PREPARATIONS

THE FOLLOWING MORNING, CLAIRE FELT refreshed and confident. Her plans were well on their way and she quickly disregarded any thought of disruption. With Charles' willingness to stand by her invitation, there was no doubt in her mind that Charlotte would be well received. Claire thought briefly on how Charles would thwart any negative actions or reactions to Charlotte's attendance with grace and dignity. She clamored out of bed and soon emerged from her room into the hall wearing a simple dress.

Claire sat comfortably before the portrait of her parents and began her communion with them. Her plans were clear and concise in her mind and she relayed them in their fullest extent to the memory of her father. She felt calm and love from him surround her like a warm blanket. He had always wished for her to think for herself and to not be bound by the shackles of social graces. He had stressed to her many times in her youth to be herself no matter the consequences. He was most adamant that her character was strong enough to withstand any trial that dared to confront her.

She stood from the foot of the portrait, reminiscing the fond memories of her father. She deposited her kiss to the frame and took a deep breath. Her tension was relaxed as she exhaled with calm and collected thoughts. Turning down the stairwell, Claire continued into the kitchen where she expected Lily to be working diligently on the morning's breakfast.

Lily turned and saw Claire standing in the doorway. Claire had a glow of confidence and security about her that morning, and Lily was pleased to see it again. "Good morning, Miss Stonewall. How was your slumber?"

"Good morning, Lily. I slept well, thank you for asking. Do you have any tasks that I may assist you with this morning? I am ready to challenge myself today."

"Yes, Miss. Do you feel ready to handle the stove? I have need to cook the pork." Lily seemed confident that Claire could handle it, if she was willing to try.

Claire looked over the stove and saw that there were a few pots and pans upon it ready to be used. Next to the stove was a plate of thinly sliced pork, striped with fat. She looked to Lily and was pleased to think that she was capable of cooking the meat. "Yes, Lily. If you believe I am ready."

Lily went to the stove and checked the heat of its surface, then ensured that the fire below was bright. She selected one of the pans that were laid out and placed it on the hot stove. Claire watched her as she moved about the stove and prepared everything. Lily collected a piece of the meat and placed it in the pan. The sizzling sounds from the meat crackled and popped. Claire felt slightly nervous due to the sound that it made as it was being cooked.

She continued to watch and listen carefully to Lily as she instructed her on the task. Taking over Lily's charge of the stove, Claire continued to cook the pork. As she turned the pork over, it sizzled wildly and it startled her. The aroma of the pork filled the kitchen and Claire enjoyed its overwhelming scent.

Lily kept watch over Claire as she cooked for the first few minutes. When comfortable that Claire had a handle on her task, Lily returned to the other preparations for the breakfast. The kitchen was busy, and the aroma was tantalizing to the senses.

As the two of them prepared the meal, the back door opened and Mary came into the kitchen, seeing the two of them working diligently. "Mary, please inform Forester that I will need him to collect Miss Edleman this late morning. We have much to prepare for the evening's assembly, and I have not had the opportunity to inform him. I will also require a bath immediately following breakfast, having little time before Miss Edleman arrives."

Mary curtsied with a "Yes, Miss" and left the kitchen promptly.

When the preparations for the meal were complete, Claire exited the kitchen feeling satisfied that she had once again improved her skills. She looked through the open kitchen door to see Charles siting in his chair looking back at her. Claire felt the blush of her cheeks as she looked down at her attire, quite covered in remnants of the work that she had done in the kitchen. She had no way of hiding it from him and decided not to try. She straightened as best she could and sat next to her brother.

"Good morning, Claire, I see you have taken a liking to cooking," Charles said calmly as he unfolded the paper before him. He continued to peruse through the paper, though he seemed to be only half interested in what it had to report.

Claire saw that it did not bother him in the slightest that she had taken on this new challenge. She took the napkin from the tabletop and placed it in her lap as she thought of a response to give him. Claire did not want to mention Thomas' involvement in her desire to put herself to work. She was worried that if she mentioned him it would raise far too many questions and she would be resorted to explaining even more. "Good morning, brother. Truly, I have found enlightenment in learning a new skill. I have deduced that if I am destined to be a lonely old maid, then I might as well start learning the trade. I do not believe that I will find a much better time than the present to gain the advice of such a masterful teacher."

"Well, good, then I should put you to work straight away. I cannot have you lollygagging about needlessly, when there are chores that need to be done." Claire looked to Charles and saw his playful expression. "You are in quite a good mood today, sister. I have so missed your cheerful demeanor. What has come over you to be in such a playful state?"

"Is it not obvious that I am quite determined to have a good day today, brother? I believe that tonight will be a night to remember, and am looking forward to sharing it with my dearest companions." As Claire was talking, the food was brought out to them. They talked and laughed about their recent adventures, but Claire was still holding back her trips to the pond. She did not want Charles to know about them nor her interludes with Thomas, thinking that he might consider them to be inappropriate.

They continued eating and enjoying each other's company. After a short recess, Claire stood from the table and Charles followed suit. "I must take my leave, Charles. I need to begin my preparations for tonight's assembly, and I have already sent Forrester to retrieve Miss Edleman. She should be arriving shortly."

"Very well, I will continue here if you have need of me. If Miss Edleman should arrive before you are ready, I will do my best to keep her entertained." Claire turned to the doorway, and as she left the room, she could hear him calling out to Lily behind her. Thinking little of it, she continued towards the bath upstairs.

Mary had prepared the bath ahead of time and the room was filled with warm steam and aromas from the various bath salts that were present. Mary followed Claire into the room, and after a short while, Claire emerged refreshed and relaxed from the experience. She went straight away to her room to begin her preparations for that evening.

As Claire was getting ready, a knock came to her door. "Miss Edleman here to see you, Miss," called out Samuel from behind the door. Mary, who had been assisting Claire, went to the door and invited Charlotte inside.

"Miss Edleman, so good to see you!" They greeted each other with a hug and Claire could see the excitement in Charlotte's face.

"Good afternoon, Miss Stonewall, I am so happy to be here. I do not know how I will ever repay your kindness."

"Oh, Miss Edleman! Do not think anything of it, besides, it is far more of a comfort to me to have your company at the event. Heaven above only knows what the night will bring, but in all hopes, it will be filled with laughter and dancing. Especially with some of the most handsome men I am confident will be in attendance."

Charlotte blushed and shied away from the comment, then the two of them giggled at the potential of such a delightful evening. Claire guided Charlotte over to the bed where the dress she was planning on wearing was neatly laid out. Charlotte took little time in putting on the dress.

The two of them spent the remainder of the afternoon talking about the approaching ball and playacting various encounters as they imagined them. The afternoon started to wane, and the two of them finished getting ready. Walking arm in arm, they went down the hall and turned at the top of the stairwell. At the base of the stairs stood Samuel and Charles. Charles had readied himself in one of his most elegant suits, complete with ruffles and a fine coat.

Charles looked up to the two of them and smiled warmly. The sight of them was breathtaking and he watched as they made their way down the stairs towards him. As they reached the foyer, Charles bowed graciously. "What generous beauty graces my eyes this evening. The two of you are the most stunning of sights. I feel so blessed to accompany you both to the ball."

Both Claire and Charlotte looked to each other and blushed their brief embarrassment. Charles went to Claire and deposited a kiss to her cheek, then whispered softly into her ear, "Father would be so proud of the woman you have become." Claire blushed even further, his admission of her father bringing warmth to her spirit, and a calming sensation overcame her as she took her brother's arm. Charles stood between the two of them, and the three of them walked out the door.

The carriage was clean and shining in the evening light. The sun had begun its late decent over the hills, with the evening just about to begin. Forester assisted Claire into the carriage, while Charles assisted Charlotte. Sitting across from the two of them, Charles was last to take his seat. Within moments, the three of them were on their way to Bedford Park.

As the carriage tarried down the road, Charlotte was beside herself with a range of emotions, from utter joy and excitement to complete terror and nervous anticipation. The dress they had chosen for her to wear was quite elegant, and complemented her appearance greatly. Her unmistakable excitement enhanced her beauty in such a way that none would second-guess her presence.

The three of them did not speak much during the trip, but Claire noticed Charles' attentive stare at Charlotte. It was apparent that Charles was pleased that Claire had invited Charlotte, and at ease to share in this opportunity.

CHARLOTTE'S
FIRST BALL

THE CARRIAGE ARRIVED AT THE entrance to Bedford Park in which a series of carriages already littered the parkway. Music emanated from the well-lit house and spilled out of the open doorway. The ball itself already seemed so festive despite the earliness of the evening. Many of the attendees crowded the entry to the home, making their way inside. Charles exited the carriage first and quickly turned around and offered his hand out to assist Charlotte. Claire was last to exit and noticed that the air was crisp, but not cold. As her feet touched the ground, Forester called out to them, "Watch your step, there were many horses along the path."

Charles examined the path, and found a way through the manure that the horses had left behind in their wake. Taking Charlotte's hand in his arm, he began walking towards the entry, his eyes on the ground. Claire followed them, though not paying nearly as much attention to her footing. Instead, she looked towards the stables, searching for any signs of Thomas that she could see.

Thomas stood in the distance, tending to a beautiful brown mare. He turned at that moment and looked back at her. Seeing him look in her direction, Claire blushed and absentmindedly touched the ribbon in her hair. The horse nudged Thomas in the shoulder as his attention was taken away. She curtsied lightly as she continued to walk behind Charles and Charlotte and Thomas bowed his head, holding steady to the leash of the horse. Claire shied away from his continued gaze and quickly caught up to Charles and Charlotte as they reached the porch.

Charles, Charlotte, and Claire slowly walked up the stairs and through the open door into the foyer. Immediately, as they arrived, the various people in attendance took notice of the three of them. Claire felt the eyes of onlookers as they looked upon her and she focused forward in an attempt to ignore them. It was only a short while ago that she and Charles were the focus of recent gossip. This was the first time that they were engrossed in a social gathering of any size since. Not only did they have to contend with the recent gossip, they now had a new face that few could recognize. Claire overheard a few of the patrons as they began their fervent questions to their attendance.

The Hawkins' family reception was near the rear of the foyer. Richard, Sarah, Michael, and Vivian stood opposite from the entry. They were greeting all of the attendees as they came into their home. Claire caught Vivian's expression as she looked in their direction, and she could not tell whether it was nervousness or concern over who Charlotte was. It was obvious to Claire that Vivian did not recognize her and knew that this was the moment of truth.

Charles guided Charlotte to them and smiled as he approached. He bowed generously to Richard and spoke confidently, looking to the rest of the Hawkins family. "Mr. Richard Hawkins, Mrs. Sarah Hawkins, Mr. Michael Hawkins, and Miss Vivian Hawkins, I am so pleased to be able to attend here this evening. My sister, Miss Stonewall, whom you well know of course. And may I present, Miss Charlotte Edleman."

The moment that Charlotte's name was mentioned, Vivian's mouth opened wide in shock. She had clearly only just realized that this was the girl that Claire had brought home ill. She knew that she was unable to decline her attendance at the event, Charles had made it quite clear that she was his guest. That being the case, she stood stunned and unable to utter a word in protest. Charlotte and Claire curtsied their respects to the hosts of the evening, paying little attention to Vivian's obvious discontent.

Mr. Hawkins was first to bow generously to Charlotte. "A pleasure to make your acquaintance, Miss Edleman. Welcome to our home, we hope that you enjoy the festivities."

"Thank you, Mr. Hawkins, the pleasure is mine to be sure."

Sarah chimed in and continued, welcoming her despite seeing Vivian's protest. "Miss Edleman, it is such a pleasure to finally meet you. I have heard much from the Devereuxes on your behalf. How is your mother fairing these days?"

Charlotte seemed to be a bit surprised that Sarah would be so informed. "Thank you, Mrs. Hawkins. My mother is doing well and she has recovered nicely. It is so kind of you to ask."

Claire had not been knowledgeable of Martha's illness, and thought to ask Charlotte about it in more detail later in the evening. "Mrs. Hawkins, the décor of the estate is absolutely breathtaking."

"Thank you, Miss Stonewall. You look lovely as well, I do not believe that I have seen that particular dress before." It was often that Sarah appreciated Claire in her appearance. Michael said nothing, but simply accepted their attendance with dignity. Vivian closed her mouth eventually, but the strain of her jaw made it clear that she was upset. The three of them bowed to the Hawkins family and went further inside the room.

As they rounded the entry into the drawing room, Charles released his company with Charlotte and turned to face them both. Claire and Charlotte were obviously a focus of the attendees, but Charles knew that they were welcome nonetheless. "I must bid you my leave for the moment. I have no doubt that the two of you will find yourselves in good company shortly." He bowed to them and then disappeared into the crowd.

"Miss Edleman, it seems as though you have gained the favor of my aunt and uncle, to the dismay perhaps of my cousin, Miss Hawkins. Do not worry yourself about it, I am confident that we will find you a partner to dance with. There is no uncertainty that every man within the estate will want to enjoy your company before the night is through."

"Oh, Miss Stonewall, this place is amazing. I am so happy that you have taken me under your wing this evening."

Claire could hear the whispering around her, and discerned their mention of Charlotte and her upbringing. Within minutes, the entire room was found gossiping about who she was and stories of her family. Claire considered that Vivian had quickly begun her devious task of defaming Charlotte as best she could. Spreading rumors and falsities about who she was and how she should not be there. Occasionally, Claire would be able to identify the voices as they spoke about them, and she found that Vivian was the most outspoken of them all.

Claire continued to give Charlotte a tour of the home. As they came in contact with one of Claire's acquaintances, she made the necessary introductions. Despite Vivian's attempts at diminishing Charlotte, Claire saw that the encounters were cordial and well received. This proved to Claire that Charlotte was generally accepted by the crowd, and her concerns were fading. Vivian's attempts were faltering, and for Claire, it was becoming more and more evident that people were dismissing her protests.

As the first dance was completed, the music ended in a flurry of clapping. Claire and Charlotte were far too involved in the gossip and greetings of the attendees to even realize that the dance had started. Instead, the two of them stood to the side of the room and watched the dancers as they moved around. Charlotte would occasionally ask who a particular person was and Claire would respond with a name and a short summary of their station.

Before the next dance began, Charles came up from behind the two of them and almost startled Claire. "Miss Edleman, would you do me the honor of the next dance?"

Claire was beside herself, not realizing why Charles would ask her to dance. Charlotte smiled widely. She seemed happy to oblige him and quite fond of the idea. Claire stood idly by and watched as the music commenced. She clapped along with the beat of the music as the two of them swirled within an elegant stream of partners. As the dance continued, Claire could hear the tone of the various gentleman behind her making comment on Charlotte's beauty and demeanor, and she knew that Charlotte was going to have a wonderful night.

The crowd broke out into a loud applause at the end of the dance. Claire struggled to look around the many patrons to see if she could find Charlotte. Charlotte was making her way back to Claire when she was intercepted by another gentleman of fine features. They shared a few words and she continued on her way to Claire. When Charlotte finally reached Claire, she was even giddier than she had been on the dance floor. With both hands, Charlotte reached for her and pulled her close. "Oh, Miss Stonewall, I have just been invited to dance with that handsome gentleman."

Claire looked to see if she could identify the man who had asked Charlotte and could not see him. "Is he amiable, Miss Charlotte?"

"Indeed, I dare say he is. You will see. Come now, we must find you a partner to join with me on the floor." Charlotte looked around and spotted a fine-looking man standing firm and straight. "What about him, the man in the blue coat?"

Claire looked to where Charlotte indicated. She was unable to identify the man and strained her gaze as they approached him. The man in question turned, and from the instant that his face was revealed, Claire's heart came to a sudden jump. It was Nathaniel, talking amongst a few of his favored companions. Claire did not know how to act. It had been so long since the man had even entered her mind. Charlotte seemed to have caught Claire's sudden change in attitude and resistance to her guidance. "What is it? Miss Stonewall, are you all right?"

She whispered into Charlotte's ear, "That, Miss Edleman, is Mr. Clayton."

Claire witnessed the sudden change in Charlotte's demeanor and quickly took a firm grasp to her arm to keep her from confronting him. Charlotte turned her gaze to Claire, showing her evident disdain for Nathaniel. After a few breaths, her expression calmed as she whispered, "I am sorry, Miss Stonewall. Please forgive me, I did not know who he was." Charlotte's voice was sincere, and Claire knew that she had never seen him before.

"It is all right, Miss Edleman. I just need some air." Patting Charlotte's hand as it held her own, Claire turned and walked from the room. She approached one of the balconies and passed by Mrs. Devereux without being noticed. However, Claire could not mistake the discussion that she was having with one of her friends.

"Yes, Mr. Clayton and Miss Hawkins are to be married," Mrs. Devereux said to the woman. Hearing the words, Claire ducked quickly out of sight, but kept within earshot of the discussion.

"But it seems so soon after his failed engagement with Miss Stonewall. What an unexpected turn of events that is. Are you sure he intends on marrying Miss Hawkins?"

"There is no mistaking the information. I have it on great authority that the engagement was accepted by Mr. Hawkins himself, two days prior. They are to be married before the winter is through. It is only the fortune that I expect Mr. Clayton has found interest in. He is a shrewd man, if ever there was one. It is to the benefit of Miss Stonewall that she refused him. Any wretched man who seeks the fortune of a woman over her character gains no favor with me!"

Claire fell further into remorse, not for her luck in escaping Nathaniel in his motives, but for the overwhelming thought that everything he had done was for her inheritance. The more she thought it over, the more it made sense to her. He was truly after her inheritance rather than her love. What she found most troubling was why he had left. If it were true that he was simply after her money, why would he be so apt to leave without putting up a fight for her?

Claire reached the balcony and stepped outside the door, closing it behind her to diminish the voices that were beginning to weigh so heavily on her thoughts. The air outside was crisp, cool, and refreshing. She took a deep breath and forced the thoughts of the situation behind her. She had made such a valiant effort to bury her feelings about Nathaniel, and they were now coming back to the surface. The music could still be heard from a window below and allowed the cheerful sound to provide some comfort. Her eyes closed and she focused on her emotions to wrangle them back into control.

The moon was full that evening, and it shone brightly upon the grounds. It was not necessary to hold a candle to see what was going on below. She stood on the balcony alone and attempted to calm her thoughts as she felt the struggle of her emotions overcome her. Claire knew that Charlotte was on the dance floor, completely unaware of the stories that were being spread around her. She felt a twinge of envy over Charlotte, almost wishing that she was in her position instead.

The music soothed Claire's wandering thoughts as she listened to it, and she opened her eyes to glance upward to the moonlit sky above. The stars were bright and shining down upon her as if watching her in return. The extent of her companionship with Nathaniel came to her in its finality, recognizing that she was far happier without him than in all the time she had been with him. She stood upon the balcony shrouded in solitude, staring off into the blank space before her as her mind churned through thought after thought. She concluded that it was not Nathaniel she had felt the attraction for, but rather the idea of what he might have been. This thought guided her emotion from the darkness that had consumed her for so long, and she felt the pressure wash away from her with a renewed confidence. It was at that moment that she realized there was no reason to feel threatened or hurt by the announcement of Nathaniel's and Vivian's engagement. The two of them were more alike in ways than Claire had ever thought of before.

With this new attitude towards the situation, Claire felt refreshed and relieved, a great weight lifted from her soul. The idea of Nathaniel and Vivian together was now accepted wholeheartedly within her as more of a blessing than a curse. It was obvious the reasons why Vivian felt threatened and wanted to remove her. Vivian was unsure and nervous about what Claire might have thought, and therefore it strained their relationship beyond Vivian's capacity. Claire felt the overwhelming understanding that accompanied such a realization, and she looked down towards the ground below and laughed lightly.

Just below the balcony were the stables, but she had not seen them, as her thoughts would not allow it. In the light of the moon and windows below, Claire could clearly see a man looking directly back towards her. Thomas had stopped in his tracks as soon as he had seen her upon the balcony. She had no idea that he was standing there, and felt the embarrassment overcome her in his attentive gaze. Thomas truly shared in Charles' gift of making her blush. Thankfully for Claire, the night was too dark for him to see the rosy color that flooded her face. Claire curtsied to Thomas playfully, mimicking that of grace and high stature.

Thomas chuckled lightly, looking upon her as she curtsied to him. He returned the act with an overexuberant bow. When he rose from the performance, he held out his hands as if to reach her in the dance. He must have been able to hear the music and known the steps of the dance within.

Claire returned the pose, and with the beat of the music emanating from the estate, the two of them danced the remainder of the song. At its completion, Claire and Thomas bowed to each other once more, with a flair of overemphasized gallantry. Claire laughed and turned to the door, returning inside. She glanced to her side and saw another person standing outside on the balcony adjacent to her own. Completely unaware of his presence, Charles had seen the two of them in the entirety of their playacting, and was grinning widely. Claire, unsure what she should say or do, stood there stunned for a moment with her hand upon the handle of the door. The idea of his having seen the two of them just now forced her to blush once again, as she felt the need to hide quickly from sight. Upon entering the room, she made her way hastily to the door leading to the balcony that Charles was on.

She opened the door and Charles was no longer there. She turned to the crowd to see if she could spot him, and to her dismay, she was unable to find him. She wanted desperately to plead for his forgiveness in her actions and stressed the need to find some acceptable excuse. As she focused on the room, looking for Charles, she felt a gentle touch upon her shoulder. Charlotte was standing just behind her, out of breath and enthusiastic as ever.

"Oh, Miss Stonewall, I just had the opportunity to dance with such a splendid young man. He wished to dance with me again, but I delayed his interest so that I might find out where you had disappeared to." Charlotte was so excited that her presence chased away any other thoughts from Claire's mind. "I have had offers from two other gentlemen in my simple attempt to collect you. Come, join me in the next dance, I am sure that you will find a partner in no time."

Claire smiled softly, allowing Charlotte to pull her through the rooms towards the ballroom. Charlotte was right, with little effort and time, Claire had a partner for the next dance. Claire and Charlotte stood alongside each other as the musicians began to play. The music was both energetic and revitalizing. Before long, Claire was too engrossed in the dance itself to pay much heed to anything else.

As the evening wore on, Charlotte's dance card was so overflowing that she had to deny a multitude of partners. The comments from the attendees completely disregarded any misleading arguments that were previously discussed, and turned to favor Charlotte and Claire in their countenance. Charlotte's rank was no longer a concern of the populace, but rather her demeanor and charm took center stage.

Claire was wandering through the rooms, watching the various attendees as she normally did. She turned the corner, and to her surprise, found herself face to face with Vivian and Nathaniel. Not knowing exactly how to react, she held her tongue for a moment and waited with bated breath, allowing them to speak first if they wished.

After a few moments of awkward silence, Claire curtsied to the two of them and they bowed to her cautiously. There were a few onlookers to their encounter, and Claire wondered if they half expected an indecent scene to break out in the middle of the room. She turned her sights back to Vivian, whose expression was more of fear than of hatred.

"It is wonderful to see you, cousin. It has been quite a long time."

It was obvious to Claire that Vivian was tense having to converse with her. Claire gave Vivian ample time to gather herself until she responded, "It has cousin, I hope that you have been well."

Claire smiled and attempted to relieve Vivian of her doubts and fears. "I have, cousin. A pleasure to see you again, Mr. Clayton, I see that you are well."

Nathaniel was obviously more concerned with the views of the crowd than the actions of Claire. Without saying a word in response, he bowed slightly and turned away from her. Claire sighed slightly, disappointed in his lack of civility. She turned once again to Vivian, who at least acknowledged her.

"I have heard rumors of your engagement, and I could not be happier for the both of you. I know that you must have some reservations in my regard. But I have no ill will toward either of you. I am pleased to see that the two of you are happy, and hope that one day we may be as close as we once were."

It was apparent that Vivian was stunned by Claire's reaction to their engagement. Vivian felt guiltier than ever and it was evident on her facial expression. Claire knew that Vivian had intended to defame her the entire evening, and now that they had the opportunity to meet personally, that her purpose would therefore be ended. Claire curtsied to the both of them and walked into the next room, wanting to cease her intrusion between them. Claire saw Anna Beth and immediately made her way to speak with her.

Anna Beth caught sight of Claire and was excited to see her. They had not spent much time together in their youth, but they always had been cordial in their shared encounters. "Cousin Claire! I did not know you were coming to see me. How nice it is to see you, you look absolutely ravishing." It was clear that Anna Beth showed little concern for the gossip that filled the crowds. Instead, she was enthusiastically enjoying every moment of the gathering.

"So do you, cousin. The assembly is exuberantly decorative, and so is your dress. How did you manage to find such elegant apparel?"

"Oh this?" Anna Beth lifted up the silken fabric of her dress. She proceeded to twirl around and the dress flowed and flittered in the air about her waist. The lights of the candles reflected off of the dress as it moved. She continued to laugh as she returned her focus to Claire. "My father brought this to me from his travels, I find it quite exquisite and suitable for such an occasion." She paused for a brief moment, and stepped closer to Claire before continuing, "I am so sorry for you. To have seen Vivian and Mr. Clayton together this evening in all their gallantry. If I had only known that they were to be engaged, I would have warned you in some fashion."

Claire smiled softly, hearing Anna Beth profess her concern. Anna Beth had always been the compassionate one of the family, and more like Sarah in her demeanor. Claire sighed a little and said softly to Anna Beth, "Do not fret over the situation, cousin. The engagement is most surprising to me this evening, make no mistake. However, I have no quarrel with them, and truly believe that Mr. Clayton will do much better with Vivian than he would ever have with me. If they are so inclined to be happy together, then I would only wish to give them my blessing for a long and happy life." Claire spoke the words confidently in an attempt to diffuse any concern from Anna Beth. As she delivered her speech to Anna Beth, the remnants of her troubles washed further away.

"To hear you say such things brings me much comfort. I had hoped that you would forgive her, the two of you have been so close over the years. It brought me great pain to see that the two of you would have such a falling out. What of this Miss Edleman who accompanied you this evening? She seems to be a wondrous and spirited girl. Do you know of her family?"

"I do, cousin, though I think it would be best if I allowed her to discuss it with you. It is not my place to tell you all that I have learned. She is truly remarkable and a thoughtful person of great interest. I would not be surprised in the least if you two were immediately friends." Claire realized in that moment that Anna Beth and Charlotte would be the greatest of friends, their personalities so similar that it was undoubtable. Claire turned and looked through the room and did not see Charlotte. "Come, cousin, let me make the proper introductions. I am sure that she would be so very delighted to meet you."

Anna Beth followed Claire toward the ballroom, and Charlotte saw them. The three of them met near the center of the room, and Claire introduced them to each other. The procession was between songs, and the musicians had taken a break from their playing. Although the conversations from the crowd were loud, they began to talk amongst each other freely and in confidence.

During their conversation, they were interrupted by a few gentlemen and all three of them had partners for the next set of dances. They took their places on the floor side by side and opposite their respective partners before the music began. The girls remained at each other's side from that moment on. Claire danced with several interesting young gentlemen, though none of them held Claire's particular favor. Anna Beth would come and go, in conversation and in accompaniment to meet some new patron of the assembly.

As the night progressed, it became evident through conversation that many of the attendees began to think less of Nathaniel. It appeared to Claire that he had slipped from favor with the general assembly. Vivian remained at his side throughout the evening and Claire felt pity for her. Vivian was seen dancing only a few rare times, and only with Nathaniel.

Charles had the opportunity to dance with a few of the young ladies at the ball. However, Charles dismissed each of them even though they swooned for his continued company. Claire knew that Charles was enjoying himself, but he had no intentions of gaining particular favor with any of the girls present at the assembly.

As the engagement came to its end, Charles came to them and bid Claire and Charlotte to come to the carriage. He afforded them the opportunity to say their goodbyes as he headed out to find Forester. Claire and Charlotte made their way through the procession of people headed out in the early morning. There were quite a few patrons who had stayed through to the end, as well as some who had fallen asleep among the comforts of the home. Vivian and Nathaniel were nowhere to be seen, and Claire thought they had disappeared towards the end of the night to escape the penance of their indiscretions.

Claire and Charlotte exited through the main entry after saying their farewells to the Hawkins family. Claire looked about the parkway, helping Charlotte, who was extremely tired from the night's exhaustive activity. Seeing the carriage, she guided Charlotte to the door as Forester opened it. He assisted Charlotte inside and she took refuge in the seat nearest to the corner, falling asleep almost immediately. Claire laughed lightly at the sight of Charlotte's condition, an obvious sign of an overjoyed and glorious evening.

Before Claire entered the carriage, she realized that Charles was not inside. She turned to look for him, taking the step to the carriage to gain a height advantage over the scene. Charles was by the far side of the home, speaking to another gentleman. Claire strained her eyes to identify who he was talking to. To her surprise, he was in deep conversation with Thomas. She gawked at them with her mouth wide open, too far to know what they were talking about.

Charles turned and saw Claire watching them, and quickly bid his farewell to Thomas. He steadily walked towards the carriage and urged Claire inside. Claire and Charles sat across from Charlotte, as she had fallen over slightly and taken much of the available seat. "I believe that she has enjoyed herself thoroughly, would you not agree, sister?"

"Yes, brother, I would think most heartily. And you? Did you find the assembly to your liking?"

"It was quite splendid. Long has it been since I have been privy to such an elegant and joyous event. The attendance was quite exquisite and charming by all accounts. Mr. Edleman seems to be quite an agreeable man, don't you think?"

Claire had not expected Charles to make such a mention of Thomas to her that evening. Then it occurred to her that Charles had seen her dance with him from the distance. She had forgotten the embarrassment with all of the events that took place shortly afterward. In a vain attempt to hide her expressions from her brother, Claire gazed out the window, holding her most steady face. "Indeed, brother."

"The stories of his family are far from believable, it is so very unfortunate. The Edleman family is held in such high regard in the general populace. If it were not for their elder brother, I am sure that they would have held the highest standards of social grace. Surely, not the state in which they find themselves now."

"I did not know that you had such intimate knowledge of the family, brother. I have spent some time with them myself and find their situation alarming. It is unimaginable to me that Mr. William Edleman would do such a thing to his own flesh and blood. It astounds me that a man with such a loving family, could—" Claire stopped short, catching the sight of Charlotte sleeping peacefully. She sighed lightly, and released the tension that had built up within her. Claire quieted her tone as she continued, "Though I do not think it our place to put such distaste into conversation while in the presence of Miss Edleman."

Charles looked to Charlotte as she slept soundly in the carriage, "Trust me, dear sister, Miss Edleman will have no recollection of the conversation we are having. I am quite sure that when she awakens from her slumber, she will be oblivious to her departure from the assembly, let alone the discussion that you and I share now."

Silence fell within the carriage, and only the sounds of the exterior were present. Charles closed his eyes and laid his head back, resting himself from the evening. Claire, however, could not close her eyes during their travel. She was thinking of Charles' comment regarding the Edleman family. Finding his extensive knowledge of them disturbing, she wondered how he would have gained such insight. Claire continued in her thoughts while she looked out the window, watching as the light of dawn pushed away the blanket of night.

The carriage rolled up to the entry of the manor, and Charles opened his eyes when they came to a stop. He exited the carriage first and lent his hand to Claire to assist her. Claire stood by the door of the carriage while Charles clamored back inside and gathered Charlotte into his arms. He held her in his embrace as he exited the carriage and carried her through the door of the manor. Claire watched and followed Charles as he took Charlotte inside and up the stairwell. Mary hurried before him, reaching to the room that she had prepared for Charlotte.

Charles carefully laid Charlotte on the bed, and was successful in allowing Charlotte to remain asleep. Charles and Claire left the room and went their separate ways to gain what rest could be afforded that morning. Claire struggled to keep her eyes open as she crawled into bed. She was asleep instantly with the thought of Thomas foremost in her mind. She knew without any doubt that he would pervade her dreams, and she welcomed that thought.

THE MORNING
AFTER

CLAIRE'S EYES OPENED THE NEXT morning as she lay comfortably in bed. She was still tired, but felt as though she was unable to sleep any longer. Her mind was troubled over the discussion that she shared with Charles on their journey home. The thought of his discussion with Thomas made her feel nervous. She sat up in bed and leaned against the headboard, using her pillow for support. The room was lit with the morning light as it shone brightly through her windows.

She knew that Thomas was an honorable man of good character, amiable and very handsome. Though he lacked the money that was taken from them by his elder brother, he still held pride in his family's name, and it showed. She was concerned why Charles would ask her of her opinion of the family. She was sure that she had hid her interest in the family well enough, but feared that perhaps Charles knew more of their interludes than he let on. She plotted various means to deny any misconceived notions that he may concoct and was determined to hide her true feelings from him.

After sitting for a few moments in bed, she peeled away the comforter and sheets and prepared herself for the day. There was some explaining that needed to be done, and she felt that it would be better to tell the truth to Charles and ask for his forgiveness than to continue with the façade. She continued to play out the scenarios in her head as she dressed herself, then continued down the hallway to her parent's portrait.

Claire looked upon the faces of her father and mother and saw the loving expression that was always present within their constant pose. She knew that the family always held love within the highest respect, and that was pressed into both of them diligently throughout their youth. In that effect, Claire knew it was better to trust in her heart above all else.

She deposited her kiss to the frame and continued down the stairwell towards the study. The aroma of food filled the drawing room, and Claire followed it towards the dining room. The door was open, and as she stepped into the room, she saw Charles and Charlotte already sitting comfortably with their plates filled with food. Claire could see that they were still tired, but were enjoying each other's company at the dining table. They were recalling the events from the night before, laughing at the various scenes as they remembered them.

"Good morning, Claire!" called out Charles as he stood, seeing her enter the room.

Charlotte turned and looked to her with a broad smile. "Good morning, Miss Stonewall."

Claire smiled, seeing their cheerful attitudes, and responded wearily through the exhaustion, "Good morning." She could not refrain the yawn that escaped her as she spoke. She sat at the dining table opposite from Charlotte. The attending servant reached over her and placed a napkin in her lap graciously. After pouring her a cup of hot tea, the servant stepped back once again. Claire gathered the sugar bowl and dropped a spoonful of it into her tea, then placed the bowl back into the center of the table. Charles and Charlotte were quiet as they watched Claire sluggishly moving about.

Claire took a gentle sip from the tea, allowing the liquid warmth to cover her throat. She could feel the slight increase in her attentiveness, and inhaled the tea's sweet aroma. Placing the tea back upon its plate, she looked to Charlotte with an endearing expression. Claire looked then to Charles and could easily see that he was enjoying his morning's accompaniment. "How was your rest, brother? I would have guessed that you stayed awake the entire evening, if it were not for your attentiveness this late morning. I know that you could not have slept before I reached my own pillow."

"There is some truth to that statement, sister. There was little sleep to be had, I found myself anxious with the night's events, and unable to calm my thoughts. Though I must admit, what sleep I did have in the early hours of the morning must have given me a temporary reprieve from the exhaustion. And thanks to Miss Edleman here, for she has kept my wits about me, being that she is the only one who must have gotten sleep through the night."

"Speak the truth, Mr. Stonewall. For it was not I that had such wondrous stories to tell of the late hours of the night. It was most assuredly your intriguing words that have given life to my otherwise exhausted demeanor. You have been so gracious with your stories to keep me entertained this morning. But I will not know the truth of them until Miss Stonewall graces me with her own version.

"Though, Miss Stonewall, you must be warned. Your brother is full of his tales this morning, having told me such vividly imaginative stories of my arrival and actions that I had supposedly performed, of which I have utterly no recollection. He has been gloriously vivid of the stories, and of my behavior last evening. I must protest that whatever it was that I did, I claim no knowledge of the transgression and request a pardon from that which I had no control over. I truly must have been coerced or out of my wits, the way your brother carries on about it!"

Charles took up his cup of tea to hide his expression as Charlotte proclaimed his actions to Claire. He chuckled lightly as Charlotte finished her statement and looked back at him for his admission. He casually put down his tea and Claire saw the nonchalant expression he forced. "Well, I may not have been completely truthful in saying that you insisted on riding the horses backwards on the journey to the estate. But I do say that you had the numerous tales coming to you, for your indecency to not stay awake for the journey to the manor."

Claire laughed aloud, realizing that Charles was teasing Charlotte with various misadventures of the return home. He had a jovial behavior, and Claire was able to relax in their presence easily. Before long, the three of them were telling fabulous adventures that were all fantasy and imagination. The morning was spent in the enjoyment of their company, the food that was provided to them, and the playful imagination that they all participated in. The morning was lost to them as they sat at the table, and the afternoon had begun despite their want for an extended morning.

They were still teasing and telling stories between them, well after the place settings were all cleared. Charles had just finished telling another story as they all burst out laughing in unison, when Samuel entered the room, gathering their attention delicately. The three of them looked to him as he announced a newcomer to their company. "A Mr. Edleman here to retrieve Miss Edleman." Samuel stepped aside and allowed Thomas to enter the room. Charles stood at the end of the table, welcoming him into their presence.

Claire remained in her seat as she looked upon him genuinely, glancing over him as he fingered his top hat within his hands. He was dressed quite finely, and Claire could not help but to emit the pleasure she found in his presence through her breath. "Mr. Stonewall, Miss Stonewall, Charlotte," he said as he looked to each of them respectively, then bowed.

"Mr. Edleman, would you care to join us this fine afternoon?" Claire looked to Charles, and realized that he must have made arrangements with Thomas for his retrieval of Charlotte. It had not occurred to Claire that their discussion as they left the assembly could have been as simple as that. She felt embarrassed to have thought more of their conversation than was now apparent. Her overanxious thoughts that she had experienced when she first awoke were purely misconceived in her own mind.

Claire looked at Thomas once again, and saw that he was quite nervous. This concerned her still, for she had no reason to understand why he was acting in such a manner. Immediately, she felt the urge to say something to calm him. Claire looked to Thomas with a curious gaze, as if to understand his anxiousness. Without saying a word, she relinquished her endeavor, and simply bit the bottom of her lip in consolation.

"I appreciate the offer, Mr. Stonewall, and to my dismay, I must decline. Mrs. Edleman is anxious to be with Miss Edleman as soon as possible. I hope you do understand."

"Of course, Mr. Edleman," said Charles, taking his seat once again. Claire looked to him, and saw a concerned look come over him. It was unexpected, and Claire began to fear that there was something wrong with their mother.

Charlotte looked to Claire and spoke softly. "Miss Stonewall, if you would accompany me to the bedchamber and assist me in collecting my belongings."

Claire looked at Charlotte and nodded. If she were to get any information of Thomas' behavior, it would have to be in private company. The two of them stood from the table and headed swiftly out the door toward the room. As Claire followed Charlotte, she could still hear Thomas as they entered the drawing room. "Mr. Stonewall, I wondered if I could have a word with you in private."

Claire stuttered in her step and almost tripped herself at hearing his request. 'Why would Thomas need to talk to Charles?' she asked in silence. Wanting to stay behind and hear their discussion, she was thwarted by Charlotte as she took Claire's hand and tugged her along. Claire turned her attention to her feet in order to watch her step as she followed Charlotte up the stairs and into the spare room. Charlotte began to collect her things and busy herself about the room.

Claire watched with a blank expression on her face, her mind focused on Thomas and what prompted him to request a private audience with Charles. As she wondered about the discussion that they were having, a multitude of possibilities rambled their way through her mind. It was not until Charlotte interrupted her that she returned from her reverie. "What has come over you, Miss Stonewall? You have not been yourself this morning, to the point that I feel as if you are hiding something."

Claire looked to Charlotte and realized that her thoughts were clearly reflected in her mannerisms. "I apologize, Miss Edleman. I am still tired from last night's assembly. Please forgive me."

"Forgive you? You would have to have done something wrong before you could be forgiven. There is nothing more that you have done these past few days but to bring me great joy and happiness. You must know this to be true, Miss Stonewall. You have been so gracious to me, and I know that I will never have the ability to repay you for your generosity." A long pause of silence came between them and Charlotte knew that whatever was on Claire's mind was profound. Charlotte sat softly at the edge of the bed as Claire stood there, motionless and in deep thought. "If you wish to tell me in confidence, I will keep it a secret, if I must. But please, burden yourself no further if you think that I hold you in anything but the highest regard and greatest of fondness."

Claire heard the words as Charlotte spoke them and slowly looked to her, seeing the innocent sincerity in her expression. "It is nothing, Miss Edleman. I am sure it is just passing worry on my part. I sometimes have the worst of fears coerce my mind, and your family is so very dear to me. I hope all is well with your mother."

"You mistake my brother, Miss Stonewall. He has taken a great liking to you, and although I know him to be quite overwhelming at times, he can come across frightfully. He simply wishes me to return home so that Mother will not be discomforted by my absence. There is much that needs to be done today, and I have not done my fair share with the events of yesterday. Think nothing of it, I can assure you that there is nothing to give you any unnecessary concern."

Charlotte was right, of course, and Claire often found herself worried for no reason, her own imagination getting the best of her more often than not. She took a deep breath and relaxed. "Have you collected all of your belongings, Miss Edleman?"

Charlotte stood from the edge of the bed and nodded. The two of them left the room and went downstairs. As they reached the foyer, Thomas and Charles were nowhere to be seen. Charlotte handed her items to Samuel, and they went to look for them.

As they entered the dining hall, they saw Thomas sitting next to Charles at the table. Thomas stood abruptly as they entered the room, causing Charlotte to let loose a light giggle. Charles followed suit and smiled as they approached. Claire could tell that he was hiding something, but to the best of her ability, she was unable to discern what it was.

"Miss Edleman, if you would not mind, I would like to show you the gardens before you leave. They are quite lovely this time of year," Charles said as Claire and Charlotte reached them. "Your brother has requested a private audience with Miss Stonewall and we can lend them this room for their needs."

This caught Claire by surprise and she looked to Thomas, who seemed to be quite stressed beyond his means. The thoughts once again ran rampant through her mind. Perhaps it was that Charles had found out the truth of their companionship and she now recognized the full impact of fear within her. Charlotte took a sharp breath and bit her bottom lip. It was apparent to her that there was a different reason for the request.

Charles led Charlotte from the room, and Claire stood there stunned before Thomas. Charles closed the door as he and Charlotte left the room, and the remaining servants exited the room through the opposite door. It was then that Claire found herself confronted by Thomas alone. The sound of her heartbeat pounded within her chest and she could not fathom what was going on.

Thomas walked over to Claire and placed his hat firmly upon the table. As he took the final step towards her, he stood there, straight and firm. Claire could see that the pressure of what he was about to tell her wore terribly upon his mind. He swallowed hard and took a deep breath before uttering the first few words. Claire waited with bated breath for what was about to take place.

"Miss Stonewall," he began. The sound of his voice echoed deeply within her. Struggling to keep her emotions at bay, she stood silent with bewilderment. "I have come to you this day in hopes of relieving the anguish within me. I have struggled to contain myself and have ultimately failed in my attempts to withhold that which is so dear to me. There is no release from my torture but to admit to you now the full nature of my desires. I have been a fool to them these many days and can bear it no longer. It is with a heavy heart that I profess them to you now, and I hope that you will know what trials I have faced in overcoming this most arduous predicament.

"I have no money to my name, my family is in utter ruin, and my station is far from acceptable. You have been too kind to me for me to ignore these faults, and I pray that they do not hold to your disfavor. I can no longer deny the feelings that I have for you, for they have plagued me for far too long. If you do not share these sentiments, then please tell me now and end this agony that I profess to you. One word from you is all that I require to end this suffering within me, and I beg of you to save me from this enduring torture."

The words filled Claire with disbelief, and the emotion within her came to its height. She knew now more than ever what had troubled him so, and what he must have gone through to come to this conclusion. She looked within herself and found that she too shared this feeling for him. Since the day she first met him and through their experiences they shared together, she knew that this was right. It had come to her now more than ever to feel the truth of what they had ignored. She loved him, and it was more than she could ever expect to have found in any person. She said nothing, and felt the love between them explode in its entirety within her, overwhelming her with joyous interpretation. The tears swelled within her, wanting to know that it was true and not just a fantasy made up in her dreams.

He took another step forward and kneeled in front of her. Claire stood there, keeping her eyes upon him, eagerly waiting to hear him continue in hopes of confirming the feeling in her own heart.

"I have little money to sustain us, and I have much burden to bear with my family. But if you will have me, I know without a shadow of doubt that the love that we share is all that we shall ever need for a full and complete life. I love you, Miss Stonewall. Claire. I love you, beyond any love from heaven and earth. I profess it to you now, in hopes that you will share with me the devotion that I promise to give you all the days of my life. You are my only one, the other half of my soul, my angel from heaven above who has given me hope. Miss Claire Stonewall, would you give me the greatest honor and allow me to offer you my hand in marriage?"

Claire stood there as the entirety of the event unfolded before her. Still and motionless, she could barely believe what was happening. Tears of joy filled her eyes, and her heart pounded heavily within her. Her mind raced through the emotions that she had felt for him from the beginning, the day she had seen him in the street, rescuing the young girl. The times that he had spent in her company when Charlotte was ill. The times that they shared in secret hence, and the lessons that she had learned from his gentle teachings. All of which came to this moment. This instant in time in which he had opened the door to her heart and soul.

Joy overcame her, the thoughts of their happiness in the forefront of her mind. The ideas that came from that moment were of love and endearment over time and troubles. She had no other want in life than to be accompanied by such a man. A smile formed over her lips, and as the tears began to fall down her rosy cheeks, all that she could manage to say to him was simply, "Yes."

Thomas smiled in reply, seeing firsthand the joy that overcame her. Still kneeling to her, he reached out his hand to take hers. Claire lifted her hand and reached to his, the joyous laughter emanating from within her, the tears spilling around her face as she was overjoyed. Thomas took her hand and pressed his lips to her knuckles, kissing them gently, and stood before her. The space between them faded away and they embraced with arms wrapped tightly around each other.

Claire looked up to him as they parted slightly, seeing the happiness in his eyes as he looked to her. They were to be joined together, and that was all that they both wanted. The moment seemed to last for an eternity before the realization of what was to come entered Claire's mind. She was suddenly nervous and worried, and the emotion was expressed unwittingly on her face.

Thomas saw the change of her demeanor and questioned it quickly. "What is the matter, Claire?"

"My brother, Charles. You will need to speak with him." She had remembered the feeling of pain and suffering that she had gone through with Nathaniel. This time it was different, she knew how much she loved Thomas, and the fear of Charles' rejection of Thomas was more than she cared to know. "But I do not want you to. Must it be that you get his approval of our engagement? Can we not escape this fate and go out to the world and prove our devotion to each other?" Claire feared more the denial from her brother than society's acceptance if they were to escape in passion. She feared the potential loss that, in her mind, would ultimately destroy her. She pleaded empathetically with Thomas to forego the requirement and elope with her.

Thomas calmed her carefully, stroking her cheek with his fingertips. He smiled softly and kissed her gently on the forehead. Taking a deep breath, he replied, "Not to worry, Claire. I do not fear the retribution of your brother. I am sure that he would have no reason to disapprove of our engagement." He brushed away the tears from her cheek and smiled to her softly. Claire felt the love as it emanated from his touch and she had no other thought than to trust in his words. He turned, taking Claire's hand, and went in search of Charles, dragging the now nervous Claire along with him.

Charles and Charlotte were coming back from the garden, and it was not very hard to spot the two of them. Charles saw them hand in hand and stopped in his tracks. Charlotte saw Claire's face and the evidence of tears, though no sign of sorrow existed in Claire's expression. When they reached each other, Thomas released his grip on Claire's hand and the four of them stood in conference.

Claire looked to Charles and saw the surprising understanding in his demeanor. He was smiling slightly, and Claire could see it even if the others could not. He was her brother, after all.

"Mr. Stonewall, I would like to share a word in private, if I may."

"Certainly," Charles replied confidently. He had obviously known more than he led Claire to believe. Charles softly smiled to Claire, expressing to her a slight nod of understanding. Claire looked to him curiously. Her emotions had already been wildly unstable since she awoke, and she could not depend on them any further. Charles opened his hand towards the direction of the study and replied to Thomas, "Will you join me in my study?"

Thomas looked to Claire and saw the fear still emanating from her expression. In an attempt to comfort her, he whispered softly, "It will be all right." Thomas turned towards the door and Charles guided him into the room. Claire and Charlotte followed them but stayed in the drawing room, allowing them their privacy. Charlotte sat upon the sofa as she watched Claire pace back and forth in front of the study.

Claire could not pause for any instant. Her nerves were rattled with excitement, happiness, worry, and fear. Unable to hear the conversation within the study, Claire could only play out the scenario in her own mind. Over and over again, she imagined the words as they could have been discussed. But to her dismay, the time seemed to move slowly and unendingly. She so desperately wanted to know what was being said behind the closed door.

Charlotte could not withstand the silence any longer, and spoke out with great concern. "Miss Stonewall, whatever is the matter? Why did my brother need to speak with Mr. Stonewall? And why are you acting in such a manner?"

Claire turned and faced Charlotte, and without saying a word, she smiled softly. She saw as it became obvious to Charlotte what had transpired, and in that instant, Charlotte's demeanor changed to utter shock and excitement. "He did not! Did he?" Charlotte blurted out with her mouth open and eyes wide. Claire's smile widened, and it was all the confirmation that Charlotte needed. Claire continued to pace, waiting what she felt was an eternity once again.

The door to the study opened and startled Claire from her constant pacing. Thomas stood at the entry and looked to Claire with a wayward grin. It was of no comfort to Claire's worry, for she had been struggling with the fear since they had spoken in private. Claire took the few steps towards Thomas, watching his movements carefully in hopes that she would interrupt any chance of his fleeing from her presence. Instead, Thomas stood there in confidence as Claire approached. This brought Claire little comfort. He spoke softly to her and his voice was heartfelt. "Your brother requests your attention, Miss Stonewall."

Claire looked toward the open door, and did not want to leave Thomas' sight. He nodded to her and she cautiously walked to the room.

"Close the door, Claire," instructed Charles as she reached the doorway.

Turning her gaze out of the doorway, she caught sight of Thomas looking back at her. A faint smile came over her face and she bit her lower lip gently. Slowly, she closed the door, keeping Thomas in her sight through the crack until the door finally closed. She turned and looked to see Charles in deep thought with his hands folded before his face, his elbows resting on the arms of his chair. He waited patiently for her to stand before him and looked up to her when she stood motionless.

He dropped his hands from his face, exposing his blank expression. "Claire, have you lost all of your senses? Have you lost sight of what you now have?"

"No, brother."

"Mr. Edleman is a fine man, of good upbringing, but he is of no class comparable to your own. You cannot be seriously accepting the man's proposal."

"Indeed I am, brother."

"Sister, you will have nothing. No money, no fine carriages, no servants to support you. You will be forced to work, hard labor and service to another family. Have you not considered what you are sacrificing for this man?"

"I have, brother. I do not need such finery," responded Claire, looking to her brother intently, her definitive understanding well-conceived within her thoughts. "I love him."

"Our father has left me in charge with specific direction. It is imperative that I impress upon you that if you were to marry this man, you would lose everything. The estate, inheritance, and all property. Are you so intent on leaving behind the life that you have lived these many years?"

"Charles, is it not enough that I love this man with all my heart? Our father has always pressed upon us the value of our devotion and love of family. There is no doubt within me, this man is my love. Regardless of fortune and stature, I pledge my heart fully and without remorse. I can only imagine myself as our father loved our mother. In that respect, I shall endure any challenge that comes to me. I care not for the condition of stature, and you know this of me without debate. This love that I feel is deeper than anything I have ever experienced, and I shall not be swayed from my devotion."

Charles paused for a moment, hearing the words from Claire, and folded his hands before his lips once again in contemplation. Claire stood there in fierce determination to prove her love for Thomas. It was several moments before Charles responded, "Then, I give my consent, Claire. I could not imagine a better man for you to marry, fortune notwithstanding. If it be your decision to renounce your inheritance in the pursuit of such a man, I am not to dissuade you."

Claire leaned over to him, pressing a kiss to his forehead and smiling down upon him. "Brother, you are family, and to that I will always remember. Thank you." She turned from his sight, reaching to the door and opening it to see Thomas and Charlotte upon the couch in confidence. Thomas rose to his feet instantly and Claire rushed towards him, embracing him fondly. Charlotte watched in wonder with tears falling from her watery eyes. Charles stood in the doorway of his study. The joy in the room was overwhelming to all who were witness.

THE WEDDING

THE REMAINING OF THE DAY was spent with the four of them together, enjoying stories of times past and the future plans that were soon to be set. As the night crept in and the excitement of the day wore upon them, Thomas and Charlotte returned home. Claire embraced Charles in happiness and then returned to her room for a well-deserved night's rest.

Each day following, Claire would spend time with Lily, continuing to learn and further her cooking skill. It was to no surprise that the servants were aware of the engagement. The first few days were filled with excitement and congratulations for both Claire and Thomas. Claire felt fulfilled in more ways than she could imagine. Thomas called upon Brookfield Manor when he was able, and Claire was so pleased to spend what time they could together. They took walks along the grounds, read together, discussed the wedding to come, and sat comfortably in each other's confidence as the waning light of day faded into the night.

On occasion, Claire took time to go into town, and even called upon the Edleman house. She found much enjoyment in spending time with them, and felt more and more a part of their family. Charlotte especially felt a fondness when Claire was around. The two of them spent many days together, and as time progressed, their relationship grew into a sisterhood as if they had always known each other. Claire could not believe the happiness she found being among them.

Charles and Claire had some considerations to account for during the next few weeks. Charles was determined to handle the arrangements for their wedding himself. Claire was so happy that he had approved of their engagement and found such eagerness to plan their day. He regularly asked Claire to make various decisions, reminding her of the pending nuptials and his determination to make it perfect.

Even though Claire was busy with preparations for her new endeavor and the change in her lifestyle, her confident acceptance never wavered from the happiness that she felt the day they were engaged. She knew it was meant to be, and she could even see the approval in the painting of her parents each morning as she looked upon it. There was no doubt in her mind, no worry and no fear in her chosen path.

As the wedding day came closer, the excitement was brimming throughout the town. Many had stopped to congratulate Claire and Thomas, and offered their approval of the match. It was not uncommon to find that Vivian and Nathaniel were together and crossed paths with Claire. Though they were civil in their encounters, it was apparent that Vivian and Nathaniel did their best to distance themselves from the situation. Claire did not know if it was due to their discomfort regarding her engagement, or the situation they found themselves in prior to it. There was nothing for her to do in either case, and she accepted that their relationship would settle into place in due time.

Charles was busy as he could be, and Claire watched in wonder as he would travel here and there, delivering instructions and making necessary arrangements. It seemed to her that Charles was intent on making the day exuberantly appeasing in every way. Claire could only smile and admire his diligence in coordinating what surely was to be the event of the year.

The day of the wedding came faster than any of them expected, Claire most of all. She was excited and nervous like she had never been before. The butterflies in her stomach were in full strength, as she stood fully dressed in the most beautiful gown that her brother had procured for her. Standing in awe in front of a large mirror, Claire saw firsthand how beautiful she looked. The tears welled up in her eyes as the thoughts of the event for the day came rushing through her mind. She was glowing from the inside and felt the warmth emanate from her heart. Never before had she felt so happy, and so assured in her decision. Claire had chosen to accept anything that came her way with her strength of character, and focused more on the love that she and Thomas shared.

A rapping came from the other side of the door, and Charles' voice rang from the other side. "Sister, are you ready?"

"Yes, brother. I am ready."

Charles opened the door and walked beside Claire as she stood in front of the mirror. The two of them looked upon the glass and admired their reflection. Charles was wearing one of his finest suits, and whispered softly to Claire, "You look beautiful, sister."

Claire turned around, wrapping her arms around his neck and held him close. "I am so happy brother."

"I am happy for you, sister, more than you know. You have found a good man, from a strong and honorable family. I could not hope for anything more for you. I am so proud of you." Charles paused for a moment and looked to her sincerely before continuing, "I know that you are happy, sister, but please understand that I will not allow this wedding to proceed unless you are confident that this man is the only one you wish to be with. If you have any doubts, tell me now and I will take you from this place, honorably and without regret."

Claire knew that he would do anything for her. She was confident that she could not feel any remorse or regret marrying Thomas. She looked to Charles and saw the love he had for her, and she knew that he would always be there, as he always had been. "No, brother. I love him, most arduously. He reminds me so much of our father, and of you. I could not have dreamed of a better man to be with."

With that, Charles sighed with both happiness and sorrow. "It is settled then?"

Claire nodded to him with a soft smile, seeing the turmoil that he was enduring in his heart. She raised her hand to his cheek and pressed it to his face, the light embrace seemed to call forth a single tear from his eyes. "I will always be your younger sister, Charles. Do not think that I choose one family for the other, I will always love you."

Charles took her hand and folded it into his elbow and turned towards the door. He took a deep breath and guided Claire beside him as he stood in their father's place. As he opened the door, the two of them entered the hall of the church. Without turning to look to Claire, they stood behind the sequence of seats filled with friends and family.

Claire saw for the first time the people who came in attendance to the event. She was amazed to discover that the elite and the common mingled together in awe-inspiring fashion. Everyone was dressed in their best attire to honorably witness the wedding itself. As Charles looked down the aisle, he nodded and music began playing at the opposite end of the congregation. Its melody filled the church and rang with sweet tones.

Charles leaned over to Claire before they began to walk down the aisle, and spoke just loud enough for her to hear. "Claire, I know that our father is so very proud of you. He and Mother are here watching this moment, and I know this to be true. They give their blessing to this day, and beam down from heaven above with their love for you."

With that, the two of them walked down the aisle, and all watched diligently as they steadily took each step. The day was beautiful and shone brightly for their wedding, and all in attendance were in awe of the assembly. Claire saw Thomas standing at the opposite end of the room and felt the urge to run into his arms. Charles held her hand tightly in his arm, obviously feeling her eagerness, and steadied her quietly.

Soon the bells of the church rang boldly, breaking the silence of the region. The crowds cheered and gathered out the door, as Claire and Thomas were now joined in holy matrimony. Thomas and Claire stepped from the entry of the church and they were showered with rice and flower petals. There were loud, congratulatory words being heard from the various patrons of the crowd. They made their way to the open carriage that stood at the end of the pathway waiting for their arrival. The carriage was dressed in flowers, ribbons, and bows that matched the décor of the wedding.

Thomas assisted Claire into the carriage and took the seat next to her. They waved to the crowd, paying their respects to their friends and family. Charles was nearest to the carriage and just before they departed down the lane, he handed two envelopes to Claire. He stepped in closer to her and leaned over to whisper to her in private.

"Sister, you have made me so proud! I could not have wished for a better wedding for you. These are from your father and me, but promise me you will open Father's first."

Claire was stunned to learn of the letter, she did not know that her father had written something for her. She looked to Charles inquisitively, then down to the letters he had given her. She easily recognized the one from her father, the lettering of which was clearly decipherable. It was a surprise to her to have received such a gift from him, and as the carriage began to ride away, she looked to Thomas.

"What is it, my dear?"

"A letter from my father. Charles just delivered it to me now, he must have been holding on to it all this time."

"Then I suggest that you read it."

"I do not know if I can. I did not expect to have such correspondence. I have no faith that I may be able to read it alone." Claire's eyes filled with tears of sorrow, missing her father now more than she could bear.

Thomas comforted her in his embrace. "Then do not read it alone, Claire. I am here with you. Allow me the honor of being here to comfort you through it."

Claire began to unfold the letter carefully, snuggling tightly into Thomas' embrace. The letter was well preserved and it was apparent that Charles had kept it safe through the test of time until that very day. Claire took a deep breath as the carriage continued down the road and felt Thomas' embrace comfort and shield her from any harm. As Claire began reading the letter, her imagination heard her father's voice ring in her mind, speaking the words to her as she read them.

My Dearest Claire,

By now you must have found love and happiness that I would be proud of. Your brother, Charles, has done what I have asked by allowing you to read this letter at the end of a most glorious day. I have always tried to stress to you the importance of love and family, and to this end I have put you through what I could only assume to be excruciating pain and torture. For that I am truly sorry, but I have had no choice but to protect you from the vile transgressions that others will surely seek to inflict upon you.

You were born into wealth and stability, along with a rank that many in these times seek for their own. If there was any other way, I would have sought it out fully. However, I know that your brother will be honorable in his intentions and will always protect you as best he can. To this I have entrusted him to carry out in my absence.

I have put in place a plan to keep you from the tentacles of those who wish to capture your heart for the treasures of fortune and status only. To all those who are to come to you and seek your hand, they are to be dutifully informed that you are to be without fortune or status. This should be enough to ward off those who seek only to ruin your love and devotion for the sake of money. In order to expunge those who are persistent, your brother is afforded to offer them a settlement of money. If they so choose to accept it, the sum would compensate them enough to rule out any deception.

By now, I am sure that you have experienced this fully, and the pain that was inflicted upon you is purely my doing. Under no circumstance are you to place any blame of this on your brother, for he has done so faithfully and in accordance of my dying wishes. Your brother loves you with all that he is, I have always known this, and have seen it in his actions every day since you were born.

But now that you have been joined with what I could only expect to be a most honorable and loving man, worthy of my love as well, you should know that I am so very proud of you. Do not worry for me, for I am surely with your mother this very day looking down upon you with great joy and happiness for the life that you now lead.

It is with great pleasure that I inform you of your true inheritance. You have been set with a grant of 30,000 pounds, and a parsonage of residence from the estate. This should be most generous for a living for you and your new family. I have prepared such a living for you because I love you, and shall always do so even beyond my time here on this earth. I know that you will be taken care of for the rest of your days, and can now live your life free of struggle and doubt.

Your mother and I love you so very much, and if there is only one regret that I have, it is that I could not be there to hold you at this time.

Your Loving Father,
Edwin Stonewall

The tears fell from her eyes as she read the final words of the letter. She took the parchment to her lips and kissed it gently, then held it tightly against her chest. She loved her father and her brother so very much, and without fail, she felt the love of her family surround her. She knew beyond any shadow of doubt that she would live a long and happy life because of their diligent efforts.

Barely able to continue, she folded her father's letter and placed it down beside her, securing it from the air that would take it to the winds, as they continued their journey within the carriage. Thomas continued to hold her tightly, and shielded her from any interruption to her reading the letters. He did not even ask anything of her, knowing that she would tell him what he needed to know in due time.

Claire still had the letter from her brother, and knowing now the contents of the letter from her father, her curiosity was heightened. She carefully unfolded the letter and began to read it, confident that it could only bring her comfort after the words from her father.

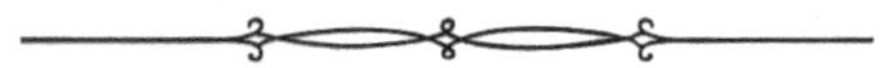

My Dear Sister,

Where to begin? That is what drives the letter I write to you now. For a long time have I watched and guided you as best as I can, in hopes that our father would be proud of my diligence. He loves us both so very much, and I cannot impress upon you the depths of his overwhelming adoration. You have by now read the letter he had provided for you on this day, and I am sure that he wrote to inform you of your birthright and his wishes for your continued happiness.

You are such a wonderfully strong and determined young woman, it has been my ultimate pleasure to watch you become the person that you are. I can only hope to find such a woman for myself, to share in the qualities that you possess, though I am quite sure that there are none who could compare. It will be my misfortune, for I could not imagine to find any woman worthy of your caliber and strength.

By now you know the truth of your inheritance, and I could not be more satisfied with what father has provided to you. But what he did not foresee was such a bountiful increase to the family holdings. Business and fortune has come to us tenfold since his departure from us. It seems as though our father provided avenues to us that could only be described as a divine influence.

I am quite aware of your love for Brookfield Manor and the staff who reside there. It is my extreme pleasure to inform you now, that you and Thomas are to inherit Brookfield Manor along with half of the estate as you know it today. I could not imagine a more perfect gift or generosity for you or Mr. Edleman, in that you are to continue to call Brookfield Manor your home.

I have taken the opportunity to indulge your fortune further by negotiating the terms of the Edleman debts fully closed and released. The Edleman family is a proud family, and would not accept the gift directly, so I have taken it upon myself to pay all debts owed on their behalf. This is the gift that I pronounce to you now, and by the time that you complete the reading of this letter, you will see the effects as they are designed.

Surely, you realize the love that I have for you, as a sister, a friend, and a woman of great character. I do these things because I am your loving brother and will always be there for you until the end of time. Our father has led the example, and as such, I walk within his footsteps in hopes of proving myself worthy to be his son.

Your Servant and Your Brother,
Charles Stonewall

It did not take long for Claire to realize what had happened. In a single day, her life had changed to something quite unexpected and glorious. She kissed the letter and closed her eyes, unable to imagine such a loving and devoted family. She looked to Thomas and smiled greatly, tears falling from her cheeks as she was overjoyed and confident in their new lives together. She recognized the background as they passed, and nodded to Thomas for his recognition of the scene as they continued onward.

Thomas looked and saw that they were entering the parkway to Brookfield Manor. He also noticed the carriage that was ahead of them. He looked to Claire who simply smiled to him in return.

Claire folded the letter and placed it along with her father's, between the two of them. She took Thomas' hand and raised it to her lips, depositing a gentle kiss to his knuckles as he looked to her in awe. Their carriage rounded the fountain and stopped as it reached the other carriage. The driver stepped from his perch and guided Claire to the grounds, followed by Thomas.

The two of them looked to the other carriage as Forester opened the door, helping out the party within. One by one, each of the members of the Edleman family were guided from the carriage, and Thomas looked with great anticipation for the reason.

Claire held tightly to Thomas, and spoke softly to him as they watched the procession of guests entering Brookfield Manor. "My father and brother have done this for us, my love. Your family and mine, together in this place, from now until forever. This place of undying devotion and love, to share with us, that is their gift and mine as well."

ACKNOWLEDGEMENTS

There are so many people to thank for their support as we have continued to evolve over time as we learned about writing and each other. Skipping Stones, in itself, is a story of how we came together to become something different. At first, it was one of us supporting the other in their dreams, and then it turned into a common dream for the both of us. This dream would not have been realized without the constant encouragement from our family and friends. In particular, our mothers, who not only provided us with the reassurance we needed, but became our first beta readers, red pens in hand. We also want to thank our three kids for believing in us and listening as we discussed our novel over and over again, even if they heard it many times before. Our youngest, Sydney, was especially patient, allowing mommy and daddy to write as she sat beside us waiting for us to play with her.

We were very fortunate to have two wonderful friends, Katherine and Michelle, to be our beta readers. Not only did they provide feedback but also the criticism we needed to improve the overall story. In addition, we had a talented editor, Stephanie Renfro from Fiction Edit who worked with us diligently in polishing the novel to become what it is today. Deranged Doctor Designs provided us with the artistic cover design that encompasses the mood of our story to be displayed for all to see. Our friends from the Southern California Writer's Association provided us with the encouragement and motivation to grow as authors, complete this novel, and continue writing.

I would be remiss if I did not mention the person who supported me the most. It is amazing to think that an idea that has been hidden within me for years was brought out from the encouragement and urging of my husband, Brett. Without him, the story would never have gotten to where it is today. I think it is fitting that Skipping Stones is a classic love story as the love story behind its creation grew as well.

ABOUT THE AUTHORS

Ananya and Brett are a husband and wife team that are partners both in life and writing. Their relationship and writing has evolved to become what it is today, a collaboration of support, ideas, and dreams. They challenge each other to create, to dream, to be more than they have become as individuals. Ananya and Brett support each other's endeavors and to that end, are passionate to help each other as a whole. While supporting and challenging each other to grow, both Ananya and Brett maintain their individuality and zest for life. Ananya's other passions include traveling, archaeology, and jigsaw puzzles. Brett loves video gaming, sewing, cooking, and movies. Ananya and Brett have agreed, that they want to share their experience and passion with others. They want to give back to the community and have made a commitment to help others with their program, Storyteller's Ethos, in which they will donate a portion of their proceeds from their novels, to various charities that enhance the advancement and passions of others. Ananya and Brett have three children, two dogs, and the occasional squirrel that likes to run along the fence.